THE THIRD FUNERAL

THE
THIRD
FUNERAL

KEVIN BOWEN

ENGAGE
PUBLISHING

ENGAGE

PUBLISHING

Published by Engage Publishing
P.O. Box 1452, Port Townsend, WA 98368
www.engagepublishing.com

07 06 05 04 03 — 5 4 3 2 1

PUBLISHER'S CATALOGING-IN-PUBLICATION DATA
Bowen, Kevin.
The third funeral / Kevin Bowen.
p.   cm.
ISBN 1-930892-14-4
Library of Congress Number: 2003092077
[1. Death—Psychological aspects—Fiction.
2. Christianity—Fiction. 3. Adventure—Fiction.
4. Mystery fiction.] I. Title.
PS3602.O946 T55   2003
813.6—dc21   CIP

Printed in the United States of America

COVER DESIGN by To The Point Solutions/www.tothepointsolutions.com
TEXT DESIGN AND LAYOUT by Mary Jo Zazueta
COPYEDITING by Mary Jo Zazueta and Audrey Dorsch

To Ruthie

Contents

	Acknowledgments	ix
CHAPTER 1	Rochelle	1
CHAPTER 2	Scott	7
CHAPTER 3	Hope	17
CHAPTER 4	Brad	23
CHAPTER 5	The Talk Show	35
CHAPTER 6	Two Funerals	39
CHAPTER 7	The First Funeral	51
CHAPTER 8	Encounters	61
CHAPTER 9	The Second Funeral	65
CHAPTER 10	The Ride Home	79
CHAPTER 11	Saturday Night	83
CHAPTER 12	Inquiry	93
CHAPTER 13	Lunch	99
CHAPTER 14	The Game	103
CHAPTER 15	E-Mail From Israel	105
CHAPTER 16	Three Meetings	107
CHAPTER 17	The Guys	113
CHAPTER 18	The Investigation	117
CHAPTER 19	The Call	121
CHAPTER 20	The Note	129

CONTENTS

CHAPTER 21	The Threat	133
CHAPTER 22	Shopping	141
CHAPTER 23	Nemesis	149
CHAPTER 24	The Plan	153
CHAPTER 25	The Team	161
CHAPTER 26	Complications	165
CHAPTER 27	Improvising	171
CHAPTER 28	The Ransom	179
CHAPTER 29	Choices	183
CHAPTER 30	Reunion	189
CHAPTER 31	Status	201
CHAPTER 32	Art	209
CHAPTER 33	Perspective	217
CHAPTER 34	News	221
CHAPTER 35	Reality	227
CHAPTER 36	Best Friends	231
CHAPTER 37	Betty	239
CHAPTER 38	Doors	247
CHAPTER 39	Changes	251
CHAPTER 40	Love, Hope, and Will	261
	About the Author	271
	A Note From the Author	273

Acknowledgments

The creation of a book involves many people. I wish to thank and acknowledge the following for their help, support, and comments along the way: Mary Jo Zazueta, editor and designer; Audrey Dorsch, editor; Alex Moore, consultant; and Terry Musclow, Dickinson Press.

In addition, I want to thank my draft readers: Dean Robnett, Brian Flanner, Sue Douglas, Dale and Pat Bowen, Linda Alger, Peggy and Jerry Maurer, Steve Hayner, Terree Lyman, Craig Bowen, Alan Wood, Ruth Roberts, Dana Herz, Florence Bowen, and Bert Roberts.

Finally, I wish to formally express my sincere appreciation to Ruth, my wonderful wife, without whom this book would not have happened.

THE THIRD FUNERAL

Death is inevitable. It is universal.
But it isn't the issue.

CHAPTER 1

Rochelle

"TOUCHDOWN!" proclaimed the announcer into the crowd's breathless anticipation. "Lincoln High has won the Division Championship! Wow! What a game!"

The occupants of one side of the stadium rushed onto the field while the other side stood frozen in silent dismay.

Twenty minutes later, the celebrating mass started to disperse. Rochelle Jackson and Estella Lopez packed up their cheerleading gear and jogged to Rochelle's car. They wanted to get to Capone's Pizzeria before the rest of the crowd.

As they threaded their way through the cars in the parking lot, Rochelle and Estella heard, "Hey, what's up, Rochie?"

They turned to see Justin Stockton staggering in their direction, his hand groping to balance himself against a nearby car.

"Whoa! You reek, Justin," said Rochelle, as Justin intruded into Rochelle's personal space. "Were you drinking it or showering in it?"

"Both," said Justin. "Drinkin' an' showerin'." He gave Rochelle a hug that would have been insufferably offensive had she not known it was the liquor and not the usually polite Justin.

"What's happening here, Justin?" Maternalism, sisterhood, and companionship merged in Rochelle. She was surprised to see him like this.

"I'm ready to party!"

"*Ready* to party? Looks like you did that already. Looks to me like you're fixin' to get yourself in a heap o' trouble."

"Relax, my Nubian princess," said Justin. He tried to hug and kiss her, nearly falling over in the process.

"Hold the phone, Romeo. I am not your Nubian princess and you are not yourself." She pushed on his chest with both hands to keep him from completely falling forward. Rochelle promised herself to hold him accountable when he sobered up. Right now, she just didn't want him to drive. She turned to Estella, who was standing fifteen feet away, arms crossed, disgusted with the whole scene. "Es, I guess we just got another passenger. We can take him home on our way to Capone's."

"I guess so." Estella shrugged, turning toward the car.

Rochelle prepared to usher the momentarily passive Justin to the backseat. Justin stiffened when Rochelle gently tugged on his arm.

"I'm not goin'," he protested in the clearest English he'd used so far.

"Oh, yes you are," responded Rochelle, more to herself than to him, taking a firmer grip on his arm.

This drunken behavior was uncharacteristic for Justin. Although his occasional volatile temper was well known, he was an uncommonly decent guy. And, though he was adamant that he wasn't a Christian, he'd been attending Rochelle's Bible study, where he'd expressed particular interest in the love of God and forgiveness.

"I 'ave my ooown wheels!"

Rochelle knew about those wheels—a souped up '66 Mustang in which Justin was known to hot-rod.

"C'mon Justin, you know you can't drive in your condition. You can hardly stand!"

"I'm fine!"

"Why don't you just give me your keys, and we'll take you home. We can come back and get your car tomorrow."

"Leave me alone!" bellowed Justin indignantly. "I'll drive myself."

With little trouble he twisted his arm free from Rochelle's grasp, unintentionally elbowing her in the ribs. Rochelle winced and stepped back. The girls knew they'd be no match for this six-foot-four varsity basketball player if he let his temper fly.

Justin stumbled away. If his blood-red Mustang had not been directly in front of him, it is unlikely he would have found it. All the while, Estella and Rochelle pleaded with him to stop.

"I said, leave me alone!" Justin turned and took two steps toward them, his fist ready to swing.

"Justin!" screamed Rochelle in alarm.

He stopped. The veins on his neck were distended and the color in his face had darkened. "I said, leave me alone!"

Rochelle and Estella took a couple of steps backward.

Justin turned and walked unsteadily to his car. The girls pleaded some more, but from a safer distance.

He managed to get into the correct car and insert the appropriate key into the ignition. As he pulled out of his parking spot, he scraped the side of the blue Chevy Cavalier parked next to his Mustang and set off the alarm on the yellow Toyota Celica behind him. His car was now pointed toward the exit. Justin's wheels screeched as he sped out of the lot, jumped the curb, and sideswiped the lamppost near the exit onto Main Street.

As the Mustang raced off to the girls' right, Rochelle dug

through her backpack looking for her cell phone. She punched three numbers.

"Nine one one," answered the dispatcher. "Is this an emergency?"

"Yes. A very drunk guy just drove out of the Lincoln High Stadium parking lot. He went south on Main Street. He's already hit two parked cars and a light pole."

"Is anyone hurt?"

"Not yet. I'm certain he's going to crash. He was driving really fast. The license plate is NUJ 365. It's a red '66 Mustang. Oh wait—oh no!" Rochelle narrated the scene before her. "Oh man! He just missed that car! He's now headed in the other direction."

"He's now headed north on Main?"

"Yes. He has to be doing ninety."

After a few more questions, the dispatcher ended the call. Rochelle shook her head, wondering if a police car had yet been sent. There was nothing else she or Estella could do. Rochelle looked at Estella, sighed her sense of helplessness, and then unlocked the doors of the '97 Taurus.

"I hope he's okay," said Rochelle, starting her parents' car.

"I hope they get him before he hurts someone," responded Estella.

Both felt helpless.

Rochelle drove to the Main Street exit. Capone's Pizzeria was three miles south on Main. She flipped on her right blinker and waited, wondering if Justin would be all right. The light turned green.

Rochelle had barely eased her car onto the street when a screech caused both girls to look to their left. They gasped. After swerving around a brown jeep stopped for the red light, Justin's red Mustang was aimed directly at Rochelle's door.

Looking across Rochelle's arms and through the driver's

side window, Estella could see the panic on Justin's face. The Mustang swerved as its tires tried to grip the road. Justin's white knuckles fought the steering wheel to no avail.

Estella's scream melded with the squeal of tires as she felt the Mustang's right front fender penetrate Rochelle's door. The Taurus jerked sideways as the airbags deployed and the entangled cars bounced over the curb, coming to rest against the lamppost Justin had hit earlier.

The elongated screech of crushing metal and shattering glass was replaced by an eerie silence.

Estella gasped. "Rochelle? Are you all right?" Estella was shaken but not hurt. "Rochelle?"

Estella fought her way through the airbags, trying to reach her friend. "Rochelle? Rochie? Rochelle? Talk to me, girlfriend!"

No response.

"Are you okay?" Estella began to panic. "Please say something!"

Finally, Estella touched Rochelle's crushed body, only to recoil as the moisture and warmth of Rochelle's blood enveloped her hand.

"Rochelle! Rochelle!—Help! Help!—Someone get some help—Rochelle!"

You are told to plan for the future.
The only certain thing in your future is death.
Why not plan for it?

CHAPTER 2

Scott

Not bad, thought Scott Kingman as he closed his laptop after downloading the day's market activity. He calculated he'd added another $700,000 to his coffers. Most of the gain was due to the positive bump in Freedom Airways' stock tied to Freedom's positive earnings report. Scott knew the positive earnings were the result of cost-cutting measures he had recently implemented, as well as Freedom Airways' recent under-the-table agreement with Advanced Chemical Products (ACP) to transport some of ACP's experimental products.

Scott looked around his Boeing 727, which technically was his as the majority shareholder in Freedom Airways. Periodically he would forgo his private jet to sample the service his company offered. His "quality assurance trips" were scheduled far enough ahead for every link in the chain to know about them; thus the employees were on their best behavior. Scott pretended to be unaware of the advance preparations, preferring the delusion that his experience was the same standard of service all Freedom's customers received.

He particularly enjoyed the personal attention of the attractive flight attendants specially assigned to first class whenever he flew. Somehow, having beautiful women treat him like royalty in the presence of complete strangers was a head-trip he could not resist.

Scott dreamed of making the whole airline first class, but the realities of the marketplace would not allow it. Clandestine agreements and questionable reductions in preventive maintenance expenses had allowed Freedom to improve its bottom line. Scrimping on the meal service and other customer conveniences had helped, but they had also earned Freedom Airways the reputation of being the low-budget-alternative airline. The immediate result was that Scott could not avoid the plebian masses that flew his airline. This meant he had to endure the pre-boarding wait, with sometimes unsavory company, and tolerate the coach passengers as they filed through the first-class section.

Today's boarding experience had been particularly trying. A men's softball team, wearing hats and jerseys that read "Buddy's—The Best Pub in Tampa," was on its way home from a tournament in northern Virginia. They were basically well-mannered except for the one called Boomer. Boomer was proof that human cloning is possible, though how they had duplicated Rodney Dangerfield's genetic code was a mystery.

Scott had witnessed Boomer's disgusting advances toward the flight attendants and had overheard some of his off-color jokes. He had also assessed Boomer's fear of flying. At one point the flight attendants even discussed not letting "the loud-mouthed jerk" on the plane. The only part Scott played in the pre-boarding melodrama was to say to the flight attendants, "You ladies are earning your money today!" What Scott perceived to be smiles of appreciation for his support hid resentment of management's uncaring attitude.

After stowing his laptop, Scott turned his thoughts to his upcoming lunch meeting with Advanced Chemical Products at their Tampa headquarters. A leak at ACP's Virginia plant had contaminated some protected wetlands. Though the Environmental Protection Agency's investigation was specifically focused on cleaning up the spill, Scott wanted assurances that the "special packages" his airline was conveying would not become an issue. The EPA had no knowledge of the product Freedom was transporting for Advanced, and Scott wanted to keep it that way.

After his meeting, Scott planned to catch a return flight to D.C. in time to share a more enjoyable meal at the home of his former college roommate, Dr. Wil Wilson, and his wife, Hope, who had been back in the States for almost two months. Wil had recently begun an eighteen-month sabbatical from the Institute of Palestinian Archaeological Research in Jerusalem. Hope was on assignment with *The New York Times'* Washington bureau.

Though Wil and Hope had made it to two of Scott's infamous dinner parties, this was the first time their three schedules actually allowed for them to get together in a more personal setting.

Freedom Airways' Flight 2652 was twenty minutes into its two-hour-and-ten-minute flight from Dulles to Tampa when the lead flight attendant, Suzanne, made an announcement. "The captain has turned on the fasten seat belt sign. Please return to your seat and fasten your seat belt. And return your tray table and seat back to the full upright position." There was a sense of urgency in her voice. "Please ensure that all of your personal belongings are safely stowed under the seat in front of you or in the overhead compartment."

Scott's inner musings faded when his gaze rested on Suzanne. He'd met her when he checked in at the gate. She'd introduced herself with a particularly friendly handshake, which Scott optimistically thought would lead to further developments. As she turned around now, Scott saw her notice that he was studying her backside. Suzanne flashed Scott a distracted smile. Something other than his hawkish stare was bothering her.

"Suzanne?" said Scott.

"Yes, Mr. Kingman." She stepped toward his seat and leaned in seductively close.

The tantalizing fragrance of jasmine bolstered Scott's desires as he brought his lips to her ear and whispered, "What seems to be the problem?"

The sensuality of the moment evaporated with Suzanne's answer. "There appears to be a problem related to the number two engine."

"Really?" Scott raised his eyebrows. "Anything serious?"

She maintained her quiet tone. "The captain thinks it might be related to the fuel tank for that engine. The other two engines are fine and—"

A surge of the plane caused Suzanne to lose her balance. She landed across Scott's lap, knocking his drink out of his hand and soaking the thirty-something woman sitting between him and the window.

"Oh! What was that?" exclaimed the businesswoman, clutching her armrests.

The seasoned travelers waited for the next jolt of turbulence. Nothing happened.

The captain's voice came over the cabin speakers. "This is the captain. The turbulence you felt was the result of a problem with our number two engine. Please do not be alarmed. This plane has three engines and the other two are functioning fine. In fact, this plane is actually designed to fly on one engine if it had to. The loss of the number two engine will, however, delay our arrival. Federal regulations require us to land at the next reasonably accessible airport to have the engine inspected. I apologize for any inconvenience this might cause. I need to ask you to remain seated for the duration of the flight. Again, please be assured there is nothing to be concerned about. Thank you for your understanding."

As Suzanne righted herself and adjusted her uniform, Boomer screamed from the back of the plane.

"WE'RE GOING TO DIE!"

He followed with further bellows. "We're going to crash. The captain is lying. It's a bomb!"

It didn't matter if Boomer was serious or not; Suzanne had to quiet him down. She passed two junior flight attendants who were also headed to the rear of the plane.

The voice of Boomer's coach echoed as he yelled, "Shut up, Boomer!" Even his teammates had had enough.

When Suzanne reached the epicenter of the commotion there was no indication that Boomer was going to comply with his coach's command. Boomer was in mid-outburst, leaning forward with a firm grip on the seat in front of him. Suzanne addressed Boomer in a calm but non-compromising tone. "Sir, you are going to have to contain yourself."

Boomer now had the attention of the prettiest flight attendant. He loosened his grip on the seat, looked up at Suzanne, and pouted. "But I'm scared. Perhaps if you held me, I'd be better."

Suzanne would have none of it. She was irritated by the hassles the delay would cause and she was anxious to talk to the captain and coordinate plans. But first she needed to deal with this fool. Boomer's ignorance was her advantage.

"Sir, do you know how to use a parachute?"

Boomer went silent, stunned by the question. Then, with a cocky smirk on his face, he said, "No, but I think you and I could—"

Suzanne ignored his leering come-hither look and cut

him off. "I am hereby informing you that, according to Regulation 1298a of the Airline Safety and Passenger Conduct Code, if you continue to be a disturbance to this flight, we will be forced to put you into the emergency evacuation chute and have you discharged from the plane, after which an Air National Guard recovery team will track your location and retrieve you before taking you into custody and filing charges for endangering this flight."

Suzanne's delivery was so convincing that even those who knew that what she had said was sheer nonsense sat back in their seats hoping they would not be next, like schoolchildren who had watched a classmate get scolded.

It worked. Boomer, wide-eyed in terror at the prospect of being ejected from the plane, even with a parachute, stopped breathing. He swallowed hard and eased his suddenly stiff shoulders back against the seat before lowering his chin to his chest and exhaling.

"Thank you! Now, put on your seat belt." Suzanne looked at the seat numbers above his head. "Seat 33D," she said to herself but loud enough for Boomer to hear. "I need to inform the captain." Suzanne briskly pivoted and returned to the front of the plane.

Boomer looked like he was trying to figure out how the eject button operated. Why had she read his seat number? He didn't move.

It was a few minutes before anyone at the rear of the plane said anything. And no one dared to look at Boomer, whose white fingers dug into the armrests on either side of him.

Suzanne knocked on the security window as she picked up the intercom handset to speak with the flight crew. This new security feature was there for good reason, but it made it difficult to communicate with the cockpit crew, who were not allowed to open the door until the plane was at the terminal.

She overheard air traffic control's confirmation of the new flight schedule as she asked, "So's everything all right?"

"Hey, Suz," flight engineer Marcos Sanchez answered.

"How's it going in there?" asked Suzanne.

"We're pretty sure we had some contaminated fuel in tank two," said Sanchez. "The other two engines are fine. When we were at the terminal, the captain noticed they switched trucks before filling tank two. Apparently, the truck that filled tanks one and three ran out of fuel. Perhaps the stuff they filled tank two with had been sitting around too long. It's an educated guess at this point, but we're pretty confident."

"Good." Suzanne was pleased it was that simple.

"Perhaps you can tell the man in first class he should get his fuel somewhere else," suggested Sanchez. "That's one place I hope his cost-cutting knife doesn't get too carried away."

Suzanne grinned. "Anything else you'd like me to tell him?"

"Yeah, tell him—"

"Shut up, Sanchez!" said Suzanne, shaking her head and smiling.

They all laughed.

"Hey, Shel," Suzanne said to the captain. "I thought you should know that I just threatened to eject a passenger if he didn't shut up."

"The softball player?"

"Yep. I think he's mellowed out for a while, and as long as you don't frighten him anymore I think he'll maintain control."

"Let me know if you—"

"Captain," first officer Bernie Bentson interrupted, "we've just lost radio contact with air traffic control."

"What?" said Captain Shel Godowski.

"It just went dead. I was verifying clearance when it went silent."

"Hey, Suz. Maybe you can ask for a new radio also," joked Sanchez.

"That's strange." Godowski wasn't taking the news as lightly. "The VHF COM radio is one of the few new things on this plane."

Suzanne wasn't exactly clear what they were talking about, but no one acted too concerned.

The captain decided to finish with Suzanne before addressing his problem. "Anyway, Suzanne, let me know if you need any support with the loudmouth."

"Thanks, I will. I'd better get back to work. It's been fun." Suzanne set down the handset and turned to walk into the cabin. She had barely taken two steps when the lights flickered out and the oxygen masks deployed.

As she turned back to the security window she could see the flight crew scrambling in controlled panic. The plane took a sudden dive, propelling Suzanne toward the cockpit. She wrenched her shoulder when her hand grasped the galley partition, stopping her tumble and preventing her face from smashing against the cockpit door.

Boomer was screaming again and there was no joking in his volume. His cries could be heard above the other passengers, whose attempts at remaining calm had given way to sheer terror.

As the passengers felt the slowly increasing angle of the plane, some of them grew silent, moving beyond panic.

Suzanne regained her focus as she held herself against the galley wall. Struggling to keep her balance, she reached for the handset and looked through the cockpit window. The cockpit crew was losing the battle. When she saw the approaching ground her eyes grew wide as icy fear stole her breath. She looked back at Scott, whose thoughts were somewhere between stunned disbelief and absolute fright.

Even if the crew had had time to access the cargo hull where the container of Advanced Chemical Products' Nitro XF192 compound had tipped over, it would have been too late. The experimental corrosive had eaten its way through the cargo compartment floor and through a bundle of electrical wires, killing communications and causing the stabilizer trim to run away to the full nose-down position. There was nothing they could do. The ground was approaching too fast.

Efforts to create life fail. Efforts to create death succeed.
Efforts to stop life succeed. Efforts to stop death fail.

CHAPTER 3

Hope

Hope Wilson drove her Acura north on I-95, heading back to D.C. She had spent the day in Richmond, Virginia gathering data related to the spill at Advanced Chemical Products' plant in Alexandria. The spill had drawn national attention, and a committee of the state legislature was closely monitoring the cleanup. Hope was talking on her cell phone to Eli Snyder, her boss at *The New York Times'* Washington bureau.

"He actually said that?" queried Eli.

"He sure did. I almost lost it. The guy is such a slime."

"And Advanced Chemical Products probably pays him a fortune."

"You got that right! The guy's face was completely straight when he said," Hope deepened her voice and imitated ACP's spokesman, "'We at Advanced Chemical Products want to be good neighbors and believe it is our corporate responsibility to do what we can to protect the environment.'"

"And the committee believed him?"

"I doubt it, but that doesn't matter. Remember, this is election season."

"How could I forget?"

"Even though the Feds are breathing down ACP's neck

regarding the leak, most of the politicians on the committee are more concerned about getting re-elected. They probably found enough to hide behind in his statements to further justify lining their pockets with ACP's campaign support."

"And since ACP is funding both parties in the state, neither group is being too critical," concluded Eli.

"Right-o! All I know is that Advanced Chemical Products is going to do whatever it can for maximum political and public relations benefit . . . period!"

"It is sickening, isn't it?"

"That it is."

"That's one of the reasons," said Eli in an arrogant tone, "it's so important for the press to remain independent. Someone's got to tell the real story."

"I agree, Eli, but don't delude yourself and pretend the press is independent. I mean—"

"Here we go again."

"You know I'm right." Hope was not conceding, but knew the debate would be best suited for another time. "Anyway, I plan on finishing my article later this evening. I'll have it on your desk in the morning."

"Great. Your first three articles on the new EPA guidelines have done really well."

"Thank you. In my next piece—"

"The one you'll give me tomorrow?"

"No, the one after that," clarified Hope. "I want to focus on how the new regulations make it more difficult to transport hazardous materials."

"That was one of the main issues behind the new regulations, wasn't it?"

"Yep. The EPA hoped the regulations would lead to a reduction of hazardous materials in the nation's transportation system. It will. Yet, contrary to Advanced Chemical's attempt to make the case that the regulations unfairly apply only to them, the impact really does go far beyond Advanced."

"Oh?"

"I'm going to point out that the guidelines are forcing everyone to rethink how they can do what they do with fewer pollutants. Hospitals have to pay more to get rid of their waste materials. Local dry-cleaning services have to reduce their emissions. And everyone who produces or uses chemicals has to pay a lot more to ship, receive, or dispose of those products."

"Sounds reasonable."

"But . . ." Hope's tone made Eli a little nervous. " . . . I also want to deal with those pandering congressmen from New York to California who drive to Alexandria for photo ops, trying to create the impression they're the people's champion against the 'evil polluters of our society.' I have no love for companies like ACP, but I'm determined to address the hypocrisy of such attacks. After all, it's American society's insatiable demand for such products that keeps 'evil polluters' like ACP in busin—"

"Hey, Hope?"

"What?"

"Will you tell me how you *really* feel?"

They both chuckled.

"Well, it does irk me," finished Hope.

After they completed their conversation, Hope called Wil to ensure that everything was in order for dinner with Scott that evening. Having received Wil's reassurances, and after agreeing to pick up some vanilla ice cream, Hope clicked the phone off and tossed it on the passenger seat.

As she leaned forward to check her lipstick in the rearview mirror, Hope noticed a large object in the sky ahead and to the left. "What's that?" she muttered, focusing on the motion. It took a second, but Hope concluded it was falling.

She instinctively slowed, as did the few other cars on the highway. As the object grew larger, Hope realized, sickeningly, it was an airplane. It was plummeting at a sixty-degree angle and would hit the ground soon and not far from where she was. Hope's stomach knotted and she flinched as the plane passed over the highway. She went pale when she looked to her right. The plane's trajectory had it on a collision course with an oil refinery she could see a few miles away. Stepping on the gas pedal, she began her pursuit, careening onto the exit she had intended to pass. She guessed it would point her toward the refinery. She guessed correctly. The compound was one mile directly in front of her.

A tremendous flash was followed by the roar of the explosion. Hope slammed on her brakes and skidded to a jerky stop. Another explosion. A giant wall of flame reached skyward, and black smoke billowed into an ominous mushroom shape. With a reporter's determination, she proceeded cautiously in the direction of the story, peering through the windshield as ash and smoke began to blur her field of vision. She wasn't sure how much closer she should get or exactly what she had just witnessed.

Fire and a swelling mountain of black vapor filled the horizon. Hope picked up her cell phone and dialed 911. She passed a few other cars headed in the opposite direction as she inched on toward the refinery until she was as close as she dared. The sky was dark and thick. Further explosions reverberated. *There's no way anyone is alive inside that cauldron*, thought Hope. In a distracted trance she answered the dispatcher's few questions. After a surprisingly short conversation with 911, Hope called Eli. He interrupted their conversation after only a few words, and left her hanging for thirty seconds. It seemed like forever.

Hope's concentration was lost in the tumultuous blaze.

"Hope?" Her boss's voice drew her back from hell's inferno. "I have Roger Hemming on the line. He's with CNN."

Hope recognized the name of CNN's evening anchor.

Eli continued. "Start over when he tells you."

A TV narrative would be an even bigger scoop. She wondered how her boss had been able to put this deal together so quickly, especially since *The New York Times* and CNN were not on the best of terms. She would find out later. Still, she knew there was no way she, her boss, or the *Times* could lose in this situation. And she trusted Eli.

Hope heard Roger's voice. "Ready, Hope? We are live in four, three, two . . . We interrupt our regular programming to bring you this breaking news. On the line with us is Hope Wilson of *The New York Times* who, with CNN, is bringing you exclusive coverage of what is unfolding as a disaster of phenomenal proportions, live from outside Fredericksburg, Virginia, where a plane has just crashed into an oil refinery. Thank you for joining us, Hope. What can you tell us?"

Hope knew her host had just divulged all his knowledge regarding the situation and that he truly had no idea what Hope was going to say. She also knew the minions at CNN would quickly uncover everything related to what she was about to report and she fully expected to know more herself by the time her interview was done. But the scoop was now. She began to tell the story.

After fifteen minutes of narrative, broken up with sensationalizing questions and intermittent repetition that Hope's report was courtesy of *The New York Times*, Roger broke from Hope and said, "CNN has just been informed that the plane that went down was Freedom Airways' flight 2652 on its way from Dulles to Tampa with 187 people on board. The total number of people killed . . ."

Choose One:

    a) *Reality can be altered.*
    b) *Truth can be a lie.*
    c) *Death can be avoided.*
    d) *All of the above.*
    e) *None of the above.*

CHAPTER 4

Brad

"NO!" cried Stewart McLaughlin, vice president of Freedom Airways, as he shot out of his chair. "Not one of ours."

Stewart, who kept CNN on in his office as background noise instead of music, was stunned.

Roger returned to Hope. "We now know it was Freedom Airways' Flight 2652 that crashed into an oil refinery near Fredericksburg, Virginia."

Stewart didn't care what Hope had to say. He was paying attention to the images CNN's helicopter camera was providing. After seeing enough, he turned and ran out the door, took an immediate left, and burst into the office of Brad Stinson, CEO of Freedom Airways.

Brad looked irritated as he raised his head. The tall, broad-shouldered former athlete had been studying a stock pro forma. "Yes, Stewart?"

Stewart shuddered.

Brad continued. "Is there something I need to know?" Brad relied on his lieutenant, though privately he despised him for his fawning tendencies.

"Flight 2652 has crashed."

Brad sat back, muttering an expletive. This would require all his attention. "Crashed? What do you mean?" It was hard to tell if he was angry or worried. "When? Where?" He wanted all the details and he wanted them now.

"About fifteen minutes ago. Near Fredericksburg, Virginia." Stewart let the first fact soak in. "There's more. It crashed into an oil refinery. Multiple casualties on the ground."

Brad took another deep breath and adjusted his camel-hide chair. He stretched his arms, put his hands behind his head, and looked past Stewart to contemplate the news.

"And, sir," Stewart took a somber breath. "Scott Kingman was on the flight."

Brad already knew Scott was on that flight.

Stewart continued. "Everyone on board is presumed dead, along with a number of people on the ground."

Brad leaned forward, bringing his hands down on the desk before him. His face had gone from white to red. "How many were on board?"

"About 180. Don't know any numbers regarding those on the ground."

"Leave me alone. Get back here with Cindy in five minutes. We'll need to make a statement. Get the word out. Cindy is the only one to talk with the press. Anyone who says anything but 'No comment' will be on my plate for dinner."

Stewart left Brad's spacious mahogany and brass office that was eclectically decorated with Chihuly glass, two Monets, one Degas, a couple of Ming Dynasty vases, and floor-to-ceiling bookcases full of rare first-edition and leather-bound books with gold-leaf lettering.

Brad began to pace his sanctuary. This was certainly not what he needed. The stock was doing well, but only he knew how fragile everything was. The tightrope was quivering under his feet and the timing was terrible. He had to get this situation under control before it was too late. But there was a bright spot. Now that Scott was out of the picture, this meant an immediate promotion to chairman of the board. Brad stopped and gazed out his thirtieth-floor glass wall. There was another bright spot. Until Scott's estate was resolved, Brad could totally control the company because Scott's large block of stock could not be traded. Perhaps there was even a silver lining in this mess.

Stewart walked into Brad's office after a quasi-knock and stood by one of the three chairs in front of the desk. He looked at Brad's back and swallowed. "Sir?"

Brad returned to his throne and sat, clasping his hands in front of him on the desk. Stewart sat. They both waited for Cindy. Within seconds a slender, attractive woman with short red hair, wearing a sleek, navy blue Christian Dior business ensemble, scurried into the room, already talking as she crossed the threshold.

"Sir, you need to see this." Cindy Henderson turned on the TV.

Stewart's failure to mention the source of his information irritated Brad.

Stewart realized his mistake as Brad turned his narrowed eyes from him to the television.

What appeared to be a Picasso slid upward into a slot in the ceiling, revealing a live image of the fiery crash on a state-of-the-art, half-inch thick, four-foot plasma TV screen. A corner inset showed Hope's face while her voice recounted what she had witnessed. Brad recognized Hope's voice even before he saw her picture. He had met her socially once or twice at Scott's parties.

Hitting the intercom, he told his secretary to hold all calls and to say he would issue a statement shortly. They watched a few minutes of the broadcast without speaking.

Brad reached for the remote and turned down the

volume as Cindy took a seat next to Stewart in one of the plush, oversized, leather wing chairs in front of Brad's desk.

"This one's big." Cindy broke the silence.

"You can handle it." Brad's leadership was never in doubt. Nor was his confidence in his press spokeswoman. "Just keep your cool, like you did on the food poisoning incident and the stock options fiasco, and everything will be fine."

"Our insurance will cover the loss," Stewart interjected. "We pay enough in premiums, it's about time we get something out of those leeches."

Brad was dissatisfied with the tangent his lieutenant was on. Freedom's insurance was part of the defense strategy, but Brad was now on offense. "The important thing is that this does not get out of control and damage our customer base."

Brad's first order was to Stewart. "Work with marketing and come up with an incentive—mileage points, two for one, free hotels with each flight, something. We can't let our other passengers get alarmed."

"Done." Stewart had taken care of this detail after leaving Brad's office a few minutes ago.

"Cindy, I want you to launch some kind of compassionate sympathy campaign thing to make the families of the victims think we care. Flowers, cards, funeral expense reimbursement, free flights, chocolates—I don't care."

"I'll come up with something."

Brad shifted his focus to Stewart. "What do we know so far?"

"The number two engine had a problem before the crash, but they had stabilized everything. Traffic control and the flight crew did not seem the least bit concerned. And then, apparently, communications went dead. All we have to go on is the immediate descent of the plane and then nothing. Could be mechanical or maintenance failure. The plane was scheduled for a complete electrical system overhaul next week."

"It is *not* related to maintenance!" Brad corrected Stewart.

"Sir," Stewart cleared his throat, hesitated, then added with the candor he believed was required, "this wasn't our best plane."

"It is *not* mechanical failure and it has nothing to do with maintenance." This time Brad also included Cindy in this factual clarification.

They understood.

"How much of the plane is left?" asked Brad rhetorically. They had all seen the film from the CNN helicopter. The commander was merely having his subordinates verify their assets and liabilities.

Stewart summarized. "Based on what that reporter said, the rate at which the plane apparently fell, and the heat in that firestorm where the plane hit, I doubt anything is left. I mean—the plane crashed into an oil refinery! Even if it hadn't hit the refinery, it would have disintegrated on impact. The fuel tanks were full and the explosion was felt thirty miles away."

Brad pondered for a second, fingers steepled to his lips, and then lifted his head, smiling. "And what are the chances of finding a black box—*any* black box?"

"Nil," responded Stewart. "I doubt they'll find anything. I mean, that fire—"

Brad cut him off. "What about air traffic control? What was the last thing they heard?"

Cindy answered this one. She had been formulating a standard press release after being informed of the engine failure. "The last transmission was about the flight delay related to the engine shutdown."

"Engine shutdown?" Brad frowned. He didn't remember hearing anything about an engine shutdown. Stewart had only said "a problem."

As Stewart cleared his throat, Cindy clarified. "When the number two engine developed a problem, the flight crew handled it according to standard operating procedures. The pilot told the tower he was convinced the engine shutdown was related to contaminated fuel."

Brad was not yet appeased.

Cindy did not want to get sucked into Stewart's doghouse, yet she didn't want to lose an ally either. "But not to worry. The situation with the engine was resolved before they lost communication with the ground."

"I don't want any more surprises."

"Relax, Brad," said Cindy, deciding to take a more personal tone before he became furious. "It's under control. The engine shutdown and the crash are not related."

Although there was no way to prove this contention, Brad accepted her guarantee. If it wasn't true, he was confident Cindy would make it true. He began to cool down, and picked up where he had left off. "Okay. Good. Then about traffic—you're certain all communication was totally terminated between the plane and air traffic control?"

"Yes," said Cindy.

"And there were no references to any other problems before communications were cut off?"

"I'm confident. That was the first thing I checked," assured Cindy.

"Fine. Good. This is going to work out," said Brad, nodding.

Cindy and Stewart glanced at each other. This did not match their assessment. Privately they were resigned that this was a deathblow for Freedom Airways. Brad had proved himself to be amazing in some desperate situations before, but even Houdini couldn't extricate himself from this box.

Brad pursed his lips and stood. He paced slowly across the room as Cindy and Stewart sat and awaited his dictate. His initial temptation was to blame terrorists, but too many people would be involved. The last thing he wanted was to make this a bigger mess. He also needed to keep the FAA out of Freedom's maintenance department. He wasn't worried about the lawsuits, because he had personally negotiated the insurance agreement. He knew he had some leverage related to the contaminated fuel, but to blame the entire accident on the fuel company was too risky; plus, it might invite an audit of their maintenance and purchasing records. What he needed was a villain. He had to blame somebody or something. This would direct everyone away from what he believed, though would never admit—that the crash had resulted from his pushing the maintenance envelope a little too far.

Brad turned back to Cindy and Stewart. "Who was the pilot?"

"Shel Godowski," answered Stewart.

"Flight engineer?"

"Marcos Sanchez."

"First officer?"

"Bernie Bentson," Stewart completed the list.

Brad picked up the phone and called the best-paid human resources director in America.

"Phil. I need you in my office—now. Bring personnel files for Shel Godowski, Marcos Sanchez, and Bernie Bentson."

Phil Reinhold didn't ask questions. Nor did Cindy or Stewart, who were equally curious about the twist this path was taking.

They sat in silence. Brad was deep in thought.

The two minutes of tension were suffocating for Cindy and Stewart, who were relieved when the door opened. Phil, a retired marine colonel who still wore a crew cut, joined the team.

"You heard?" inquired Brad.

"Yes, sir."

"What's the latest?"

"We need to do something fast or—"

"What can you tell me about them?" Brad pointed to the folders.

Phil did not need folders. He knew every detail of every employee's life. With the exception of Brad, everyone at Freedom was intimidated by Phil. Even Scott, who had let Brad hire Phil, hadn't liked him, though he liked the results.

"Godowski. Fifty. Squeaky-clean. Devout Catholic. Family man. Twenty years' experience. No holes."

Brad's expression didn't change.

"Sanchez. Thirty-two. Climber. Living with his girlfriend, who's a fast-track exec with IBM. One kid. Fast car. Tough."

This was a side of Phil that Cindy and Stewart knew about but had never seen in action.

"Bernie Bentson." Phil slowed the pace. He knew this one would work. "Forty-three. A loner. Lots of time on the Internet. Gambles and loses. No known family. Recently diagnosed with diabetes and—here's the kicker—denied promotion due to his chief pilot's recommendation. We wanted to let him go, but the union objected."

"Perfect." Brad smiled.

Cindy was the first to catch on and immediately joined the burgeoning conspiracy. "But we need a smoking gun." She had worked in PR for the Postal Service at the time "going postal" worked its way into American slang. By portraying assailants as lunatic attackers, the Postal Service was able to shift attention completely onto demonized employees rather than focus on the work environment that might have contributed to the assailants' lunacy. The result was that post offices around the country, rightly or wrongly, remained safe places in the eyes of the public.

Brad hoped to so demonize Bernie Bentson that this potential corporate disaster would be passed over as a one-time anomalous attack by a lunatic. If they did it right, the public would merely chalk it up as another tragedy rather than blame Freedom Airways. But they needed evidence. "And," said Brad as he stood behind his desk, "nothing works better than a suicide note."

Phil took the ball and ran. "If specific enough, such a note could expedite the investigation and allow overworked detectives to get on with more important and less obvious crimes."

Brad calmly sat and lifted his hand innocently. "Bernie Bentson caused the crash; we simply need to prove it."

"Hold it. I'm a little lost." Stewart had to admit his ignorance. "Smoking gun?" Stewart was an asset to Brad for his unscrupulous and unconditional loyalty, not for a quick mind.

"Bernie Bentson caused the crash. He was an employee who went wacko and left a suicide note." Cindy filled in the spaces for her colleague.

"He did wh—?" Stewart caught himself and an enlightened grin slowly covered his face. "And the union wouldn't let us fire him." Once Stewart got it, he got it.

"Let me see that file." Cindy took the folder from Phil's hand.

"What about an e-mail?" Stewart offered, now up to speed with the rest of the team.

"That'll be tricky. How are you going to electronically

date it so it looks like it was created before the crash?" Phil sounded skeptical.

"No problem," boasted Stewart. Loyalty wasn't Stewart's only asset. He had been one of the first hackers to break into the Department of Defense.

"What about an affair?" offered Cindy.

All three men looked at her. Their unison caught her off guard.

"What? Why are you looking at me that way?" She had piqued their interest. "I could pretend I had a one-nighter with him—"

"No way," said Stewart.

She continued, not sure what the basis of his objection was "—and I also had an ongoing thing with Scott."

This one could be true.

"And Bernie was jealous of Scott and I was beginning to get worried for my safety." She completed the motive.

Brad raised his eyebrows as he mused to himself, *This could be good.*

Cindy changed her tone, holding her hands to her cheeks, caricaturing cute and innocent, and said, "But I never imagined he would do anything like this."

"C'mon Cindy," interjected Stewart. "You and Bentson? Did you even know him?"

Brad was smiling. He appreciated her willingness to sacrifice herself, though her idea was a long shot.

"I knew what he looked like. Even better, it would be believable. Who would confess to having an affair with a lunatic who killed hundreds of people because he was jealous of your 'relationship' with your boss, if it wasn't true? And coming up with evidence of a one-time fling wouldn't be tough." She thought about the personal implications of her plan. "Besides, my sex life hasn't been anything of note lately and this might even help."

"And Scott's reputation did precede him." Brad looked at Cindy.

"It worked for Monica Lewinsky," added Phil.

"Oh, right. Thanks," choked Cindy, her eyes narrowed at Phil.

Phil felt the invisible darts from her death glare. Even Cindy wasn't certain if her reflex response to his Lewinsky reference was due to resentment of the three men's easy acceptance of her troubled sex life or Phil's willingness to associate her with Clinton's White House intern.

Phil shook off Cindy's curse and moved on. "What about a witness to corroborate Bentson's plan to kill Scott and destroy the plane?" Phil was considering who owed him a favor.

"Yes to all three of your suggestions," said Brad, resolved. "Tighten it up. I want the details and the facts in thirty minutes."

Brad reached for his phone. He pushed his secretary's extension. "Notify the press. Tell them I'll make a statement in an hour. Schedule my meeting with the FAA immediately after the press conference. You should also invite the FBI."

As the unholy team was leaving Brad's office, he attached a few addenda. His first comment was to Cindy, who was still slightly offended that her offer of fictitious sexual promiscuity had been so easily accepted. "Cindy, you need to make it clear we are fully cooperating with the authorities." Brad then addressed Stewart. "I want you to call the FBI first, then the FAA. I assume our damage guys are already on site—and keep me posted."

Their orders were clear. Cindy wanted more information, but at this point there was none to be had. Brad had given them the framework. It was now up to her to keep the team informed of any new details as she, Stewart, and Phil made them up.

Stewart held the door open for Cindy, who was given a wide berth by both Stewart and Phil.

"And, Stewart," Brad said as Stewart was closing the door. "I'm trusting your assurance about the total destruction of the airplane. That means there will be no black boxes showing up."

"I understand." He drew the door shut behind him.

On the TV monitor in Brad's chambers Hope's voice could still be heard, though she was now only one of many providing commentary. The CNN camera crew had arrived and arranged a makeshift set with Hope's car and the burning refinery as the backdrop. Roger routinely introduced her with, "And now back to Hope Wilson from *The New York Times*, who was an eyewitness to the disaster and is on site."

It was thirty minutes into the broadcast before Hope learned that Scott Kingman had been on the plane. It wasn't until she called her old friend Senator Henry Newcastle that she was able to find out who she needed to talk with at the FAA to get the inside scoop. And when Brad called her at home later that evening and promised to keep her personally informed, it was undeniably obvious to Hope—she was in the middle of her moment of fame. She had become a media celebrity.

Based on the inside information from Brad, Hope was also the first to formally report the details regarding the cause of the crash in her lead article in the morning edition of *The New York Times*. The headline read:

CRASH CAUSED BY DISGRUNTLED EMPLOYEE IN LOVE TRIANGLE

CHAPTER 5

The Talk Show

Cindy finished reading Hope's article and looked up with a grin. The four conspirators restrained themselves, not wanting their celebration to be heard outside Brad's office.

Brad's feet were on the desk, his chair was tilted back, and his hands served as a pillow. He unclasped his hands and reached forward to push a button on his desk. The Picasso slid out of sight as the CNN logo appeared in the bottom corner of the television screen. His smile got bigger.

It was the "Royal Lawrence Live" show. Hope sat across a U-shaped table from Royal Lawrence. Beneath Hope's name on the screen it read, "*The New York Times* reporter, eyewitness to the Freedom Airways disaster."

Royal began his interview. "So, tell us what you saw."

Hope was prepared. It had been twenty-four hours since the accident. She had stayed up most of the night gathering and reviewing her notes and practicing her delivery. She was, after all, a newspaper reporter, not a "talking head," and this would be the first time she had been on national TV, other than yesterday's ad hoc reporting.

"I was outside Fredericksburg on my way back to D.C. when I noticed something falling from the sky. At first I didn't know what it was, but it didn't take long to figure that out. It became apparent the plane was headed in the direction of an oil refinery I could see off to my right. Call me crazy, but I drove in the direction of the refinery. I was less than a mile away when it hit. A massive fireball exploded out of the refinery. I didn't want to get too close since everything was on fire and I was concerned about other explosions.

"By the time the fire crews arrived, I was at the entrance gate to the refinery. Even at that distance, the heat was tremendous. I learned later that, with the exception of those people who were in the administration building on the south-eastern side of the compound, there were no survivors. To the best of my knowledge all the casualties were either in the refinery compound or on the plane."

It was Royal's turn, but first he needed to insert the contracted endorsement of *The New York Times*. "By now most everyone knows that *The New York Times*, primarily because of your phenomenal reporting, has taken the lead in informing the public about this disaster." Royal continued with his interview. "For those viewers who haven't been able to follow the details as closely as others, please tell us what you know about the cause of the accident."

"According to my sources . . ." said Hope, beginning with the four words press people have used more than any others to justify even some of the most outlandish stories, ". . . allegedly, the first officer deliberately caused the crash."

"You mean Bernie Bentson?" Royal clarified.

"Yes. According to my sources, they are still trying to verify exactly how he carried it all out, but they are confident he caused the accident and that the evidence will support their speculation."

The villain had been created, tried, and hanged.

Hope continued. "Because of the note he left behind, which Freedom Airways turned over to the FBI shortly after the accident, the authorities are convinced that co-pilot Bentson cut off communications with air traffic control, allegedly by manually disabling the communication system. After that, according to Bentson's note and FBI speculation, he subdued the rest of the cockpit personnel before steering the plane into the ground by setting the stabilizer trim to the full nose-down position."

"Any ideas on how he subdued the rest of the cockpit?"

"Not yet. They're speculating he used a weapon of some sort, perhaps the crash ax."

"Was there any indication he had intended to hit the refinery?"

"Not yet. According to the information Bentson left behind, it is quite clear that his primary target was Scott Kingman, chairman of the board and president of Freedom Airways, who was on the plane. The authorities are currently speculating that the refinery was a coincidence, or perhaps Bentson picked the target once he had control of the plane."

"But what about the issue of the engine that died earlier?"

"Based on everything I've heard from Freedom, the FAA, the FBI, and others, everyone is convinced it was merely coincidental and unrelated to the accident."

"How do they know?"

"They don't know for sure, of course, since there is no hard evidence left to look at because everything was incinerated in the crash. However, based on what they do know from the last communication with air traffic control, the engine failure is apparently wholly unrelated to the crash. After all, the Boeing 727 is designed to be able to fly with only one engine operable."

"I've heard there might have been some contaminated fuel involved with the shut-down of the engine."

"Correct. As it turns out, contaminated fuel is the most likely cause of the engine failure. I've been told the fuel tank of the engine that was shut down had been filled from a different fuel truck than the other two engines. That particular fuel truck is currently under heavy scrutiny, as is the driver of the truck. At this point the belief is that, when the driver realized he didn't have enough fuel in his truck after filling the first two tanks, he took a shortcut. Rather than refill his truck and be blamed for delaying the flight, he filled the third tank from a truck that hadn't been in use for eight weeks. In my opinion, the driver made a big mistake and is very lucky his shortcut wasn't the cause of the accident."

"So, the fuel guy isn't being charged with causing the disaster?"

"Not to the best of my knowledge."

"What can you tell us about the infamous black boxes that are supposed to record the flight data and other information?"

"The fact is, if they weren't destroyed in the crash, they were certainly destroyed in the explosion and fire at the refinery. You've seen the pictures. There wasn't anything left of the place. It was so hot in that inferno that the metal of the plane melted into what looked like pools of mercury. Though black boxes are made to withstand almost anything, there is no way they could endure such extreme heat, which even caused some of the surrounding fences to melt."

"And what can you tell us about Bernie Bentson?"

With that lead-in, Hope began the story of the villain devised by Brad and his team. She spoke of Bernie Bentson's affair with Cindy Henderson, the reports of his jealousy, his rejection for promotion, the notes, and the now famous e-mail suicide note. The evidence was so compelling that, rather than question the validity of the smoking gun, the nation began to use the concocted villain's description as a profile for other employees who might try a copycat attack.

Satisfied smirks covered the faces of Brad, Cindy, Stewart, and Phil. They had just heard the very words they wanted to hear.

CHAPTER 6

Two Funerals

The alarm at the side of Wil's bed blared. "Ugh," moaned Wil. His right arm, with one practiced, semi-conscious motion, hit the snooze button and then settled back into place next to his lethargic body. The clock said 8:30. It had been a tough week. Today was the climax.

"Good morning, Wil," came a much softer and welcoming sound.

Wil rolled over and pulled his beloved wife into his embrace. He pressed his lips to her forehead and thought how lucky he was. Ten years after he had broken off their relationship to pursue his career, he'd been reunited with his true love. The past three years, since their marriage, had been the happiest of his life.

"Meow." Napoleon, their huge and aged tabby, began to nestle between them. Hope and Wil reached to give him a pat and then continued in the routine the three had perfected. Napoleon's vociferous purring required them to talk a little louder.

"How'd you sleep?" asked Hope, her voice muffled on Wil's shoulder.

"Okay," yawned Wil. He was less than truthful.

"Me too."

The events of the past week had rattled them, particularly Wil.

First there was Scott Kingman's death in the plane crash. Then they heard the news that, on the same day, a drunk driver had killed the daughter of their new friends, Franklin and Rebecca Jackson. Incredibly, hours before Rochelle was killed, Wil had gone to lunch with Franklin after delivering a guest lecture at George Washington University, where Franklin was a philosophy professor. During lunch, Franklin had not been reserved about how fortunate he was to have Rochelle as his daughter. Wil could not imagine Franklin's emotions hours later when he learned of his daughter's senseless death.

The deaths had intensified Wil's reflections about life and what really mattered, issues that had surfaced after he became a husband and father. Making matters worse, Wil's restless thoughts about death compounded the difficulty with sleep he was already having due to the time zone change and his recent need to use the bathroom more often, especially at night. The net result was that sleep was not happening.

"Today's a big day," said Hope, trying to sound buoyant.

"I still can't believe it," groaned Wil. "*Two* funerals."

"I know."

"I haven't been to a funeral since my father's—when I was just a kid."

"I'm not exactly an expert at this either."

"Do you think there'll be a lot of people?"

"Probably." Hope glanced at Wil inquisitively.

Wil didn't know why he'd asked.

Hope kissed Wil lightly on the lips, ignoring Napoleon's complaint at being squeezed between them. Hope then scooched out of bed to make her way to the kitchen, where she poured two mugs of coffee that had already brewed. They loved their timed coffeemaker.

A minute later, she returned.

"Here you go, hon. Perhaps this will help."

He reached for the good medicine. This new dark-roasted Colombian blend by Starbucks was his favorite.

"Thank you."

"Such sincerity. You'd think I'd just offered to quench the thirst of a dying man."

Wil contemplated how accurately that analogy matched the way he felt.

Hope's attention turned to the mound of fur that had occupied her place. "Out of the way, you claim-jumper."

Napoleon, who had been known to attack deliverymen he mistook for trespassers, acquiesced to the alpha female. He also knew the routine. He slowly stood, arched his back, washed his right paw, and then tilted his head to look at Hope for clarification.

Hope pointed to the foot of the bed and said, "Now."

With a look of insult, Napoleon sauntered nonchalantly to the foot of the bed, circled twice, and curled up on his side.

"Do you think he understands English?" asked Wil.

"Yes."

"Just wondering." The performance had been convincing.

Hope slipped into a maternal mode as she slid back into bed. "So, how many times did you have to get up last night?"

"A couple." Again Wil slighted the truth. He hated doctors, and he didn't want to give his wife any more ammunition.

Wil and Hope adjusted their pillows and settled in, backs to the headboard, shoulders touching, letting the heat of their coffee mugs warm their hands.

"Your mom left a note on the counter," said Hope. "She went for a walk with Steven. I guess he was awake and playing when she went in to see him."

"Steven will be fine." Wil knew the real issue was Hope's

reluctance to trust anyone else with their child. "Mom knows what she's doing. Look how well I turned out." He smiled.

Hope glared at Wil. Such weak reinforcement did not help. She loved Wil, but she also knew that Wil's mom, the battered wife of an abusive alcoholic, had not been a good mother.

Yet Hope also knew that Wil's mom had gone through a transformation following her husband's death. And though it was too late for Wil's or his older brother's childhood, Hope assumed it was the new Betty whom Wil was actually asking her to trust with their two-year-old son.

"Really. It will be fine," said Wil, drawing Hope closer with his left arm, trying not to spill any coffee. "Really." He pressed his lips against the top of her head.

Regardless of his childhood, Wil appreciated how quickly his mom had arranged to come stay with them following the events of the past week.

Betty Wilson seemed to sense this would be a good time to visit. She was also eager to spend time with her grandson, whom she hadn't seen since visiting them in Israel eighteen months earlier. At that time she'd been astounded at how much Steven had grown during the eight months following Wil and Hope's spending Christmas at her house in Hazel Dell, Washington. Betty also welcomed the chance to see Wil, with whom her relationship was gradually improving. She seized the opportunity to come, and both Wil and Hope had appreciated her help during the hectic week.

"Do you think they'll be like church services?" Wil refocused on the funerals.

"Possibly." Hope tried to track with her husband.

"I find it odd. Scott spent his whole life rejecting religion and now, after he's dead, everyone's gathering in a church for his memorial."

"It's because of the facilities, not the sentiment," noted Hope. "Saint Peter's Episcopal is a nice place after all."

They both knew Scott would have chosen another site, had he been asked. They knew Scott was in no way religious, which didn't mean he wasn't a nice fellow. In fact, most of the people who had known Scott liked him. He was the life of most parties. He worked to support the United Way's fund-raising campaigns. His personal charitable contributions had been well publicized. He had maintained close ties with nearly all his college buddies and was genuinely caring toward his friends. And he would never have hurt anyone; that is, unless they were on the opposite end of a business transaction. Though he'd had difficulty with personal relationships, he'd never been mean, and it was highly likely that the five women he had been most involved with over the past nine years, four of whom he had lived with at one time or another, would all show up at the funeral with kind things to say about him. It was a measure of his compelling personality that Scott could break off a relationship and leave a woman thinking she still loved him and wishing him well.

"It's still odd, though," concluded Wil. "And I have no idea what to expect at the Jackson funeral. I'm even wondering why I agreed to go."

Wil's best friend, Steve Halterman, had persuaded Wil to accompany him to Rochelle's funeral. Four weeks ago, Hope and Wil had met the Jacksons at a dinner party at the Haltermans' home. Steve and Franklin had become close friends through their involvement with an inner-city program where they both volunteered. Steve knew of Franklin's fascination with Wil's work in Israel and thought the two would enjoy an interchange.

Since Wil and Franklin hadn't met each other through the university or the Smithsonian, where Franklin was a consultant, Steve took matters into his own hands and invited both men and their wives to dinner. It was a hit. One of the more interesting discussions that night concerned a book Franklin was writing that compared Hesse's *Siddhartha* with the Bible's *Ecclesiastes*. So, when the subject of the funeral came up during Wil and Steve's weekly lunch together, Wil agreed to go.

"What was I supposed to say?" Wil was still rationalizing. "I didn't want to look like a racist or like I was afraid to go to a church. Besides, even though we've only known them for a month, I really like Franklin . . . and Rochelle did baby-sit Steven twice."

"I can hardly believe she's dead," Hope said quietly.

Wil sighed. "Going to the funeral is the least we can do. My guess is I'll see a number of folks from the University or the Smithsonian there, too. Did I tell you Franklin started an inner-city tutoring program?"

"Yes."

Wil was rambling, his uneasiness evident. Thoughts about the upcoming funerals forced him to think about the last funeral he attended twenty years ago, which he remembered perfectly. He also remembered the beatings he and his mom received at the hands of his drunken father, a church deacon who would talk about Jesus even while he beat the daylights out of them. He remembered how things had gotten particularly ugly when there was another woman involved, like there had been the night his dad died in the car crash.

Wil hadn't been inside a church since then, except when it was related to his archaeological work. Their wedding had been held in a community hall in Oshkosh, Wisconsin, Hope's hometown. They consented to his mom's request to hold a reception in Wil's hometown of Hazel Dell only if it wasn't held in a church. Now he would be attending two funeral services in two churches in one day.

The first service would be in a church named after a dead disciple of a man Wil loathed. The second would be in an African Evangelical Methodist Bible church.

"I really do not want to go to the Jackson funeral," Wil said resignedly, knowing his candor wouldn't change anything.

"Steve said we would find it interesting." Hope reminded Wil of the original justification for saying yes to Steve's invitation.

"I wish I knew what he meant by 'interesting'," responded Wil. "The last time he used that word was when he had me taste some slimy Vietnamese fish concoction at the restaurant of one of his church members." Wil was seriously second-guessing his decision, but knew it was too late to back out.

Wil's friendship with Steve went back to Wil's youth and was a mystery to everyone who knew them. The two had met at a youth outing where Steve was the youth leader. Steve was now a nationally known evangelical Christian pastor. Wil was a renowned atheist archaeologist and as anti-Christian as one could be. Their friendship had spanned more than twenty years and had even survived the time when Wil had turned the world upside down by claiming to have found the bones of Jesus, which, had it been true, would have killed Christianity.[*] Steve had even spoken at their wedding, although in somewhat peculiar circumstances as neither Hope nor Wil was a Christian, and Steve's beliefs about marriage did not coincide with theirs. The three agreed Steve would not officially perform their wedding. Instead, he was to deliver a message at a public ceremony, more like the captain of a ship than a Christian minister. Hope and Wil's marriage was actually

---

[*] See *Wil's Bones* by Kevin Bowen. ISBN 1930892128

made official by a visit to the justice of the peace. This was, again, at Hope and Wil's insistence that their marriage ceremony not involve any form of capitulation to Christianity. Yet Wil and Steve's friendship bridged their differences, and their mutual respect and integrity remained intact.

The snooze alarm sounded for the second time.

"I guess we'd better get going," they said simultaneously.

Wil kissed his wife one more time before heading to the shower. Hope staggered in the direction of the kitchen, hearing Steven's voice. She nearly tripped over Napoleon as the cat shot out to the kitchen to see the only person he liked more than Hope.

"Papolion!" shouted Steven as Hope walked into the kitchen.

Steven reached for his best friend. The eighteen-pound cat willingly let the two-year-old try to pick him up, but Steven lost his balance and sent both of them sprawling in a tangle of little hands, feet, fur, and paws.

"I torry kitty." The two-year-old meant it.

"I wish I had my camera." Betty knew it wouldn't have mattered if she had found her camera because she had used up her film the day she arrived. "That is so cute!"

Napoleon snuggled against the little boy sitting in the center of the kitchen floor. Hope looked slightly jealous until Steven looked up and saw the face of someone he liked even more than his cat.

"Mama!" Steven's arms went out toward Hope.

Hope's motherly envy dissolved. Steven's smile beamed as Hope moved in his direction. "Mama pick up."

"There's my little boy!" said Hope as she scooped up Steven, swinging him high into the air.

Steven's screams of delight mingled with Hope's laughter as they spun around until Hope almost lost her balance.

Betty moved toward the kitchen sink and instinctively began to do the dishes.

"Mom, c'mon, you don't have to do those."

"It's not a problem. Go ahead and relax. Why don't you let me fix you some breakfast? Do you think Wil would like some eggs? I'd be happy to put something together." Betty was unusually eager to please. "I know what a day you and Wil have before you, and I don't have anything else to do."

Regardless of what was behind Betty's extreme servitude, Hope sighed thankfully and said, "That would be wonderful."

Hope now turned her attention to the two-year-old attachment clinging to her neck. She eased herself into the large wing chair in the kitchen corner, perching Steven on the arm of the chair with one of his arms still around her neck. Napoleon soon joined mother and son in the chair, purring, rolling over, and arching his back. As Hope stroked the delighted cat, she looked at Steven and said, "How's my sweetie?"

"Papolion thoft." Steven's hand stroked the cat.

"He sure is, isn't he?" Hope cuddled Steven who, now in the complete comfort of his mother's arms, was directing his attention to the motorized fur ball.

Napoleon's eyes were closed, his paws were making little kneading motions, and his engine was at maximum purr.

"Okay, sweetie, Mommy has to get ready to go." Hope stood up sideways, placing Steven in the chair and letting Napoleon slide from her lap to settle beside Steven. She bent down one last time to kiss her son's head. "Grandma's going to take care of you."

Whether he didn't understand or didn't care, Hope wasn't certain. Rather than say bye-bye or beg her to stay, Steven struggled to his feet and headed toward the back door he had come through with his grandmother a few minutes earlier. Napoleon followed him.

Betty glanced over her shoulder at Steven then quickly turned back to the sink. She began to scrub the dishes more attentively, her shoulders tense with anticipation.

Steven reached for the door. "See doggie. Nice doggie."

Hope looked inquisitively at Betty who was looking intensely at the dishwater, trying to avoid the next and obvious question.

"Dog? What dog?" asked Hope.

Betty was silent. The two-year-old pulled open the door, revealing the happiest-looking canine Hope had ever seen. Napoleon hissed and fled the scene. Attacking strange humans was one thing; a seventy-pound dog was not in the cards.

The surprise, which was not wearing a collar, had the coloring and build of a chocolate lab and the wavy fur of a cocker spaniel. The dog's feet were moving, as if running in place, but he didn't leave his spot. *Should he stay or should he go see the nice lady?*

"What is this?" said Hope, spinning around to encounter the back of Wil's mom, still focused on the dishes in the bottom of the sink. "Betty?"

Betty turned to Hope, but not before Hope turned back to Steven, who had wrapped his arms around the dog's neck. The appreciative animal gave Steven a lick right across his face. Steven began to laugh hysterically, lost his balance, and sat hard on the floor. The dog, apparently thinking it was his duty to right the child, began to nudge Steven, trying to help the fallen child stand. Steven only laughed louder in contagious joy.

When Betty saw Hope smiling and fighting not to laugh, she decided it was safe to disconnect from the dishes.

With a glare that was betrayed by a giggle, Hope turned to the grinning grandmother. "Explain!" She pointed at the dog.

Betty was prepared. "Steven and I were sitting on a bench in the park when we heard whimpering coming from the bushes a few yards behind us. Because Steven was intrigued, we went to investigate."

Hope listened patiently.

Betty continued her confession. "When I pulled the branches out of the way, there was Boo—"

"Boo?" interrupted Hope.

"Boo. That's what Steven calls him. Well, anyway, Boo was just staring at us. He looked so sad." Betty paused. "I tell you, Hope, I don't think I've ever seen a more expressive dog. You'd think he was part human or something."

Hope raised her eyebrows.

"Before I knew what was happening, Steven rushed up to Boo and began patting the dog on the head. Obviously this made me uncomfortable, you know, a strange dog and all, so I picked up Steven and took him back to the bench and . . . wouldn't you know it, he began to cry, 'Doggie, Doggie, Doggie.' Steven wasn't hurt. He was crying because I had just taken him away from his new best friend."

"Oooh." Hope's face softened. She could hear Steven's cry.

"Boo walked over to us to investigate, but I told him to stay back."

"And?" Hope wanted the rest of the story.

"Boo immediately stopped when I told him to stay back and just sat there, staring at us with those big black eyes, and whimpering his request to come to us. I tried to tell Steven we couldn't keep the doggie. It didn't help that the dog slowly scooted closer to us. Finally, I gave in. I looked at Boo and said, 'It's okay. You can come over here.' And he did! He walked right up to us, put his head on my knee, and begged me to take him home."

"Begged you to take him home?"

"It was the darnedest thing!"

Betty smiled as Hope turned to look at Steven and Boo. Steven was climbing on the back of the dog. Boo didn't stand up, somehow sensing his rider lacked the balance to stay in the saddle.

Betty strengthened her case. "They do get along pretty well. Don't they?"

Next came the anticipated interrogation. "Whose dog is it? What if he has fleas? What if his owner comes looking for him? You don't really think we can keep him?"

Betty didn't need to say another word. When Hope was done having the conversation with herself, the decision was made that they would post some signs in the park and, if no one claimed the dog, they would keep it. Betty knew Steven had a new pet. She only wondered how Hope was going to break it to Wil.

"I'll give Boo a bath today while you're out," Betty offered. "Now, about breakfast. I'd better get started on it if you're going to get out of here on time." Betty was relieved to have that part of the morning behind her.

Feeling both hoodwinked and stunned at how life changes so quickly, Hope walked to Steven, picked him up for another hug and kiss, and set him down saying, "What's the doggie's name?"

"Boo."

Hope was surprised at the clarity of her two-year-old son's voice.

"They are a sight to be seen," observed Betty.

"Indeed they are." It was time for Hope to get on with her day. But first, she had a surprise for Wil.

CHAPTER 7

The First Funeral

Saint Peter's Episcopalian Church was packed. The priest, a woman in her late forties, wore a black robe and a clerical collar. The organist played a selection from the Brahms *Requiem* as the ushers tried to persuade the stragglers to sit further forward in the cavernous sanctuary. The narrow, recessed, stained-glass windows provided the only lighting, which was barely enough for Wil to make out the faces of people a dozen rows in front of him or behind him. His eyes met those of one man he hadn't seen since college. There was another fellow whom both Wil and Hope had met at one of Scott's dinner parties. Wil reasoned the majority of folks knew Scott from Freedom Airways or through Scott's charity work.

Two women a few rows in front of Wil and Hope had their heads bowed and held tissues to their eyes. Wil thought one looked like girlfriend number four.

Wil also easily identified the attendees from the press, cameras and notepads not being standard-issue funeral attire.

Eventually the ushers managed to settle most of the audience. The priest stepped to the pulpit as the organ sounded its last chord. "On behalf of Scott Kingman's family," she began, "I want to thank you for coming to this memorial for Scott, who was tragically killed only a few days ago. Today we celebrate the life of our friend and associate who gave us so much. While we know it was hate that took him from us, it is kindness and a giving spirit that Scott leaves behind as his legacy. Today we will remember a good man, a man who knew how to put others before himself and who was always willing to help when someone was in need."

Wil began to wonder if he was at the right service. True enough, Scott was a nice guy and he had done a lot of nice things. But Wil could not bring himself to think of Scott as some sort of saint. His combative spirit, which during his college days caused him to go to functions solely to be contrary with the speakers, was more revealing of who Scott was than the minister's introductory comments. Scott also had the ability to sell anything. Wil remembered the day Scott told him he was going to buy an airline company. Wil was in England to receive an award and Scott was there on business. They were having lunch at Yamamoto's of London. Wil clearly recalled the place because the aggressive, sushi-eating Scott had made him eat a foul-tasting sea slug morsel that almost sent Wil home. Without being too specific, Scott told him he had secured the financing to buy a bankrupt regional carrier. Five years later, Scott's picture was on the covers of *Forbes* and *Fortune*, he was living in a mansion, and he had begun to collect classic cars like they were T-shirts. Over the same time frame, Scott had also told Wil about some of the lawsuits he was involved in. Though Wil didn't know the details, it wasn't difficult to read between the lines to know that a number of people would not concur with the reverend's description of Scott.

"Let us begin our service of remembrance with Scott's mother, Carolyn Kingman."

Mrs. Kingman ascended the stairs from her front and center seat. From the podium, composed and confident, she smiled at the assembly and began to tell stories about Scott. Wil had met Scott's mother previously, but had never taken the time to talk with her, and Scott certainly had never told Wil his mom was a comedian. Her stories were funny in and of themselves, but her delivery was incredible. One thing Wil had not expected to see at a funeral was tears of laughter. He began to understand the roots of Scott's irreverence and wit.

Mrs. Kingman concluded with a story that had taken place after their family had moved to Rochester, New York. A seventeen-year-old high school thug had been bullying the elementary school children at the bus stop, taking their lunches and lunch money. After one particular day at the bus stop, Scott decided he would not tolerate the situation. He organized the other children to deal with it. "I remember—it was about a week after moving to town—Scott asked me if we had any rotten eggs. I didn't, of course, which disappointed him. He settled for an extra thick and juicy egg salad sandwich. I had no idea what he was up to and he didn't tell me. That evening I received calls from mothers of the other children. They wanted to thank me for the confidence their children now had. Apparently, all twelve children took extra gooey sack lunches that day. When the bully told the children he wanted to see what they had brought him, Scott gave the command to attack. I remember one mother of a six-year-old girl telling me her daughter had been given the honor of rubbing her peanut butter and jelly sandwich in the bully's hair. The best part was when I received a call from the bully's mother, who wanted to protest that my son's gang had ruined her child's clothing. When I explained my son was only seven and none of the other children were over nine, she didn't know what to say. When I told her the children had, apparently, grown tired of financing her son's cigarette habit, the mother ended our conversation by actually thanking me."

Mrs. Kingman took a deep breath. "Scott never changed. He was someone who didn't accept obstacles or bullies. He was unique, and I am and always will be proud of him." Her eyes shone with tears as she looked at the audience one last time. "And I want to thank all of you for being such an important part of my son's life." Mrs. Kingman's composure began to crumble, but she mustered her last bit of strength and said, with intense sincerity, "Thank you for being here today."

The next speaker was one of Scott's associates. Some of his jokes were slightly off-color and made sense only to the 120 or so Freedom employees in attendance. He wasn't as entertaining as Scott's mom.

The seventh speaker was Scott's sister, Melissa. Her face was reddened, though her tears had dried. She began, "Those of us who were close to Scott know he was not a religious man."

This brought a few laughs that quickly died down as the audience realized this was not intended to be a continuation of the levity they had enjoyed the previous thirty-five minutes. The mood of the service had changed.

"He told me one time that, while he didn't believe in a god or heaven or anything like that, he did believe in eternal life. Perhaps this surprises some of you. It certainly caught me by surprise. Scott told me he believed all of us have eternal life in our accomplishments and in the memories of those who know us. Maybe that is one of the reasons he was so supportive of the United Way. He knew he wasn't going to live forever and that agencies like the United Way were going to long outlast him. Consider the Boys and Girls Clubs he helped to fund in Washington.

"Think of all of the lives of the children who will benefit, even today, because of Scott's willingness to donate his time and money to those projects. And think of Freedom Airways.

The last I heard, there were 3,200 people who earn their livelihoods because he had the courage to create this company." Melissa paused to let her words sink in. "Yet, beyond those things, in some mysterious way, Scott lives on in each of us. Close your eyes for a moment. Think of one of the pleasant times you and Scott had together."

She paused, expecting compliance.

"Can you see him?" The whispered question was rhetorical. "He is there, and he is here with us now." Melissa took a breath before articulating her closing statement, making eye contact with the jury. "So, today, as we honor our friend, my brother, let us pledge not to forget him. He has given much to us and he has changed us. We are thankful for his life and for him." She paused. "Thank you." Her eyes declared her true appreciation of the people at her brother's funeral.

Melissa descended the altar's center stairs and sat in the front row next to her mother, who was crying as she reached up to embrace her daughter.

"Wow, that was moving," said Wil to Hope.

"Thank you, Melissa," said the priest. "Next, we will hear from Brad Stinson."

Brad stepped up to the pulpit. He exuded confidence. His relaxed and dignified poise matched his oratorical skills, both refined through experience. Scott had hired Brad as CEO primarily because of his commanding presence and easy self-assurance.

Scott and Brad had known each other since Yale Law School. Following graduation, they practiced law while working for competing brokerage houses. After a few years they decided, in the era of corporate takeovers, public offerings, and leveraged buyouts, they might do well on their own.

"Why *guide* the conqueror when you can be the conqueror?" was the pitch Scott had used to persuade Brad to join him a year after he had started Freedom Airways. Scott remained the largest shareholder and Brad quickly became the second largest. Brad had proven his worth after Freedom Airways' stock took a severe hit on the market following a food poisoning incident. According to Scott, Brad was able to single-handedly "fix" what could have been a major disaster. Until six months ago, Scott had never said anything negative about Brad to Wil. As far as Wil recalled, the comment, which was only in passing, had something to do with control and shareholder relations. Wil had thought nothing of it at the time.

Brad spoke in the well-modulated tones he had culti-vated. "I've known Scott for over fourteen years. In all my professional dealings and experience, I have never met a greater visionary or a harder worker. And this wasn't only at Freedom. I had the unique privilege of sitting on a number of charity boards with Scott. I sincerely doubt anyone cared as much as Scott. His generous giving was proof of this. In fact," Brad paused as he appeared to recall a special moment, "I remember a time when we were working on a particularly difficult permit process in a city where we wanted to set up a new office. We had to attend the full city council meeting. As it turned out, the director for a local nonprofit homeless shel-ter was on the docket right before us. The director's presentation concluded with a rather painful dialogue between her and the council members, who wanted to support the homeless shelter but knew the shelter's fund-raising efforts were not going to meet the city's minimum requirements to justify their ongoing support. As the council was about to vote to close the program, which was contrary to everyone's desires, Scott and I came up with an idea on how we might be able to help. At my urging, we stood and received permission to speak."

He's good, thought Wil, who saw through Brad's façade.

"The funny thing was, only two members of the city council knew who we were. I asked the shelter's director how much was needed to keep the shelter running for the next three years. The director, stunned by the question from a stranger, quickly did some calculations and said $200,000. The director then added that whatever the amount was, it would soon be immaterial since, without immediate funding, the shelter would have to close. Scott and I quickly discussed the situation. We concluded the right thing to do was to help. Scott addressed the council and said, 'We work for Freedom Airways. We firmly believe being part of a community involves supporting what the community thinks is important. Such being the case, on behalf of Freedom Airways, we are hereby pledging $200,000 to support the homeless shelter over the next three years.'"

Brad paused, allowing the audience's murmurs and sighs to be fully appreciated before continuing. "The good news is, because Scott and I did this, the rescue shelter is still helping poor and disenfranchised people today. I tell this story to point out what a truly special person Scott Kingman was."

A few insiders had heard this story before. They'd heard it was all Scott's idea, and that Brad had actually objected. Hope and Wil had heard an even more personal version from Scott when he boasted how he had saved more than $1,000,000 in delay costs and tax breaks by throwing a couple of hundred thousand dollars at "some pathetic local charity." Scott was now silent on the issue and Brad had just made sure everyone, regardless of the truth, knew the official version, of which he was a co-star. And, courtesy of the press attending the funeral, Freedom Airways' kindness and charity giving would be well publicized.

Hope was swift enough to know a spin when she heard

one, and could not believe her colleagues in the press were buying it.

"He's good," said Hope, echoing Wil's thoughts about Brad. Hope's mumbled compliment included a hint of disdain for Brad as she thought: *What kind of person would use a friend's funeral as an opportunity for self-aggrandizement?* For the first time since the crash, Hope began to wonder if she really liked, let alone trusted, Brad Stinson.

Having dealt with the public relations issue, Brad now turned to the personal. His chameleon faith could adjust to any ceremony. Unlike Scott, who was a sincere atheist, Brad would become whatever benefited him at the time. He picked up on Melissa's comments. "I agree with everything Melissa said earlier, and I do and will remember all the good times we used to have." He took a deep breath. "But I also know I will miss him." Brad's eyes shone as he blinked. "Even though I know Scott will live forever in our hearts and in the good things he has done, I am going to miss him terribly." Brad bowed his head away from the microphone and cleared his throat. With his head and shoulders slightly turned sideways, he appeared to be struggling to maintain his composure. Most were convinced, and many in the audience began to cry. With the poise of a premiere Shakespearean actor, Brad turned his body toward the audience and looked to the ceiling. With convincing tears in his eyes, he said, "Scott, buddy, I am going to miss you." His speech didn't seem finished, but Brad clearly was. With his head lowered, Brad made his way back to his seat in the front row opposite the family. He put his head in his hands and leaned forward over his knees.

Even the priest looked overcome as she stood. She walked to the pulpit for the last time and, after pausing for a moment while people refocused, said in a welcoming tone, "Thank you all for coming. Please join the family for refreshments immediately following the service in the fellowship hall, out the sanctuary doors, down the corridor, and to the left."

The organist began Bach's *Fugue in D Minor,* and the audience began to make their way to the exit doors.

Wil and Hope stayed at the reception only long enough to pay their respects to the family. Time urged them to leave for the next funeral.

There is always more to a story.

CHAPTER 8

Encounters

Hope and Wil were on their way to the exit, which would take them back down the hall toward the entrance to the sanctuary.

"How much time do we have?" Wil's question betrayed his anxiety about the next funeral.

"About forty-five minutes. We'll be fine. We're only fifteen minutes from Steve's house."

Wil noticed the rest room sign and let go of Hope's hand. "I'll be right back. I've been holding it since we arrived."

Hope mumbled her disapproval of her husband's candor as she watched him hustle down the hall. Wil didn't look back.

This is a first, thought Hope, realizing she was alone in a church foyer. Like a tourist she looked at the photos on the wall and read the captions. Based on the dates on some of the pamphlets, the '50s look of the interior, and the fact there was only one priest for the massive structure, Hope speculated that Saint Peter's membership had significantly declined since its heyday. She guessed, because of the architecture, that the building was at least 150 years old. All Hope really knew about St. Peter's was that it had recently been at the heart of a well publicized brouhaha having to do with the doctrine of the trinity, the authority of the New Testament, and the sexuality of Jesus. The conflict was substantive enough that the national Episcopalian leadership was debating the future of this congregation.

Hope's eyes drifted to the stained-glass window above the main door. "Wow, someone spent a lot of money on that one," she muttered. The window was nearly fifteen feet in diameter, about the same size as the one behind the pulpit. It looked especially huge from where she stood. Its intricate detail invited analysis, yet the parts did not detract from the whole. The bright sunlight streaming through the glass cast the full splendor of its colors around the vast narthex.

Hope wondered what the metal was that held all the little pieces together. *It must be lead of some sort*, she mused. She also wondered how many people had worked on it. Hope let her eyes follow the flow of the pictures.

There were four main sections, each a wide oval that narrowed and met the others in the middle of the window, forming a shape somewhat like a four-leaf clover. The rest of the circular window was filled in with an intricate web of ivy teeming with birds and blossoming flowers. The leaf on Hope's right was filled with the image of a baby in a manger. Surrounding the manger were the traditional characters in a Christmas nativity scene. Under this scene, yet inside a clover leaf, was the word "Birth."

The bottom leaf contained three smaller sections. Hope assumed the main character in the three sub-scenes was Jesus because He had the same halo as the baby. In one scene Jesus was touching clay jars at some kind of gathering. The second scene portrayed the haloed Jesus pulling a man from the water while Jesus himself was standing on the water, with a boat in the background. The third scene looked a little like da Vinci's *Last Supper*, though the detail was lacking. Under the set of three scenes and within the bottom clover leaf was the word "Life."

Hope's gaze moved to the leaf on the left. It was Jesus on the cross. Under this image was the word "Death."

Hope's eyes were drawn to the final leaf—the one on top of the clover—the designer's focal point of the whole mosaic. The fragments of colored glass formed the scene of a cave entrance in the midst of a garden, with a large, stone disk lying near the opening. *The empty tomb*, thought Hope. She recognized the scene from having been in Jerusalem with Wil, who had invested the greater part of his career trying to refute the resurrection of Jesus. Under this scene was the word "Resurrection."

Hope was struck by two things. The first was the undeniable artistry of the window. The second was a memory from her college days, when she had learned in an art history class that the reason for such religious art was to convey messages to the masses, who were often illiterate. Hope continued to look at the window, her enjoyment changing to contemplation of the message. She was jostled out of her reflection by the sound of footsteps coming toward her from the opposite direction of the men's room. She turned to see a small man in a dark suit hurrying toward her. Her curiosity was heightened as she recalled the man from earlier at the reception, when he had seemed to be staring at her. She had passed it off as nothing.

"Hope Wilson?" He stopped in front of her, looking relieved he had found her. "Are you Hope Wilson?" he whispered, breathless.

"Yes, I am." Hope hesitated before asking, "And who—"

"With *The New York Times*?"

Hope wondered whether his comment was a question or a statement. Perspiration glistened on the man's forehead, and his voice was a shaky whisper. Hope did not answer.

"The reporter investigating the Freedom Airways crash?" He completed his clarification.

"Yes." Hope responded with curiosity. "And you are . . .?"

"Never mind that. I must be anonymous. Please take this." He looked both ways before removing a sealed envelope from his inner jacket pocket. His hand was trembling as he extended it to her. "This is for you."

Hope gingerly received the envelope. The man, uncertain of his next move, was breathing heavily and shifting from foot to foot.

It was an awkward moment. Hope was expecting him to say more, to elaborate, to explain his unusual behavior. Instead he said, "That's all. I need to go now." He turned and hurriedly walked out the main door. Once outside, he picked up his pace and went in a direction away from the lot where Hope and Wil's car was parked.

Hope took a step to follow him but stopped when she heard, "Sorry I took so long. Something isn't settling with my stomach. And man, did I have to go!"

Hope turned to Wil, shaking her head in puzzlement at the mysterious man and in appreciation that her overly candid sweetheart was back.

"We'd better get going," said Wil as he grabbed Hope's hand and began to drag her out the door and toward their Volvo. "Who was that you were talking to?"

"I have no idea," said Hope letting go of Wil's hand. She put the envelope in her purse then took Wil's hand again. She would look at the envelope's contents later.

Glancing at her watch, she realized Wil had used up the ten spare minutes they'd had. Now they might be late.

CHAPTER 9

The Second Funeral

"Hallelujah!" said the elderly man in the pew in front of Hope and Wil.

"Preach it! Amen!" cried a woman sitting across the aisle. She was adorned in an elegant dress with a vivid floral pattern and matching hat.

Others throughout the congregation echoed her remarks as the bishop stepped to the pulpit to begin his sermon.

Hope and Wil welcomed what they hoped would be a more conventional element of this funeral, which, so far, had them befuddled. Though they had not been overly comfortable at St. Peter's, they at least had been able to blend in. No matter how hard Wil and Hope tried to blend in here, it was not working. Beyond their skin color and their ignorance about hand raising, their unfamiliarity with saying "Amen" and "Hallelujah" left them looking stupefied. When the colorfully dressed woman across the aisle began to dance in front of the congregation after the choir's song, Wil and Hope exchanged looks of shocked disbelief.

There were probably only forty white people among the thousand-plus attendees. One of them, Steve, was up front with five other ministers. Another was a woman from the Smithsonian, whom Wil recognized but did not know. About thirty looked like Rochelle's classmates. The rest of the congregation, other than a smattering of Asians and Latinos, was black.

As staunch atheists, Wil and Hope did not participate in the songs and prayers because it would have been hypocritical. Though this maintained their integrity, it had the result of making them feel even more isolated. In order to be a little less conspicuous, they stood when everyone else stood and sat when everyone else sat. Yet, they knew that any thought that they were blending in was only wishful thinking.

Most troubling to Hope and Wil was how much they'd been caught off guard. The church, though bigger and newer, wasn't that different from the one they had been in forty minutes earlier. Since Steve was to read a Scripture passage as part of the service, they had arrived early and were seated by the time others arrived. At least fifteen people had come over to welcome Wil and Hope and to introduce themselves. It wasn't too hard to conclude that Wil and Hope were visitors.

Five minutes prior to the service, the organist played something that sounded like a rendition of *Amazing Grace* on steroids.

The service began when one of the church's associate pastors walked to the pulpit, made a few announcements, and then encouraged people to squeeze together "so more folks can come in." Such a request appeared futile to Wil and Hope. It was obvious the sanctuary was at capacity. Nonetheless, the associate minister made the request. He also informed the latecomers there was still some space in the overflow room—"down the hall and to the right, where the service can be seen on a closed-circuit big screen."

With those details out of the way, another minister stepped to the pulpit and said in a slow, fluid tone, "Now let us pray."

The crowd of more than 1,000 people grew quiet.

"God. We come before you this day to thank you." The extended pause made Hope and Wil wonder if he was done, but his head was still bowed and his eyes were closed. "God. We come before you this day to thank you for the precious life, oh Jesus, the precious life that you allowed your people to share." Another pause. "Almighty, all loving, everlasting, and wonderful God, we come before you to thank you for Rochelle, your precious . . . most precious . . . lovely child. God. We come before you today to worship you. We come before you to worship you who alone are worthy of our worship. You, oh great and glorious God, we come before you to worship and praise your name and celebrate the new life, the life eternal, the life glorious, the life which our sweet sister is now fully partaking of . . . in your most holy and beautiful presence . . . our precious Savior and God." The minister took a breath, which he held for a moment before continuing. "We come before you today to thank you and praise you and worship you."

There was another brief pause. This time half of the congregation said "Amen!" though not in unison. The cascading chorus of amens settled into silence before the minister concluded with one more petition.

"Hear our prayer, O God."

And then everyone said "Amen" in unison.

So far, so good, thought Wil, as Steve readied to step forward to read the Scripture.

The associate pastor introduced Steve. "The Scripture will be read by our dear brother and friend, the Reverend Dr. Steven Halterman, pastor of First Church D.C., who, in addition to being a dear friend of our own fellowship, was especially close to the Jackson family." He turned and nodded at Steve.

Steve stepped to the podium and smiled down at the

Jackson family in the front row. Wil had heard Steve speak from the pulpit a few times before, via some videotaped sermons Steve had given him as fodder for upcoming lunch debates. Steve's presence was warm and friendly, yet, compared to the other ministers, a little stiff.

"First of all, it is an honor to be here. I knew Rochelle from the time she was thirteen, when I first met her father." His eyes shone in fond reminiscence. "I was new in town and decided that, as the pastor of a sister church in the D.C. area, it would be good for me to visit the different ministries and services for the homeless to get an idea of what was happening to help the poor and disenfranchised in our community. I remember visiting one soup kitchen where the primary mission was to feed the hungry. I'd been invited to give a devotional after the meal. I walked in the door and noticed the office was on the other side of the dining hall. I set off in that direction.

"I was reaching for the knob when the door, which I suddenly learned also led to the kitchen, opened. Out blasted a bundle of energy with the largest platter of spaghetti I'd ever seen. The problem was, I was square in her way. Somewhere between running into me, trying to stop, and slipping, Rochelle fell flat on her back with the plate of spaghetti landing upside down on her chin and chest.

"A second later, Franklin Jackson was kneeling by his daughter's side. When tears began to form in Rochelle's eyes, we were concerned she might be hurt. Franklin asked her if she was okay. With an expression that tore at my heart, Rochelle looked at her dad and said, 'Daddy, what will all these poor people eat for dinner now?' Franklin asked her again, 'Are you all right?' Rochelle answered, 'Yes' but then asked—and I will never forget the look on her face—'But, Daddy, what will we do? The people are hungry. I am so sorry.'

"Then Rochelle, completely covered in spaghetti, looked at me and said, 'Mister, are you okay? I'm so sorry I got some on your shirt.'" Steve chuckled. "It was hardly a drop. When she reached to wipe it off my shirt a pile of goop that had affixed itself to her chest plopped into her lap. She paused, finally aware of her appearance, and touched her head with her hand. As she pulled some spaghetti from her hair, she said, 'Oh, I guess I got some on me too!'"

Steve joined in the congregation's laughter and then continued. "Maybe it was her delivery. Maybe it was the spectacle. But her comment also sent Franklin, the kitchen crew, Rochelle herself, and me into stitches. Within a few minutes some of the volunteers in the kitchen had politely informed the patrons that more spaghetti would be coming soon but there would be a brief delay. The rest of the crew, once they were certain their princess Rochelle was okay, went back into the kitchen. As we cleaned up the original dinner, I introduced myself. From that point on Franklin and I have been the closest of friends."

Steve paused to reflect on the night he had learned of the accident. "Rochelle was unique and one of the most special girls I've ever known. When Franklin called me on the night of the accident, I went directly to their house. We both cried for a long time, only saying a few words. What could be said? And then Franklin said, 'She has gone home. She has gone to be with her Lord and my Lord. I guess she'll be watching over me now rather than the other way around.'"

Steve opened the Bible he had placed on the pulpit. "The passage I am going to read was one of Rochelle's favorites. I remember her quoting it to me at dinner one night. It seems appropriate that it be the text for Bishop Jordan's message later in today's service."

He read, "For God so loved the world that he gave his only begotten Son, that whoever believes in him shall not perish but have eternal life. For God did not send his Son into the world to condemn the world, but to save the world through him. John 3:16 and 17."

As the congregation quietly said their amens, Steve closed his Bible and started back to his seat.

Wil and Hope heaved a collective sigh. So far so good.

While Steve returned to his seat, the choir director positioned himself in front of the fifty robed singers who awaited their cue. The church grew silent. One single organ note sounded and faded away. And then the choir and the organ hit their first chord in a clean, loud, and harmonious staccato.

"Praise!"

This was followed with an equally magnificent, "The!" Pause. "Lord!"

Then silence.

Wow! That was cool, thought Wil.

The choir then repeated the line, this time an octave higher, but every bit as crisp.

What a treat, thought Hope.

Absolute silence again.

Then the organ exploded with sound as the harmony of the swaying, singing, thunderous, smiling choir filled the sanctuary. Hope and Wil had difficulty making out some of the words, not because of a lack of clarity, but because of the abundance of harmonizing and overlaying of chords and musical lines. All were swept up in the glorious sound, which grew and burst forth and surrounded everyone in the church until, precisely at its apex, it stopped in deafening silence.

The choir director was on his toes, his arms fully extended above his shoulders. Anticipation. Then his arms dropped and rebounded, eliciting a deluge of harmony as the word "Praise!" rose in intensity, filling the air. It ended with a slight twitch of the director's wrists, his arms again fully extended toward the ceiling, his head back, his eyes looking into the glories of heaven.

It was as if the congregation didn't know what to do. They were caught up in the beauty of the moment. Hope started to clap, but Wil caught her hands before they came together. It didn't matter. A sea of "Amen!" and "Hallelujah!" began to roll. It started with a few voices around the church, then it grew. Soon more than half the crowd was involved. Praises and prayers and expressions of thanksgiving and worship permeated the air. The entire congregation was on its feet, Wil and Hope included. Many people had their hands raised. A few appeared to be jumping in place. It sounded like ocean waves, except there wasn't any lapse between waves. It was then that the colorfully dressed woman started to dance up front. After a few minutes of jubilation, things started to calm down and a semblance of order, not that anything had been disorderly, was restored.

Hope and Wil, eyes wide and unblinking, hadn't said a word or even looked at each other. Their thoughts were identical. *That was WILD! This is a funeral?*

"Praise the Lord! Praise the Lord!" came the voice of the associate pastor as he ended the celebration the way it had started. He took a deep breath on behalf of the whole congregation and then said with anticipation, "Bishop Obadiah Jordan, our pastor, will now deliver the Word to us."

Bishop Jordan, in his sixties, towered over the pulpit in a robe that cascaded from his broad shoulders. He wore narrow, dark-rimmed reading glasses. His demeanor was that of a supreme court justice, his disposition that of a coach, his presence that of a loved elder. After setting his large, black Bible on the pulpit, he said, "Bow with me as I ask for God's blessing on the message I am about to deliver . . . and for His blessing on this time." He bowed his head, as did the entire congregation, save Wil and Hope. "Father God! This . . . this . . . this . . . is *your* time . . . not mine. These are your people, not mine. And . . . I ask that the words I am about to speak, be your words . . . and not mine. To you be all glory and honor and praise. Amen."

In one voice the congregation said, "Amen."

Bishop Jordan's delivery reminded Wil and Hope of an Eddie Murphy parody of black preaching. But something was different. Although he repeated his statements in multiple ways, each time emphasizing a different word or phrase, and while he did settle into the stereotypical singsong rhythm in which the congregation's amens supported his discourse, the whole thing was mysteriously refreshing to Hope and Wil. They were compelled to listen. What is more, they understood the message even though they did not agree with what was being said.

They were surprised by Bishop Jordan's perspective regarding Rochelle's death. He didn't talk about a permanent good-bye; he talked about missing her for a time. He didn't talk about the tragedy of death; he talked about Rochelle's triumph over death. He didn't talk about some esoteric, wishful concept of life after death as memory or legacy; he talked about her really being alive, maybe even more alive now than she had been on earth. And he talked about the love of God that made this hope possible through the birth, life, death, and resurrection of Jesus.

Wil had heard it before. So had Hope. Today it caught their attention.

At the end of the spellbinding thirty-five-minute sermon on eternal life, heaven, hell, and the love of God, the bishop concluded with, "And never, no never, no never, forget that this eternal life, this eternal life now known by Rochelle and available to all those who will call upon the name of Jesus, is the result of the unending, unsearchable, unmistakable, unrelenting love of God demonstrated in Jesus' life, death, and glorious resurrection. Amen."

"Amen," echoed the congregation.

After a moment of silence, Bishop Jordan looked at Rebecca and Franklin Jackson and asked them to come forward and say a few words.

Rebecca Jackson stepped up to the microphone first. She was keeping it together better than her husband, who stood by her side holding her hand, tears glistening on his cheeks.

"First of all, thank you for coming and thank you for all your cards and calls. We sincerely appreciate your gifts and generosity to the Rochelle Jackson Scholarship Fund and to the Share the Gospel Foundation. Rochelle would be so proud."

Rebecca paused and swallowed her tears.

"Over the last few days we have had the opportunity to think about our little girl in a way we had not really done before."

Franklin's chest sank as he sighed.

"We have had time to reflect on what a special gift of God she was to us. Though she was only seventeen years old, I honestly cannot count all the lives she has touched. This was made very clear to us through the many cards we received from the people at the mission, from her classmates, and even from school board members, including those who opposed what she was fighting for. So many people have told us they didn't understand what the love of God had to do with their lives until they met Rochelle. So many people, in cards and conversations, have told us that they believe they have eternal life through Jesus Christ because Rochelle took the time to listen to them, and even to pray with them. They are not alone. This little girl was also an inspiration to us. There were times when

Franklin and I would wrestle with financial issues or with job issues. It was often Rochelle's believing voice saying something like, 'What would Jesus do?' or 'God knows what He is doing,' that would help us get re-centered away from our useless fretting … and now she is gone."

Rebecca paused, trembling, her words resonating from her soul.

"I can only imagine what she's doing now. Chances are she's running around the streets of heaven making friends. If I know her, she's probably already had a great conversation with the apostle John and with Ruth from the Old Testament, two of her favorite people. She has probably tracked down some of her other heroes, like Saint Augustine, the African saint who is so important in the history of our faith, and the Ethiopian eunuch from Acts who was perhaps the first Christian in Africa. I'd also be surprised if she hasn't had a nice visit with Mother Teresa. Beyond this, I know she's been singing with the angels in the choir of heaven. I imagine her face so full of light and life that, in a way, I am a little envious."

Rebecca's voice broke and then, after pressing her lips together, she said, "I have to do something for you, because I know Rochelle would do it if she were here."

Rebecca focused her kind eyes at the congregation. "Many of us have heard Rochelle sing this song a hundred times. I'm not a singer, but I'd like to sing it one more time for Rochelle."

Rebecca paused and stood a little straighter, chin up. Her presence changed to that of an ambassador announcing a message, or a spokesman for a king. The mandate was that the messenger sing a song. So she sang.

Do you know that Jesus loves you?
Do you know that God really cares?
Do you wonder where you're going?
Amidst all life's pain and snares.

Let me tell you a story of love;
Let me tell you how you can be free.
Our God has made it possible.
Let me tell of Mount Calvary.

Try as she did, Rebecca Jackson couldn't continue the song she had sung with her daughter hundreds of times. So the congregation helped. At first there were only a few tentative voices, then everyone joined in until the sanctuary was filled with Rochelle's song.

Do you know that Jesus loves you?
Do you know that God really cares?
Receive God's gift of His forgiveness,
And say good-bye to all your fears.

Let me tell you a story of love;
Let me tell you how you can be free.
Our God has made it possible.
Let me tell of Mount Calvary.

By the time the last line was sung, Rebecca's composure was restored. Her joy had overcome her tears. She stood, beaming at a congregation that had heard her daughter sing this song countless times. Rebecca mustered up one last thank you and stepped back, allowing her husband to approach the podium.

Franklin stepped forward. He cleared his throat and leaned toward the microphone. "I know what Rochelle is doing right now." He picked up on his wife's theme. "She's telling Gabriel and Michael and heaven's head choir master, 'Now *that* is what the song is supposed to sound like!'"

Joyful laughter filled the sanctuary, punctuated by the ever-present amens.

Franklin was well known to the congregation. By the looks on the faces Wil observed, he was also extremely well liked.

"I want to read a letter to you." Franklin pulled four folded sheets of paper from his breast pocket. "As you know, Rochelle was killed in an accident in which a young man did something very stupid. He got drunk and drove a car and he killed my daughter. What many of you do not know is that Rochelle knew this young man and she had been spending a lot of time praying for him. He had even been attending her Bible study at school.

"This young man could not be here today, even if he wanted to, since he is currently in legal custody. He has already said he will plead guilty to manslaughter, with which he has been charged. Since he turned eighteen just a few days before the accident, he will serve up to three years in prison. I received this letter from him yesterday. While I can't read it all," he held up four pages, "I want to read a portion of it."

Franklin put the sheets down in front of him and cleared his throat before beginning to read.

"Dear Mr. and Mrs. Jackson:

"I know there is no way I will ever be able to pay for the terrible thing I have done. I also cannot even come close to knowing what pain I have caused you. I do want you to know one thing though. Prior to that night, your daughter, Rochelle, told me she wanted nothing more for me than that I would open up my heart to God and receive the love and life that is available through Jesus.

"Even now, I do not fully know what that means, or why God would even have me. But last night in my cell, after realizing there was no lower place for me to go for the terrible things I have done, I prayed for the first time in my life. I asked God to forgive me. I asked God to come into my life and be my Lord. I figured I had made such a mess of it, it was time I gave Him a chance.

"I don't know what is ahead for me, but I do know Rochelle would be happy to hear the news. No one ever cared for me the way your daughter did. No one ever believed in me the way your daughter did. And, if there was any way I could go back in time and prevent from happening what happened, I would. But I can't. Rochelle always spoke so highly of you and about how you loved God and showed it in your life. All I can say is that you apparently rubbed off on Rochelle and, because of Rochelle, for the first time in my life I can say I am alive. It is because of Rochelle. . . ."

Franklin paused.

"He goes on to say that he met with someone from the Prison Fellowship organization that day and he only wished he could tell Rochelle how much everything has changed."

Franklin looked up from the letter. "The Bible says, 'All things work together for good for those who love the Lord and are called according to His purposes.' This applies to Rochelle. And, while God knows I wish His plan didn't involve the loss of my daughter, I am confident Rochelle's death was not in vain, and this young man's letter is only the first fruit of what I am convinced our wise and holy God is going to cause to come out of this. For my wife and the rest of our family, I want to thank you from the bottom of our hearts. We shall not forget these last seven days . . . ever.

Thank you." He could say no more. Rebecca put her arms around her husband as he fought back his tears.

The choir director stood to lead the congregation in one last song. It was the one song Hope and Wil both knew. Though they still didn't sing it, they did hear the words in a new way.

> Amazing grace, how sweet the sound,
> That saved a wretch like me!
> I once was lost, but now am found,
> Was blind, but now I see.

CHAPTER 10

The Ride Home

Following a preliminary conversation about the weather and a couple of acquaintances Wil had bumped into, there was a moment of silence in Steve's car. No one mentioned the service.

Wil, sitting in the back, was the first to bring up the subject they all wanted to talk about, albeit for completely different reasons. "The choir was amazing," noted Wil.

"They certainly were," Hope agreed from the front passenger seat. "I've never heard a choir like that before!"

"And I love that song," said Steve, making it a consensus.

"And Bishop Jordan sure is a good speaker," added Hope. Another point of consensus.

"And you did good," said Wil.

"Thank you." Steve accepted the compliment with humility.

The silence led to a change of subject.

"So . . . two funeral services in one day. Were they very different?" asked Steve.

"Different? I'll say!" Wil exclaimed.

"Night and day," added Hope.

"What do you mean?"

"For one thing," said Wil, "the first one wasn't a circus."

Wil knew the main difference was philosophical, yet he didn't want to discuss that.

"Circus?" Steve glanced at Wil in the rearview mirror.

"Or carnival or whatever you want to call it. There were parts of Rochelle's funeral service that were pretty entertaining, but frankly, I thought a lot of it was weird."

"There was also a difference of perspective about death and the afterlife," added Hope, not intimidated by the essence of Steve's question.

Wil didn't want to go there. "All I know is that two funerals in one day are too much and I'm beat." The subject was closed. "We'll need to leave as soon as we get to your house," said Wil.

"Hopefully your car is still there," said Steve, who didn't live in the safest of areas.

"Funny!" said Wil.

"We need to get home and see Steven," added Hope. "Betty is expecting us home around nine." They had half an hour.

Wil regretted his derogatory comment about Rochelle's service but still wanted to justify his position. "I have to tell you, Steve, I never imagined any funeral would be like that!"

"Like what?" Steve picked up as if the earlier conversation hadn't been derailed.

"The amens and hallelujahs and arm waving—you know."

"The woman dancing up front after the song was a little much for me, too," said Hope, as a form of honesty, and because she truly found the behavior aberrant.

"I know what you mean," said Steve. "That church's traditions and style are very different from what I am comfortable with. But I know those people. They love and serve the very same Jesus Christ I do. While our practice is different, our Jesus is the same. You might not understand this, but what matters to me is not format, but substance. Because of this, I've learned to enjoy worshipping God alongside my Christian brothers and sisters, even when they do so in a very different manner."

"Different is an understatement," snorted Wil. "That'll be the day when I see you dancing around on the stage and hear your congregation start hollering amen and hallelujah as you preach—not that I believe your format is any better. Personally, I think all you Christians are a little wacko."

Steve let the insult pass. Hope didn't.

She looked over her left shoulder at Wil. "William! Don't be so negative."

Hope didn't like hearing Wil be so superficial and insulting, even though his comment was a true reflection of his opinion.

Steve was unfazed. "It's okay, Hope." He knew Wil tended to lump all Christians into one pile that included his hypocritical, drunken father, the Crusaders, Adolf Hitler, David Koresh, and anyone else who said they were Christians, regardless of their theology. By so doing, Wil could discount the whole and avoid dealing with the parts, even though Wil knew, for instance, that Steve's faith was genuine and Hitler's wasn't. "He's got a point." Steve caught both Hope and Wil by surprise.

"What, that Christians are wacko?" Hope reminded Steve of Wil's last point.

"Just a second," said Steve as he checked over his shoulder. He had been paying so much attention to Wil and Hope that he almost missed the highway exit. "Wil could be right. I mean, people who sincerely follow the Christian faith are either wacko, mistaken, or . . ." Steve put extra emphasis on his next word ". . . *possibly* right!"

"I hate that argument," said Wil.

Steve chuckled.

"Ugh," moaned Wil.

"But, Wil, what are the other options?" Steve asked for the umpteenth time.

Hope was not in the mood for the conversation to get any more intense. It had been a long day. She also knew that Wil and Steve had plenty of material to talk about at their weekly lunches. She changed the subject. "So, is Wendy feeling better today than she did yesterday?"

Steve politely went along with Hope's diversion. "Yes. We're thinking it might have been a case of food poisoning from something she ate the other night."

"You mean the night you cooked Chinese food?" Wil elaborated. Anyone who knew Steve knew the only thing he could cook was his renowned lasagna with anise-flavored sausage. Anything else inevitably ended in disaster.

"Shut up," Steve said, laughing.

"I can't believe you poisoned your own wife. Wendy is such a great woman."

"I didn't poison my wife!"

Hope felt as though she was watching a tennis match.

"Did you manage to get your daughter at the same time?" asked Wil.

Hope fought back a laugh. Steve was stymied.

"Okay. I confess. I poisoned my wife *and* daughter. But it was an accident. I promised them I would never cook anything but lasagna again." Steve smiled mischievously. "Hey, Wil, why don't you let Hope drive on home and see your son? Perhaps we could hang around the house and watch a movie or something. Besides, I have some great leftover Chinese food I'd like you to try."

CHAPTER 11

Saturday Night

"Thanks for letting me use your bathroom," said Wil as he opened the car door for Hope.

"No problem," said Steve. "You're sure I can't interest you in some Chinese food?"

Steve, Hope, and Wil chuckled. Wendy was puzzled.

"How 'bout to go?" added Steve.

"Get in," said Wil as he held the door open for Hope, "before he forces it on us."

Hope laughed and slipped into the car. Steve turned to Wendy. "I'll explain later."

Little was said on the drive home. Though their dread regarding the funerals had proven to be substantially unfounded, it had been an exhausting day.

With what little energy they had left, Wil and Hope gathered the day's paraphernalia and climbed out of the Volvo. Wil pushed the button next to the door into the kitchen and the garage door began to close. Hope held the door for Wil as he followed her into the house. A note from Betty was taped to the refrigerator. She had gone to bed early and, based on the absence of any noises from Steven or the two animals, it sounded like everyone else was asleep, too.

Hope read the note out loud. "Welcome home. Your

dinner is ready. All you need to do is put the microwave on high for eight minutes."

They looked at each other and smiled, reading each other's minds. *Wouldn't it be great to have Mom around all the time? I mean she cooks, she cleans, she baby-sits . . .*

"Not!" Their silent communication was broken by their concurrent conclusions. It was a treat, but then there was reality. Still, more frequent visits were definitely within the realm of possibility.

Wil threw his jacket over a chair back. Hope unwrapped the casserole she'd taken from the refrigerator and placed it in the microwave. She set the microwave on high for eight minutes and pushed start.

Wil set two plates on the table then opened the silverware drawer as Hope collapsed in the wing chair and kicked off her shoes. Once Wil had finished setting the table he joined her, pulling his kitchen table chair around so he could stretch his legs out onto the same footstool as Hope. They finally began to unwind and let their muscles relax.

Hope suddenly remembered the envelope in her purse.

"Wil, can you hand me my purse?"

The object in question was on the far end of the table. *Why do I have to be the one to get up?* thought Wil. Without verbal objection though, he retrieved the purse, handed it to his appreciative wife, who rewarded him with a smile and a kiss, and then returned to his chair, groaning as if he'd just run a mile.

Hope dug out the envelope.

"What's that?" asked Wil.

Hope slit the envelope with the blade of a dinner knife she'd been able to reach without leaving her chair. "I'll soon find out. Remember that fellow I was talking with while you were lollygagging in the men's room after Scott's funeral?"

"Yeah, sort of … kind of … well, not really." Wil's voice trailed away.

"He gave this to me and walked away."

"What'd he say?"

"Nothing much. He asked who I was and if I was with *The New York Times*. Then he handed me the note. He didn't tell me his name or anything."

"That's odd."

"I'd noticed him looking at me earlier, before the service and at the reception."

"A love note?"

"Somehow I doubt it," she said, as she slid the contents of the envelope into her hand. She unfolded the single sheet and inspected it, intrigued.

"Well? What's it say?" Wil feigned jealousy. "I can't believe the nerve of this guy—to give a love note to my wife while I'm in the bathroom!"

Hope studied a sheet of white paper with letters that had been cut from a magazine and glued to the page in a pattern that resulted in words and sentences.

"Nice work," said Hope as she quickly flashed the collage in Wil's direction.

He barely caught a glimpse.

Hope began reading the note to herself. Wil waited with curiosity.

"It says he works for Freedom Airways." Hope's head tilted toward the bottom of the note. "And it doesn't say who it's from."

"Read it!"

Hope read:

I WoRk fOr fReedom aiRwAYS
I Knew sCOtt AnD bErNie
TherE iS mOre To tHe CRaSH
BerniE is being FraMEd

Hope read the rest of the note. "I have been with the company a long time. I am on the inside. I am afraid for my safety. I must be anonymous. Check the maintenance records. That is all I can say. The company is hiding something."

"Cryptic son of a gun, isn't he?" commented Wil.

Hope pursed her lips and read the note again, this time to herself.

Wil could hear Hope's wheels turning and knew there was a significant chance he would be spending a large part of the night sleeping alone.

"Ho-o-o-pe!"

Hope lifted her gaze from the note.

"Will you at least try and get some sleep tonight?" he asked.

She smiled. "Yes, but you've got to admit this is extremely interesting." She resumed her scrutiny of the letter.

The timer on the microwave dinged. Hope set the paper down to get their dinner. Wil, slumped in his chair, halfheartedly offered to help her bring the casserole bowl to the table. Hope turned to her pathetic-looking husband and tossed a dishtowel at him.

"What? Do you think it might be too heavy?" However, seizing on his offer to help, she directed him to get two glasses of water.

They served themselves from the steaming dish and began to eat.

It may have been the microwave's bell or its door slamming closed that woke Betty. Clad in her robe and slippers, she joined them in the kitchen. "How was your day?" she asked.

"Fine," they replied in unison.

"Thank you for the dinner, Mom." Wil had just taken his second helping. "It's really good. I haven't had this since I was a kid." Wil was referring to the tuna and noodle casserole

made with peas, water chestnuts, and Durkee onions sprin-
kled on top.

Hope was eating it, but without as much enjoyment, and
certainly without the memories it evoked for Wil.

"So . . . what were the services like?" Betty pressed.

Neither Wil nor Hope wanted to talk about it, so they
again said, "Fine."

Betty picked up on the topic-closing cue, shrugged, and
began to tell them about her day with Steven. Soon Hope and
Betty were immersed in their own conversation.

Even though Wil wasn't very interested in the women's
conversation, he felt a little neglected. He settled for catching
up on the news, and reached for the newspaper lying on the
corner of the table. Wil read silently as Hope and Betty chat-
ted. Soon it was 10:30.

Ten minutes later, Wil moaned as if he had taken a shot
to the ribs. "I can't believe it."

Betty and Hope broke off their conversation, startled by
Wil's outburst. They looked at him.

"I can't believe it," Wil repeated.

"What?" asked Hope.

"Those politicians disgust me. I wonder whose back got
scratched for this one! They're all a bunch of crooks."

"What are you talking about, Wil?" Hope couldn't understand what was so important that he had to interrupt their
conversation. She also felt obliged to challenge his statement.
"And besides, you know not everyone holds your sentiment
on that issue. For example, Senator Newcastle and, I hate to
admit this, Congressman Jones. Those two are okay."

Wil disregarded Hope's statement.

"It's just—I just—I can't believe it!" Wil pointed to the
right-hand side of the opened newspaper. "Do you remember
all those clowns I helped Jones and Newcastle put behind

bars?" Wil was proud of the role he had played a couple of years ago when he helped expose corruption and illegal campaign-financing activities. "You know, associated with 'The Bones Project' I was on a few years ago?" He looked up.

Hope and Betty nodded. They knew exactly what he was talking about. How could they forget the time Wil had turned the world upside down with his archeological claims, only to end up in the middle of one of the biggest corruption scandals ever to hit Washington? They also remembered the enemies Wil had made.

"You'll never believe this. The President just pardoned a bunch of those degenerates."

Wil turned the newspaper so Betty and Hope could see a small article buried at the bottom of page eleven of *The Washington Post*.

"I only wonder what this President got in exchange for pardoning all those jerks who used to work for his despicable predecessor."

"How many were pardoned?" asked Hope. She pretended to be interested.

Wil studied the article. "Six altogether. But the one that really irks me," said Wil, "is Kathreen Steele."

Hope was suddenly wide awake. "You're kidding?"

Kathreen Steele was one of the former President's closest advisors. Until the congressional hearings, few had ever heard of her. During the investigation it came out that even the President's closest "official" advisors feared her. Some credited her, post-investigation, with her boss's earlier political success. The only things that eclipsed her power were her ego and selfish desire to win at all costs.

Wil's interaction with Kathreen had been related to one of her assignments involving Israel. The President had dispatched Kathreen to "deal with" Wil after Wil had angered and alarmed the President. Not only did Kathreen and her henchmen nearly kill Wil, they beat Wil's secretary, Beth, so badly she had to be hospitalized for two weeks. During the congressional hearings, it was blatantly evident that Wil had earned Kathreen's seething hatred.

"Geez, I can't believe they let that sadistic witch off the hook." Wil stood and began to pace the kitchen floor. "Perhaps threatening to kill a citizen like me isn't that big a deal. And . . ." his tone became even more sarcastic and bitter ". . . as for beating Beth and nearly killing her, well . . . Beth isn't an American citizen, so she definitely doesn't matter!"

Wil's tirade continued. "I mean, think about it—that despicable sadist broke Beth's arm and beat her within an inch of her life. At least her two goons aren't on the list." Wil blamed himself for the whole chaotic, awful mess and was still haunted by what had happened to Beth. Wil had not fared much better when Kathreen and her two goons tried to "persuade" him to talk, but Beth's beating was largely the result of her protecting Wil. He still had nightmares, seeing Beth beaten and bruised after Kathreen had finished with her.

"Maybe it pays to be corrupt." Wil had now begun to sound rabidly cynical. Neither Wil's mom nor his wife liked this side of him.

"How I would like to give that President and all those corrupt, money-grubbing politicians a piece of my mind." Wil was approaching the end of his outburst, as Hope and Betty knew he eventually would. He crumpled the newspaper and threw it in the direction of the kindling box next to the fireplace. "Bah," he said. "What difference would it make anyway?"

"Well, how about a piece of chocolate cake?" Betty decided to help Wil move on. Since the pantry cupboard was still closed, Betty deduced Wil hadn't seen the cake she'd planned to surprise him with before he took her to the airport in the morning. But, from a mother's perspective, her son needed the chocolate cake now.

"What?" asked Wil distractedly.

"I said, how about a piece of chocolate cake?"

"Yeah, honey, how about some cake?" Hope didn't know what cake Betty was talking about, but thought a conversation about fictitious cake was better than hearing Wil's diatribe against politicians this late at night.

"What cake?" He didn't want to look easy, but he knew he was outnumbered. "Don't you two care about what I just said?"

"Of course we do, honey," said Hope, supporting Betty's diversion. "But it's 10:45 Saturday night and neither of us feels like talking politics right now."

Wil growled, slightly offended they were not showing more interest in his concern.

Betty retrieved the cake.

Hope saw this as an appropriate time to excuse herself. She wanted to get a few hours of sleep before getting up early and going to the office. She needed to finish her latest article on the EPA guidelines and wanted to pursue the lead she had been given in the form of the cryptic note.

"And besides," said Hope. "I'm exhausted, sweetie. Why don't you and your mother have a few minutes together before she leaves in the morning? I need to go to bed."

Though he wouldn't have admitted it, he welcomed the chance to have a few minutes with his mom alone. Over the past few years, they had finally started to communicate. A glass of milk and chocolate cake set the ambiance for one more positive conversation.

"Okay," said Wil, " I'll join you in a bit. I love you, Hope."

Hope walked out of the kitchen, blowing a kiss to her

husband. Wil and his mom settled into their chairs, milk and cake in front of them.

"We sure have appreciated having you around, Mom."

A man trained a dog to ring a bell when the dog needs to go outside. Now, whenever the dog rings the bell, the man opens the door. Who trained whom?

CHAPTER 12

Inquiry

Hope walked into her office at seven o'clock Sunday morning with a triple-shot latte in her hand. She began searching through her notes and unauthorized copies of FAA reports on Freedom Airways. She decided to put off the EPA article so she could focus on what had kept her up all night. She came across a few references to the maintenance logs, but these were almost exclusively related to the engine failure.

Hope was struck by the way Flight 2652's investigation had progressed. There were the initial questions about the failed engine, which concluded with consensus that the engine failure was directly caused by contaminated fuel delivered by a negligent employee of the fuel company. Then there was the investigation into the crash itself. Unlike the engine failure investigation, where truly objective evidence substantiated the investigative teams' conclusion, the crash inquiry lacked physical evidence because the explosion on the ground had destroyed everything. This meant that the teams were forced to rely almost exclusively on corroborative evidence provided by Brad and his team at Freedom Airways. It appeared to Hope that the unusual sense of agreement and cooperation, which resulted from the earlier consensus, had contributed to a hasty decision regarding the cause of the crash. Without objection, the investigators had expeditiously concluded that first officer Bernie Bentson had deliberately caused the crash as revenge on Scott and Freedom Airways. The investigation then moved from what had happened to what needed to be done to prevent similar tragedies.

Hope sat back and took a sip of her latte.

No one, herself included, had questioned the conclusion's foundation. No one had questioned the evidence provided by Freedom Airways. The more she thought about it, the more incredibly suspect things appeared. Hope decided to start over and refuse to accept the dead end resulting from the destruction of physical evidence at the crash site. As she looked more intently, she thought she saw chinks in the armor of the conclusion.

It was now noon. Hope picked up her phone and dialed.

A smooth baritone voice answered. "Hello."

"Brad?"

"Who is calling?"

"Brad, it's Hope Wilson."

"Hope Wilson with *The New York Times* or Hope, my friend? What can I do for you?" It was no secret that Brad did not like or trust the press, and the numerous conversations he'd had with Hope since the crash were out of character. Hope supposed it was because they had a slight social acquaintance through Scott.

"Brad, I'm sorry to trouble you at your home on a Sunday, but I have a question."

"Personal or business?"

"Business."

"Just a second Hope, my friend. I'm on the phone with a reporter from *The New York Times*, and I need to put on a different hat." Brad's tone changed ever so slightly.

"Thanks, Brad. I appreciate your time."

"Well then, Ms. Woman-of-the-Press, what is it that has

piqued your curiosity so much you needed to call me at my home on a Sunday morning?" Though she had placed the call, Brad was clarifying that it was his dime.

"I know, Brad." Hope acknowledged his warning. "I apologize. But something came up and I needed to talk to you." Hope prepared to ask her calculated question and wished she could see his face when he heard it.

"Yes?"

"Are you positive Bernie Bentson caused the crash?"

Silence or a pause were indicators Hope would measure. His pause was a split second too long. Her ambush had worked. She just didn't know what was next. She held.

"Yes, of course—why are you asking?" he inquired, his voice measured and smooth.

Hope dealt the next card. "I was just wondering if there might be more to it. Perhaps there were some mechanical or maintenance issues." Hope pictured Brad sitting down.

"What?"

Who would speak next was crucial and they both knew it. Who would reveal a card?

Hope bluffed. "I was just wondering. It could be nothing."

"What could be nothing?"

Hope had upped the ante and he matched her. Brad could not see her fidget in her chair or that her neck and cheeks had flushed with anxiety.

"Oh, it could be nothing." She hesitated. "That's why I called you at home. I didn't want to make a big deal out of this."

"Out of what? Hope, why are you asking me these questions?" He had matched her again.

She decided to show some of her cards and break the impasse. "I was led to believe, by someone who might be in a position to know, that the accident was related to maintenance issues."

"By whom?" He wasn't satisfied.

"A man gave me a note that said there was more to the crash. It said I should look at the maintenance records."

"A man? C'mon Hope."

Hope was relieved by the chance to simply be candid about the contents of the note, and she told him most of the story. She deliberately left out details such as where they had met. She also was meager in her description of the informant.

Brad pursued it further. "What did he look like?"

Brad sounded paranoid enough that Hope assumed her bluff had worked. Rather than ask why her informant's appearance mattered, which would have made Brad more defensive, she fattened the pot with a generic description that could have matched anyone who was between thirty and sixty years old and wasn't black, female, or shorter than five feet. Ironically, as she gave the generic description, Hope noted to herself that she hadn't paid too close attention to his appearance, other than his dark suit and his possibly disguised voice.

Brad was obliged to accept her vague response.

"Did he say anything else?"

"No. That's what was so strange."

Brad folded. "Probably just a troublemaker. I wouldn't pay any attention to it."

"I thought that might be the case." Hope's last comment could not have been any more passive-aggressive.

"And besides, Bernie Bentson didn't leave a smoking gun. He left a smoking cannon." Brad knew he'd lost the hand and became aggressive. "And—are you accusing me of something?"

Hope was done playing and gracefully excused herself from the table. "No. It was just so unusual. I thought I'd give you a call and ask you for myself."

"I'm glad you did." That was both the truth and a lie. "Why don't you stop by my office and take a look at our maintenance records—see for yourself that the rumor is ludicrous." Brad already had that base covered anyway. From the moment the plane fell from the sky, he had ensured that the records were sanitized.

"Thank you, Brad. I appreciate your time and understanding that I'm only doing my job." Hope knew they would play again. She hung up the phone and sat back in her chair. The can of worms had been opened, and the closer she studied them the more the worms looked like snakes. She knew well enough that if there was foul play the last place any evidence would be found would be in the place it should be. And, though she intended to take Brad up on his offer to look at the maintenance records, she didn't expect to find anything. Something wasn't right, though.

After looking through her notes again—for what, she didn't know—Hope reached for the phone one more time. This time she called her friend at the FBI who had been assigned to the Freedom case. She didn't intend to tip her hand, but there was something she had to know.

"Connie Donaldson here," a clipped voice answered. Hope assumed that meant Connie was in the middle of something.

"Hi, Connie, this is Hope."

"Hope. Good to hear from you." Connie's lighthearted cheeriness belied her commanding professional presence. "What are you and Wil doing? We're about forty-five minutes away from the best smoked chicken you have ever tasted. Want to come over?"

"Connie. This is work."

"Criminey, Hope. Don't you ever take a day off?"

"I know. It's just—I had to ask one question."

"It's a beautiful Sunday afternoon!" Connie was a little

perturbed by Hope's weekend business call. But she'd known Hope for too long to let it upset her. "What is it? But you'd better hurry. The salad is calling my name and the cherry pie needs to come out of the oven. Are you sure you don't want to come over?"

"Not today. But thanks." Hope asked her question. "How much effort was put into verifying the authenticity of the evidence Freedom Airways provided on Bernie Bentson?"

"What?" That was not the question Connie expected.

"I was just wondering. A source who works for the airline contacted me, and I've been asking some questions of my own."

"A source?" Connie was skeptical but intrigued. "You are one odd chick, Hope, but I'll look into it Monday."

The conversation concluded with a plan for a girls' night out on Wednesday and Connie's anxious announcement, "Oh no! There's the timer for my pie."

Hope was beginning to see a way out of the evidence dead end.

CHAPTER 13

Lunch

"Monday lunch. So, you couldn't wait until Wednesday night," said Hope. She knew something was up when Connie called her Monday morning, insisting they meet for lunch. "I take it this means you have some questions?" Hope was enjoying the fact that her FBI friend was obviously going to ask her for a favor. Normally it was the other way around.

Connie gave Hope a rueful smile. "Tell me, what do you know about your informant?"

"Why?"

"Let me just say . . . we're looking into some things in a little more detail."

The waitress returned for their order. Neither Hope nor Connie was interested in the daily specials.

"I'll have the Reuben," said Hope.

"Big surprise," commented Connie.

"I like them," said Hope, not compromising.

"I'll have one, too. And iced tea."

"Sweet?" asked the waitress.

"Sure."

"Me, too. With lemon," added Hope.

"Two iced teas. Both sweet. One with lemon. And two

Reubens. Got it." The waitress walked away wishing all her customers were that easy.

Free of distraction, Connie looked at Hope and said, "Okay, tell me about this guy."

Hope told Connie everything she knew, starting with the strange meeting in the church and ending with her conversation with Brad.

"You really don't know who your informant is—"

"—or how to get in touch with him." Hope finished Connie's sentence.

"I thought that might be the case." Connie handed Hope a stack of papers. "I haven't had time to sort through all these, but I think this might help you locate your informant. It's a list of the employees who work for Freedom Airways. I've highlighted the ones who are based in the D.C. area."

Hope was impressed.

"I've taken the liberty to delete all the women and I high-lighted those with recent disciplinary actions in their personnel files."

"Hold it." Hope sat back and reached for her glass of water.

Connie raised her eyebrows.

"Are you asking me to tell you who he is if I figure it out?" asked Hope.

Connie shrugged.

"But, Connie, my informant demanded anonymity."

"So?" The FBI always seemed to have a problem with the confidentiality of press informants.

"Connie!"

"I'll work with you." Connie acknowledged Hope's protest. "You might want to start with these folks. Let me know what you find out."

Hope sensed she had just been enlisted in something

much bigger than she had imagined. But then again, maybe this was the way the FBI made everybody feel. The two friends discussed business a little more and then got down to a serious conversation about their husbands' peculiar habits.

As their plates were cleared, they stood to leave, gathering scarves and coats. Connie picked up the tab.

They left the restaurant, which exited into the hotel lobby, and said good-bye. Connie turned toward the front door since her office was within two blocks of the building.

Hope headed toward the elevators that would take her to the parking garage. The stack of papers Connie had given her was crammed into Hope's swollen purse. She pushed G3 as the doors closed. When the elevator doors opened again, Hope walked into the quiet, dank, full parking garage.

"Darn," she muttered in protest as she approached her Acura. A white paper was held against the windshield by the wiper. "A parking ticket."

It wasn't. It turned out Hope didn't need Connie's list to make her next contact with the informant. The handwritten note on a napkin from the restaurant where Hope and Connie had just dined read, "I am the man you met at the funeral. I'm on the inside at Freedom. My boss was too detached and didn't know what was going on, but I did. I have more information, but you must respect my anonymity."

Though Hope was pleased to know she would be hearing from the informant again, it gave her the creeps knowing she'd been followed. She quickly unlocked the car door and slid into the driver's seat, locking the doors again. As she gathered her wits, she decided Connie's request would have to be put on hold, at least as far as it involved her informant.

She started her car, backed out, and followed the exit signs. She didn't notice the black Lincoln Continental a few rows down from where she had been parked. Even if she had, the tinted windows would have prevented her from seeing the four occupants—and that one of them was gagged and terrified.

Inside the Continental, the leader was talking to the one who was terrified. "So, when Clarence takes that gag out of your sorry mouth, you're going to tell me who you are and why you put that note on Mrs. Wilson's car. Do you understand?"

The fear in the man's eyes indicated he was going to do whatever his captors asked.

"And don't leave out any details."

Five hours later, there were no more details left to tell.

CHAPTER 14

The Game

Hope's meeting with Brad went as expected. He provided copies of the maintenance records on the plane that crashed. He also informed her she was welcome to look at the originals if she didn't trust the copies.

Stewart, coincidentally, stopped by Brad's office on a completely unrelated matter. Acting surprised to see Hope, he asked, "By the way, did you ever hear from the fruitcake again?" Not waiting for her answer, he added, "How absurd."

Hope smiled. The truth was she hadn't heard from her informant except for the note on her windshield. She didn't answer Stewart's question. Instead she said, "Today was very helpful."

"That's good," said Stewart. "We're doing all we can to address this terrible tragedy that Bernie Bentson caused."

"I can tell." Hope looked to Brad. "I want to thank you for your time today and I apologize for the inconvenience."

Brad and Stewart were pleased with the outcome, convinced of Hope's ebbing curiosity.

Hope left the office looking as convinced and appreciative as she could. She knew the hard part was done, but she was perspiring under her navy blue jacket as she walked quickly to her car, unable to shake her nervousness. Connie had reassured her that she was doing the right thing.

She drove out of the lot and out of sight of the Freedom Airways building before dialing a number on her cell phone.

"Yes?"

"Connie?"

"Hope?"

"You're positive it's legal?" asked Hope.

"I have the warrant right in front of me."

"I'm glad of that. The microphone is stuck to the bottom of the chair I was sitting in, right in front of Brad's desk. I hope that's a good enough location."

"You did great, Hope. It's perfect. I can hear him talking now. The judge only gave us seventy-two hours. Now we wait to see what happens."

"And you will keep me in the loop, as you agreed?" Hope had consented to Connie's request only after a two-hour meeting involving Hope, Connie, Eli Snyder, a lawyer for the paper, and a lawyer for the FBI.

"As we agreed," concurred Connie. "But nothing to the press until I say . . . as *you* agreed."

"Got it."

Hope smiled. With or without the legal agreement, their trust in each other as friends was assurance enough.

CHAPTER 15

E-Mail From Israel

Wil read the e-mail from his secretary in Israel:

Hello, Dr. Wilson. Everything is going fine at the Institute. The Institute has not collapsed with your departure as you feared it would. However, the Israeli government is being bothersome again, but nothing out of the ordinary. Still, you are missed.

Oskar Gunderson and I have decided to be married. This probably isn't much of a surprise to you, but it is quite exciting for us.

I wanted to let you know that Oskar and I were driving by your house yesterday and noticed a bouquet of flowers on your porch. It looked like it had been there for a couple days. All the note said was, "Thank you for the good time. I owe you one." Since I didn't think you would be using them and a few were still in pretty good shape, I took them home and made up a nice arrangement for my coffee table. They are so beautiful. I doubted you or Mrs. Wilson would mind.

The note didn't say who sent the flowers, but just in case someone asks about them, they did arrive.

Hello to Hope and little Steven. I bet he is getting really big. Maybe you could send me a few photos. Got to go. Bye.

Beth

Hmm, thought Wil, scratching his chin. *I wonder who sent us flowers? Oh well.*

Wil clicked on the next ten messages, all of which were junk mail, then closed his e-mail program.

"Well, Boo," said Wil to the lump of brown fur across his feet, "maybe Hope will know who sent the flowers."

CHAPTER 16

Three Meetings

"See you later, Connie," said Hope. They had just concluded their second lunch meeting in three days. The
restaurant was located on the fifth floor of an office building
halfway between each of their workplaces. Connie had
parked on the fifth floor of the attached parking garage and
was headed to the bridge that led to her car. Hope had parked
on the second floor and waited for the elevator.

Hope waved good-bye as the elevator doors opened. She
stepped into the elevator, still reflecting on how much she'd
enjoyed her time with Connie and the news that the judge
had extended the warrant even before the first one had
expired.

Lost in her musings, Hope bumped into a man who was
equally distracted. Both began to apologize for the collision
before doing double takes.

"Hope!"

"Brad!"

"What a surprise," said Brad. "How nice to see you."

As the elevator doors closed, Brad noticed Connie exiting
through the door that led to the parking garage. "Say, wasn't
that the FBI agent involved in the crash investigation?"

"Yes." The truth couldn't hurt. "She's a good friend. We
just had a delightful lunch making fun of our husbands'

habits." Hope was trying to diffuse the tension and evident suspicion.

"At Michael's Bistro?" Brad was playing along.

"Yes. We really like their Reubens."

Silence.

"What brings you to this part of town?" Hope finally broke the ice.

"I had a meeting with a shareholder upstairs. It went well." Brad was trying to keep it light as well, but he was not comfortable with what he had just learned. "Did you talk about business at lunch?" He was trying to joke.

"We tried not to." Hope's voice was innocent.

"Say," said Brad, in a tone that implied an affirmative answer to this question would be preposterous, "did you ever tell your friend," his head gestured toward the elevator door, "about the ridiculous note the nutcase gave you?"

Brad's bluntness put Hope in a difficult position. All she could do was deflect. "Why would I do that when you told me there was nothing to it?"

They were dancing, but both were leading. Brad knew his next step. He let go. "Just curious."

"Besides, why would I have reason to doubt your truthfulness?" Hope slipped in one last move.

The elevator door opened. Brad let Hope step out first. She headed toward her car and hoped he was headed to his.

After a few steps, their routes to their respective cars led in opposite directions. Brad was going to make his last move count. He stopped Hope, lightly touching her arm. "Hope, I appreciate your keeping dangerous accusations, such as the one that fruitcake made, to yourself." He knew she hadn't. "With all the other stuff on my plate, the last thing I need in my life right now is an FBI investigation pointed at me. I'm not sure how I'd handle it."

Hope looked at Brad's hand that had tightened on her upper arm. After keeping it there a second longer than he needed to, Brad let it drop to his side. He smiled, turned, and then calmly strode away.

Hope waited for a moment, stunned, speechless. Shaking her head, she turned and walked to her car. Chills ran down her back as she forced herself to stay calm. She knew she had been threatened and was eager to be in a different place.

After watching Brad's red Lamborghini drive away, she began to breathe more easily. Hurrying to her car at the far end of the parking garage, Hope noticed that the shivering that had started moments earlier was abating.

She had walked about one hundred feet before she heard footsteps approaching from behind. Resisting the urge to look, Hope calmly retrieved the can of pepper spray from her purse. She didn't want to appear fearful, yet the footsteps were accelerating. With her finger ready to fire, she whirled around.

The person following her stopped and took a step back. It was the informant from the funeral. "Hope Wilson?" He took a hesitant step toward her.

Oddly, she felt safe. For some reason she trusted this man, even though it bothered her that he was following her.

"May I talk to you?" he asked.

Hope stopped. She was actually glad to see the enigmatic man who had sparked the flame that had turned into a fire. His voice was different, a little higher—maybe because he wasn't whispering as he had been at the funeral. Hope relaxed her trigger finger and stowed her weapon.

"Yes. But first I need to know your name."

"Sorry. No go. I'm anonymous. Got it?"

Hope studied his face. She tried to recall their first meeting, cursing herself for not being more attentive to details at that time. He looked smaller than she remembered, but his suit appeared to be the same one he'd worn at the funeral. The lighting wasn't very good and it made him look rather sickly. His hair was perfectly combed.

"But I know what you look like. Why can't I know your name?"

"Wrong. You do not know what I look like. This is a mask."

"What?" This candid disclosure of his disguise surprised her. She took a step closer to examine his face in more detail.

"Pretty convincing, isn't it? My wife didn't even recognize me."

The mask *was* convincing, and it wasn't until he allowed her to touch his cheek that she was fully persuaded. Why hadn't she noticed this at the funeral? Still, he couldn't disguise his size. He wasn't a football player or a weight lifter. His gloved hands were on the small side. Obviously he'd gone to a significant amount of trouble with the disguise. Why was he so afraid?

"Okay, I get the anonymity bit," said Hope. "I'm sorry you had to go to all the expense. If there's one thing about me I want you to know, it is that I'm trustworthy and I do not expose my sources."

"I believe you. I just needed to make sure."

"Thank you for trusting me."

"Have you come up with anything yet?"

"Not really," admitted Hope.

This was mostly truthful. The reason the judge had extended the warrant for the listening device Hope had planted in Brad's office was related to a conversation between Brad and an executive from Advanced Chemical Products, which, at this point, seemed wholly unrelated to the crash. The FBI was suspicious that ACP was trying to extort money from Freedom, or the other way around. The cryptic conversation, including Advanced Chemical Products' suggestion that perhaps something could be slipped into Freedom's insurance claim, was particularly confusing since no one was aware of any official relationship between the two companies. The possibility existed that it had something to do with a shady stock deal, since Advanced had recently acquired a block of Freedom stock. The FBI knew something was up; they simply weren't sure what it was. Connie had speculated, off the record, that the two companies were possibly concocting an insurance scam.

Hope refocused on the man's question. "I'm sorry. I looked at the maintenance records and they were clean as a whistle."

"What did you expect?" the informant said angrily.

Hope was playing him. "I need more. You didn't give me much to go on. Besides, how do I know you're not some sort of crackpot?"

"Phuh." The informant exhaled and stiffened his back, his tone indignant. "Check the maintenance logs of other planes on the same day as the crash. See if they are as clean as the plane that went down. It will be obvious the records you were provided were doctored."

"Are you saying Freedom Airways cleans its logs after each incident?" Hope contrived a look of surprise.

"You should also check purchase orders to see if you can find evidence of Freedom actually buying all the parts they say they replace. Each time an engineer figured out how to not replace a part deemed obsolete according to code, Freedom would increase that employee's year-end bonus."

"Really?" Hope wanted him to keep talking. This was good.

"And I was punished for bringing it to Stinson's attention."

"Punished?"

"I'd made a mistake in the past and Stinson knew about it. I didn't want that mistake made public."

"Did you go to Scott Kingman or was he in on it?"

"Kingman was out of town. I made the mistake of going to Stinson first. I don't think Kingman knew about it. Maybe he did. I didn't want to risk getting Stinson madder at me, so I just let it go."

"Why?"

The informant had said all he wanted to but, after a moment of hesitation, added softly, "And I think you might want to be careful, too."

"What do you mean?"

"Stinson. I tell you, he can be ruthless. Knowing what I know about him, I would rather deal with a cornered Mama grizzly than Brad Stinson, especially if he feels threatened."

"You're not suggesting—"

"I'm not kidding. I'd watch my back if I were you. Why do you think I'm wearing this costume? It ain't 'cause I'm chicken." He stood a little straighter. "But he'd probably have me killed if he found out what I was up to."

"No way. Brad? He can be a creep, but not a killer."

"Hey, I warned you, lady. I appreciate that you're looking into this situation. You'll find out there's more to it. I'm merely protecting my back. I'd suggest you protect yours."

Hope had been warned.

"I gotta go." He walked away, knowing she would not follow. Hope respectfully turned away, opened her car door, climbed in, and started the engine. She ignored the informant as he walked to the left and disappeared.

CHAPTER 17

The Guys

As Hope drove away from her three encounters, Wil, Steve, and Franklin Jackson were finishing lunch.

Wil pushed his plate back and patted his stomach. "Now, that was good."

"It sure was," said Franklin as he set down his last rib and wiped his hands on his napkin. "I haven't eaten like that for two weeks. Thanks for asking me to join you."

"Sure," said Steve, who had invited him.

"And thank you for picking the place!" inserted Wil. "Your taste in restaurants is certainly better than Steve's! He usually picks some exotic place where my cultural horizons are supposed to be expanded, and I sometimes feel inclined to stab my food before eating it."

"Knock it off, Wil. It isn't that bad," protested Steve.

"Okay, Steve. Let's go with an impartial jury." Wil looked at Franklin, who had just been assigned jury duty. "Mr. Juror, what do you call good food? A rack of ribs with a side of seasoned applesauce, garlic-roasted french fries, barbecued baked beans, corn on the cob, fresh-baked biscuits with honey, and horseradish-tinged coleslaw . . ." Wil had just described the banquet the three had shared ". . . or little tiny helpings of sea animals and plants delicately cut from uncooked and sometimes undead items lying on ice in front of you, which are prepared by a highly paid, artistic chef who does not speak English?" Wil described last week's outing to a sushi bar.

Steve looked at the jury, hoping for support.

"Sorry, Steve. Wil's right." Franklin reached for the final piece of honey-soaked biscuit on his plate. Franklin held the morsel, evidence before the court, and said, "You can't beat this," then popped the treat into his mouth. His smile of pure pleasure sealed the case.

"Okay, okay," said Steve. "I'm outnumbered. But at least it's been interesting, hasn't it, Wil?"

"I'm just glad we alternate on who chooses the place."

Steve was tired of the beating and changed the subject. He turned to Franklin. "I heard the donations to the two funds in Rochelle's name have topped $250,000. That's amazing."

"She was an amazing girl," Franklin said matter-of-factly.

"She sure was," added Wil. He hadn't known Rochelle long, but he'd been impressed by their brief conversations when Rochelle baby-sat Steven and by what others had said about her.

"Thank you," Franklin said proudly, as he directed his attention to Wil. "I didn't get a chance to talk to you at the reception."

"I'm sorry about that."

Franklin smiled. "Tell me, what did you think of the service?"

Wil swallowed. It had been four days since "two-funeral Saturday." He was reluctant to express himself the way he had in the car with Hope and Steve. He'd also had more time to think about the two services and the differences between them. "It was . . . interesting," he smiled.

Franklin tilted his head slightly.

Wil elaborated. "First of all, I haven't been to that many church services, let alone funerals. I felt a little out of place."

"Oh?" Franklin nodded. "Did you enjoy the choir?" Franklin was looking for a point of agreement so Wil could save face.

"Now, that was impressive."

"Wonderful," added Steve.

"Did you enjoy Bishop Jordan's sermon?" asked Franklin.

"He's a very good speaker but . . ." Wil didn't want to give the impression he'd been influenced, ". . . you do know, Franklin, I don't believe the things you and Steve do."

"I know."

With that clear, Wil continued. "Still, I must admit, I found his statements about John 3:16 and 17 to be quite different from the way I heard those verses used when I was a kid. In the church where I grew up, the whole emphasis was on people burning in hell if they didn't accept Jesus. I never heard anyone talk about God's underlying love, let alone the reason Jesus came in the first place—at least as the bishop said it. Best I can recall, those verses were used as a tool to scare the hell out of people. The bishop made it sound like a message of love. While I don't agree with him about Jesus, I do like his perspective more than the one I was familiar with."

Steve struggled to keep his jaw from dropping. Franklin had just elicited from Wil more personal reflection on Jesus than Steve had been able to in more than twenty years of friendship.

"That's too bad," said Franklin. "You see, though identifying and accepting responsibility for our sins is a big part of Steve's and my faith, there's a lot more to it. Unfortunately some of us Christians get so focused on the problem of sin that we neglect the solution to it. Some forget that God's love for us is more important than our sin. Romans 5:8 says, 'But God showed His love for us in that while we were yet sinners Christ died for us.'"

Wil was not only listening to Franklin, he was actually hearing him. Steve couldn't recall, in all their years of friendship, Wil ever listening to him the way his friend was now hearing Franklin. But Steve also knew Wil could tolerate only so much before his deep-seated disdain for Christianity would surface and overshadow the valuable information he had just received.

Steve leaned into the conversation. "Well, how about some dessert?"

Both men looked at Steve like he had grown another nose.

CHAPTER 18

The Investigation

"So," said Hope to her assistant, Shelly, "they thought you were a sales rep with a software company."

"Yep."

"Being young and attractive didn't hurt either."

"I guess not." Shelly appreciated but deflected Hope's compliment. "I still can't believe the access they gave me."

"What did you wear?"

Shelly blushed. "Okay . . . so maybe that had a little something to do with it. But, as I was saying, only four people in the maintenance department have ever been let go or quit in the entire history of the company."

"Oh?"

"And of the four, two were let go in their first week for performance issues. One long-timer was killed in a car accident two days after giving his notice, and the fourth person was a woman who, according to John—"

"John?"

"John—the archivist. He liked me. He even left me alone with the files. I told him I didn't want to keep him from doing his other *extremely* important work." Shelly batted her eyes and smiled sweetly.

Hope's look was somewhere between pride and disgust.

"Anyway," Shelly continued, "John told me this woman

left the company supposedly claiming sexual harassment. He said it was settled quickly and the terms of the settlement are confidential."

"Still, four is a remarkably low number, all things considered."

"Right. Perhaps one reason is that Freedom Airways pays its maintenance managers, on average, thirty percent more than the industry standard."

"Thirty percent? Wow! Are you certain?" asked Hope.

"Yep."

"That's a little out of character when you consider that Freedom skimps in every other area."

"They also have a unique bonus program for their non-managers, which I could not figure out."

"My informant said something about that," Hope mused.

"I couldn't prove it, but my guess is the bonus program is somehow tied to purchase orders related to parts replacement."

"Why do you think that?"

"I'm not sure, but John said something when I asked him about a number of entries that said 'new part ordered per code.' I asked John where they kept the department's copy of these purchase orders. He told me they were locked in the manager's office. When I asked why, he said it had something to do with the mechanics' paychecks."

"'Something to do with?' What does that mean?"

"I don't know. He didn't say how or anything, and I didn't pursue it. But the more I thought about it the more fishy it sounded."

Hope tapped her fingers on her desk. "Anything about the maintenance logs?"

"Keep in mind that I'm not an expert on this kind of thing, but your informant knew what he was talking about.

The maintenance logs for the plane that went down were spotless. The other logs were clean, but not that clean."

"Were they suspicious?"

"The logs?"

"No, Freedom."

"Oh. No. They never knew I was looking at the logs of other planes. Of course, I do have a dinner date with John."

"No!"

"Well, he is kind of cute in a nerdish, adolescent, puppy kind of way."

"Are you going?"

"Are you kidding? No way! I'm planning to catch the flu or the Ebola virus or the plague or some other highly contagious disease on the afternoon of the date. Too bad—that'll mean I need to cancel."

Hope smiled ruefully as her assistant gathered up a pile of papers.

"Oh, well." Shelly put the back of her hand to her forehead and leaned against Hope's desk. "And I thought our relationship looked so promising."

"You did great, Shelly."

Things are not supposed to be broken.
Sometimes they are.
And sometimes, after they are fixed,
they are even better.

CHAPTER 19

The Call

The phone rang as an exhausted Wil staggered back to bed after his seventh trip to the bathroom. He debated not answering it, but the demanding ring overruled his desire. And since Hope had unplugged the phone in the bedroom, thinking it would ensure their effort to sleep in, this meant a detour to the phone in the kitchen. Mumbling, and then yelping after stubbing his toe on Steven's Tonka truck, Wil fumbled the phone to his ear on the fifth ring.

"Hello?" grumbled Wil.

"Is that you, William?"

"Mom!"

"Good morning, Wil."

"For heaven's sake, Mom, it's Saturday morning!"

Betty paused then said, "You're right," with true contrition. "I should have waited a bit longer before I called."

Wil glanced at the clock next to the refrigerator. Nine-thirty. He realized his mom didn't need to be quite so apologetic. In fact, he began to realize how lucky he was that Steven hadn't awakened them yet. Then he began to wonder if Steven was okay. "What's up, Mom?"

"Oh nothing. I was just missing my grandson and was thinking of you and Hope, and thought I'd check to see how you all are doing."

"Who is it, honey?" inquired Hope from the bedroom. "Oh my gosh, it's nine-thirty!"

"Just a second, Mom." Wil put his hand over the phone. "It's Mom. Hope, honey, could you check on Steven?" Hope was already heading in that direction.

"Sorry about that," said Wil informing his mom, "I guess we slept in a little later than planned."

"So how is Steven?"

The peculiar feeling that everyone—even your own parents—is more interested in your child than in you made itself known to Wil as he considered the question.

"Hope's checking on him. We were all exhausted after staying at the Haltermans' a little longer than expected. Steven also insisted on playing with Boo once we got home."

The answer to Betty's question was clear when Boo came flying through the kitchen with Steven in pursuit and old Napoleon as the caboose.

"He's fine," said Wil, smiling at the spectacle. A few seconds later the three playmates came out of Wil and Hope's bedroom, careening through the kitchen again, but this time Napoleon was the lead and Steven the caboose. "That dog you brought home from the park has definitely become part of the family."

"Can I talk to him?"

"Boo?"

"Steven!"

"Sure." Wil lowered the receiver from his ear. "Steven, Grandma is on the phone."

It is difficult to know which Steven enjoyed more—Grandma or talking on the phone. In any case, an abandoned dog and cat followed him to the phone. When the two animals realized Steven was not paying attention to them anymore, they turned to the next best thing—Wil, sitting in

Hope's wing chair. Napoleon jumped onto his lap and attached himself, like a baby, to his master's chest. Boo nestled up next to them and plopped his head on Wil's thigh. As Napoleon began to knead contentedly, Boo, with his eyes, beseeched Wil to pet him.

"Now, that is a sight," said Hope, as she joined the family in the kitchen.

Steven had crawled onto Wil's other leg, holding the receiver with both hands. Wil had a cat on his chest, a child on one knee, and a dog resting his head on the thigh of his other leg.

Wil grinned. He was at the top of his game. *It doesn't get better than this.*

Hope picked up on Wil's mood and understood his non-verbal communication. She reached for the camera and clicked off a few shots before Steven lost interest in his conversation and took off running, followed by a cat and a dog. Wil heard the TV come on in the living room, and the inarticulate sounds of the Teletubbies floated into the kitchen. Steven was now occupied for a good twenty minutes.

Wil put the receiver back to his ear as Hope sauntered over and sat in his lap. She put her arms around her husband who, after the departure of Boo, Napoleon, and Steven, looked dejected and lonely.

"I won't run off and leave you," Hope whispered in a seductive tone that, at another time, would have been much more appreciated. Wil smiled at his wife and sighed.

Hope had planned to sleep in, but not past eight or eight-thirty. Though she needed the sleep, the work waiting for her at her office made her feel a little frantic. Hope kissed Wil on the top of his head, and then set off to the bedroom.

"So, Mom," said Wil, now free of distractions, "our circus is currently on intermission."

Betty laughed even though she was not completely clear what Wil meant.

"How are you doing, Mom? We miss having you around."

Wil and his mom were on the road to reconciliation. It had been a challenge, a repercussion of Wil's years of not-so-repressed anger at his mother for tolerating his abusive father. In the early stages, when Betty had lacked the honesty or ability to even see the need for reconciliation, the rift had grown. A few years after his dad's drunken death in a one-car crash, and after Wil and his brother had moved out of the house, Betty had changed. Wil, who was angry to his core, channeled most of his anger into an intense desire to destroy his father's religion. The balance of his anger, in the prolonged aftermath of his dad's death, had been directed at his mom.

It baffled Wil that, while he had concluded that God doesn't exist and had specifically rejected the Jesus of Christianity, Betty had become even more "Christian." However, her Christianity wasn't along the lines of the non-sense and hypocrisy of her late husband. Instead, it appeared to be a sincere faith, similar to Steve's. Still, Wil responded cautiously to the changes he'd observed in her. It was only due to Betty's persistence that reconciliation had even begun.

"I'm fine," answered Betty. "I miss all of you, too." It had been six days since Betty had left D.C.

"I've been thinking about our conversation regarding the funerals," said Betty.

Wil and his mom had stayed up until two a.m. the night before she left, talking about, among other things, the differences between the two funerals Wil and Hope had attended.

"I owe you an apology," confessed Betty.

"What?"

"Do you remember your father's funeral service?"

The subject was so unexpected, Wil almost said, "You

mean the one where everyone lied and pretended Dad was a saint, when in fact he was probably one of the meanest and most despicable people on the planet? You mean that great day when he died? You mean the one where I had to leave the sanctuary and vomit when I heard you paint him as a decent man, the very man who beat you and me and had a stable of other women in your bed?" But Wil compressed his lips and tried to figure out where she was going. He also felt that, though he probably needed to say those things someday, now wasn't the time. He liked his improving relationship with his mom and didn't think a nuclear blast would help.

"Yes," Wil said cautiously.

"Well, I was wrong and I'm sorry."

"For what?" Wil wasn't sure what she meant. He thought he'd track better after his first cup of Starbucks, which he'd just begun to pour.

"For not being truthful when I had the chance. Wil, your dad was not a good man. I was weak and I'm responsible for my bad choices. I don't have any excuse for letting him hurt you and your brother the way he did."

Wil set down the coffeepot and returned to the wing chair, his half-filled cup forgotten on the counter. He no longer could hear the Teletubbies or his son in the living room.

"Wil, I don't know how to say this. But . . ." Betty hesitated ". . . in many ways, I also died at that funeral."

Wil could tell that his mom had thought intensely about this phone call. He could also tell she was fighting back tears.

Betty continued. "That was, in many ways, the beginning of a new life for me. It took many years for me to begin to heal from all the pain and the eighteen years of awfulness with your father. Still, I began to heal that night, even as I lied to everyone who attended the funeral and I said all those nice things about your dad. Maybe it was some kind of emotional release or just my low point. But since then, things really have been different in my life. However, I haven't been able to get over the pain I caused you and your brother."

"Mom—"

"No, let me finish."

Wil had never heard her say that before.

"Wil, I was wrong and I am sorry. Please forgive me. Thankfully we've grown closer over the last couple years. If only you knew how happy this has made me." She began to lose the battle against the tears. "But, Wil, I could not go another day without you knowing how bad I feel for putting you through what you went through and how much I've always loved you, even when, for whatever reasons, I was not able to show it. I love you, Wil. Our conversation the other night about the funerals, and then remembering your dad's funeral, got me thinking about my own funeral, which is getting closer with each year. I could not bear the thought of going to my grave without you knowing how sorry I am and how very much I love you, and have always loved you and always will."

Wil had been paying so much attention to his mom's emotions as she struggled to articulate her thoughts and fight back her tears, that he lost track of his own. It wasn't until a warm drop fell from his cheek to his hand that he realized he also had begun to cry.

"Mom . . ." stuttered Wil, "I think I'd better go see what Hope and Steven are up to."

His mom understood. She could see him through his shaky voice.

"Thanks for calling, Mom. I'll talk with you later, okay?"

"Okay."

Wil set down the receiver, put his head in his hands, and

began to sob. Hope, who had been standing in the doorway in her bathrobe, had an idea of what was happening. She walked over and put her arms around Wil as he released a flood of tears that had been stored up since his childhood.

Clues are great when you know the game.

CHAPTER 20

The Note

"Honey?" Hope paused in the doorway between the kitchen and the garage.

Wil was attempting to convince Steven the cereal was supposed to go into *his* mouth and not Boo's.

"Did you leave the garage door open?"

"Ahh . . . mmm. . . . No. Why?"

"Are you sure?"

"Yes. . . . Mmm, yummy cereal! . . . I know I closed it last night when we came home from the Haltermans'. . . . No, no—not for Boo! . . . I even checked it when you sent me back to the car to get your purse. Why?"

"It's just . . ." Hope said hesitantly. She wasn't sure what was wrong, but something was. "It's just . . . the door is wide open."

"Maybe the garage door gnomes did it." Wil was more concerned with the contest going on with his son, the dog, and himself. He directed Steven's spoon away from Boo. "It's for you, Steven. Is anything missing?"

"I don't know. I just noticed the door was open." Hope glanced around the garage. "Nothing's missing that I can see."

"Perhaps Boo and Steven were playing tug-of-war with the opener again."

Wil and Hope knew they lived in a safe area and a break-in was the least likely alternative. Plus, nothing seemed to be missing or even disturbed.

"Hmm. Oh well." Hope stepped down into the garage. Just before the door closed behind her she called to Wil. "I'll be home around six."

Not twenty seconds later, Hope opened the door again. Steven had just spilled the whole bowl of cereal, and Wil was trying to decide whether to clean up the mess or allow Boo to do it. In either case, he had to prepare another bowl for Steven.

"Wil?" Hope was puzzled.

"Back already?"

"Did you cut out this article?"

Wil took a quick glance, which wasn't necessary because he knew he hadn't cut out any articles. "No," he said.

"That's bizarre."

Wil looked up when he heard the mild alarm in Hope's voice.

"Neither did I," added Hope.

"Where'd you find it?"

"Taped to the steering wheel."

"What?" Wil was now interested in the article. He set the fresh bowl of cereal in front of Steven, giving him a look that meant, *Don't spill this one*.

"It's my latest article," said Hope.

"On the EPA guidelines?"

"No, about my investigation of the plane crash."

"Why was it taped to the steering wheel?"

"Got me." Hope shook her head.

"This is odd," said Wil as he opened the door and went into the garage. A minute later he returned to Hope, who was sitting at the table where Steven was faithfully eating his cereal. Boo was doing his job and cleaning up the floor. Perhaps Boo's example was inspiration for Steven.

Wil sat in the chair next to her. "Was there anything with the article?"

"No."

"There doesn't appear to be anything missing from the garage either. This is really peculiar. Should we call the police?" Wil voiced the question both were thinking.

"And say what—that somebody got into our garage and taped my newspaper article to the steering wheel of our car and nothing is missing?"

It did sound rather ridiculous. Besides, Hope had kicked into her I'll-figure-this-out mode even as she admitted to herself there wasn't enough to go on. When she looked at her watch, she realized there wasn't enough time either. She started toward the garage again. "I've got to get to the office." She opened the door. "We can figure it out tonight. You might want to check around to see if any other gnomes have been at work. I'll see you at six."

Wil whirled around when he heard the crash of Steven's bowl on the floor.

"Doggone it, Steven."

"Theven full. Theven love Dada. Want down."

Boo began work on cleanup job number two.

*The line that divides your professional life from
your personal life is in your heart.*

The Threat

With no rush-hour traffic, it took Hope only twenty minutes to drive to the office. The rest of the morning was spent finishing her article on the new EPA guidelines. Unexpectedly, this article would also reflect poorly on Advanced Chemical Products. During the final stages of the cleanup at the ACP plant in northern Virginia, the EPA had discovered a "compound of unknown origin" and concluded that the plant had been manufacturing a corrosive that had yet to be reported to the EPA. When the same substance, later identified as Nitro XF192, was discovered in their Tampa facility, the question of how the substance had been transported bubbled to the top, since it was precisely this type of activity the new EPA guidelines were supposed to stop. No one was certain how the chemicals had been shipped to Tampa, and Advanced Chemical Products wasn't telling. The result was that Advanced Chemical Products was in scrutiny's furnace again.

Hope dialed the extension of her assistant, who was working another weekend day. "Hi, Shelly. Can you come see me? I want to hear what else you've found out about Freedom's maintenance logs."

"Be right there."

A minute later Shelly seated herself in the chair in front of Hope's desk.

"So, Shelly, have you come up with anything else?"

"Well . . ." Shelly wasn't sure where to start.

"Well what?"

"Hope, I hope you don't mind, but I took the liberty of reading your article on Advanced Chemical Products before I dropped it off at editorial."

"Was something wrong?" Hope was aware that her protégée read all her articles. Yet, the way Shelly was looking at her made Hope wonder what major mistake she had detected.

"Oh, there's nothing wrong. It's just that something caught my attention and made me think."

"Yes?"

"While I was going over the logs this morning I came across a few references to Advanced Chemical Products."

"What? Are you talking about the Freedom Airways' maintenance logs?"

"Yes."

"And?"

"It's probably nothing."

"Well," said Hope, gesturing with her hand, "what is it?"

Shelly hesitated. She didn't want to overstep the line and also didn't want to speculate only to be proven wrong. "I don't really know if it's related to anything."

"Okay, Shelly. I understand you think this is a long shot. But out with it."

"It actually might be more related to the story you were doing on Advanced Chemical Products."

"Uh huh?" Hope was lost.

"The logs of the plane that crashed had a couple of entries that referenced Advanced Chemical Products. It caught my attention since I didn't see any references to them in the logs of any other planes. The entries had something to do with special parts for the cargo compartment, which John told me were only available from Advanced Chemical Products. I didn't know ACP even made parts for air cargo compartments! Maybe this isn't unusual, but I thought you might find it interesting, particularly since you'd been investigating Advanced Chemical Products before all this stuff happened."

"Hmm. This is good, Shelly." Hope was excited. "Are you wondering if ACP shipped those chemicals to Florida by way of Freedom Airways?"

"And I was just thinking . . ."

"This is good, Shelly, really good."

"Thanks." Shelly's confidence had returned. "But there's more. Every one of the log entries related to these parts was signed off by the same person—the company's lead mechanic."

"How do you know it was the company's lead mechanic?"

"I gave John a call."

"No! He's still talking to you after you stood him up?"

Shelly pushed on her throat with her index finger, which caused her voice to have a choking sound. "He understood that I am still not up to par."

"You are bad!" said Hope, with a chuckle.

"Yeah, I know," said Shelly, grinning impishly before becoming serious again. "Hope, do you think there's something there?"

"Shelly," Hope said, with confidence and appreciation, "at this point, it appears you might have just opened Pandora's box."

Courtesy of Hope's connections at the FAA, they learned that the FAA had discovered evidence of an "unknown substance" at the Freedom crash site. Hope worked her magic and was able to convince the two departments of the government, the EPA and the FAA, to actually work together. Within an hour Hope confirmed the unknown substance the FAA had discovered at the crash site: Nitro XF192.

Hope combined this information with her knowledge of the cargo compartment parts that Advanced Chemical Products had provided to Freedom Airways. She linked this with the recent unexplained revenue Freedom had begun to record about the same time the Nitro XF192 started to show up at Advanced Chemical Products' laboratory in Tampa.

The puzzle began to look like a picture, an extremely nasty picture.

Hope had been pestering, baiting, and tormenting Brad and his gang for more than a week. Her articles, such as the one taped to her steering wheel, had put so much pressure on Freedom Airways that the FBI, FAA, Securities Exchange Commission, local police, and even the IRS had begun to converge on Brad. Freedom's stock price had plummeted. Connie Donaldson even told Hope that within a week the Justice Department would be issuing indictments of Freedom Airways related to everything from their recounting of the plane crash to insider trading.

With the information regarding the Nitro XF192 and the cargo compartments, Hope was confident she would put the final nails in the coffins of Freedom Airways and Advanced Chemical Products. Though it would be difficult to prove the crash was related to the corrosive, she knew Freedom Airways, Brad, and Advanced Chemical Products were in for very difficult times. When Hope told Connie about this new twist, Connie okayed Hope's article for publication, suggesting it might even cause the conspirators to make a fatal misstep.

The deadline for her article was five p.m. Hope ignored

everything else on her desk and wrote knowing this could possibly be the most important article of her life. She had been nominated for a Pulitzer six years ago for a series on welfare reform, but the plane crash had thrust her into the national spotlight. This article had the potential of being bigger than anything she had ever done before.

Two hours later she sat back and hit the print button. It was time to edit her work in hard copy. She had only ninety minutes to finish the article. As she tried to ease the knots in her shoulder muscles, she noticed her message light. Now was as good a time as any to listen to her messages.

She put it on speakerphone. There was only one message. The voice was disguised. The words were clear.

"You shouldn't leave your garage door open. Some very troubled person might sneak into your car and put a dangerous article on the steering wheel. Perhaps you should close the door before something bad happens."

Her tense muscles forgotten, Hope pushed replay and listened again. She picked up the phone and hit speed dial number one.

Her home phone rang. Hope counted silently. *One. . . two . . . three . . . four . . .* "Where are you, Wil?" Hope muttered through clenched teeth. *Five . . .*

"Hello." It was Hope's voice. "You have reached the Wilsons . . ."

"Hello, hello . . . Hold it. I'm sorry about the machine." She heard Wil's voice over the recording, but she knew she had to wait until after the long beep before Wil could hear her voice.

"Sorry about that. This is Wil. Can I help you?"

"Hi, honey. Is everything all right?" asked Hope.

"If you count a game of tug of war and chase between a cat, a dog, and a two-year-old who has volunteered his dirty underwear as the object of the game as 'all right,' then everything is all right." Wil was breathing hard. He'd been doing some chasing of his own when the phone rang.

"Good." Hope sighed.

"Good? Perhaps I should tell you where Napoleon decided to hide the treasure before I found it!"

"I just wanted to make sure everything was okay." Hope's voice was unsteady.

Wil sensed her uneasiness. "What's up, Hope?"

"Wil, I think we should call the police."

"Why? What's wrong?"

"I just listened to my message machine at work. Someone is threatening me. They apparently are upset about the articles I've been writing."

"C'mon, honey. Now why would Brad Stinson be upset?" His sarcasm was not helpful; nor was his ready confirmation of her suspicion it was Brad. "It's not a secret you're not his favorite person, but what would be the point of harassing you?"

"Wil, someone came into our home last night and put a note in our car and then called my office and left a message telling me what they'd done. I don't think they're kidding."

"Okay, I'll call. But what do I tell them?" Wil wanted to be supportive, but things were not as clear to him.

"No, I'd better call. Perhaps you should just keep a close eye on things. Look, I'll call the police and get home as fast as I can."

"Okay, whatever you say, Hope. Be careful." Hope's anxiety had spread to Wil.

Hope set down her phone and jogged the twenty-five yards to Eli's office. She told him about the garage and the article and the message on the machine.

Connie arrived at Hope's office fifteen minutes later. The

local police took thirty minutes longer than Connie, which was actually relatively quick for D.C.

After a powwow, Hope, Eli, Connie, and the local police agreed that Hope's article needed to run. Since threats had already been made, they thought the article might help flush out the person making the threats, whom they speculated was associated with Freedom Airways. Eli made it clear nothing was running unless a twenty-four-hour police guard was posted at Hope's house. The FBI agreed to provide support and to monitor incoming phone calls at the Wilson home. Ever since Brad had discovered the listening device, Connie felt responsible for Hope's safety, even though Brad had not, apparently, realized it was Hope who had put it there.

Hope arrived home about thirty minutes after the first shift of police protection had introduced themselves to Wil. The FBI crew was just setting up the phone tracking system. Boo and Napoleon had been banished to the garage. Boo had been a little too willing to help and Napoleon had been a little too territorial.

Crucial moments are seldom planned.
They just happen.

CHAPTER 22

Shopping

The expedition to Nordstrom department store on Tuesday morning was Wil's idea. After being barricaded in their home for more than forty-eight hours, Wil knew, Hope could not take being cooped up much longer. Wil also knew that few things helped his wife unwind more than a couple of hours at her favorite store. When he floated the idea, the police and FBI strongly opposed it.

Hope's article had stirred up more commotion than anticipated as the rest of the press attacked the bloodied Freedom Airways and Advanced Chemical Products like frenzied piranha. Though nothing had happened since the voice message and the note on the steering wheel, the police and Connie were concerned that whoever had made the initial threats had likely become more upset by the last few days' events. After Wil offered to pay an off-duty officer to act as an escort, the idea of Hope's mall visit became more palatable, but not by much. Connie reluctantly agreed, but only on the condition that Hope and Steven never be out of view of their armed chaperone.

Hope and Steven headed to the children's clothing section of Nordstrom. Their police escort was less than thrilled about being at the mall. Not only did Pete hate shopping, the drive had been stressful because of an accident near the mall entrance, which momentarily distracted him from watching to see if anyone was following them. Yet, once inside the store, the sound of Mozart lofting up from the piano near the escalator calmed both Hope's and her chaperone's spirits.

It was early, the mall wasn't busy, and Nordstrom was blessedly quiet. Hope found the warm elegance, enhanced by intermittent scents of lavender candles, potpourri-filled gift baskets, and Oscar de la Renta perfumes, particularly soothing. She sighed contentedly as she looked through a rack of children's shirts. Steven vroomed his red fire engine at her feet. As she moved to the next rack she looked up to see a six-foot-four staff member with short blond hair, a mustache, and vivid blue eyes walking toward her from the dressing area. He was straightening his clothes and nametag, fully prepared to be of service.

"Welcome to Nordstrom. Is there something I can help you with?"

Hope loved the customer service and, since she was alone in the department, nobody else would be competing for the employee's assistance. "We need some new clothes," she said, tousling Steven's hair.

"I believe I can help you. I'm Marc." Hope already knew his name, courtesy of the Nordstrom name tag that had "Marc" imprinted in dark gold ink.

Marc squatted on his haunches and shook hands with Steven. "What's your name?"

Steven liked him right away. The cherry-flavored DumDum lollipop also helped.

"I Theven. I two." Steven's fingers were extended in the shape of a peace sign.

"Good to meet you, Steven. My name is Marc. What's your favorite color?"

"Bu."

"I like blue, too." He smiled. "Are you ready to do some shopping?"

"Yep!" Steven was eager to do whatever his new friend wanted.

Hope was wondering where Nordstrom had found this guy. He was great. "We need some warmer clothes. He's grown out of most of his things and we don't have much for the cooler weather."

As they walked toward the racks filled with clothing for two-year-olds, Marc turned to Hope and inquired, "Do you mind if I ask something?"

"No." Hope shrugged. "What is it?"

"Are you that famous reporter with *The New York Times* investigating the criminals at Freedom Airways?"

"Yes." Hope smiled, still amazed that the word "famous" should be linked with her.

"I really hope you get them," Marc sounded sympathetic, "but don't you get a little worried that those high-powered crooks might retaliate?"

Marc's concern sounded more like movie promotional hype than believable reality. Still, she responded appreciatively. "Thank you for your support and concern. But I'm only doing my job as a reporter. Truth be known, though, that's why Pete's our chaperone today."

"Ah," said Marc glancing at Pete and then smiling at Hope. "Shall we, then?" Marc began to pull items that looked like Steven's size and then stood back, ruminating with Hope as she shopped.

For the next few minutes, the two adults picked, matched, sampled, and discussed the appropriateness of this or that style of clothing for a walker versus a crawler. Pete thought it particularly cute when Steven decided, unknown to Marc or Hope, to dispose of the candy he'd grown tired of.

Pete knew someone would find the sticky lollipop when they tried on the shirt.

By the end of the brief fashion show, which Steven tolerated like a *GQ* model, Hope and Marc had managed to come up with five sets of clothing they agreed could be combined to make almost any number of outfits. Steven was more interested in finding hiding places than in looking at clothes. But he was easy to locate since he could hide only the upper part of his body in the hanging forests of children's clothing. Pete yawned and was reminded again of how much he hated shopping.

"Now all we need is a coat," summed up Hope.

Marc paused, not wanting to interfere in the shopper's decision to buy more.

"And it seems to me, I saw a perfect one—one floor down. I saw it as I was getting on the escalator. It was blue."

"Ah, good," Marc said hesitantly. "Would you like to take these items with you?" Marc gestured to the mountain of clothing. "Or would you like to bring the coat up here?"

Hope understood his implication. "Oh . . . you're not supposed to leave your department, are you?"

"Not really."

Hope decided. "Okay. Why don't you go ahead and start ringing these up and I'll go get one or two of the coats and be right back." Pete's frown deepened, revealing his reluctance with this plan, though he said nothing. His job was to be an observer, not a director.

"Perfect." Marc endorsed Hope's plan. "Steven, Pete, and I will stay here while you get the coat."

Hope's chaperone resented Marc's collusion in the conspiracy to split his flock.

"Sure. I'll be right back. I won't be but a minute." Hope turned toward the escalator and the jackets.

"Oh—and Mrs. Wilson . . ." said Marc.

Hope turned back.

"While you're getting the coat, there's a really cute pair of overalls I'd like you to take a look at. I think you might like them."

Hope smiled. The soft sell worked with Hope.

The shepherd wasn't pleased. He could not be in two places at once. As Hope walked past him, she whispered, "Keep an eye on Steven." Now, he was being asked to be a baby-sitter.

"Excuse me, Mrs. Wilson." Pete could not be quiet any longer. "I really don't like this. I'm supposed to be keeping an eye on you, and now you have me watching your son. Perha—"

"It'll be fine. See?" She pointed to the rack of blue jackets near the base of the up escalator. "I'm just going right there." She appealed to his paternal ego. "And, what better baby-sitter could I leave my child with?"

"But—"

Hope was gone, the heels of her beige pumps tap-tapping across the wood floor. She knew she'd be back in less than two minutes and it wasn't worth the time arguing about such a trivial thing. As Hope went down the escalator, Pete noticed that, if he stood a little closer to the escalators, because of the open area in the center of the store, he could see the rack of blue jackets, the entire route Hope would have to travel to return to home base, and still have a perfect view of Marc's entire department.

"I'll go get those overalls," Marc said to Pete.

Marc stopped after taking a couple steps. He turned to Steven, who was on the floor playing with his fire truck and had been abandoned between the baby-sitting guard and Marc. "Hey, little guy, why don't you come with me?"

Steven clasped Marc's extended hand and followed him, his fire truck in his other hand.

Marc looked at Pete and said, "The overalls are right over there near the dressing rooms."

The entrance to the dressing rooms was clearly within Pete's sight, so he nodded his approval.

"Let's go," said Marc.

The two buddies set off on their journey to the overalls.

Hope was holding a blue coat, looking at its size label.

As Marc and Steven walked in the direction of the dressing rooms, Marc leaned down and said to Steven, "Let's surprise your mommy. I have the perfect blue teddy bear that will go with your clothes. Do you think she'll like it?"

Steven's eyes lit up in the affirmative.

"Okay, we have to go this way." Marc stepped through the threshold that said "Dressing Rooms."

Pete frowned and took a hesitant step toward the dressing rooms. Steven and Marc were temporarily out of sight. *Perhaps the overalls are just inside that area on a rack or something.*

Pete didn't know that the entrance to the dressing room area also led to a service corridor that exited to the parking lot.

Hope was on her way up the escalator.

Steven held on with enthusiasm as his new friend took him on an adventure. They walked past the dressing room stalls and a storeroom. Instinctively, Steven pulled back when Marc opened the back door and pulled him through the exit. The self-closing fire door automatically shut behind them. Steven looked up at Marc when he saw the big black car drive up to the curb in front of them.

Marc had stopped talking to him.

Steven asked, "Where teddy bear?"

No answer.

Pete grew uneasy after ten seconds of Marc and Steven being out of sight. He started toward the dressing room area. Hope, who had just stepped off the escalator with two blue coats in hand, followed, quickening her pace when she noticed Steven was not in sight.

"Steven?" called Hope.

Pete did not look back. He entered the dressing room area and stopped. "Marc? Steven?"

Pete heard the door latch at the end of the corridor. His Beretta was out of its holster as he ran down the corridor toward the back door.

Steven began to whimper when Marc scooped him up and put him in the back seat of the Continental next to a woman he didn't know. Marc climbed in beside him and the car pulled away from the curb even before Marc had closed his door.

"Mommy?" Tears began to well in Steven's eyes. Something was wrong.

"Hello, Steven," came the woman's voice from behind a cold smile. "It's okay. Here's a nice blue teddy bear."

Steven was even more confused and began to cry. "Mommy?"

"It's okay, little guy. I'm an old friend of Daddy's."

Marc, or correctly Clarence, ignored the conversation between Kathreen Steele and Steven. Panting heavily, Clarence was having a hard time believing he'd actually pulled it off.

By the time Pete and Hope exploded out the exit door, Daryl, the driver of the car, had steered around the corner of the mall and the car was out of sight.

The difference between imagination and insanity is being able to tell the difference.

CHAPTER 23

Nemesis

The New York Times lead story:

REPORTER'S CHILD KIDNAPPED
NORDSTROM EMPLOYEE MURDERED

Yesterday morning at 11 o'clock the two-year-old son of *New York Times* correspondent Hope Wilson was kidnapped at Nordstrom department store in downtown Arlington, Virginia. During the investigation of the kidnapping, the body of a Nordstrom employee, 23-year-old Arlington resident Marc Jamison, was discovered in a storeroom near where the boy was last seen.

According to Arlington police, no one has claimed responsibility for the kidnapping. One source, who requested not to be named, indicated authorities are not ruling out the possibility that the kidnapping could be related to the recent series of articles by the kidnap victim's mother that has led to the investigation of alleged corruption at Freedom Airways.

The boy's father, archaeologist Dr. William Wilson, has gone on record as saying they will do whatever is necessary to get their son back. Because of concern for their child, he and his wife will not be answering any questions. Instead they have asked that all questions be directed to the local police or to the FBI, who have taken over the investigation. Dr. Wilson also asks anyone who has any knowledge of the incident to call 804-212-9878.

There is one suspect in the kidnapping, a male described as about six-foot-four with blond hair, a blond mustache, and blue eyes. This man is also being sought in connection with the murder of Mr. Jamison. According to a police spokesperson, they believe the two crimes are directly related because the suspect was wearing the murdered Nordstrom employee's nametag at the time of the kidnapping.

Kathreen continued reading the article, which contained further details of the crimes and subtle speculation that Freedom Airways was allegedly behind it all. After she had finished she began to carefully cut the article from the paper.

"This will make a nice addition to my scrapbook." She looked at Clarence. "I must admit, even though you botched it up when you killed that worthless Nordstrom employee—"

"I told you, he got in the way and I was improvising."

"—this does definitely turn up the heat on ol' Mr. Stinson and company and keeps the Feds off our backs."

"That was the plan, wasn't it?" asked Daryl.

Clarence was still defending his performance at Nordstrom.

"I had to come up with something. I thought I was pretty creative. Besides, I got the kid, didn't I?"

"You also aren't exactly anonymous anymore, are you, Mr. six-foot-four, blond, blue-eyed kidnapper?"

Daryl, who had been listening to Kathreen and Clarence squabble for almost twenty-four hours, wanted to change the subject. "How are we going to get the money?"

Clarence used the opportunity to go on the offensive. "Yeah, Kathreen. How are we going to get the money?"

Kathreen ignored them. She was sitting on the sofa of their two-room apartment hideout. Though there were positive side effects of Clarence's poor judgment and tactics, the death of the Nordstrom employee had added a complication Kathreen had not anticipated; nor did she welcome it.

"Perfect." Kathreen placed the article on page eight of her scrapbook. The cover of the scrapbook read, "Something To Remember Me By." The first page was a crumpled article that had been folded and unfolded numerous times. Kathreen had clipped the article from *The Washington Post* two years ago when it became obvious she was going to jail. It read, "Renowned Archaeologist Exposes Cover-up. Presidential Advisor Kathreen Steele Identified as Ring Leader of Corruption." The next few pages were filled with Polaroid photos of Steven playing with Kathreen. There was also a receipt for flowers delivered to the Wilson home in Israel.

"I have that under control," she snarled at Clarence.

Clarence grunted.

"Do you really think it's necessary to kill the kid?" asked Daryl.

"Yes . . . but not yet. We need him to get the money."

"I still don't understand why you don't want to knock off Wilson, too." Clarence was incapable of comprehending the depth of Kathreen's desire for painful revenge.

"Because, you buffoon, I don't want him dead. I want him to suffer. He will experience more pain when I give him this little souvenir, with the last page being a lovely color photo of his dead son." She held up the scrapbook.

"And then to Cuba?" Daryl wanted reassurance.

"Relax, Daryl. I have everything under control," said Kathreen.

"I'm hungry," mumbled Clarence.

Sometimes the most helpful person is your enemy.

CHAPTER 24

The Plan

"Hope?" The FBI tape was rolling.

"Yes?"

"This is Brad Stinson."

Even those who were tracing the call could not believe Brad's gall.

He continued. "I'm at my office and I know this phone call is being taped. So everyone can relax."

Hope looked to Connie for a clue. Connie made a gesture with her hand indicating that Hope should keep him talking.

Hope swallowed. "Brad, I'm surprised to hear from you."

"I figured I'd better call before I came over to see you. I'm afraid one of those police revolvers, which the maggot media have so effectively pointed in my direction, might go off if I just happened to stop by."

"What do you mean?" Hope knew the jibe was not aimed directly at her. It was aimed at the press that had, in the three days since the kidnapping, all but convicted Brad of orchestrating the kidnapping of her son and the murder of the Nordstrom employee.

"May I have your permission to come over? We really need to talk."

Hope again looked at Connie who nodded.

"Yes."

"I'll be there in twenty."

True to his prediction, Brad arrived twenty minutes later. The taxi driver, who was being paid $200 an hour to keep his mouth shut and wait, parked in the driveway behind two police cruisers. Brad's anonymity was maintained courtesy of his overcoat and sunglasses and the assistance of the police greeting party. The front door of the house opened as he approached, and it quickly closed behind him. A plain-clothes officer requested permission to check for weapons, which Brad tolerated irritably.

"Do you really think I would bring a weapon?" he grumbled. "It's hard to believe I'm going to help you jerks."

Brad was shown into the living room and, after a few unsettled greetings and his rejection of coffee, water, or tea, sat in the one chair that didn't seem spoken for. Connie occupied the matching chair next to him. Across the coffee table, sitting on the sofa, Hope and Wil were holding hands as if in anticipation of Ed McMahon telling them they were the lucky winners.

"I appreciate your providing witnesses," Brad said to Wil and Hope, trying to diffuse the tension caused by the seven people staring at him. "First of all, I want it clear—everything I'm going to say and do is completely unrelated to the unpleasantness concerning a series of articles and ongoing investigations involving Freedom Airways."

Everyone in the room acknowledged Brad's position. After all, he had not been charged with anything and his presence was voluntary.

"Hope, Wil," Brad started his presentation. "If you've been reading any of the rags called newspapers or listening to those talking heads on TV, you're probably convinced I had something to do with the kidnapping of your son. I did not."

"Then why are you here?" asked one of the officers, who expressed the curiosity of everyone in the room.

Brad looked at Hope. "I want to help."

"And how do you plan to do that?" asked Connie quietly.

He turned to Connie. "And I also want to clear my name. It's bad enough people are attacking me for my business practices, but the latest round in the demonization-of-Brad-Stinson campaign, which apparently includes my virtual lynching for kidnapping, has pushed me to my limit."

There was silence except for Boo's pawing at the door and Napoleon's meowed complaints that he could not attack the strangers in his house.

"There's another reason," said Brad in a low voice.

The group waited.

"Ten years ago," Brad began his story, "before I became a successful businessman, I was married to a wonderful woman named Adriana. We had met two years previously and were married less than three months later. We had planned to wait before having children, but . . . well . . . things don't always work out the way they are supposed to . . . and Adriana got pregnant. Ten years ago, while we were shopping on Fifth Avenue in New York, we were attacked by three muggers. One of them was jerking on Adriana's purse, which was wrapped around her arm. She was going to give it to them, but she couldn't get it off her arm because of the baby."

Brad stopped and took a deep breath. His mind was back on the streets of New York and his gaze was focused beyond anything in the room.

His voice was subdued. "He kept tugging on the purse and I was afraid that little Bradley was going to fall. And then . . . Adriana slipped. She fell away from me and into the street precisely as a taxi was passing." Brad closed his eyes and paused. Still distant, he said, "She was killed instantly. I thought Bradley was going to make it. I sat by his crib for three days, and I really thought he was going to make it. . . ."

Brad stopped. The room was silent as he brought himself back to the present, not needing to complete the story. He looked directly at Hope and Wil. "As much of a demon as everyone in America seems to want me to be, I am probably one of the few people who can begin to identify with the pain you are both feeling. Please believe me. I had nothing to do with the kidnapping of your son. And, if your friends here will let me, I am willing to do whatever is in my dimming power to help you get your son back."

A skeptical cop broke the silence. "Thank you, Mr. Stinson. We will consider it."

Hope was not that cynical. She was also a mother. She stood and walked over to the man she had all but brought down and put her arms around him. "Thank you, Brad. We do want your help."

Everyone in the room was aware of the battle the two had been engaged in for the past couple of weeks. Perhaps none more than Connie, whose investigation of Brad had gone into high gear and was getting close to resulting in a number of indictments against him and Freedom Airways. However, something more important was now in front of them.

At that moment an agent came in with the mail that had just been delivered. With Wil's unspoken permission, the gloved FBI agent sat next to him and began to go through the mail. A couple of bills, a magazine, some junk mail, and, at the bottom of the pile, a U.S. Express Mail envelope addressed to Steven Wilson.

The agent opened the envelope, careful to preserve any area where prints might be found. Inside were a Polaroid snapshot of Steven, crying, and a plain piece of typing paper with the demands.

"Oh, Steven." Hope's voice broke into shuddering sobs as she looked at the photo of her son. "Steven!"

"What does the note say?" demanded Wil.

The agent laid the note on the coffee table in front of Wil, next to the photo.

Wil read: "Deposit four million into Swiss Banc Nationale Account 634-9998765-65 within seventy-two hours. Then we will discuss your child. I have nothing to lose."

Wil looked up from the note, wild desperation in his eyes.

"What are we going to do?" Hope pleaded. "Oh, Wil, what are we going to do?" Hope leaned into Wil's embrace. Wil stroked her hair and looked blankly across the room.

Hope, clutching Wil's hand, took a breath, and then looked to Connie. "Connie, what can we do?"

"First of all, we will check out the note." Connie gave orders for the note, envelope, and photo to be processed through forensics.

One of Connie's assistants thought out loud. "The demand of ransom money after nearly three days of silence is unusual and the personal comment about 'nothing to lose' does not fit any patterns."

Another of Connie's assistants came up to her and whispered a little too loudly, "His story checks out."

Brad heard him. "Ten minutes. Not bad. You FBI people scare me."

"Sorry, Mr. Stinson," said Connie. "We had to."

"Are we sure Mr. Stinson should hear all this?" asked the officer who had first questioned Brad's presence.

Connie, who realized how desperate they were for clues and knew she would not be able to convince Hope to exclude him, relented and said, "For now."

"Thank you," said Brad, Wil, and Hope in unison.

"First the kidnapping," Connie began to sum up the situation, "then, nearly seventy-two hours of silence. Now this. We obviously can't send the money. The money is our only guarantee to keep Steven alive."

Wil winced. Hope gasped.

Connie's statements were true, yet the moment she said them she realized she should have softened the potential outcome in front of the parents.

"This is the first you've heard from the kidnappers?" asked Brad, who was now privy to the investigation.

"Yes," said Connie, still reluctant to so readily confide in their prime suspect.

"What else do you know?" Brad knew how to strategize, and knowing the facts was usually his first concern.

Connie was silent, and the other officers avoided looking at Brad.

"Nothing," conceded Hope, who had been completely won over by Brad's offer to help.

"Nothing? You're kidding! Almost three days after the kidnapping and no one knows anything about the kidnapper!" This was unmistakably a rebuke aimed at the detectives and investigators in the room.

"We have the newspaper article," offered Hope.

"What article?" asked Brad.

"And the phone message," added Wil.

"What phone message?" Brad's sincere ignorance had the effect of dampening suspicion related to the pre-kidnapping threats. He was somewhere between curious and frustrated. He wanted to know everything in order to assume the helm and solve this problem. But the authorities weren't completely certain they wanted to answer his questions.

Hope and Wil decided it was worth the risk and brought Brad up to date.

Brad said nothing else. Instead, he sat back in his chair,

steepled his fingers to his lips and stared into space, thinking. Hope stood and walked over to look at the picture of Steven again, as the agents prepared to take the items to the lab for further testing. Wil took a drink of his coffee and began to work his way through the other mail. Perhaps there was another clue in there. The officers and agents were conferring with each other.

After fifteen minutes of unproductive brainstorming, Brad stood and announced, "I have an idea." The murmuring voices stopped.

Perhaps it was his intensity. Perhaps it was the newness of his voice being added to the last fifteen minutes of commotion. In any case, those standing and those seated looked at the airline executive, who was positioning himself in the center of the unofficial huddle.

"It's unconventional and it's risky." Brad began to lay out his plan. "But the way I see it, we don't have many options. I also think it will work. Follow me. The kidnappers—the hunters—have Steven—the bait. The kidnappers are going to use the bait to lure the prey—us with the money—into their trap. What if we remove the bait?"

Wil was puzzled.

Hope asked, "What are you talking about?"

"What if we pretend I did kidnap Steven? We could even say I killed him. Maybe that would force the hunter to come out of hiding to reset the trap—to show he still has the bait."

"Ah." Connie understood. "But how will we inform the hunter? How do we convince him he needs to reset the trap?"

"First of all, we need to pretend that we never received the note. They have no way of knowing whether or not we received it. If the only contact they intended to make with us was the letter, well, let's change the rules. The second thing we need to do is put the ball back in their court. Let's get the press to announce that I confessed to kidnapping the child. That would change the game!"

"And how are we going to get the press to buy it?" asked Connie's assistant.

"Unless I'm mistaken, the mother of the child is fairly well connected to some folks in the media," responded Brad.

"We could stage Brad's arrest and convince CNN to cover it!" Hope interrupted.

"This is crazy!" exclaimed another officer.

"But it could work," said Wil. "Who'd believe the FBI convinced Brad Stinson to be a decoy? From my estimation the kidnappers have been trying to make it look like Brad was the kidnapper anyway. Why not call their bluff?"

"As crazy as this all sounds, I like it." Connie approved the plan. "It will definitely throw the kidnappers a curve ball. It will force them to contact us, and maybe they'll make a mistake."

"But, if we do it, I have to be informed of everything," added Brad.

No one responded. His terms were not worth rebutting.

Brad leaned into the tightening huddle. "Now, what if . . ."

CHAPTER 25

The Team

The CNN logo faded and the news anchorman appeared. "Good evening from CNN. Today's top story concerns a major break in the Wilson kidnapping and the Marc Jamison murder investigation.

"Earlier today, Brad Stinson, CEO of Freedom Airways, voluntarily surrendered to the Arlington Police Department. He is currently being held without bail, having been charged with coordinating the kidnapping of two-year-old Steven Wilson.

"One other individual, whose identity has not yet been released, has also been detained for questioning related to the case. Brad Stinson is shown here exiting the police station on his way to the Arlington jail." The screen showed a tearful and disheveled Brad, handcuffed and wearing a black bullet-proof vest, being escorted from the police station by a ring of eight officers in the direction of a police cruiser.

"According to the spokesman for the Arlington police, Mr. Stinson stated he surrendered to authorities as a way to bring closure to this terrible tragedy, which had spiraled out of control. The spokesman also said Mr. Stinson emotionally recounted details that corroborated his confession. Stinson claimed the child has been murdered and is buried in a field outside Arlington.

"Speaking through his attorney, Stinson issued a statement asserting his innocence of the murders. He admitted to
participating in the kidnapping, which, as was widely speculated in the press, was intended to persuade Hope Wilson, the
child's mother, to stop her investigation into the Freedom
Airways crash. Mr. Stinson's attorney also stated that at no
time was there any intention for anyone to be harmed.
According to Mr. Stinson's attorney, the alleged kidnapper
murdered Nordstrom employee Marc Jamison without Mr.
Stinson's knowledge and then killed the child after a dispute
with Stinson. According to sources, the other man will soon
be charged with both murders.

"The Wilson family has issued a formal statement thanking the nation for the support they received over the past few
days. According to a family spokesperson, Steven's parents
have requested their privacy be respected as they deal with
the terrible loss. The family of Marc . . ."

Kathreen and her two associates were sitting at the dilapidated table watching the TV. All three had stopped eating
their Subway sandwiches, the two men with their mouths
poised to bite.

"What!" Kathreen broke the silence as she sent her sandwich flying in the direction of the CNN reporter who was
talking about the case. "What sort of rubbish is this? Didn't
they get the note?"

She marched over to the door of the abandoned kitchen
where Steven was imprisoned with a few toys, some Barney
videos, and the Teletubbies. She pushed the door open and
pointed at Steven, who was sitting on the floor near the
garbage chute, his clothes soiled, dried food on his face, clasping a blue teddy bear.

Seeing Kathreen, Steven squeezed the bear and began to
rock gently.

"Does he look dead to you?" She was screaming at her partners, who were still speechless. "What is going on?"

Pacing the floor, arms akimbo, Kathreen tried to reason it through, but gave up and began to concoct another strategy. She stopped pacing, put her index finger to her lips and thought. *No problem. The plan has changed. How am I going to let them know I still have the kid and also maintain my anonymity? I don't want to risk a phone call.*

"If they think the kid's dead, why would they give us the money?" asked Clarence, as he took another bite of his sandwich.

"Shut up, you fool," snapped Kathreen.

"What's the matter?" chided Clarence. "I thought you had this all figured out." He was concerned about his share of the money and his irritation with Kathreen had made him careless.

Kathreen ignored him. She had called in every chit owed to her from her days in politics in order to assure herself safe passage to Cuba after getting the money and killing the child. The situation would be complicated by this delay. "This changes everything," she mumbled to herself.

"I'll say," added Clarence sarcastically, uncomfortably aware that his decision to kill the Nordstrom employee had made matters more complicated from that point onward.

"Would you please be quiet! I'm thinking." Kathreen was not in the mood for any lip from Clarence.

"Well . . . what are you going to do now?" said Clarence, unrelenting.

Daryl continued to eat his sandwich, keeping an eye mostly on Kathreen.

"I'll come up with something." Kathreen moved closer to Clarence, and to the gun resting on the fireplace mantel. "I'll come up with something—just like I did when you fouled up and killed that guy at Nordstrom."

"At least we're off the hook for that one now, thanks to that bozo Brad."

"That wouldn't matter to you anyway, Clarence." Kathreen's voice was icy.

"What?" Clarence felt a chill run down his back. He looked up from the sandwich he was holding with both hands.

"You see, now that things have changed . . ." Kathreen's pacing had slowed. Though she was not looking at the gun, she was only a few steps away from the H&K 45, its silencer still in place. "My feeling is that our team needs to be a little more refined. I am of the opinion the team only needs people who will not make mistakes."

"What are you saying, Kathreen?" Clarence sat up in his chair, dropping his sandwich onto his plate.

"I'm saying I think you have caused enough problems." Clarence tensed.

"And, now that circumstances are different, we need to do a little downsizing and . . ." she took the H&K 45 from the mantel, ". . . you have just become expendable."

Clarence saw Kathreen's movement but never heard the gun. The force of the shot to his forehead sent his immediately lifeless body and chair tumbling backward.

Daryl, whose initial thought was to flee, sat motionless, splattered with Clarence's blood. Was he next?

"And you, Daryl. Are you planning to make any blunders like Clarence?" She was using the gun as a conductor's baton.

"N-no!"

"Good, because if we are going to pull this off, we need to be sharp. And here is what we are going to do."

CHAPTER 26

Complications

By eleven-thirty Friday night, the day after Brad's staged arrest, for the first time in four days there were no press vehicles among the neighborhood cars parked near the Wilson home. Inside an unmarked car, across the street and down ninety feet from the Wilson driveway, Matt Turlow, the senior officer on surveillance duty that night, was calling headquarters to get the make on the motorcycle that had just pulled up near the Wilson home. He and his partner, Tyrone Borden, watched as Daryl took off his helmet.

"The bike's hot," said the dispatcher. "Reported missing earlier this evening."

Daryl walked toward the house.

"Should we go in?" asked Matt into the two-way radio.

"Not yet," replied the duty sergeant on the other end of the call.

"He just pulled something from his pocket." Matt turned to his colleague, who was looking through night-vision binoculars. "Is it a gun?"

"No," responded Tyrone. "It's a garage door opener."

Matt continued with his play-by-play description as the dispatcher informed him that backup was on the way. "It's not a gun," relayed Matt. "The garage door just opened."

The officers could see into the garage. Wil's Volvo was parked next to Hope's Acura.

"Should we go? I think we should go." Matt was edgy.

"He just tossed the opener into the bushes," said Tyrone.

Daryl walked between the cars.

"He's opening the driver's side door of the Acura," narrated Matt.

"Maybe he'll leave another note and we can follow him," suggested Tyrone.

Matt tapped his fingers, waiting for permission from his commander.

Tyrone said, "He's pulling something from his vest pocket and is leaning into the Acura. It looks as though he put something on the steering wheel—wait! He just ducked down between the cars."

Matt spoke into the radio. "A light just came on in the kitchen. I can see someone in the kitchen—the wife—she just opened the refrigerator door."

"Should we go?" Tyrone asked.

"Do we have permission to go?" Matt pleaded for approval from command.

"Not yet," said the sergeant. "We don't want Mrs. Wilson to panic." The sergeant spoke to another dispatcher. "Dial the Wilson home. Now! Now! It's imperative she does not go into the garage. Hurry!"

Too late.

"She's going toward the door into the garage," said Tyrone.

"We're going in." Matt made the decision.

The officers ran across the street toward the driveway. Tyrone stopped briefly to provide cover for Matt, who approached the garage ordering, "Police. Freeze!"

Daryl ducked in front of the Acura, seven feet from the

kitchen door and out of sight. As he pulled the H&K 45 from his jacket, he was distracted from the approaching officers when the kitchen door began to open.

"See, there's nothing out there," Hope said to Boo as she opened the door. Hope froze when she saw the open garage door.

"Get back in the house," yelled Matt to Hope, who stood in the doorway in her pajamas and robe, a cookie in one hand. "Get back in the house!"

Boo took off and charged the officers.

Hope hesitated a split second too long.

Daryl took two steps toward Hope as she called for Boo. With one jerk, Daryl pulled Hope into the garage, putting his left arm around her neck and the gun in his right hand to her head. When Hope screamed, Boo turned and charged Daryl. With one shot, Daryl hit Boo between the chest and foreleg, leaving him immobilized and whimpering.

Napoleon attacked next, an orange blur flying through the air. The cat affixed himself to the intruder by sinking his claws into Daryl's right shoulder.

Daryl cursed and then, with one seamless motion, grabbed the cat with his left hand, choking Hope in the process, and violently threw Napoleon across the garage. Hope gasped for breath and screamed in pain as Daryl rammed the gun's barrel against the side of her face. Napoleon hit the tool wall and fell limply to the ground.

"Stop right there." Daryl's order could be heard above Boo's whimpering. The officers, who had stopped short when Daryl fired, held their positions.

Wil came to the kitchen door, having been awakened by the ringing phone. Betty, who had returned to D.C. after the kidnapping, was right behind him.

"What's going—" Wil stopped mid-sentence when he

saw the gun at his wife's head. He gestured to his mom to stay back and call the police. Wil stood in the open doorway, not daring to move. "Don't hurt her. Take me instead. What do you want? Please don't hurt her."

"Dr. Wilson, go back in the house," came the order from one of the officers. They still had their guns trained on Daryl, sheltered behind a terrified Hope.

"No!" Daryl was not done giving orders. "Dr. Wilson, I suggest you stay where you are and listen."

This was not the way Daryl's mission had been planned. He now had to improvise. He ordered Wil, "Get the keys for your car."

Wil reached to his right and grabbed a set of keys from the kitchen counter.

"Will you promise not to hurt her?"

"I will more than hurt her if you don't shut up and do exactly what I tell you. I'll blow your wife's head off right here."

"Okay. Okay." Wil looked at the officers, who gave him the nod.

"Now, take those keys and get into the Acura and back it out of the garage into the street," ordered Daryl.

Wil started to edge uneasily toward the car.

"Now!" yelled Daryl.

As Wil climbed into the car, he noticed the envelope taped to the steering wheel.

"What's this?"

"That's yours. Now do exactly what I told you," ordered Daryl.

As Wil put the key in the ignition, Daryl made his final announcement.

"The good doctor . . ." Wil cringed at the reference. That is what Kathreen Steele and her two thugs had called him when they beat him up three years ago. ". . . is going to back this car into the street and then get out. You fine officers are going to come into the garage along with Dr. Wilson, who will bring you the note that is taped to the steering wheel. You will then close the garage door and Mrs. Wilson and I are going to get into that car and go for a ride. And you—now listen closely because this is the important part—are not going to open the garage door or follow me. If you do, I will kill her. Is that understood?"

Within sixty seconds Daryl and Hope were gone.

The police backup arrived a few minutes later. It was too late to follow.

*Being in the driver's seat doesn't mean
you are in control.*

CHAPTER 27

Improvising

"You know, you're never going to get away with this," said Hope, trying to sound confident and believing it highly unlikely he would shoot her while she was driving sixty miles per hour.

"Maybe. Maybe not. What matters to you is that my gun is aimed at your head and," he sneered, "I also have your precious little boy."

"Steven!" Hope gasped. Her grip on the wheel tightened. "You—"

"And he will end up dead if we don't 'get away with this.'" He spat out the last few words with venom.

"Is he all right?"

"Take a right at the next exit."

"Is he all right?"

He ignored her.

"IS STEVEN ALL RIGHT?"

"Look here, Miss. I'm a desperate man. You messed things up tonight by coming into the garage. All you need to know is my gun is pointed at your head and I don't want to hear any more of your annoying questions. Got it?"

Hope complied.

After a few moments of excruciating silence, Daryl spoke again. "Take a right here."

"It says 'Dead End.'"

"What do you know—the reporter can read."

Hope took a right that led them down a road headed nowhere. No one else was going or coming.

"Pull over."

"Why?"

"Missy, your questions are irritating. I said pull over. What part of that are you having a hard time understanding?"

Hope pulled over.

"Turn off the car and give me the keys."

Hope obeyed.

"Now, listen closely. You are going to do exactly what I say. Understand?"

Hope, nervous and uncertain, nodded.

"Take off your pajama bottoms."

"What?"

"I said take off your pants."

"You're kidding me!" Hope was frightened. She was also baffled. "What? Are you actually going to rape me?" Her questions were laden with disgust and condescension at his repulsive machismo.

"Lady, I'd just as soon kill you as rape you. If you cooperate, I do not intend to do either—at this point. But if you keep up with your irritating questions, you might make me change my mind." His tone reflected frustration on the edge of rage. "You should be more worried that I don't care if I shoot you. I'd recommend you just do what I say."

Compliance was her only option. Hope positioned her buttoned terry-cloth bathrobe in such a way as to cover her bare legs and then took off her flannel pajama bottoms.

Though not in the least apologetic, Daryl seemed vaguely embarrassed as she handed him her pants. "Look here, lady. I'm not some kind of pervert. If you had some spare rope in the car, or duct tape, I wouldn't need your pants. But since you messed everything up, I'm having to improvise." That was the end of his self-justification.

"Now listen closely, because I'm not in the mood for anything cute. I'm going to get out of the car and you're going to slide across to this side and get out after me. I will aim my gun at your pretty legs so, if you try something, it won't kill you, but I guarantee it will hurt. Remember the sound your dog was making? It's worse with people."

Daryl climbed out of the car. His H&K 45 was pointed at Hope's legs as Hope slid toward the passenger door, climbing over the gearshift before getting out and standing beside the open door.

"Now, turn around and lean up against the car with your arms behind your back." She did as she was told.

"You know," said Daryl, "now that I look at you, you're pretty fine."

Hope ignored him.

"It's a shame to have to do this to such a pretty woman."

With one blow of the gun's handle to the back of her head, Hope collapsed. Daryl ripped her pajama pants into a few strips and began to tie her hands and feet. Opening the trunk, he lifted her limp body and placed her in the compartment. He used a piece of her pajamas as a gag, balling it up and jamming it into her mouth. The last piece he tied around her head to hold the gag in place. After slamming the trunk, he climbed in the car, did a U-turn, and sped off.

Daryl drove for ten minutes before taking the exit that led him to the abandoned building where he and Kathreen had been holing up. A few minutes later Daryl was carrying Hope up the stairs to their hideout.

"This ought to be good," Daryl mumbled to himself as he moved sideways through the door with Hope's inert body.

Kathreen was waiting on the other side of the room. She was not pleased. She had watched from the window as he carried the body up the stairs. "What in—"

"She came into the garage while I was leaving the note," he said, pleading for understanding. "Their possessed cat even attacked me." Daryl showed Kathreen the blood stained rips in his shirt to prove it.

Kathreen didn't care. "Who else saw you?"

"A couple cops and her husband. They didn't follow me. I'm positive. I closed them in the garage."

"Cute."

As Daryl deposited Hope's limp body on the sofa, he responded, "It worked." Kathreen was his partner and boss, but he didn't trust her. Clarence's scent, even after he'd been dumped down the garbage chute in the kitchen, still lingered in the air.

"You're sure no one followed you?"

"Absolutely."

"But they did see your face?"

Anonymity had been their strength. Now that had been compromised—again.

"So what? Are you gonna kill me, too?" Daryl went right to the crux of the matter. "You need me. Besides, by the time they figure out who I am, we'll be in Cuba."

"Is that right? From my perspective, you just complicated things."

"But now," Daryl hesitated, "maybe we have even more leverage on your buddy Dr. Wilson." He was thinking as fast as he could. "Perhaps some photos of you with his brat *and* his wife might be a nice addition to Dr. Wilson's scrapbook."

Kathreen smiled. Daryl had passed the test.

"But no more slipups. Got it?" Kathreen moved on. "Is she alive?"

"Yes."

Kathreen's surprise was giving way to a plan. "How long has she been unconscious?" She stood next to the inert, robed body of her enemy's wife.

"About fifteen minutes."

"Hmm." Kathreen eyed their latest acquisition. "Throw some cold water on her. I want to see the look on her face."

Daryl walked into the kitchen, ignoring the child sleeping on the floor, and returned with a two-quart saucepan full of water that he dumped on Hope's head. She didn't stir. Daryl began to shake her.

"I hit her pretty hard, but I know she's alive. Hey, lady, wake up. Time to get up."

Hope began to move. When her eyes opened, she was looking directly into Kathreen's gloating face, which cleared away all cloudiness of thought. Hope kicked back against the cushions on the couch and tried to cry out.

"Get that gag off of her."

Daryl sat on the sofa next to Hope. He pulled her face to within a foot of his and said. "Look here, Lady. I'm gonna take this off you. I have hundreds of bullets. I only need one to make you permanently quiet—and besides, don't you want to see your little boy?" With one motion he jerked the gag off her head and shoved her back against the armrest.

"Kathreen Steele!" Hope's words rasped from her dry mouth. "I can't believe it. Why . . . why are you doing this?" Hope's eyes scoured the room looking for Steven. What had that witch done to her baby?

Kathreen, who never demonstrated a reluctance to use violence, struck Hope across the face with a firm backhand. "That, my dear, is a dumb question, but one I can hardly wait to hear your husband answer. He ruined my life. Quite simply, he is going to pay for that. In a matter of days, I will have four million dollars and be settling into a new life at his expense. Even more, your pathetic husband will be minus a child, and now a wife. You have only made my revenge sweeter."

The blood on her lip and her swelling cheek didn't matter. Hope's only concern was her son. "What have you done with Steven?"

Kathreen ignored the question. "It was nice of you to dress up for the occasion," said Kathreen with feminine disgust, pulling on Hope's collar, making Hope flinch.

"Where is my son? Please untie my hands. They hurt. I won't do anything."

"Would you relax?' Kathreen mocked, as she straightened Hope's collar using both hands. "You know, I really wish you had come better dressed."

"What are you talking about?"

Daryl had already retrieved the scrapbook. He was even beginning to enjoy this part.

"You see, I've been preparing a little present for your hubby. We'll need to get a couple photos of you and me, and then maybe of the three of us—me, you, and the brat."

"What?" Hope shook her head, trying to understand the surreal conversation.

Daryl handed the scrapbook to Kathreen. She pulled up a chair next to Hope, who lay on the couch with her back to the armrest.

"I've called it 'Something To Remember Me By.' Here, let me show you what we have so far."

Kathreen showed Hope the book, slowly, page by page, without narrative. Hope's expression changed from curiosity and fear to revulsion and terror.

"You are a sick woman, Kathreen!"

Kathreen ignored her. "Go get the kid."

Daryl did as directed.

"I'll get the camera," said Kathreen. "I want to get some pictures of this."

"Please, don't make him see me like this. It will scare him," pleaded Hope.

"That sounds like your problem, honey—not mine."

Daryl woke Steven. The fussing child staggered in behind the man who was pulling him by the arm. "Come see your mommy."

Steven stopped when he saw the hog-tied woman on the sofa. Then he saw her face and heard her voice.

"Come here, sweetie." Hope did her best to hide all fear.

Steven pulled away from Daryl and ran to his mom. When she didn't hug him, he looked at her again. Something was wrong.

"That'll be a good one," said Kathreen as the Polaroid snapped its first shot.

"It's okay, honey." Hope tried to sound reassuring. "It's just a game. I can't hug you now, but I can give you a kiss! Come on, give Mommy a kiss."

Steven hugged his mom and began to cry softly.

"Oh, my baby . . . my little Stevie. Don't cry. Everything will be all right." Hope tried to hide her uncontrollable tears of fear from her child.

When it comes right down to it, what does matter?

CHAPTER 28

The Ransom

By nine-thirty the next morning the team of police officers, FBI agents, and Wil had reassembled in the Wilson living room. Daryl's envelope had contained a Polaroid photo of a dirty and tearful Steven. On the back was a black spot, slightly smaller than a dime, and a handwritten note telling them to expect a call at ten o'clock. The note didn't mention Hope, which substantiated the team's speculation the kidnappers had not anticipated last night's events.

Betty was at the veterinarian's with Boo. Boo would recover, but only after $1,500 of surgery. Wil rationalized the expense on the dog that had adopted them a few weeks earlier as compensation for the other decision he had had to make. Napoleon's fifteen-year-old body had sustained too many injuries when he was thrown against the wall. The vet said the only future for Napoleon was tremendous pain and inevitable death. Making the decision to put down Napoleon had been particularly tough for Wil. Not only had the cat been part of his and Hope's relationship from the time they met, but any thoughts of death, after recently attending two funerals, were strangely uncomfortable.

As the rest of the room readied for the ten o'clock call, Wil sat quietly. His eyes moved from the clock to the phone and then back to the clock.

"Remember, Wil," said Connie, "keep the caller talking as long as you can. And do not mention the Express letter. Remember, we do not know anything about the letter."

At ten o'clock the phone rang.

Wil put the receiver to his ear.

"Dr. Wilson." The voice was Daryl's.

"Yes?"

"I know this call is being taped and I don't want any interruptions."

"Who are you? What have you done with my son and my wife?"

Daryl ignored him. "The photo and the spot of blood that were delivered last night—yes, it is your son's blood—only a prick on the finger, and he didn't cry too much—will hopefully be convincing enough for you to give me my money."

"What money?" Wil asked, making a show of his ignorance of the earlier ransom letter.

"The four million dollars."

"What are you talking about? This is the first I've heard about four million dollars."

"Enough games, Wilson. Now shut up and listen. Regarding your wife . . . she's pretty. I still haven't figured out what to do with her."

"You'd better not—"

Daryl disregarded Wil's interruption. "Maybe I'll let you know what I'll do to her when I contact you in exactly forty-eight hours. But more importantly, I want four million dollars."

"I don't have that kind of money," Wil protested.

"One million in cash and three million in U.S. treasury bills."

"I said I don't have that kind of money."

"Not good enough, Wilson. I have your wife and kid. Get

it!" he growled. "I want the four million dollars in a briefcase, ready for you to deliver where I say and when I say. And . . ." Daryl's articulation was excruciatingly clear on the next point ". . . you also have forty-eight hours to convince those who are listening to our conversation that if the police attempt to intervene, your wife and child will die." The line went dead.

Wil heard the FBI eavesdroppers in the background cursing. The caller had been on a cell phone, but not quite long enough for them to pinpoint the exact location. It wouldn't have mattered anyway because Daryl had tossed the phone into the Potomac and driven away.

Wil looked at Connie in desperation. "How am I going to get four million dollars?"

Connie touched Wil's shoulder. "We'll figure it out."

"What do I need to do?" He was willing to do anything. "They're going to kill them."

"No, Wil! We won't let that happen." Connie tried to sound confident.

"I have to do what he said or they will kill them." Wil's statement left nothing undecided.

Doing what you think you have to do sometimes means doing things you shouldn't. Should you?

CHAPTER 29

Choices

O ne of the advantages of fame is that people pay for your
story. Wil had received a two-million-dollar advance for
his story about the discovery of bones he had claimed
belonged to Jesus—the discovery that eventually uncovered a
presidential corruption scandal and sent Kathreen Steele to
jail. He also had saved a good deal of his income, including
scholarly award money, since graduate school. In addition, his
retirement account was worth about one million, courtesy of
the stock market boom in the '90s and his lucky decision to
move into a cash position a couple of months before the
World Trade Center disaster. Hope also had saved a couple of
hundred thousand dollars before they were married. All of
this added up to three and a half million dollars. Personal
loans, loans secured with the equity in their homes, and the
good graces of a banker friend of Steve Halterman's, brought
the total to four million. The banker also helped Wil convert
the money to T-Bills and cash, as was required to meet the
kidnappers' conditions.

Wil did all this without giving it a second thought. The
kidnappers already possessed everything of real value to Wil.
He'd give up anything to get them back. Nothing else mattered.

The phone rang again, exactly forty-eight hours after the first call. Wil put the receiver to his ear. No introductions were made.

"Go to the phone booth near the tourist trolley kiosk at the corner of 17th and L. Answer the phone." It was Daryl's voice, short and brisk. "You have twenty minutes."

"Twenty minutes? It will take me that long to get there. Do you know where I am now?"

The phone went dead halfway into Wil's question.

Wil grabbed the large and heavy briefcase and started out the door.

"Dr. Wilson," said Connie. "You can't do it this way. We—"

"I don't have a choice. And don't follow me. Please." Wil ran out the door.

As he drove away in his Volvo, Connie gave the order for them to activate the tracking devices that had been put in place without Wil's knowledge. "Remember, no one moves until I say. Got it?"

Wil drove as quickly as possible to the corner of 17th and L but could not find a parking spot. Through his open window he could hear the phone ringing. Leaving his car running and double-parked, he ran across the street to the phone booth, dodging traffic on his way. Shifting the briefcase to his other hand, he caught the phone on the fifth ring.

"Get on the Metro at Farragut North. Take the Red Line South. Get off at the 12th and G Station. A note is taped under the bench."

"Which bench—"

The phone was dead.

Wil abandoned his car and ran the two blocks to the Metro, unaware that this switch to the Metro rendered useless the tracking device the FBI had planted on his car. He dug for change in his pockets as he ran. He found a quarter, two nickels, and a penny. He reached for his wallet. All he had, besides the money in the briefcase, were two fifties and four credit cards. The line for the subway tickets was ten deep. Five of the machines were out of order. He didn't have time to stand in line.

Wil walked up to two high school kids who had just gotten their tickets, took a breath, and asked the first one who looked at him, "Where are you going?"

The teenage boy he'd addressed looked skeptically at Wil. "What's it matter to you?"

"Is that ticket for the Red Line South?" Wil pressed

"Yes," said the teen, stepping backward to be closer to his comrade.

"What's this? A stickup by Grandpa Jones?" said the other teenager.

Wil grabbed the ticket from the first kid's hand and handed him a fifty. "Today is your lucky day." As the two teenagers looked at each other in bewilderment, Wil ran toward the loading area just in time to catch the train as its doors were closing. Frantically he checked the map above the windows and was relieved to see he had guessed correctly.

12th and G was the next stop. The train was crowded and his heavy breathing and frenzied appearance invited curious glances. But no one talked. The pause allowed him a moment to catch his breath.

As soon as the train stopped and the doors opened, Wil bolted out of the train ahead of the throng of commuters. "The caller said under the bench," he mumbled to himself. He went to the first bench he saw. The bench's four occupants gave Wil disparaging looks and walked away when Wil got down on his hands and knees in front of them, talking to himself. People stared at the frantic man. One of them called him a pervert.

No message. Wil stepped up onto the bench to look for his

other options. There were three more benches on his side of the track and four on the other platform. He jumped down and jogged to the closest one. As he approached the occupied bench, he slowed his pace to a brisk walk, straightened his coat, and tried to look less frantic. He decided to try a different tack this time and addressed the five people sitting on the bench. "Excuse me."

The unsuspecting commuters looked up at him, slightly startled.

"I need to look under that bench for a note someone has taped to the bottom of it. It's very important." His smile pleaded for their assistance.

Whether it was Wil's emphasis on the words "very important," his look of desperation, or simply the unbelievable nature of the request, all five politely stood and made way for him as he got down on his hands and knees to search for the all-important note.

"Is it a love letter?" asked a middle-aged woman wearing a bright red dress that was slightly too small for her well-endowed body.

"There it is," said the college age kid who had gotten on all fours to help look.

"I'll be," said the gray-haired lady who had been the last one to stand. "There actually was a note."

"Thank you. Thank you!" said Wil as he snatched the note and walked away.

The group sat down again, somewhat disappointed they didn't learn the contents. The five people, who had not said a word to each other before Wil's arrival, now began to chat about their common experience.

Wil walked forty feet to where the crowd was thinner. He stopped and leaned against the wall, letting the stream of humanity flow past him. Opening the note, he steadied himself and read.

"Get back on the Red Line. Take it to the Rhode Island Avenue Station. Walk four blocks south on Rhode Island." Wil looked up just in time to see the Red Line spill another mass of humanity onto the platform. He heard the metallic voice announce the imminent closure of the train's doors, instructing people to stand back.

This was getting out of control. He was beginning to realize that his decision to go on this adventure alone was taking him far away from anyone who could help him. He didn't like the idea of meeting the kidnappers without at least some backup plan. But how could he get help? What to do?

First of all, he had to get on that train. He forced his way through the crowd waiting for the next train. He was only a few steps away from the door when the recorded voice's final warning came over the loudspeaker.

"The doors are closing. Please stand back."

Two female tourists and one businessman, who was negotiating with someone on the other end of his cell phone, stood between Wil and the closing doors.

Not planning or even thinking, Wil grabbed the phone from the man's hand and stepped onto the nearly vacant train. The businessman was so stunned by the disappearance of his phone that by the time he had said, "Hey, that's—" the doors had closed behind Wil and the train had started to move. The women, who had observed the theft, unconsciously gripped their purses more firmly.

Without verifying whether the man's business associate was still on the other end of the phone, Wil pushed End. As he did, he noticed the flashing battery indicator light. The phone battery was nearly gone.

Wil dialed his home.

"Hello. The Wilson residence."

Wil didn't wait to find out who it was.

"Listen closely. This is Wil. I do not have time to explain."

The static was already building up, though Wil believed the person could still hear him. "I'm on the Red Line leaving the Metro station at 12th and G heading toward the Rhode Island Avenue Station. I don't have time to explain. I'll be getting off at Rhode Island and walking four blocks south."

"Dr. Wilson, you're breaking up."

"Do not be seen. I just want you as backup."

"What station?" The voice was surrounded with static.

"Remember. Do not get too clo—" the phone went dead. Whether it was the reception or the battery, it didn't matter. Wil shook the phone in vain. It was dead.

"Wouldn't you know it?" Wil muttered, oblivious to the few people who could not help but eavesdrop. "I steal my first cell phone and get fifteen seconds use out of it!"

After giving the phone a few useless shakes, he threw it the length of the car, causing the four expressionless commuters to flinch and then hurriedly return their attention to their newspapers, books, and maps.

CHAPTER 30

Reunion

Nine minutes later the train arrived at the Rhode Island Avenue Station. Wil exited before the doors finished opening and ran up the vacant escalator until his breathing grew so heavy that he had to slow to a more reasonable pace for the last third of the fifty-foot rise. At street level he found himself in an area of D.C. that had not been the beneficiary of any redevelopment funds. He went to his left as directed by the sign. He became painfully aware of the briefcase he was carrying and knew this wasn't a good place to be walking by himself, let alone with four million dollars. He tried not to run, but walked as fast as he could. After two blocks, a black Lincoln Continental pulled up beside him and a door opened.

"Can I give you a ride, good doctor?"

Horror and shock jerked Wil to an abrupt stop as the familiar voice mocked him. "Kathreen Steele!"

"Get in," came the command from the back seat.

"What have you done with my family?" demanded Wil, as he climbed into the back seat on the passenger side.

Kathreen pointed her H&K 45 at Wil. "Shut the door."

Wil did as he was told.

"Put both your hands on the back of the seat in front of you and don't move them. I don't want to shoot you . . . at least not yet."

Wil slowly put his hands on the seat in front of him.

"Where is she? Why are you doing this? Where are Hope and Steven?" Wil knew the situation required finesse, but he didn't have any finesse. It was all he could do to control his shaking and catch his breath.

"It's been a long time Dr. Wilson. We have a lot to talk about."

Wil choked back a response.

"I heard you didn't get the flowers I had sent to your home in Israel. Pity." Kathreen grinned. "For what it's worth, that made finding you a little more difficult. Fortunately, your darling's sudden celebrity made my task easier. Lucky, yes?" Kathreen was enjoying herself.

"Where are Hope and Steven?" Wil's words were clear and measured.

"I appreciate your bringing my money." Kathreen reached for the briefcase.

"First my family." Wil took one hand from the back of the seat and held the briefcase between him and the door.

"Look around, Dr. Wilson. Unless I am mistaken, or you have an army stuck up your sleeve, you are not in a position to ask for anything."

She's right, thought Wil. *What can I do? What on earth can I do?*

"I'd shoot you right now, but I don't want the mess in my car. Besides, I have a gift for you, though I'm not done with it yet. Now that I have my money, I can complete the last few pages."

Wil had to make something up. Fear gave speed to his thoughts. "Here's the deal," he said, still keeping the briefcase out of Kathreen's reach.

"Deal?" Kathreen was intrigued. "I thought I told you you're not in a position to make any deals, Doc."

He spoke with deliberate certainty. "I'm afraid you're mistaken."

"Mistaken?"

Wil's confidence was building. "You said no police intervention. I complied. However, you did not say no explosives."

"Explosives?" Kathreen's cocky smile wavered for a split second.

"I brought you your four million dollars all right. I even have it in the denominations you demanded. But, what's more important is that I know the combination for the lock and you don't. I also know how long the timer is set for. You have everything of value to me. I have the knowledge of when this thing is going to blow as well as the voice command to make it blow right now if I wanted to."

"You're bluffing."

"Kathreen—that's your call."

"A stand off?"

"You are the most evil and despicable human being I have ever had the displeasure of knowing."

"I'm hurt."

"Personally, I can think of few things I would rather do than give the voice command right now and blow you and me to smithereens. I would rid the world of the blight you are and, unless I am mistaken, I would also prevent you from killing my wife and child. And . . ." Wil's cathartic confidence grew, ". . . if you've already killed them, I have nothing to live for anyway. And, if you haven't, I wouldn't have to watch you do it. So—I would suggest you consider your options, witch, and take me to see my family."

Kathreen didn't see any reason to call the bluff. There were still a number of hands to be played and she had the deck fairly well stacked.

"Hurry up," she barked at Daryl, who had driven down

Rhode Island Avenue. He took a right on 12th. The neighborhood was not improving. Daryl turned into the dilapidated parking garage under the abandoned warehouse he had carried Hope into two days earlier. "You know, Dr. Wilson, I have a lot to repay you for. The last two years have not been very good to me. If it hadn't been for you, I would still be running the country with that weakling I made president."

"You weren't that important." Wil took a shot at her ego.

Kathreen caught herself just before she returned volley. "Nice try, Doc. Tell that to my friends in the Department of Justice who got me out of prison or, better yet, tell it to my friends in Cuba who can hardly wait for my arrival."

Neither said another word until the car was parked.

Daryl went around to the passenger side and yanked open Wil's door. "Come on. Get out," he growled.

They walked out of the garage and thirty feet down the street to the exterior metal stairs that ascended to the second-story hideout. Daryl was now holding the gun. They climbed the steps, Kathreen nearly triumphant and Wil sick at heart. When the door opened, Wil saw Hope gagged and tied in a chair, with Steven gagged and tied in a chair next to her. He thought the best thing would be for him to restrain his feelings. Psychology had never been his best subject, but he knew better than to reward Kathreen with a show of helpless emotion.

Hope gazed at Wil, wide-eyed, her buttoned terry-cloth robe soiled with blood that must have come from her swollen lip and bruised cheek. One eye was black, and chunks of her hair had been cut. Steven began to wiggle and make noises muffled by his gag. With Herculean effort Wil stifled any response.

"So," snarled Kathreen, "here's your family. Now give me

the briefcase and show me the money, or I'll start shooting."
Kathreen relieved Wil of the briefcase and then walked over
and stood directly behind the two captives. "I don't suppose
you would want me to try to open this thing by myself now,
would you?" She held the bomb against Hope. "It might go
boom and hurt someone."

"Okay. Okay," said Wil who had to follow through with
his bluff. "But first, untie Hope and Steven and let them go."

"A little pushy aren't you? I need someone else to explode
with me." She looked at the combination numbers on the
front of the briefcase.

"Don't touch the numbers!" Wil yelled, his panic not difficult to pretend.

Kathreen narrowed her eyes at Wil. She took the gun
from Daryl and put the muzzle to the back of Hope's head.

"I mean . . ." Wil modified his demand. "Okay, just Hope.
I'll stay here with Steven until you get the money. At least
Hope will be safe in case you go insane, or should I say more
insane." Diplomacy gave way to hatred.

"Deal," said Kathreen, who knew Hope wouldn't get far
looking like she did. Kathreen had also concluded that
having two hostages and the money was preferable to Wil
blowing them all up. She looked at Daryl. "Untie her."

Daryl, Wil, and Hope were surprised.

"Hope," Wil said. "Do exactly as I say. Go now. Get to the
Metro Station on 10th Street. I'll take care of Steven."

"But Wil—" Hope's dry, weak voice cracked.

"Just do it!" Wil ordered.

Even Hope wasn't sure whether it was due to her exhaustion, Wil's intensity, or her complete trust in Wil, but she left
the room and her child, stumbling down the stairs and into
the vacant street. She ran a block and a half before she
stopped, frozen in indecision. She couldn't leave them. Hope

turned and started back towards Kathreen's lair, deciding to go around the block and approach from the opposite direction. She was a half block away from her destination when she heard a familiar voice.

"Hope!"

A hand gripped her upper arm. Before Hope could resist, she was pulled through the doorway of an abandoned storefront bakery. The door shut quickly behind her.

"Connie?" Hope was confused.

"Good to see you, Hope." The FBI agent gently hugged her friend.

"Oh, Connie." Relief made Hope's knees weak and Connie guided her to the chair next to the door. "How did you—"

Hope winced as Connie gently reached to touch her friend's bruised face. "Are you okay?" asked Connie, observing the destruction done to Hope's hair by Kathreen's shears.

"Yes." Hope's voice was weak, reflective.

Connie got down to business. "There's a tracking device in the briefcase. Hope, tell me what you know."

"There are two people." Hope licked her cracked lips and made herself think. "Kathreen Steele and a man named Daryl."

"Who's the leader?"

"Kathreen," answered Hope. "They have Wil and Steven. Wil threatened to set off the bomb if—"

"The bomb?"

"The bomb in the briefcase. Kathreen is afraid to open it without the code because it might explode. Wil told Kathreen he'd open it for her if she let me go."

"He said there's a bomb in the briefcase?" Connie was impressed.

"What?" Hope was taken back by Connie's look of surprise.

"That's a good one. There is no bomb."

Hope's face turned white. "What do you mean, there's no bomb?" Hope stared at Connie.

"There isn't a bomb in the briefcase. He made that up."

"Well, she believes it. Oh, no! What is he going to do? I have to get back there. She's going to kill them. I know. Her plan is to kill Steven and leave the country with the money. They're going to Cuba this afternoon."

"Hope, they're not going anywhere," said Connie confidently. "We're here. We'll get them. Now, tell me what the room looks like."

Hope quickly described the room.

"Any exits other than the front door?" asked Connie.

"No."

"You're sure?"

Hope squeezed her eyes shut, picturing the room. "Hmm, yes . . . I think so . . . yes."

The SWAT commander relayed the information to his waiting team.

"We have the situation under control, thanks to Wil's leading us to them. This is going to work out," Connie said, trying to encourage her friend.

Hope couldn't take it anymore. She stood and began to pace like a caged tiger. "Connie, I have to go now or she will kill Steven and Wil."

"Trust me, Hope."

"This isn't an issue of trust. I'm going. I'll get your SWAT man a shot." Hope went to the door, opened it, and began to run in the direction of the stairs leading up to Kathreen's hideout.

"Hope, no!" It was too late. Connie promptly shut the door and threw her hands in the air in exasperation. "Dang it!" Hope was the second Wilson in a few hours to ignore her and force her to change plans. "Captain, do your snipers have a shot?"

"Negative."

"The first shot must be the woman. Once she's hit, fire the tear gas and storm. Got it?"

"Affirmative." The SWAT commander turned to his radio.

Connie paused to listen to indistinct words coming through the open window. "Now what?" Connie stepped to the window and looked. Her eyes grew wide in disbelief. Hope, disheveled in her dirty white bathrobe, was walking down the middle of the street waving her arms and screaming.

"Hey, you dog-faced witch. Yeah, you, Kathreen, honey. Let's do this thing. Woman to woman, you wretched, pathetic excuse for a human." Hope wanted her litany of insults to provoke her opponent into making a mistake. Soon, however, she realized the error of returning to the battlefield with nothing but her mouth.

Inside the room, Kathreen's negotiation techniques—Daryl giving Wil a few blows to the face and ribs—had finally convinced Wil to open the briefcase. The sweat on Wil's brow, as he pretended to concentrate on the precise combination for fear one mistake would blow them all up, convinced Kathreen there really were explosives. In truth, Wil knew he was running out of cards to play. His charade was interrupted by Hope's tirade.

"What's that?" Kathreen snarled through clenched teeth. She looked at Daryl and said, "Check it out."

Daryl moved to the window and looked down into the street.

Daryl was in perfect view of the sharpshooter who informed his commander. "I have a shot of the man. Should I take it?"

"No," the captain responded. "It has to be the woman. It has to be the leader."

Daryl spoke over his shoulder, "You won't believe this, but it's the wife."

Kathreen's head snapped up. "What's she doing?"

"She's standing in the middle of the street screaming that you are not a nice person. Wait. Now she's coming up the stairs."

Wil glanced up from the briefcase, bewildered.

"What an idiot." Kathreen calculated her next move. "Let her come in."

The door opened and Hope walked in, continuing her verbal barrage. "And did I ever tell you that you are ugly and fat and you shouldn't dye your hair and—"

"Shut up," demanded Kathreen.

"And you really looked fat on TV and I am glad you went to jail and—"

"I said, SHUT UP." Kathreen lowered her gun slightly, aimed, and fired.

Wil collapsed on the floor, his knee shattered by Kathreen's shot. Steven started crying again. Wil was on his side, gripping his leg, moaning in pain.

Hope paused for a second, fighting the urge to scream, then tightened her fists and started her verbal attack again.

"And you wear ugly clothes and your nose is too big and you—"

"Lady, you're really irritating me." Kathreen pointed the gun at Wil's head. "And you," she said to Wil who was writhing in pain, "that shot was to keep you on track. Open that briefcase." Kathreen wanted to shoot Hope but was hesitant for fear Wil might still blow everyone up if she did. "Do I need to shoot your son's leg also?" Kathreen walked toward Hope. "I will, you know," said Kathreen.

Daryl, who had assumed the role of guard and spectator, stepped back from the window and toward the center of the room. Kathreen was now a few feet away from the window, her gun pointed at Hope.

"I know you would. And, you probably will anyway," said Hope as she leaned over and grabbed the lamp off the end table, snapping the cord from the outlet. She cocked her arm to throw the lamp at Kathreen. "You despicable scumbag."

"A gun versus a piece of furniture. Now, I wonder who is going to win?" Kathreen looked at Daryl. "Relieve the dingbat of the lamp."

Daryl stepped toward Hope, whose face was bright red, her chin high, her other fist clenched.

Wil was certain Hope had lost control.

Hope screamed, "You've shot my husband. You've terrorized my son. I am not going to stand here and let you do it without a fight."

"Hope, stop!" Wil knew her battle was futile. "Put the lamp down."

"No!" screamed Hope and threw the lamp at Kathreen, who easily dodged the slow-moving projectile by moving one step to the side and toward the window.

At that moment, the sniper's bullet shattered the window, grazing Kathreen's left arm. The shock sent her spinning to the floor.

Hope saw the look of surprised anger as Kathreen realized that somehow she had been duped.

The tear gas canister came through the window next, landing beside Kathreen and rolling toward Wil, who lay helpless on the floor. The only one who seemed to know what was happening was Daryl, who ran toward the back of the room. But the front door burst open before he got there.

Hope instinctively fell to the floor as a SWAT commando hit the ground, rolled, and dropped Daryl with one shot.

Kathreen, who had not dropped her weapon, fired next, hitting the officer, who had assumed his sharpshooting colleague had killed her.

Hope had not moved and was too shocked to make a sound. Steven was crying. Wil was in the direct line of fire of the tear gas canister on the floor five feet in front of him. He was choking and screaming in pain.

By the time the next SWAT officer came through the door, Kathreen had gotten to her feet, scooped up her duffel bag, and made it into the kitchen, running over Daryl's limp body and slamming the door behind her.

Two officers entered the room and ordered Hope to stay down. The smoke from the tear gas hindered everyone's vision.

"She went into the kitchen," yelled Hope.

One officer scooped up Steven, chair and all, and carried him from the building.

The other officer took up a position behind the sofa and began to order Kathreen to surrender since there was nowhere for her to go.

Kathreen did not respond.

Hope ignored the officer's demand that she stay still. She crawled to Wil, who had nearly lost consciousness before the canister stopped spraying. She began to pull him toward fresh air.

"Mrs. Wilson, I said stay down."

"I have to get him to fresh air."

Two more officers entered. One joined his colleague behind the sofa. The other took over for Hope. "I've got him, Ma'am. Get out of the building."

Hope let go of Wil's hand and stumbled out the door to look for her baby.

The standoff in the apartment ended fifteen minutes later when infrared cameras indicated no one was in the kitchen. Entering the kitchen they noticed the blood stains on the garbage chute. At the bottom of the chute they discovered the decomposing body of Clarence. They also discovered the motorcycle tracks, which led, via an access tunnel, to the adjoining building's parking garage and exited on the opposite site of the block from where Connie and her team had mustered in advance of the assault.

In the aftermath, the three Wilsons were reunited. Steven's tight, little fists fiercely gripped Hope's neck, his face buried on his mom's shoulder. Hope clutched Wil's hand as she walked alongside the stretcher, releasing it only long enough for them to load Wil into the ambulance and for her to climb in after him.

Wil tried to keep his composure for his son, who had finally stopped crying. "It's okay, kiddo," he whispered, his voice hoarse from the gas. "Daddy's okay. Mommy's okay. You're safe and the bad people are gone."

The wounded officer and Wil were transported to the hospital.

CHAPTER 31

Status

"Hi, honey," said Hope, as she walked into Wil's room at George Washington University Hospital. Hope's hair had been cut to repair the damage done during her captivity. The pixie style accented her beautiful green eyes.

Hope had just eaten dinner with Steven and Betty in the hospital dining room.

"Hope?" Wil slowly turned his head toward his wife.

"Hi, honey," repeated Hope, as she kissed him on the forehead.

"Did you have a nice dinner?"

"You betcha," said Hope sarcastically. "I had a meat thing and a vegetable something-or-other, and something that had rice in it."

"Me, too. Yum."

"Hospital food! I'll bet they make it taste that way as an incentive for people to get better."

"That's a thought."

"Steven liked it," said Hope. "But then again, he likes everything except what we feed him at home."

"Steven . . ." mused Wil. "I still can't believe how close we came to losing him."

"Wil, I really don't feel up to talking about that. I . . ."

"I almost lost you too, Hope." Wil's tears of thanksgiving fought with tears of terror.

"I know, but . . . it's just . . . I'm not far enough from it yet. It hurts too much to think about it. Even though I know it's over, I just don't want to cry anymore."

"I am so glad I didn't lose you." Wil took Hope's hand.

"And I want you to get through this surgery so we can get our lives back."

"Deal. I do love you, Hope."

"And I love you, Wil, more than you will ever know."

Wil changed the subject as requested. "So, they're off to the Haltermans?"

"Yep. They were beat. Your mom got more than she bargained for when she flew out here this time."

"She's been great." Wil paused. "You know, Hope, it's getting hard for me to believe she's the same woman who tolerated that jerk I had for a father."

"Maybe it has to do with her faith."

"Maybe. All I know is I like this mom a lot better."

"Say, while I was talking on the phone with Connie—"

"When were you talking with her?"

"After dinner. But—"

Wil interrupted again. "Any word on Kathreen?"

"No, but I'll get to that." Hope started over. "Anyway, while I was on the phone, I thought I saw Franklin Jackson."

"You might have. He stopped by to see me. He'd heard about my injury and wanted to let me know he was thinking of me."

"How nice."

"You know, I don't get that man. I mean, I hardly know him and he's so kind to me. He offered to help any way he could. I told him we were doing fine." Wil reflected a second and then added, "I have to admit, though, I sure do like him."

Hope mused, "To think he lost his daughter just a couple weeks ago. It's amazing he's not holed up somewhere. I can't imagine what I'd be doing if we'd lost Steven."

Wil stirred. Hope's comment haunted him. "He says it has to do with his faith." This time Wil used the words.

"Maybe it does."

"All I know," said Wil, "is if more Christians were like Franklin Jackson, the world would be a better place." He drew a breath. "Anyway, Hope, what did Connie have to say?"

"I'll get to that. But first, how are you feeling?"

"Truthfully—terrible. The pain has spread from my knee to my whole body. One of the nurses told me my pain wasn't that unusual after a major injury like this." Wil adjusted his position. "At least I don't have to get up to pee." He glanced at the catheter bag hooked to the side of his bed and raised his eyes to his wife's smiling face.

Hope leaned forward in her chair and touched Wil's arm.

Wil took her hand, gave it a squeeze, and sighed. "Now—are you going to tell me what Connie had to say about Kathreen?"

Wil's question was driven by curiosity more than fear. The police were keeping an eye on Hope and Steven. An officer had become a fixture outside Wil's hospital room. In addition, Wil had hired professional security. Hope and Steven each had their own chaperone at all times.

"Have they found her?" Wil asked. "I can hardly wait to hear she's behind bars again."

"Not yet," answered Hope. "Connie said they had some strong leads though, and they were confident they'd catch her. But that's all she'd say."

"Oh." That wasn't what Wil wanted to hear.

"You know, Connie's my friend and all, but there are

times she irks me," said Hope. "I know she could tell me more, but she's being stubbornly maternal. It's not like I don't deserve to know where the person is who shot my husband and kidnapped my son and me." Hope was venting. Still, she was appreciative for all Connie had done.

"Frankly," said Wil wincing in pain as he tried to reposition himself, "I'm glad they're on it and we're out of the picture." It was difficult for him to carry on a conversation, yet he wanted to comfort his wife.

"I know," she said. "And besides, I don't want to talk about Kathreen. It isn't like we don't have enough on our minds with the surgery tomorrow afternoon and all. Besides, there's nothing we can do."

Wil agreed to move on. "The therapist said my leg would be out of commission for about a month. At least I'll be able to get around with a wheelchair."

"I was thinking. We might want to make some modifications to the house and—"

"For Pete's sake, Hope." His objection was clearer than his earlier speech. "I'll be in the wheelchair for less than a week. I'll be on crutches after that, and soon I'll be back to normal."

"And exercising at the gym every week?"

"Hold it there, honey. I said back to normal, not healthy. You know I hate to exercise."

"And eating healthy foods," said Hope, ignoring him.

"Hah!" Wil objected.

"And seeing a doctor for regular checkups."

"We know that won't happen."

"Come on, Wil, you've been seen by a bunch of doctors over the last couple of days and it hasn't killed you."

"That's because you have been protecting me." Wil grinned.

Hope did not relent. "After all, if something did happen to you, Steven and I would be the big losers."

Wil pushed himself up on his elbows and looked toward the open door. "Nurse, will you please come tell this lady to quit badgering the patient."

Delilah, the nurse on duty, who happened to be Wil's favorite, had been listening to the conversation. "No, I won't. And, why should I? I agree with Mrs. Wilson."

"Hey, wait a minute here," protested Wil, who did not appreciate his nurse's lack of support. "I thought you were supposed to be on my side."

"Oh, I am on your side, Dr. Wilson," said Delilah slyly. She now stood in the doorway. "But the doctor's orders are specific that, in addition to your medical treatments, badgering by a woman who loves you is part of your plan of care."

Wil groaned. They had ganged up on him. "Thanks for the help," said Wil, collapsing back onto his bed.

"You're welcome," answered Delilah, as she walked away. "Just let me know if you need anything else."

Wil looked at Hope. "She's *my* nurse. Why is she on *your* side?"

"Because I'm right."

"Hmph!"

"And you're wrong."

Wil scowled in submission, then took a breath and said, "Moving on—what else did Connie have to say?"

"She was quite pleased with my decision to take a little time off from work. She'd been telling me to do that even before you were hospitalized. I can only imagine the harassment she'd have given me if I'd turned down my boss's offer of three weeks paid time off."

"You got that right."

"She also filled me in on the Freedom investigation. As I

suspected, the 'evidence' regarding co-pilot Bernie Bentson has begun to evaporate."

"Really?"

"The FBI computer hacks have proven the suicide note was created after the accident."

"Oops."

"And regarding the so-called love triangle between Bentson, Scott, and Cindy Henderson—well, Cindy is having a tough time with the details of both liaisons."

"So Bentson didn't do it?"

"Doubtful."

"But Brad and his gang certainly tried to make it look that way."

"And they almost got away with it. But, according to Connie, they're going to be issuing indictments against Brad tomorrow evening."

"I was wondering when it was going to happen."

"You know, it's still hard to believe that someone as ruthless and corrupt as Brad could have come through in such a difficult time for us."

"I know," conceded Wil.

Both Hope's and Wil's feelings were jumbled as they tried to balance Brad's corruption with his help in rescuing Steven.

"We never really thanked him," said Hope.

"It isn't exactly like we've had an abundance of time or anything." Wil knew they needed to, but he was hiding behind extenuating circumstances.

"Why don't I go tomorrow morning and thank him? Your surgery isn't going to happen until tomorrow afternoon anyway. I could see him and be back in plenty of time for your operation."

"That's probably a good idea."

"I'll make an appointment and stop by. I'll also let him

know I won't be working for a couple of weeks. My guess is he'll be glad to not hear from me so often."

"Probably."

Hope shifted in her chair next to Wil's bed. "Connie told me something else that was kind of disconcerting."

"What?"

"Did you know Scott's assistant, Art Middleton?"

"No. I recall Scott mentioning Art, but I never met him."

"Me either. Anyway, Connie told me he was found murdered."

"Murdered?"

"She said they found his body in his home."

"You're kidding me?"

"He'd been dead nearly two weeks when they found him."

"Geez. What happened?"

"Shot in the back of the head. Apparently he'd been badly beaten before being shot. Their guess is it started out as a burglary. The local police are handling the investigation."

"Any family?"

"Don't know."

"Do they know who did it?"

"Connie didn't go into too many details, but she told me the authorities were convinced it was unrelated to the crash investigation or anything else at Freedom."

"How so?"

"She didn't tell me much, but she did say it was Phil Reinhold, Freedom's HR director, who discovered him. Supposedly, Art had been on vacation. When he didn't return to work or answer their calls, Phil stopped by on his way home from work and found him."

"Man!"

"I know."

Wil sighed pensively and then asked the question Hope had asked Connie. "Are they certain it wasn't Brad?"

"I thought the same thing. Connie told me Brad's alibi is rock solid."

"Oh, come on!"

"All she said was the circumstances were so clearly unrelated to her investigation that they decided to assign the murder investigation locally. She was adamant it was unrelated to her investigation of Freedom."

"How do they know?"

"I told you, I don't know. Connie didn't tell me. Hey, weren't you the guy who, just a few minutes ago, said you were glad you weren't in the middle of all that stuff?"

"I know, but a murder of Scott's assistant? It's just ... well ... so coincidental."

Hope shrugged. There was nothing she could do about it. "Besides," she said, "I'm on vacation. Hey, Connie also invited us over for a barbecue, wheelchair and all, after you get out of this place."

"Great! I'm already sick of this food. A good barbecued bratwurst ..." Wil licked his lips in ecstasy.

"Or veggie burger."

"Bratwurst." Wil repeated himself louder. "*Bratwurst* would be great."

"Wil!"

"And lots of potato salad and beans and pork rinds and ice cream and chocolate and sugar-coated pork fat and sausage and biscuits and gravy ..."

"At a barbecue?" Hope looked at him with disgust.

"And cheese cake and boiled egg yolks and ..."

Hope ignored her exasperating husband.

CHAPTER 32

Art

"Hope Wilson to see you," announced Brad's secretary over the intercom.

"Show her in."

"Brad." Hope strode in and stopped next to one of the three wing chairs in front of Brad's desk. Her security chaperone had consented to wait in the lobby.

"Hope." Brad stood from his desk chair. "Please, have a seat."

Hope sat in the center chair. She glanced around the office and back to Brad. Each of them waited for the other to start.

Brad initiated. "That was great news about your son."

"Thank you."

"And, he's all right?"

"Yes. He's a little shaken, but he should be fine." Hope tried to sound upbeat.

"The poor kid went through a lot."

Hope didn't respond right away. It was all still too close. She took a breath. "The doctors were amazed at how resilient he is. And it appears those thugs didn't physically harm him."

"That's good."

"He certainly was dirty though, and he'd lost a little weight."

"And your husband?"

"He's doing fine. The doctors are running some tests. He'll be having surgery later today, but they expect close to full recovery, except for maybe a slight limp."

"That's good," Brad said mechanically.

"Thank you." Hope appreciated Brad's appearance of goodwill.

"I was happy to hear you'd gotten your son back." Relief and envy tinged his words.

"We might not have—if you hadn't helped."

"I'm sure it would have worked out anyway. But, thank you." He welcomed her appreciation, even though he knew he'd done it more for himself than for anyone else. "Any word on Kathreen Steele?"

"They still haven't caught her, but I have been reassured, ad nauseum, they will."

The conversation lagged as it waited for a topic.

"Really, Brad, I still don't understand. I'd been hounding you for days and I'm part of the reason you'll be going to—"

"Hold it. *We* are not sure what's going to happen. I understand malicious and unmerited accusations have been leveled at me and that I will be formally indicted this afternoon. But, Hope, I'm not in prison yet, and I do not plan to be."

"I mean—"

"Hope, as despicable as you—and now millions of people—think I am, you above all people should know there's something about being a parent that goes beyond all this." He gestured to his office and it was obvious he meant his work, her work, and the day-to-day routine of living. "I did what I did as a father who had lost a child. I believed I could prevent the horror I experienced from happening to someone else. Anyone would have done it."

"I don't know about that," said Hope.

"Since there is probably another bug hidden in my office . . ." Brad glared at Hope, not accusing her of involvement in the bugging but expressing a warning ". . . I'm still being rather careful what I say." His tone relaxed. "But, Hope, for what it's worth, your willingness to let me help you get your son back has lifted a weight I'd been carrying for ten years. Perhaps I should thank you."

Hope didn't know how to respond, and the moment of tenderness was so out of the ordinary it shocked both of them.

Brad cleared his throat. "Now, are you here on business or just for this personal stuff?"

"I'm not here on business. I'm not going to be doing any business for three weeks. I'm taking some time off."

"Does that mean the articles and harassment will stop?"

"I'm afraid not." Hope smiled ruefully. She knew *The New York Times* was not going to take the heat off Brad and that he was in for a very unpleasant future. She'd turned over the Advanced Chemical Products and Freedom Airways investigations to her assistant, Shelly, who would have her moment in the sun. "But my byline won't be on anything for a while."

"At least no one's accusing me of killing your secret informant."

"What?"

"Oh, didn't you hear? Your informant was found murdered. Your friend Connie and her cronies even had the audacity to interrogate me. As if I—"

"I heard that Scott's assistant, Art Middleton, had been murdered."

"One and the same. They found him a couple of days ago in his home. It's a good thing my alibi was rock solid. I'm a businessman . . . not a murderer."

"How do you know he was my informant?" Hope didn't

understand Brad's correlation of Scott's dead assistant with her informant. All she knew was that Scott's assistant had been killed. Yet, as she thought about it, she realized it had been nearly two weeks since she'd last heard anything from the enigmatic man—when he met her in the parking garage and warned her to watch out for Brad.

"We know," said Brad.

"It's just that I . . ." Hope was trying to hide her bewilderment as she thought, *My informant's fears have come true. He warned me. Am I next?*

"Do the authorities know Art was my source?"

"I didn't tell them."

Perhaps her informant had been right. Hope began to plan her exit, not fully convinced by whatever alibi had appeased the FBI. *They don't know he was my informant.*

Hope hesitated. "And you're not a suspect?"

"Why, Hope!" Brad pretended to be shocked, then stood up from his desk. He walked toward one of his massive mahogany bookcases, and picked up a letter opener that was out of place on one of its shelves.

Hope shifted. Her adrenaline was flowing. She did not want to panic.

"No," said Brad. "I'm not a suspect. I didn't kill anybody. Why would I want to? I haven't done anything that would push me to such extremes." He returned to his chair and nonchalantly used the small sword to slowly open a letter he did not read. He placed the letter opener on his desk and spun it like a compass needle.

"He warned me you might do something like this if you found out," said Hope.

"Like what?"

"Well, you know . . ." Hope's voice trailed away.

"He did, did he?" Brad was not denying he could do

"something like this." But he was denying he did it this time. "Hope, I'm the guy who helped get your son back." He called in his chit.

Hope thought about the two times she'd met with her informant, and then thoughtfully volunteered, "That's why he wore a disguise."

"A disguise. Really?"

"Uh huh. He wore a mask."

"So, you don't even know what Art looked like."

"No. And, by the way, how *do* you know Art was my informant?"

"He—" Brad didn't like that Hope's question put him on the defensive. "Before I answer your questions, let me first mention how much it disturbs me that you attacked someone of my standing based on the unsubstantiated claims of a goofball in costume whose identity you didn't even know."

Brad had the upper hand in the ethical debate, but that didn't discount her anonymous source being right about the maintenance records or his prediction he would be killed if Brad found out.

Brad continued. "I knew he was your informant after I had our human resources director do some investigating of his own."

"Before or after the authorities did their search?"

Brad's eyes smoldered with indignation. "Would you knock that off?" He then smirked at her. "Remember, I have nothing to hide."

Had a jury seen his look, they would have convicted him on the spot, regardless of what he was accused.

Hope knew there was more to the story but said nothing.

"It's not our fault they didn't check a particular computer an employee told us Art had been using, which happened to be in an unoccupied office."

Hope was surprised at his candor. Still, it helped assuage her anxiety, as did her awareness of her chaperone in the lobby outside Brad's office. "And what was on that computer?"

"Notes."

My informant was an idiot, crossed Hope's mind. Instead she asked the obligatory, "Notes?"

"Yes, notes. I don't know what form the notes were in that you received, but he obviously spent a fair amount of time trying to figure out exactly what he was going to say."

"I don't understand."

"It seems he wanted to be very precise in what he put in the notes. Only he was unaware of our data backup system. He thought he had erased his files. Well—"

"I get it." Hope cut him off.

Brad continued anyway. "One of those notes sounded a lot like the one you told me about when you first brought up the subject."

"That doesn't mean he was my informant and—wait a minute. Why didn't you tell the authorities this?"

"I thought you weren't working anymore," jibed Brad.

Hope shrugged.

Brad sat back in his chair. "Our attorneys are working on making sure we inform them in the proper manner. Plus, since it is unrelated to their investigation, we're not convinced we even need to tell them. Besides . . . you know . . . there's a lot of paperwork involved in situations like this."

Hope was still trying to convince herself that her informant and Art Middleton were really the same guy. It was possible Brad was only fishing for information. She wondered if this merited breaking the vow of confidentiality she had made to her informant. "What's to keep me from telling the authorities?"

"Trust."

Hope wasn't clear if he was threatening or honoring her. She wanted more information. "Can you tell me more about Art? Did you know him very long?"

"About five years."

"Why would he turn against you?"

"Your guess is as good as mine." Brad was not going to take the bait.

Brad turned to his credenza and reached for a five-by-seven framed photo of four men standing in front of a golf cart. He looked at it for a moment and then flashed it in Hope's direction, but not long enough for her to make out the faces. "I thought we were on good terms," said Brad as he studied the photo of Art.

Hope was suspicious as she pondered why Brad just happened to have this photo so readily available. She wondered if it was part of his charade. Perhaps he kept a "sentimental photo" like this with all of his key employees.

"Did he have any children?" Hope asked.

"No. Never married either."

"What?" Hope was startled. "What did you say?"

"I said he didn't have any kids." Brad look surprised with the intensity of her response.

"He wasn't married?" Hope was puzzled.

"Nope. Single. Never married. Kind of a recluse. I never could understand what Scott saw in him. Maybe he felt sorry for the guy. Anyway, that's enough about his personal life."

Brad returned the photo to its place and turned back to Hope. "Is that all?" His question indicated it was time for her to leave.

"I guess I'd better be going." Hope took the hint.

"Well, then . . . Thanks for stopping by."

Hope hesitated. "But, before I go, may I look at that photo? I'd at least like to see what Art really looked like."

"Sure." Brad took the photo from the credenza and held it out to her.

Hope looked at the photo. "That's strange."

"What? He's the one on the right. Is there a problem?"

"It's just that this *is* the guy I was talking to." Hope pointed to the man on the right in the photo, turning it so Brad could see which one she meant.

"I know, Hope."

"No, I mean this *is* the guy. He wasn't wearing a mask after all."

"Sounds to me like your informant has a real credibility problem. Of course, it's a little too late to find that out now, isn't it?"

"Hmm." Hope set the photo down on Brad's desk.

Brad could see she was puzzled. "I guess the crack reporter who relied on information from an unidentified and non-credible source has her work cut out for her."

Hope ignored his taunt as she turned to leave. Her steps were slow and her thoughts distracted as she walked to the door. She reached for the knob and paused, chasing a fleeting thought.

Brad joked. "Don't stay away so long next time."

Hope turned, the thought gone. "Oh . . . right." Standing in the doorway, Hope remembered why she had come in the first place. "And Brad . . . thanks."

"Sure."

Hope drew the door shut behind her. Her chaperone set down the copy of *Newsweek* and rose to greet her.

CHAPTER 33

Perspective

The doors of the elevator opened. A bald woman looked up from her wheelchair and smiled at Hope. Hope waited as two nurses assisted the thirty-something woman, one pushing the wheelchair, the other carrying some paperwork and pulling the IV pole.

"Thank you," said Hope, expressing appreciation to the man who instinctively held the door open. Hope and her security guard stepped into the elevator with the man, a woman, and a child.

"What floor?

"Five," said Hope.

"And you?" the man asked, looking at Hope's escort.

"Five."

The man pushed the fifth-floor button and glanced at Hope, whose smile was tight with anxiety. Hope had intended to be here an hour ago, but a six-car pile-up on the freeway a mile from Freedom Airways had slowed her down. To make matters more stressful, her cell phone battery was dead and there had been no way for her to get off the freeway since she was halfway between exits. Her chaperone had taken it all in stride.

"Tough day?" asked the woman. Hope assumed she was

the man's wife and the mother of the rosy-cheeked boy grasping her hand.

"Tough day?" repeated the child.

"Todd, shhh," said the mother.

"Yes." Hope smiled at Todd. "A big traffic accident. I was stuck in one place for an hour."

"Was anyone hurt?" asked Todd.

The question penetrated Hope's self-absorption. She had worked herself into such a fury due to her delay that she had not even asked that question about the people in the accident, who may have been hurt, or worse, killed. Suddenly, her hour-long delay wasn't such a big deal anymore.

"I don't know," said Hope, ashamed. "I hope not."

"I'm going to get my tonsils out," Todd volunteered. "See!" He turned his face up and opened his mouth wide for Hope to look.

"Really?" asked Hope, as she obligingly examined the back of the boy's throat. "I didn't know they did that anymore."

"Once in a while," added the father. "But he'll get to have lots of ice cream."

Hope remembered when she'd had her tonsils out. The promises of unlimited ice cream never quite made up for the discomfort and trauma of having a part of her body snipped out.

"Chocolate," announced Todd.

"What are you here for?" asked the mother, sincerely interested. The light on the elevator read four.

"My husband is having knee surgery. They'll be doing it this afternoon."

"I'll bet he'll be glad to have that over with," said the father. "I had a bum knee from an old football injury." He sounded as if he were bragging about a war wound. "After my knee surgery, I felt like a new man."

"It'll go fine," said the mother. "They're getting so good at those nowadays."

"Six weeks and he'll be good as new," said the father, bending his knee to demonstrate his surgeon's success.

Hope smiled. She was looking forward to Wil's recovery and to everything returning to normal.

The elevator stopped at the fifth floor and Hope and her escort stepped out. She turned toward the little boy. "I hope you enjoy your ice cream, Todd."

The beaming child waved good-bye to his new friend as the door closed.

Hope started down the corridor to see her husband.

Birth: A terminal diagnosis.

CHAPTER 34

News

Betty was sitting in a chair at the end of Wil's bed. Wil lay on his back with the head of his bed angled at thirty degrees and Steven perched beside him playing pat-a-cake, though his partner seemed to be somewhere other than in the game.

"Whew! I'm back," said Hope.

Steven looked to the door as Hope entered. "Mommy!"

The little boy planted a wet kiss on his mom's cheek as she picked him up and gave him a big hug.

"Are you glad to see Mommy?"

"Uh huh!" said Steven, kissing her a second time.

"Okay, Steven," said Wil. "Why don't you let Mommy and Daddy talk to each other? You can go with Grandma to get some candy."

"Yippee!" Steven wriggled to get down. Hope and Wil both were a little concerned by how easily their son could be manipulated with the offer of candy.

Steven reached for his grandma's hand and skipped out of the room at her side. Steven's private guard followed them. Hope's chaperone remained in the hallway, talking to the police officer at his post.

The nurse, who had followed Hope into the room and

delivered some medications, excused herself. "I'll leave you two alone."

"Was it my breath?" asked Hope. "Or have I done something to offend everyone?" She giggled as she leaned down to kiss Wil.

"No," said Wil, smiling. "Your breath is fine."

"Why aren't they getting you ready for surgery?" Hope brushed off the room's evacuation as coincidental.

"They decided not to do it."

"They?" Hope was ready to do battle with an HMO representative or clerk who was still trying to get the authorizations.

"I decided not to do it," said Wil quietly.

"You decided? Why?" Hope shook her head. "What are you talking about?"

"Hope, there's something I have to tell you."

Hope grew quiet. She saw the tension in Wil's jaw and felt her own stomach tighten. She glanced away, not wanting to continue reading his eyes. "Did the Haltermans come by? You know, I can't get over how helpful they—"

"Hope."

"—have been and I've also really—"

"Hope."

"What, Wil?"

"While they were doing tests in advance of the surgery they found something."

"Something?" Hope's heart sank.

"Doctor Olsen told me about it yesterday. But I wanted to wait until we had the results from some other tests before I told you."

"Told me what? Is this why they postponed the operation? What does this have to do with the surgery?"

"Dr. Olsen said I had an extremely high white blood cell

count—some kind of special white blood cells and some other sort of 'markers' is what he called them. He also did a brief physical and some radiology tests—"

"When? I was here all—"

"Not all the time." Wil felt bad about being so secretive, but he hadn't wanted to worry Hope in case it was nothing.

"I told you that you should have gone to see the doctor for a physical. I was concerned because you were peeing all the time. And I know how much you hate going to doctors, and yet I knew you needed to and—" She didn't want him to say any more.

"He also noticed some unusual lumps."

"Lumps?" Hope tried to look unfazed. "But at least they know now so they can give you medicine and—"

"Hope, I have a very advanced case of cancer—prostate cancer with metastases to my bones. It has also gone into my liver and kidneys." Wil's eyes said how difficult this was for him. He couldn't hold back the tears. "I guess that's why I've been peeing so much and—" Wil broke off, breathing hard, fighting for control.

Hope sank into the chair. Her chest felt tight and a rushing sound filled her ears.

"The doctors could hardly believe I hadn't been in a lot of pain. I guess I have a higher pain tolerance than I realized."

Hope could tell by the look in Wil's eyes that he was not worried about himself. She opened her mouth but couldn't speak.

"But after the shot to the knee, that tolerance seems to have been compromised, which is why I feel so terrible now."

"What—what does this mean?" Hope's voice was barely above a whisper.

"Hope, I'm going to die." He choked in a breath so he could say his next words. "And it's going to be really soon—"

"Hold it." She'd come to the hospital expecting her husband's knee surgery. Instead, she was asked to believe her husband is going to die—and soon. She wasn't ready to accept it. "What about chemotherapy and surgery? I've heard they have new treatments now." Hope was reaching for straws Wil had already rightly concluded were useless.

"Hope. There's nothing they can do. It's throughout my whole body. I couldn't believe it either, but then they showed me the test results and . . ." Wil began to sob. His effort at being strong had given way to the overwhelming reality that he had only a few weeks, or maybe days, before the cancer would finish its destruction and he would die.

"No. It's a mistake. It's not possible." Hope abruptly stood and left the room, walking briskly to the nurses' station.

The officer and Hope's security guard, who had overheard the conversation, sat helpless.

"I want to see Dr. Olsen, and I want to see him now!" Hope yelled at the nurses.

"Hope," Wil called weakly, both embarrassed and broken. She didn't hear him.

"Ma'am. Please lower your voice," said the charge nurse. "Is there something I can help you with?"

"No. I want to see the quack who convinced my perfectly healthy husband that he's going to die of cancer in a few days." Hope's volume had increased.

"Mrs. Wilson. Please lower your voice. There are other patients."

"I want to see Dr. Olsen, and I want to see him now." Her outburst was over with this last volley, but she was not moving until she received satisfaction.

"I'll page him. I believe—"

"Mrs. Wilson." Dr. Olsen walked up. He'd observed the outburst from down the hall. "I was just coming to see your husband. How is he doing?"

"You tell me!" The volume had been replaced by indignation.

Dr. Olsen sighed. "Hope, your husband is very sick."

"What do you mean by saying he can't have the knee surgery? He needs it done in order for him to walk again. What do you mean, it has to wait? Is there a problem with the insurance? Can I help get the authorization? Perhaps there's another doctor who would like our business . . ."

Dr. Olsen reached forward and gently grasped Hope's arm. "Why don't we go have a seat?"

"No! I just want to know what's going on. I mean . . ." Hope's hand went to her mouth. Her spirit broke and she began to cry.

Dr. Olsen held her while she sobbed and then he gently turned her toward the nurses' station.

"Let's go and have a seat over here." The doctor guided Hope to a small conference room behind the station. The nurses were acting as ushers and honor guard, one opening the door and the other offering a chair and a box of tissues. The one who held the door struggled to keep her own emotions in check. After closing the door behind Hope and Dr. Olsen, she walked to her chair at the station and put her hands to her face.

The other nurse had tears in her eyes. "I've been doing this for too many years. Maybe I should get another job."

Death is everyone's common destination.
    Some fear it.
    Some don't.
For those who do,
    do they fear the destination,
    or are they concerned it isn't the final one?

CHAPTER 35

Reality

Wil and Hope didn't talk about the cancer until after breakfast the next morning. Nor did Betty, who had the unspoken mandate to keep Steven safe and occupied. Nor did Steve, who arrived around eight o'clock, his eyes reddened from tears and lack of sleep.

By lunchtime they had decided the best thing to do was to get Wil home, at least for a week or two, while they waited for the cancer to win. The charge nurse secured authorization from Dr. Olsen for discharge and supplemental home health and hospice care.

The hospital staff had arranged for a visiting nurse to go to the Wilson home to help with bathing and medications. This would afford Wil a measure of dignity and protect Hope and Betty from the discomfort of providing primary care to a forty-year-old husband and son.

Steve had volunteered to drive. His church owned a van with a wheelchair lift. Though it would have been possible for Wil to transfer from his wheelchair to the front seat of their Volvo, Wil's useless leg and the cancer pain, which was rearing its horrific head, made the wheelchair lift a preferred option.

"So, are you ready to go home?" Dr. Olsen stopped by to

sign the discharge paperwork and ensure that everything was in order. He wasn't totally sold on the idea of sending Wil home because he knew how quickly things would deteriorate. Yet, Hope's plea for Wil to be able to die at home, and Wil's determination to pretend he wasn't that ill, made the physician's agreement inevitable.

"Yes," said Hope.

Wil concurred with a nod, his lips tight with pain.

"And you must be the designated driver?" The doctor and Steve knew each other.

"Yes. I'm not the regular driver of the van, but at least I know how to operate it."

"I guess this is the last time you're going to let me torment you," said Delilah. Her banter and helpfulness had smoothed some rough times. "Let's get you into the chair and then you can be rid of me forever."

Wil reached for the over-bed trapeze to pull himself up so Delilah could slide her arm behind him. Hope stood at the ready to assist with the bed-to-chair transfer. Betty watched closely since she anticipated filling in for the nurse once Wil was home. Steve steadied the wheelchair and moved the catheter bag.

Wil had been up only half a dozen times since arriving in the hospital four days earlier. The last time was shortly after lunch when Hope, Delilah, and Wil had practiced for this evening's performance.

Hope's encouraging smile masked her heartache.

"Wow, I'm really getting sore." Wil grimaced as he pulled himself up and Delilah steadied him for the next move. The color drained from his face and his teeth clenched.

His nurse continued the procedure with narrative instruction. "The next thing to do is bring your legs around like this." Delilah held and guided Wil's injured leg as his good leg followed. He was now sitting on the side of the bed. The pain was worse than ever.

"Are you okay, honey?" asked Hope. Delilah waited for Wil's response.

"The pain has really gotten worse," Wil groaned.

"Perhaps he should have some more morphine," commented Betty, keeping one eye on her grandson in the hallway and one eye on her son.

"He had some thirty minutes ago. We even upped the dosage because of the increased pain he was having this morning." Delilah stated what everyone already knew. She was willing to give him more pain medicine if he wanted it. "Dr. Wilson—"

"I don't want any more drugs. I am not going to be turned into a zombie. All I have left is my mind."

"Okay, if that's your decision," conceded Delilah.

"Right then, let's get this done," said Wil, determined. "I want to go home."

Everyone resumed their positions. Wil readied himself for the next move, which would be to stand and pivot on his good leg into the wheelchair that Steve had positioned next to the bed.

"On three," said Delilah.

"On three," confirmed Hope, who was positioned on Wil's other side.

The nurse counted, "One, two, three."

"Augh!" Wil's cry was heard down the hall.

Hope and Delilah immediately aborted the transfer and sat him back on the bed.

They were joined by another nurse who had heard Wil's cry and run past the security personnel into Wil's room. Betty turned away and left the room, her shoulders shaking with silent sobs.

"Let's see if I can help," said the second nurse, politely excusing Hope.

"Oh, man! That hurt!" Wil's chest was heaving. Tears of pain welled in his eyes.

"Honey?" Hope's hands were clasped tightly as she looked to Wil for guidance.

"Babe, it hurts too much."

"Okay . . . sure . . . okay. Maybe we can try later."

"Are you sure, Dr. Wilson?" Delilah wanted to respect her patient's desires, but also didn't want to let him abandon his earlier determination so quickly.

"I can't," he moaned, his face pale and strained.

Betty had started down the hall. Steven was holding her hand and looking up at her.

"What wrong? Daddy sick?"

Betty wiped away her tears and gave Steven a shaky smile as she squeezed his hand.

CHAPTER 36

Best Friends

"I think you made a good decision to stay here, Wil," said Steve. It was two hours after the aborted discharge. Betty and Steven had gone home for the evening and would gather some things Wil might want now that he would be staying in the hospital. Hope sat in the corner by the large picture window, reading and attempting to respect the two friends' privacy. She had determined not to be gone if—when—Wil died.

"Me, too," said Wil. "I really wanted to go home, but it'll be easier for everyone if I just stay here."

"Is there anything Wendy or I can do for you?"

"You're already doing enough by letting my family live with you." The Wilson clan had discreetly moved in with the Haltermans. "At least until they can guarantee me our home is safe for Hope and Steven—that means locking up that witch Kathreen."

"One thing's for sure, the police presence provided by those still looking for Kathreen has made it a little quieter around our neighborhood, though I'm concerned about their impact on my reputation. My neighbors are getting a little curious about the pastor who's under police surveillance."

Wil smiled.

"And Steven has certainly changed the chemistry of our house. Boo's a little confused, but he's settling in."

"I can't thank you enough."

"I wouldn't hesitate if you were to ask again. It's the least we can do. Besides, my daughter is enjoying her time with Steven, and I have liked getting to know your mother better. Why didn't you tell me she was so strong in her faith?"

"It never came up," said Wil with a shrug.

"She's quite a lady."

"That she is." Wil's gaze shifted to the window and toward Hope, who was keeping her eyes directed at her book.

"Anyway, is there anything else we can do for you?" Steve drew Wil's attention back.

"There's one thing. Hope has never been much for paperwork."

Hope looked up. She was slightly offended but knew Wil was right. Sighing, she returned to her book.

"At least her financial situation will be fine since the ransom money was recovered and the loans are paid off. But I know there's going to be a lot of stuff that needs to be done. Will you help her with it?" Wil was aware the government, banks, investment houses, social security administration, etcetera, sometimes required more paperwork for a dead person than a live one.

"Sure."

"Thanks." Wil was confident his best friend would take care of his wife and child.

"How are you doing—really?" Steve asked.

"Really?" Wil skirted the deeper meaning behind Steve's question. "I hurt like hell. That's how I'm doing."

Wil realized his choice of the word "hell" would be particularly poignant. Their recent theological/philosophical lunch conversations had been on the subject of the torment and agony associated with the doctrine of hell.

"I'm dying and leaving everything I have ever known and loved—Hope and Steven." Wil said cautiously, then stopped. He wasn't ready for another cathartic event. Nor was Hope.

"Are you afraid of anything?" Steve was Wil's best friend, indeed, but Steve was also a pastor at heart.

"Afraid? I don't think so." Again, he knew what Steve was asking. "I am a little curious though."

"What do you mean?"

"To be perfectly honest, until two-funeral Saturday a couple weeks ago, I hadn't done much thinking about death," admitted Wil. "I've always been more concerned with life." His second sentence had a hint of arrogance to it, as if thinking about life was, of course, more noble than thinking about death.

"And?"

"I wonder what it'll be like."

"What do you think it will be like?"

"I don't know. I'll probably just go away."

"Go away?"

"Yeah, go away. I don't buy this stuff about an afterlife and a spirit and a soul and all that. We're merely biological creatures, the result of random genetic evolution over billions of years. My time in the mire has about ended." Wil did not sound very convincing, even to himself. Still, he went on the offensive. "Steve, do you really believe, considering how big this universe is and how minuscule we humans are, that we are really so special—that somehow we have access to life beyond the grave in a different manner than, say, a rabbit or an ape or our microbial ancestors in the primordial swamp?"

"First of all, I disagree with you quite a bit about our origins. And, yes, I do think humans are different." Steve paused. "Do you really want to have this conversation?"

Wil shrugged. "We're not going to have many other chances."

Steve spoke softly. "Wil, the reason I believe in eternal life and all the things you so easily disparage, is largely based on Jesus' resurrection."

"But I don't believe in the resurrection of Jesus."

"I know," acknowledged Steve. "May I be candid?"

"You might as well," said Wil waving his hand in assent.

"Wil, we have known each other for more than twenty years. I've always had respect for you and I've grown to know you as a man who has incredible integrity, but perhaps even more stubbor—"

"Determination," corrected Wil.

"Stubbornness—than any other person I've ever known. However—"

"Here it comes." Wil knew Steve's major points always followed his "howevers."

"—on the issue of the resurrection, you have been negligent because you have refused to think it through."

"That's awfully judgmental of you," said Wil, smiling.

"You're probably right. But so am I."

"Whoa, you're serious about this. Don't forget, I'm the one dying." Wil tried to make light of the conversation.

"Wil, look." Steve prepared to state his argument one last time, crisp and clean. "The resurrection of Jesus is the key."

"I'll give you that," said Wil. "And I agree the belief in Jesus' resurrection is what Christians have based their faith on for two thousand years. I, quite simply, believe they are wrong."

"But you've examined the other explanations—that He never died, that He never existed, that His bones are in Japan or France or Kashmir or England. You know the evidence of the resurrection is stronger than all these bogus theories combined. Why can't you accept it?"

Wil turned away, choosing not to respond.

"For heaven's sake, Wil, your position takes more faith

than mine!" Steve did not relent. "You know the evidence, perhaps as well as anyone: the testimonies of people who saw Him, the changed lives of the disciples who died defending their claims of actually seeing the resurrected Jesus, the inability of the Roman and Jewish rulers to find the body—which would have killed Christianity right then and there—the continuing absence of Christ's body, the Old Testament prophecies, the reality of Christ's presence in the lives of Christians around the world today. There isn't an explanation that makes more sense."

"Well . . ." responded Wil.

"Well, nothing!" There was love-driven frustration in Steve's voice. "Why do you refuse to accept the conclusion that fits the data? Why do you persist in ignoring, or worse, changing the data so that it fits your unfounded conclusions?"

"Calm down, Steve." Wil's voice had also risen a little.

Steve sat back. He seldom let himself become so impassioned.

Hope was peering over the top of her book and listening intently.

It was Wil's turn. "Okay. Okay. I agree with your premise. I agree Jesus either did or didn't rise, and Jesus either is or isn't who He claimed to be. I just don't know which is true. I don't know what to believe."

"If Jesus did rise, what I am saying is true," said Steve. "If He didn't, I am an idiot who is completely deluded and following a dead, thirty-year-old Jewish radical nutcase who went around claiming to be God, either foolishly thinking He was God, or evilly knowing He wasn't." Steve took a breath and put his hand on Wil's bed. "I am convinced He was who He said He was, and I want you to know Him and to receive His love and spend eternity with Him. You simply need to decide."

"I don't want to decide," said Wil, who resented being told he had to make a decision.

"Whether you want to or not, Wil, you can't avoid it. And, whatever you decide is going to be permanent when you breathe your last breath in what might not be too long from now."

"What are you saying?" said Wil, mildly indignant at Steve's blunt statement of the truth.

Steve leaned forward slightly. His volume had softened. "Wil, one day we're all going to stand before God. I believe, at a minimum, those of us who have heard of Jesus are going to be asked who we believe Jesus to be. I don't know in what form the question will be asked. But I am convinced the one answer that's not going to be acceptable is, 'I haven't decided.' You have the evidence and you have the capacity to make a decision—just like you've made decisions about countless other things in your forty years of life, even when you had less to go on. You also know, more than most people, the approximate date of your death. All I can say is, God loves you immeasurably, Wil. All of us have been separated from God by our sins. Yet, God, in Christ, has paid the price for our sins so that, if you accept His forgiveness, you can have a relationship with Him and experience life to the fullest, now and throughout eternity."

"Or, I will go to hell?" Sarcasm laced Wil's words. "So, now you're telling me I'm going to hell?"

"No, Wil!" Steve was irritated. "That is not my point and you know it. Besides, that's God's decision, not mine. What I am telling you is, God has provided you with a way of salvation, a way to have eternal life. All you need to do is receive the forgiveness and love manifested in Christ Jesus."

Steve had, as succinctly and compassionately as he could, shared the heart of his faith, as a gift of love, with his best friend. Yet, when it came down to it, Wil interpreted it as, *You want me to believe that stuff my dad said in a drunken stupor as he would beat me and then jump in the sack with countless women, in our home, while my mom was at church doing her Christian duty.*

"Steve, I know you meant everything you said with the best intentions." Wil's voice was tinged with academic condescension. "But I will never believe what you believe. Jesus was the wall my dad hid behind. If you want to believe it, that's up to you. As for me, I will take my chances with hell. Or, better yet, I will just go away like the billions of Christians and non-Christians who have gone before me, returning their molecules to the ground out of which they came."

Defeated, Steve's chin dropped as he let out a sigh, his heart broken. He loved Wil deeply, but he could not get past Wil's blockade of resentment, pain, and pride.

Wil was resolved, and since he had ended the theological conversation, he decided to choose the next subject. "Hey, honey, what are you reading over there?"

Both Steve and Wil knew Hope had not been reading during their conversation, even though she had made a pretense of turning pages.

"Just something I picked up in the gift shop. It's about this woman who . . ."

Steve sat back in his chair.

Why is it that people who do not believe in heaven or hell sometimes have the most intense feelings about them?

CHAPTER 37

Betty

Franklin Jackson and Hope walked from Wil's hospital room into the hallway, greeting the police guard and Hope's bodyguard, who were discussing the weekend's games.

"Thank you for coming," Hope said to Franklin.

"Sure."

"I know you and Wil haven't been friends for too long, but . . ." Hope lowered her voice so Wil couldn't hear, ". . . your kindness has meant an awful lot to Wil."

"Thank you."

"And to me," added Hope.

Franklin took Hope's hand as they walked down the hall.

Hope's eyes began to fill with tears. "I just don't understand why, if there is a God like you and Steve say, this could happen."

Franklin knew this was not the time to answer that question. Instead, he listened. As they strolled down the corridor, Franklin gave Hope his full attention, only occasionally responding to her introspective meanderings.

As they approached the elevator, Hope turned to Franklin. "I don't understand why you are so kind to Wil and me. Your faith is so important to you. Yet, you are still so accepting of us, even though you know Wil and I disagree with what you believe."

"Hope," Franklin said gently, "that's your choice. And, I wouldn't be truthful if I didn't tell you that I pray you two will change your mind on the matter. You see, God has given Wil and you and me the freedom of choice. It's up to each individual to receive God's love or reject it. But, regardless of what you or anyone else decides, for those of us who call Jesus our Lord and Savior, we have no choice but to love those God loves, and that includes you and Wil."

"You really believe that, don't you Franklin?"

"I do, Hope."

"You're a special man, Franklin."

"And you are a special woman." Franklin gave Hope a hug and said good-bye as he stepped into the elevator.

Hope headed back down the corridor in the direction of Wil's room.

Betty had just settled into the chair next to Wil's bed.

"I talked to your brother today," said Betty. "He's planning on getting here next weekend."

"That's eight days from now," calculated Wil. He knew he couldn't last that long. He didn't want to either. The pain had become so great even the morphine and Dilaudid and other painkillers were not controlling it. There was still room to increase the amount of pain medication they could give him, but he refused to take more. His body was dying and there was nothing he could do to stop it. Since he believed the next few days were all he had left in existence, he was not going to let them slip away, as unpleasant and painful as they were, in a painkiller-induced stupor. He wanted to ensure he was not susceptible to making foolish comments or agreeing to something when he wasn't in his full mind. Integrity was all he had left and consciousness was the only means he had of ensuring it.

"Mike said he couldn't leave until then," Betty responded.

"He said that was the soonest he could come because of his job and his responsibilities with Rocky."

"Why couldn't he leave Rocky with Sue?"

"It is Mike's weekend. Sue is on a trip to Las Vegas with her new husband."

"Timing is everything, isn't it, Mom?"

"Yes."

"At least he'll be here for my funeral."

"Wil!" Betty was still not comfortable with Wil's bluntness about his impending death. "You've become so morbid."

Wil had become quite candid about his funeral. He'd even picked out a casket and persuaded Steve to do the funeral, as a favor, even though Wil's criterion was that the service not be turned into a religious affair. Steve had agreed, reluctantly.

"C'mon, Mom. You know as well as I do—Mike would just as soon see me dead as alive anyway."

"William, please stop. You know that isn't true."

"It is. It's as though Mike has become Dad and feels obligated to hate me."

"I'm sure his delay is not related to anything other than what he told me on the phone—his job and his child."

"Okay. Whatever you say."

"He sends his best wishes. In fact, I believe those flowers over there are from him." Betty pointed to the smallest vase on the bedside stand, which looked like a runaway display table from a flower shop.

Wil glanced at the table, then turned back to his mom and looked into her eyes. "So, Mom, are you going to be okay?" Wil's tone softened. "This has to be tough on you."

Betty sighed. "It is, Wil. But I'll be fine. It's you I'm concerned about."

They both fell silent.

"How are you two doing?" asked Hope, as she walked in on the tender moment, unintentionally bringing it to a timely close.

"Fine," they said in unison, each with a smile.

The unison made Hope suspicious. "Why do I have the feeling you two have been plotting?"

"We were just having a mother–son moment," Betty replied softly.

Hope looked from Wil to Betty and then at the clasped hands. "That's good."

Hope walked toward the huge windows that took up two-thirds of the wall. "Steven is fine at the Haltermans. I just talked to Katie and she's agreed to baby-sit again tonight and will see that Steven is fed and gets to bed at a reasonable time. She said she doesn't have any homework and wanted to hang out with her parents tonight anyway. She's been awfully helpful, as have Wendy and Steve."

"Good friends," said Betty.

Hope picked up her book, which she had set on the foot of the unused bed, and sat in her chair in the corner. "Well, I've been burning with curiosity to know what happens next." Her sarcasm was not lost on her listeners. "And I didn't mean to interrupt your time together. I'll just be over here in my chair in the corner, reading my book."

Both Betty and Wil suddenly felt like children who had just been introduced and told by their parents they need to get to know each other. Where to start?

"Wil?" Betty knew what she wanted to say.

"Yes?"

"There's something I need to say."

"Uh huh." Wil politely opened the door.

"My faith in Christ must be a real quandary for you."

"That's an understatement." Wil went right to the point.

He sincerely could not understand how she could ever accept the religion of the husband who had beaten and otherwise abused her.

Betty knew this. "Yes . . . well . . . about your dad's Christianity. Your dad told me over and over, sometimes before beating us, sometimes after, sometimes during church, and sometimes in bed—he told me he never believed 'this religious stuff about Jesus.' The words he used about Jesus make your hatred of Christianity look mild."

"So . . . I guess that means Dad's in hell." Wil didn't believe in hell, but he liked the thought.

"That's between God and your dad."

"Hmph."

"Wil, hating your dad doesn't help anything. I finally found freedom from hating your dad when I admitted that I also am a sinner. Besides," Betty hesitated, "ultimately, regardless of how awful your dad was, we're all going to be held accountable for our own lives—our own sins—not anyone else's. Even you, Wil."

Wil looked away. Her direct communication had caught him off guard.

"But the God revealed to us in Jesus isn't a God who is waiting to pounce on us and punish us when we mess up. God loves us, you and me, in spite of our being sinners, so much so that He died for us—because we are sinners."

Wil shook his head. He could not miss the sincerity or integrity of his mother's comments. He just wished the conversation would go away.

"Okay, Mom. Thank you." He gently squeezed her hands that still held his, but he was done listening. "I know you believe that. But the fact remains, I do not. While faking a conversion might make you and my best friend much happier, I cannot and I will not do that. Please, let's not spend the last few days of my life talking about religion. We don't agree. Okay?"

Betty nodded, her eyes brimming with tears. While their reconciliation had been miraculous, she would have traded it all for Wil to be reconciled with his loving God.

She stood and leaned forward, gently embracing her son, who lay with the head of the bed at a forty-five degree angle. She kissed him on the forehead and cupped his cheek with her hand. "I love you, William."

"And I love you, Mom."

Betty lowered her hand from Wil's cheek and looked at the clock. "Would you look at the time? It must be getting close to your dinner time."

"I already had it. Right before you got here." Wil knew she was trying to gracefully end their conversation.

"Really? That's earlier than normal. Are you going to be okay for the night? Should I get you a snack?"

"I'll be fine."

"Well, I'd better go on home and get something for myself to eat. I might even get some rest tonight. I'll be back first thing in the morning." Betty turned to find her sweater and purse.

"Thanks for coming," said Wil. He meant it.

"I'll see you tomorrow," Betty nodded to both Wil and Hope, then looked back to Wil. "Try to get some sleep tonight."

Wil knew that was not going to happen. "I will," he said anyway. "Have a good night, Mom." Betty started to walk out of the room.

Hope rose from her chair. "I'll walk you to your car, Mom."

Betty and Hope left the room, Hope's guard following

them. The duty officer stayed put in his chair outside Wil's room. Wil was alone for a rare moment.

"Delilah." Wil called for his favorite nurse, who was just beyond the doorway.

"Yes, Dr. Wilson?" said Delilah, stepping into the room.

"Do you think I could get a heavy-duty sleeping pill for tonight? I'd really like to try to get some sleep. I'm beat."

Freedom of choice is a blessing and a burden.

CHAPTER 38

Doors

W il awoke and found himself standing in the hospital corridor, fully clothed. After taking a few steps he looked down at his knee. No pain, not even a limp. He was surprised no one was at the nurses' station. He looked back toward his room and noticed his sentry was also missing. More unsettling was the quiet. As he tried to get his bearings, he observed that the swinging fire doors at the end of the corridor had been replaced by a narrow white door with a circular window about one foot in diameter. As he moved toward the door, he could hear peaceful yet celebratory music coming from the other side. The music grew louder and richer as he approached. He looked through the window and was amazed at the beauty of a banquet hall. The carpeting was rich green grass and, though he couldn't see the sun, he knew the brightness in the enormous room could not be from any other source.

The magnificent table was overflowing with pies and chocolate cake with dark fudge icing; barbecued ribs dripping with hickory-smoked sauce; steaming anise-filled lasagna; bowls of bright blueberries, raspberries, and strawberries surrounding pitchers of crème anglaise; succulent lobster tails bathed in melted butter; fresh breads; ice cream;

roasted bratwurst; deep red watermelon slices and cheesecake with a buttery graham cracker crust. It was endless. The bountiful table had thousands of sides. Yet, no matter what side a person was on, no one was farther than anyone else from the host at the head of the table.

Children were skipping and giggling as their elders played chase and hide and seek. Those at the table were of every age and color. And, as Wil looked closer, he saw faces he knew, Rochelle and Franklin, his mom, Steve and Wendy. Even Hope was there. He didn't know some of the people, but they seemed to know him and they liked him. They were eating and singing and laughing and dancing and celebrating. Everything was centered around the one at the head of the table who was their best friend, yet he looked like a king. The king looked directly at Wil and said, "Come here, my child, and share in my love."

As Wil reached for the doorknob, he heard sounds coming from behind the door to his left. It wasn't a beautiful sound, like what was coming from the banquet room, but it was a familiar sound. It drew him. Wil took a step to the left to peer through the window of the other door. This muddy reddish-colored door was larger than the white door. It was also coated with jewels and fine carvings, but its window wasn't as clear. As he looked through the hazy window, he began to realize he was hungry. Perhaps it was the thought of all the food he had seen at the party. But that didn't explain why, all of a sudden, he began to feel lonely. Staring through the window of the wide door, he tried to make out the figures in the distance. They were the source of the familiar sound. When the scene finally crystallized into view, his heart began to pound and his face reddened with a rush of blood. His fists grew so tight he had to forcibly relax them when his fingernails bit into his palms.

There, in the distance, he could see his mom tied to a chair. Behind her was his dad. His brother, Mike, lay on the floor cowering in fear, his forearms protecting his bloodied face. Wil's dad was berating his mom; another woman clung to his dad's arm begging for his affection. Behind them, Wil could see his secretary, Beth, limp, moaning as Kathreen drew back her clenched fist to strike her again. And there, inside the door, directly in front of him, lying on a small plain table, was a gun.

He opened the door. The atmosphere was damp but he couldn't decide if it was extremely hot or extremely cold. As he approached the gun, he felt as though his strength was oozing out of him. His mom's empty screams and Beth's heart-wrenching cries grew louder.

He had to get the gun, but he could barely lift his arms. Maybe his hunger had grown to such a point that he didn't have the energy. And somehow, each time he reached for the gun, it was a little farther away.

The agonizing weeping of his mom, and now others, grew louder. Sadness and helplessness and loneliness began to overshadow him. He tried to turn around. Perhaps if he could get some food from the other room he would be able to regain his strength. But he could no longer move. Suddenly he was in the room with his dad, his mom writhing in pain next to him, Beth pleading for Kathreen to stop.

His dad was coming directly toward him, fist raised, his eyes mocking, burning pits of hate. Wil tried to move, but he was tied to a chair. Wil forgot about the gun when his dad's fist smashed into his cheek, knocking over his chair and slamming his head against the stone floor. Something had happened, though. His hands were no longer restrained and the gun was within arm's reach. Beyond the gun, his father was kicking his mom, who had curled into a fetal position.

Wil grabbed for the gun. He had it, but he couldn't pick it up. It was there, but it wasn't. He rolled over to defend himself as his dad kicked him in the side. He was struggling. He was fighting to escape. The sounds of Beth's screams and his mom's crying grew louder. He began to kick and—

"Dr. Wilson. Wil. Dr. Wilson. Wake up."

CHAPTER 39

Changes

Wil managed to get a few hours of sleep after his dream. In the morning he actually felt better, though he shuddered when he thought about the dream. *It must have been the drugs*, he thought. He told no one.

The room was quiet. The morning light flooded the room. Hope sat reading in her corner next to the windows.

Wil broke the silence. "You and Mom must have had a lot to talk about."

Hope looked up, having heard only the last part of his statement. "What?"

"I said, you and Mom must have had a lot to talk about last night."

"We did."

Wil shifted his hips, trying to find a more comfortable position. He was not successful. He tried to concentrate on something other than his pain. They heard the duty officer ask Hope's bodyguard to cover for him while he went to use the rest room.

"So what did you talk about?"

Hope began to answer but stopped when she heard a man's gravelly voice address the nurse at the station, "Dr. Wilson is in room 548, right?"

"Yes," responded the nurse.

"I decided I would deliver his breakfast personally this morning."

"Oh?" The nurse sounded hesitant since she didn't recognize the employee. But his uniform, hospital ID badge, and breakfast tray qualified him. She decided to be helpful. "He really likes the chocolate Ensure."

"I'll keep that in mind."

Though not enthusiastic about talking with anyone, Wil welcomed the diversion of an unexpected visit from the dietician. Hope welcomed the reprieve from Wil's questions and returned to her book.

The security guard in the chair outside Wil's room let the dietary employee enter. It wasn't until the door clicked shut that the guard's curiosity changed to concern.

Hope looked up from her book to greet their visitor and her face turned ashen.

By the time the security guard heard the meal tray hit the floor, the door had already been secured and a note had been slipped under the door. The note read, "Open the door and I will kill them." The guard retreated and called for reinforcements.

"Art Middleton?" Hope gasped as she stared at her informant, who was dressed as a hospital dietary worker. "I thought you were dead."

The H&K 45, which had been hidden under the tray cover, was now pointed at Hope. The intruder correctly assumed he didn't need to worry about any sudden movements from Wil.

"I thought you were dead," Hope repeated.

"Wrong." The voice was flat, clear, and female.

"Kathreen!" Wil gasped, tense and breathless.

Kathreen kept the gun aimed at Hope as she spoke in a

venomous tone. "And, Mrs. Wilson, I'd suggest you just stay put. Otherwise, my gun might mess up your cute little hairdo."

Kathreen used her free hand to unbutton the top of her shirt. Then, reaching into her shirt, she grasped the bottom of the mask and peeled it from her neck to the top of her head, shaking her hair free. Her face was matted pink from the adhesive.

"I'm glad I won't have to wear that again," said Kathreen.

"You killed Art Middleton?" said Hope in disbelief.

"And to think you led me to him. In fact, if I hadn't bumped into old Artie after he left the note on your car, I wouldn't have come up with this handy disguise."

Hope thought back to the last time she had seen her informant.

"And, while things didn't work out the way I'd planned, the disguise did get me past that gorilla outside." Kathreen motioned to the door before tossing the mask at Wil, who flinched and then moaned because of the pain the movement caused.

"A little sore, are we?" asked Kathreen, not taking her eyes or aim off Hope. The last time she was in this position the crazy woman had thrown a lamp at her and a bullet had nicked her arm. "Well, isn't that just too bad."

"What are you doing?" Hope implored. "Why would you come here?"

"You have something that belongs to me."

"What are you talking about?" Wil's rush of adrenaline didn't cut his pain, but it did increase his strength. "There are two officers outside that door. How in the world do you think you're going to get out of here?"

"Frankly, Doc, you have other things to worry about. A couple days ago I had to leave behind four million dollars.

You and your sweetie pie are now going to get it for me. The other option is that I will shoot you. Perhaps I'll start with your other leg—and then your hands and then maybe your lungs so you can still curse me while your wife listens to you suffer as you die in front of her."

"You are a sick woman," Hope said in disgust.

"At least I'd be rid of you once and for all. I would much rather be the one to cause you to suffer than merely stand by and let the cancer have all the fun."

"What do you want us to do?" asked Wil.

"Simple. I want my four million dollars and I want a police escort to my plane at Arlington Community Airport. And," she directed her gaze at Wil, "if I do not land safely in Havana with your wife in twelve hours, she will have a hole in her head and you will have the privilege of knowing you allowed your wife to be tortured and killed before yourself died."

"Cuba?" asked Hope, surprised.

"Friends from my days with the President—before your worthless husband messed things up."

"But—" Wil needed assurances.

"Don't worry. I'll let her fly back to the States. I don't want to kill her in Cuba. Killing her before I left the States wouldn't be that big a deal, but your wife's blood on Cuban soil might create a problem. Besides, by then, I'll be ready to let bygones be bygones."

Kathreen glanced at the door as the guards shouted that the room was surrounded.

"Those fools don't know when to give up do they?" She knew they had read the rest of the note she'd slipped under the door, which informed them of her plans and demands.

"I might not live that long," said Wil.

"Pity. Then who would take care of your little brat? You

see, either I get my money or you both die. It's that simple. Besides, don't you want to know whether your wife lives or dies? I suggest you hang on. Now, pick up the phone and make the call."

Wil tried to reach the phone.

"Give him the phone," barked Kathreen.

Hope stepped toward the phone and picked up the receiver. "Who's he supposed to call?"

"I suggest your bank."

"But how are we supposed to get the money to you?"

"One step at a time, Sherlock." Kathreen was growing weary of Hope's questions. "Now shut up and dial the number."

"Call Larry at First Union," Wil told Hope. "He can take care of it."

"What's the number?"

Will dictated the number. "I have it memorized from the last time I went through this," he said.

"Wil?"

"It will be okay," Wil assured her.

Hope began to dial, then stopped, letting her hand fall to her side.

"Hope?" said Wil.

Hope hung up the phone and turned slowly to her dying and confused husband. "I'm sorry, Wil. I won't call."

Wil sank back on the bed, bewildered and silent, his energy ebbing rapidly.

"I'm not going to take it anymore," said Hope, gritting her teeth.

Hope turned to Kathreen. "This charade ends now. The way I see it, you shoot me and you lose. You shoot Wil and you lose. I fully expect you to kill me in Cuba anyway, so I'm not going for the ride. Look here. These are my terms."

"What?" Kathreen hissed. "Terms?" She sneered.

"Here is what you are going to do," stated Hope.

"You are forgetting something, sweetie. I have the gun."

"And you won't use it. The way I see it, I'm your only ticket out of this room alive. You shoot me; the police shoot you. And, as pathetic and miserable a creature as you are, I know one thing. You do not want to die."

"Are you saying you do?"

"No, I'm saying you don't."

Kathreen brushed her off. "I'd recommend you shut up and dial the number."

"No." Hope was defiant. "Shoot me."

"Don't push me. You listen—"

"No. You listen to me. My husband is dying. I know my son will be well cared for. And I am, quite simply, not afraid to die."

Hope's confidence in her last statement surprised even Wil. He looked at his wife. The anxiety and fear in her face, present when she had confronted Kathreen with the lamp, were non-existent. This time, Hope's face was self-assured, resolved, peaceful. He was baffled by her next words.

"Last night I finally came to terms with my Creator and, if I am going to meet Him today, that is just fine. I figure, all things considered, today is as good a day as any. Besides, there's no way—and I guarantee it—if you shoot me and I go to meet my Maker, that you will ever leave this room alive. Are you prepared to meet your Maker?"

Kathreen was cornered.

Wil didn't know what his atheistic wife was talking about.

"Nice speech, honey," said Kathreen. "But you might want to reconsider your options after this." Kathreen yelled over her shoulder. "Okay, you bunch of cowboys out there. Don't try anything foolish. You are going to hear a shot and a scream. Don't panic. I will not have killed anyone. Hope here has just volunteered to experience the pain her husband felt when I shot him in the knee."

"No . . . no!" pleaded Wil, turning and raising himself on one elbow.

"Got it?" Kathreen yelled toward the door making sure the security force on the other side understood. "Enter the room, and someone will die."

Kathreen took their silence as acquiescence.

"Are you ready?" she said to Hope as she pointed the barrel at Hope's leg.

"You're not going to shoot me, Kathreen."

"Wrong." The sound of the gun in the small room was deafening.

Hope's leg collapsed under her as the bullet sliced the outside of her leg just above the knee then created a crater in the wall behind her. She screamed and fell at the foot of the empty bed near the window.

Wil pulled himself up, wrenching in pain, to verify that Hope was not dead, and then collapsed in exhaustion and agony.

"All here and accounted for," yelled Kathreen over her shoulder. The gun was still pointed at Hope. "Are you ready to do it my way now?" Kathreen was flushed, her eyes flashing with anger.

Swallowing her pain, Hope climbed up the end of the bed and stood. Blood oozed from her leg.

Wil lay pale and silent. Hope's chest heaved as she struggled to remain vertical.

"No," gasped Hope in unyielding defiance. "Nothing has changed."

Kathreen's tensed body shook, as her red face grew darker. "Nothing has changed?"

Hope swallowed, her will barely holding the pain at bay. "You have two choices. Kill us and die yourself, or lay down that weapon. I'll make sure you get out of here alive."

Kathreen glared, her teeth clenched.

"Do you want to die?" Hope screamed.

This was not an option Kathreen had considered. Dying was something others did, not she. Perhaps it was Kathreen's arrogant optimism leading her to believe she might be given another opportunity after her arrest. Perhaps it was the inescapable reality that Hope's assessment of her fear of death was true. Regardless, Kathreen knew Hope was correct about her chances of getting out of there alive.

"So, what is it, Kathreen? Are you ready to die today?"

Hope's synopsis reverberated in Kathreen's mind. She did not want to die, but refused to concede. One option was killing them and then surrendering before the police had a chance to shoot her. She coolly inspected Wil and Hope.

With her gun pointed in Hope's direction, and keeping one eye on Hope, Kathreen turned to sit in the chair by the door. Seated on her puny throne, Kathreen rested her arms on the sides of the chair, allowing the gun's muzzle to dip as she took a contemplative breath. Her diabolic countenance was rigid with anger.

"You know, Hope, you are re—"

From behind Hope came a horrendous cracking sound as a SWAT officer, hanging from a rapelling rope, bounced off the window, the strength of the glass too much for his weight. The shaken officer now dangled helplessly outside the window. Hope stood frozen between him and Kathreen. While the officer fought to steady himself enough to get off a shot, Kathreen stood and aimed.

Kathreen's movement broke Hope's immobility and she dived for cover behind Wil's bed. As Kathreen squeezed the trigger, an explosion at the door startled Kathreen. Her shot shattered the window and hit the officer in the leg, setting his suspended body twirling like a marionette.

Kathreen spun around and fired at the door, which now hung limply from its hinges. Before she could fire a second shot, the officer suspended from the rope managed to steady himself enough to aim his quivering revolver. The recoil from his shot sent him spinning but his bullet hit Kathreen in the shoulder. As Kathreen fell toward the door, the door came off its hinges, propelled by an officer using a wheeled four-drawer filing cabinet as a battering ram. Kathreen collided with the door, which sent her reeling onto Wil's bed. Wil groaned in agony as Kathreen's battered body fell, full force, onto his chest. The officer released his battering ram and looked for his target, who was now behind him. He whirled around and froze. Kathreen was ready for him. She was leaning against Wil's bed with her gun aimed at the officer's head. He didn't stand a chance.

The instant before Kathreen squeezed the trigger, Wil shoved Kathreen, expending his last ounce of energy. Her shot hit the officer in the center of his bulletproof vest. The blast drove him against the wall and rendered him unconscious. As he fell, his gun dropped to the floor next to Hope.

Kathreen, shaking with fury and gasping for breath, held her weapon to Wil's head. She was bloodied but not beaten. "Anybody moves and I'll blow Wilson's head off." She was yelling to those in the hallway. "Do you hear me?"

The silence after the chaos was haunting.

Kathreen continued. "If I even hear anything that sounds like movement, Wilson is dead. Now, here are my—"

Hope pulled the trigger. Kathreen screamed and dropped her gun as her leg shattered beneath her. An officer yelled "Now," and two policemen rushed into the room and restrained Kathreen. The policemen were followed by two paramedics and a nurse.

Hope's adrenaline and endorphins finally succumbed to the pain and loss of blood. With one last moan she passed out.

"Dr. Wilson. Dr. Wilson," said the nurse tending to Wil, who had lost consciousness after exhausting his energy to push Kathreen.

Wil moaned.

"I think he's going to be all right," said the nurse, who reached for the blood pressure cuff and began to take his vitals.

"We are going to need four gurneys in here and we need them now," said the paramedic who was assisting the officer dangling from the rope.

Within minutes, Hope, Kathreen, and the two officers had been transferred to the emergency room. Wil passed out again and would not wake for hours.

CHAPTER 40

Love, Hope, and Will

Hope was treated in the emergency room, where the doctors told her she was lucky the bullet had only nicked her femur. They stitched up the wound, put a soft cast on her leg, and transferred her to the other bed in Wil's room. The doctors were convinced that time, rather than surgery, was the best treatment, but they wanted to observe Hope for a couple of days. The expectation was that in three to four weeks she would be back to normal.

Wil's condition was deteriorating rapidly, but he still refused to be doped up on pain medications. He did agree to take a short-acting sleeping pill as long as it wasn't the kind he had taken the night he'd had the dream.

That night they both slept well. By morning, Wil's mind was the clearest it had been in days, though the pain was back with a vengeance. Soon after breakfast, which Hope had merely nibbled and Wil had pushed away, Steve and Wendy arrived with Betty and little Steven. They made known their collective relief that the Kathreen episode was over. She was finally in police custody.

"For good, with any luck," said Betty.

As noon approached, Betty announced it was time to take Steven home for lunch and a nap. Steve and Wendy had left an hour earlier after a brief visit from Franklin.

As Hope and Wil lay in their beds, they listened to CNN anchor Roger Hemming sum up the day's top stories. Kathreen Steele, who was still in critical condition, would be arraigned as soon as her condition improved. Hope's standoff with Kathreen had drifted into the realm of legend via the rumor mill and courtesy of the hospital personnel who had been interviewed the previous evening.

"In other news," said Hemming, "the investigation into alleged corruption at Freedom Airways and Advanced Chemical Products has intensified, even as the board of directors at Freedom Airways announced the removal of Brad Stinson from all board and operational responsibilities associated with . . ."

Hope and Wil already knew this story from Connie, who had stopped by that morning. Though Brad and his co-conspirators vehemently denied any wrongdoing, it was doubtful they would see freedom for a number of years. Tying the knot of their noose was the confession of the plant manager at Advanced Chemical Products' refinery where the corrosive that brought down Freedom Airways' Flight 2652 was manufactured. The manager's recounting of his meeting with Brad and ACP's vice-president of product development resulted in criminal charges against both. It also started an avalanche of civil and criminal actions against each company. Though many of the top officers of ACP and Freedom were genuinely unaware of the corruption, their liability would not likely be diminished by their ignorance.

After lunch, both Wil and Hope drifted to sleep. The sound of dishes breaking on the hallway floor, followed by the cursing of a nurse, woke them.

As they lay there, adequately rested and alone, Wil asked the question that had been nagging him since the middle of the Kathreen episode the previous day.

"So, what was that about you and your Creator?"

"I was wondering if you were going to ask."

"Either that was the best bluffing you've ever done or there's something you haven't told me."

"Wil . . . hmm . . . there's something I haven't told you."

"And that would be?"

Hope struggled out of bed and, with the aid of a walker, hobbled over to the chair next to Wil's bed.

"Wil. . . I know you'll have a hard time believing this. It's even strange to hear myself say it. Please understand, it isn't a whim. God knows my disdain for Christianity ran as deep as yours."

"Hah! And?"

Hope swallowed. "One of the things that has happened to me . . ." She thought about her feeble beginning and started over. "As you know, I overheard your conversations with Steve about the resurrection and with your mom about her faith. I also had a long conversation with Franklin and then last night with your mom—"

Wil interrupted her. "You've been talking to Mom and Franklin about this?"

"Yes."

"Enemies in my midst," Wil sighed.

"Wil, they are not your enemies, and you know it."

Wil waited, anticipation masking his pain.

"For the first time in my life, I decided to look at things objectively rather than through my whatever-the-case-may-be-Jesus-was-not-who-He-said-He-was lenses."

Benedict Arnold was about to justify her behavior.

"Wil, I've given my life to Jesus. I've accepted Him as my Lord and Savior."

"Geez, Hope! Not you, too!"

"Wil—"

263

"No!" said Wil as Hope tried to talk. "I can't believe it. I'm on my deathbed and you tell me you've become a Christian." Wil was hurt and angry. He temporarily forgot how painful it was to speak. "Hope . . . how could you choose this moment to announce you've become a Christian? All my life I've been fighting that awful, pathetic religion of my father. I only have a few days to live, and now the woman I love with all my heart tells me she has abandoned me . . . given her life—whatever that's supposed to mean—to the very myth I have spent my whole life hating. Geez, Hope. I can't believe what you're saying."

"Wil. It's true."

"What's true? That you have just made Benedict Arnold look like an American patriot? What? That you have abandoned me on my deathbed? What's true? What in God's name is true?" Wil's intensity and volume left him gasping for air.

"Wil." Hope wasn't hurt. She gently touched his hand. "We all have to make a choice. I made mine. Somehow I had justified rejecting Jesus, thinking I possessed a superior knowledge to many of the most intelligent people who have ever drawn breath. Well, I don't. Though there are brilliant people on both sides of this fence, I finally admitted, whatever side one is on, it ultimately comes down to faith. Everybody has faith. It's just a matter of in what or in whom. I finally gave Jesus and His claims a fair chance. Nothing makes more sense than Jesus' resurrection and that Jesus was who He said He was."

"But, Hope—come on!"

"But nothing." Anger flared briefly and quickly faded. "You know I've never been the religious type. But I couldn't deny the emptiness in my heart any longer."

"Emptiness? Boy, that makes me feel great!"

Hope ignored his sarcasm. She knew Wil was aware the emptiness had nothing to do with him. "Since I acknowledged that Jesus died for me and I asked God to forgive my sins, things have changed."

"Changed." Wil said cynically.

"Wil, I have peace. For the first time in my life, I have peace."

"Peace!" Wil spat out, turning his face from her. As he lay there he recalled Hope's confident expression as she faced down Kathreen. He looked back at her. "But, Hope—"

"Yes, Wil—peace." Hope stroked Wil's hand.

"Hope. It's too much." Wil's shoulders slumped back weakly against the bed. "I'm tired."

"I know." Hope laid her hand on his moist forehead. "Oh, Wil, the last thing I want to do is hurt you … and I really don't want you to think I'm badgering you. But Wil, I only get a few more hours with you. I have to say these things. If the tables were turned, I would want you to say them to me. I love you so much."

Wil looked into her eyes. Intense emotion and love were shining from Hope's face. Her motives were pure.

"Wil," Hope said, "it isn't too late."

Oh brother, he thought. *This is getting irritating.* He was not going to change sides now. As much as he loved her, he could only conclude she was weak. He was going to be strong. *What good are convictions if one doesn't have the courage to uphold them?*

"Wil, please, listen to what I have to say."

He would not. He knew what she was going to say. An enemy often knows his adversary better than the enemy knows himself. So it was with Wil and Christianity. But things were now so confused. Hope was not his adversary. She was his love. It was this cursed Jesus and Christianity he hated.

"Wait, Hope." Wil held up his hand and took a minute to regain some strength. It was his turn. He knew it would take all the energy he had in him to say what he was going to say. It had to be said. Love and integrity were at issue and he was not dying with those two issues compromised.

Hope waited.

"Hope, I love you." He took a breath. "My life with you could not have been better. You are my love and always will be. Nothing will ever change that."

"I know, Wil," said Hope quietly.

"And it is because of this that I can say, from the bottom of my heart, I'm absolutely happy you've found something you believe in. I hope it brings you all the joy this life can provide. I want nothing more for you."

Hope squeezed his hand.

"But," Wil paused, knowing the permanence of his statements, yet full of compassion for his wife, "my darling, my dear sweet Hope, I do not believe Jesus was who he said he was. I also don't believe there is a heaven and I certainly don't believe in some kind of judgment by God … or in hell."

Hope drew a breath to speak but decided to remain silent.

Wil went on. "I actually think I hate Jesus for what he did and who he claimed to be and for this travesty called Christianity, which my dad—"

"Wil," Hope interrupted him. "For one time in your life, get over it!" She couldn't bear the thought of being separated from Wil again. His impending death was inescapably real. If there was life after death, beyond being in the memories of other people who also die, the thought of their being separated for all eternity haunted her, cut her so deeply she could hardly bear the thought.

Her words were soaked in sincerity. "You have fought against your dad long enough. I know, and you know, the resurrection is the only thing that really makes sense. I believe you also know, in your heart, as I have finally admitted, that God's love for you in Jesus is true. Do not leave me again because of your hatred for your father."

Wil was stirred but did not respond.

Hope's imploring words settled on their target as she added in desperation, "Do you want to spend eternity where I will be, in heaven with your heavenly Father who loves you, or in hell with your dad?"

Wil swallowed, trying to moisten his dry throat. "I told you, I do not believe Jesus—"

"But what if you are wrong?" Hope was not judgmental. She was a desperate wife, pleading with her husband who had just confidently stated he would return safely from an ill-fated battle.

"Hope, darling," Wil did not want to continue. "I'm sorry my decision causes you to be so upset, but my love for you is so great that it requires I be honest with you."

Hope's gaze now included tears of compassion, remorse, and helplessness, which began to flow down her cheeks. All she could breathe was, "I love you, Wil. I love you so much."

"I know."

Hope's voice softened. "But Wil, it isn't about what I want. It is about truth and integrity."

Wil looked away as his thoughts turned inward. *Hasn't she heard me? If she only knew that ever since Scott's and Rochelle's funerals I've been thinking about my beliefs more intensely than ever before in my life. I've even been thinking about my unanticipated death. I never dreamed the next—the third—funeral would be mine. I wonder what my funeral will be like?* Wil shook his head. *Why am I defending this position I've held all my life. Why? What if . . .* he could barely bring the words to mind . . . *the resurrection is true?*

"Wil?" Hope brought Wil out of his introspection.

"Hope," said Wil, raising his eyes to meet hers, "I don't want to believe in Jesus."

Hope's words were bathed in love. "Wil, there is nothing more that Franklin or Steve or Betty or I can say or do. It's up to you." Her tenderness penetrated his wall. "But whatever you do, nothing will ever change my love for you."

Wil began to weep and so did Hope as she clasped Wil's hand and lifted it to her lips. Wil reached across with his other hand and caressed her cheek. They looked at one another—memorizing contours and colors, reliving moments from the past, thinking. Wil let his arm drop. Hope leaned forward from her chair to rest her head by her lover's hand, still held tightly in hers.

It was the nurse's entry an hour later that woke Hope. She lifted her head, smiling.

Wil's eyes were wide open, his stare empty, his lips slightly parted.

Hope released Wil's cool, unfeeling hand. The nurse compassionately touched Hope's shoulder before initiating an unnecessary routine, attempting to take his vitals. He was gone.

And Hope wept.

~

Yesterday is gone.
Tomorrow never arrives.
Today is what you have.

And death will come.

But, as today determines yesterday,
And on today does tomorrow depend,
So today can shape death's tomorrow,
From yesterday 'til the end.

~

About the Author

Prior to the release of his first book, *Wil's Bones*, Kevin Bowen owned a health care consulting business, owned and operated a bed and breakfast, and managed several skilled nursing facilities. He has worked for an engineering firm, worked in a soup kitchen/shelter in Los Angeles County, and served as a missionary in India.

Since writing *Wil's Bones*, Kevin has spoken to groups ranging in size from two to twelve hundred and as diverse as a mystery club in Oregon, a public high school English class in Georgia, a senior citizens reading group in Arizona, and a college chapel service in Arkansas. He has also appeared on various radio and TV programs and done numerous book-signing events around the country. Kevin thoroughly enjoys dialoguing with people, both those who agree and disagree with him, regarding issues of faith. He hopes his writing will continue to stimulate such conversation.

Kevin has a Master of Divinity from Fuller Seminary; a Master in Health Care Management from California State University, Los Angeles; and a Bachelor of Arts in History from the University of Washington. He lives in the Victorian seaport of Port Townsend, Washington, with his wife, Ruth, their two children, three cats, and six ducks.

A Note From the Author

I have been told that, in order to maximize the sales of my books, I need to pick a desired audience and a specific genre, and then stick with it. I have not done that. Instead, I hope that my writing appeals to a wide variety of people who want a good story, enjoy adventure and twists, and like having their minds provoked to think about issues that are much more important than a few brief hours of reading.

My first book, *Wil's Bones*, received positive and supportive reviews. More gratifying to me, however, was that many reviewers, who sincerely liked the book, had a hard time classifying it. Some called it a suspense thriller. Some called it a mystery. A few called it Christian fiction. Most called it general fiction. One reviewer called it a historical romance. That one truly surprised me.

Even more pleasing, though, was that my book appealed to both Christian and non-Christian readers, albeit for sometimes opposite reasons. In a world that fosters unproductive conflict between these two fundamentally different groups, it was nice to hear that my writing bridged this gap without downplaying the existence of the gap.

It has been said that fiction writers can't be trusted because they make things up. This is partially true, and it is important that the distinction between fiction and nonfiction be maintained, lest fantasy be presented as fact. It is, however, also important to recognize that, though fiction is fiction, fiction can also present ideas, facts, issues, and truth in a way no other form of literature can.

Finally, in my opinion, fiction is seldom written solely for entertainment purposes, and fiction writers who say they do not have an agenda in their writing are not telling the truth. I am no exception. In my case, though I sincerely hope you enjoyed *The Third Funeral*, I also hope that the book has provoked thoughts about our mortality and the need for reconciliation.

Thank you for reading *The Third Funeral*.

Sincerely,
Kevin Bowen

Mr. Bowen welcomes your comments. He can be reached via e-mail at TheThirdFuneral@engagepublishing.com. Letters can be addressed to him care of Engage Publishing, P.O. Box 1452, Port Townsend, WA 98368.

Other Works by Kevin Bowen

Wil's Bones
(ISBN 1930892128, October 2000)

Archaeologist Wil Wilson makes a discovery that turns the world upside down. When the President of the United States grows concerned that Wil's find could threaten his re-election prospects, a cover-up ensues. Driven by a concern for truth and his personal disdain for Christianity, Wil goes public with his discovery. The President is furious. Spin-doctors shift into overdrive, Congress calls for hearings, and a world religion is on the brink of collapse. With the FBI in pursuit, Wil flees for his life . . . and then things get intense.

Wil's Bones is a fast-paced adventure thriller that reviewers have compared to Grisham, Cussler, and Clancy, as well as to the *Left Behind* series. *Christianity Today* called Wil's Bones "an entertaining page-turner." The *Midwest Book Review* said, "*Wil's Bones* is the type of book that is almost impossible to put down. . . . The plot is fantastic; the characters are engaging. . . . A great read."

Wil's Bones will entertain you and cause you to think . . . What if?

And Introducing
The exciting sequel to *Wil's Bones* and *The Third Funeral*

Faith
(ISBN 1930892160, August 2004)

After two men confess to faking miracles on Elijah Matheson's television show, investigative journalist Hope Wilson exonerates the scandal-ridden televangelist of this specific accusation of fraud. When the diamond-adorned

Matheson announces that Hope has converted to Christianity, Hope's *New York Times* editor and the police begin to question her motives and objectivity.

Infuriated by their suspicions, Hope takes a hiatus from their recriminations and leaves for Israel to deal with some personal matters. While in Jerusalem, Hope has a harrowing experience following a terrorist attack. In the aftermath, Hope befriends a Palestinian who has experienced incredible hardships because of his religious beliefs.

When Hope returns to the States she discovers a note from the two men who were involved in the miracles on Matheson's show. Unprepared for what lies ahead, Hope becomes entangled in a web of murder, international conspiracy, money laundering, and fundamental questions of faith.

————

Henry points to the glass-enclosed case that everyone, including Mr. Wilkins, passes by every day.

"I don't know how long it's been there. I just noticed it," Henry tells us.

At first, all I see are the usual trophies: WiHi's 1994 Sectional Wrestling Trophy, 1953 City-Wide Baseball win, 2011 Girls' Varsity Basketball champs, Debate Team Champions of 1966.

At last, though, the fakes become apparent. Once I notice them, it's impossible not to stare at the two "added" to the case. They're the type of trophies a little kid gets after soccer season, but the first one is more menacing than anything from a recreational center league. A thin rope loops around the girl's neck. The other end is attached to the shelf above so that the trophy hangs. The original nameplate has been replaced with "Roving Reporter."

The second fake is scarier. The player's head is chopped

* *

Books by Carol M. Tanzman

from Harlequin TEEN

dancergirl

CIRCLE OF SILENCE

CAROL M. TANZMAN

HARLEQUIN®

entertain, enrich, inspire™

Recycling programs
for this product may
not exist in your area.

ISBN-13: 978-0-373-21062-6

CIRCLE OF SILENCE

www.HarlequinTEEN.com

Printed in U.S.A.

For Jack, Liana and Dylan

with love and gratitude

Bad idea, bad idea, bad idea…

The words keep time with my pounding heart. Dashing, darting…hurtling forward. It's like a nightmare. Chasing after the school bus, the train, a minivan. No matter how fast I run, I can't get there in time. I'm left stranded, alone, surrounded by abandoned warehouses, darkened streets and smelly drunks…. This isn't a dream. I know where I'm going. I just can't move fast enough.

Jagger. Jags! I asked you not to do this. Begged you…

My cheeks feel wet. How did I not see the approaching storm? But the streets aren't slick and the pitter-patter of rain does not mingle with the sound of my feet slapping against rough cobblestones.

I touch my face. Taste the droplet. Salty…

That's when I know I'll be too late. Instinct, ESP or maybe just plain terror breaks through. Because it's my fault. I pushed too hard; it went too far.

Whatever terrible thing I am about to see, I could have stopped. No matter what anyone tells me, no matter who insists, "You can't blame yourself," I will always know, deep down, that it's a lie.

SEPTEMBER—OCTOBER

1

My sweaty palm pushes the Media Center door open on the second day of senior year. The single most important class of my life is about to begin.

"Don't look so worried, Val," Marci tells me. "We got this covered."

I give my best friend since eighth grade a pained look. Sunny Marci. Always seeing the bright side. Except this time, she's especially naive. There's no way it's a sure thing.

Together, we move to the table Mr. Carleton assigned to us. Yesterday, he divided the class into two permanent *Campus News* teams. First order of business today: each crew votes for producer. The job I covet. The position I worked really hard, during both sophomore and junior years at Washington Irving High School, to get. If mine, it could propel me straight into the college of my dreams.

I steal a glance at my competition. Raul Ortega. His dark chocolate eyes take everything in. Taller by about three inches than me, he wears his hair in a brush cut that tops a solid body. Raul's definitely the guy you want on your side in a fight. Not that he's a hothead. On the contrary, the dude's cool. He knows his way around TV Production almost as well as I do. Exactly the reason he might get more votes than me.

He feels my look, turns. Grins nervously. Oh yeah, Raul wants it, too. The real question is: which of us does the group want? Besides Marci Lee, the team consists of Omar Bryant and Henry Dillon. With five votes, there won't be a tie.

Mr. Carleton takes attendance and then says, "Okay, folks, you know what to do."

For a moment, our table is silent. Afraid that I'll come off as either too confident or too bossy, I resist the urge to take charge. Raul's busy giving the other two boys meaningful glances. A sinking feeling hits the pit of my stomach. Did he talk to them last night? Make them promise to vote for him?

That would totally suck.

Marci jumps in. Energetically, she tears a piece of paper into five pieces. "You all have something to write with?"

Henry whips out a pen. A classic overachiever, he skipped both second and third grades, won a national award for drawing in eighth and captains the chess team.

"I've got extras!"

Underneath the curtain of brown hair that covers his forehead, Henry shoots Marci puppy dog eyes. He's been quietly crushing on her for at least a year. Quietly—since she's dating a football player. Doesn't matter to Henry. He'd probably faint if Marci actually kissed him.

Omar extends a well-manicured hand. "I forgot a pencil."

"Forgot?" Marci counters. "Or never had one in the first place?"

He wriggles his eyebrows. She indulges him a laugh before handing over a slip of paper.

At first glance, Omar Bryant's a diva. When he was eight, he put on a sparkly cape for Halloween and refused to take it off until Christmas. Didn't care what anyone said—then or now. But dig deeper and you'll hit the sensitive soul of a true artist. Everyone in *Campus News* knows he has a great eye and a steady hand. When he gets behind the lens, his focus is total.

Marci hands out the rest of the paper. Names are scribbled. Without a word, we all fold the slips into tiny squares, as if that can disguise who voted for whom. Five tiny bundles are tossed onto the table.

"I'll count." Carefully, Marci unfolds the first piece of paper. "Valerie Gaines."

I keep my face neutral because that doesn't mean much. It's either my vote—or hers. The second paper has Raul's name on it. So does the third.

A wave of disappointment hits. I *told* Marci I might not win. Not if it's boys vs. girls—with the boys outnumbering us.

Marci gives me a cheerful look after unwrapping the fourth vote. "ValGal."

Obviously, that's hers. The score's tied. Raul leans forward, triumph etched across his face. I can practically see the writing inside the final piece of paper.

Raul Ortega.

"Valerie," Marci says.

"What?"

She waves the slip. "The last vote's for you. You won!"

The shock on my face is genuine. As is the surprise in Raul's eyes. Marci shoots me an "I told you" smile before prancing to the whiteboard. She grabs an orange marker and writes *Valerie Gaines, B Team Producer.*

Mr. Carleton nods. "Team A, you have a winner?"

Scott Jenkins raises his hand. His stick-up sand-colored hair and square jaw make him look skinnier than he actually is. Given who's on A Team, he's the person I'd vote for, too.

Scott's good but I'm better. I work harder. I care more. I won't ever let my team down.

The teacher heaves himself out of his chair. "Good choices, folks. Now listen up! Rule review so you can't say you didn't know 'em when you break 'em. Each show consists of four segments, no more, no less, interspersed with anchor ins and outs. Sixteen minutes total. Remember to look for the angle. What's the way into the story? Teams alternate weekly broadcasts. B Team's up first, then A."

Which doesn't make sense. You'd think A Team would start because, well, it's first in the alphabet. But that's how Mr. Carleton thinks. Roundabout. And backward.

"Last three rules. First—" he holds up an index finger "—a Question Sheet must be filled out before every interview." Two fingers go up. "Rude behavior or fooling around in hallways when you're shooting Will. Not. Be. Tolerated. Third. Do not open a case unless it's on a table or the ground because equipment in said case *will* fall out. If it breaks, your folks pay. Trust me, they Will. Not. Be. Happy."

Mr. Carleton, a portly African-American man, keeps his head shaved smoothly and his desk immaculate, proof positive that he's a fan of the "less is more" theory. Tightly edited sequences, one-word sentences.

He continues with basic equipment sign-out procedures. When he's done, he glances at the clock. "Okay, teams, with whatever time's left, start planning your first broadcast."

Excited, I pull out my *Campus News* notebook, but before anyone can say a word, the door flies open. Every head turns.

"Omigod!" Marcis hisses. "What's *he* doing here?"

My heart takes a nosedive straight into my stomach.

Jagger Voorham! Pouty, rocker-boy lips, hazel eyes that change color according to his mood, and yes, supercute. Slacker Jagger crosses the room without bothering to look at anyone, including me. As if he doesn't know I'd be front and center.

He hands Mr. Carleton a mustard-yellow Schedule Change form. The teacher frowns.

"Don't worry, Marci," I whisper. "Carleton'll never let him into the class. Jags didn't take Intro. He can't be in Advanced."

Resolutely, I tap the notebook and try to discuss stories for the first broadcast. But everyone's focus is on the quiet conversation at the front of the room. Finally the teacher nods.

"B Team!" Mr. Carleton points a finger at Jagger. "New member."

Do something, Marci mouths.

Like what? Throw myself under a bus? Jump off the Brooklyn Bridge? Drop the class?

Jagger saunters over. I look down, refusing to give him the satisfaction of acknowledging his existence. There's no way I want him—or anyone else in the room—to see the tears of frustration forming hot in my eyes.

How could Jagger do this to me? My triumphant moment—ruined!

My BFF, a four-foot-eleven, barely one-hundred-pound Korean dynamo, kicks me. I don't have to look at Marci to know what she's thinking.

Who wants to deal with Jagger all year?

That's the moment the bell rings. Everyone in class jumps up, as if electroshocked into obedience. Mr. Carleton gestures. "Stay a moment, Val?"

Marci glances at me, but I wave her on. Scott Jenkins smirks as he passes, knowing my team's just been saddled with a complete neophyte. Hailey Manussian, on the other hand, shoots me a look of sheer hatred—or maybe it's jealousy. Like most girls at WiHi, Hailey's probably going through an *if only Jagger wanted to get into my pants* phase.

Backpack on shoulder, I walk to the teacher's desk.

"I put Jagger Voorham on your team," Carleton tells me.

The blood rushes to my cheeks at the mere mention of his name. "I noticed."

"He can't fit Intro into his schedule. I let him in because he's a senior like the rest of the class. Although that doesn't mean you let him slide. He needs to do his share. Show him the ropes, won't you, Val?"

Despite the fact that I find it hard to breathe, I put on a tough act. "Sure, Mr. Carleton. I'll kick his butt."

The teacher laughs. "I bet you will." He points to a couple of Student Emmy Awards gathering dust on the shelf above his desk. "Get those stories, girl. I'm counting on you to win us another."

"No pressure," I say.

His bald head gleams. "Would it be *Campus News* if there wasn't?"

The last bell of the day is like a tsunami warning on a Pacific island. The halls explode as almost two thousand kids run for higher ground—which in this case means lockers and exit doors. I elbow my way down the corridor with just the tiniest bit of amazement. Even though the school was cleaned over the summer, initials are already chalked across the walls.

Marci stands in front of her locker, fiddling with her lock.

"Maybe you should try your new combination," I tell her. "That's last year's."

She frowns as she searches her backpack for the combo paper the homeroom teachers hand out. "Why can't they let us keep the same lockers every year?"

"The mysteries of WiHi are…mysterious, Marci."

The metal door pops open. She switches a book and we head down the steps. "I can't believe I forgot to ask at lunch. What did Carleton want?"

"We're supposed to show Jagger the ropes."

"Not we. You're the one who knows everything. I only take TV so we can hang." She lowers her voice. "Think you can get him to switch Jagger to A team?"

"What am I supposed to say?"

"The guy's a killer. Broke your heart and scattered the pieces without a second thought."

Ouch. Rip the scab right off the wound, why don't you?

Outside, the afternoon sun makes me blink. At least, that's what I tell myself. September in Brooklyn Heights is like an iPod on shuffle. Summer weather, fall weather, and everything in between. This week it's end-of-summer-with-hints-of-autumn. That means it's too nice to have been stuck in school obsessing about Jagger Voorham for the past five hours.

"Mr. Carleton gave me permission to kick his butt if he screws up," I tell her.

"Like that'll help. He was my dialogue partner in French III, remember? I wanted to murder the kid, but I swear Mademoiselle Reynaud's in love with him. Two-faced dog if ever there was one."

"Jagger or Mademoiselle Reynaud?"

The French teacher is ninety years old and mean as a pit bull. She's been teaching so long they're thinking about naming the language hall bathrooms after her. Or maybe just a stall.

"You know who I mean," Marci sniffs.

I do—and I'm just as pissed off as she is. Why does Jagger have to ruin twelfth grade the way he did eleventh? For months, we were lip-locked and then one night, he finds *someone else* to soothe his tortured soul. Or whatever that stupid cliché is. The fact that I wasn't enough for him, that I didn't even *know* I wasn't enough, left a cavernous hole deep inside me.

"I can ask Mr. Carleton to switch him," Marci pleads. "I don't mind."

I shake my head. "Scott'll never take him. Plus, Mr. C. specifically asked me to help."

"Worse and worse," she mumbles softly.

"I heard that! You're not helping, Marci."

"Sorry! It's just…I don't want to see you hurt again."

Again? I almost laugh. Watching Jagger walk into the Media Center made it clear that the hurt had never gone away. It just got buried inside the hole at the center of my life.

"I'll just have to deal with it. With him. What doesn't kill you makes you stronger, right?"

My best friend shakes her head. "Not exactly the choice I was going for!"

2

Tony's Pizzeria is a Heights institution. Old-school booths with Formica tables, cracked leather seats and the best pizza in a town known for excellent pies. It's on Montague, Brooklyn Heights' main street, in between Moving Arts Dance Studio and an antique shop.

Marci waits in line while I scout a table. The place is packed with WiHi's hungriest. I zero in on a couple of newbies. I can tell they've just launched their high school career because they have that haunted *how did I survive the second day of ninth grade?* look—damn! Bethany!

My sister started WiHi yesterday, too. Mom made me promise I'd walk her home all week.

I hit my cell. Bethany has the same lame one I do because my parents get a "two for the price of one" deal. It's not hard to imagine my sister staring at the caller ID while she decides whether or not to answer.

She does—an instant before it goes to voice mail. "What do you want?"

"Are you at your locker? I—"

"I'm home. Did you really expect me to wait?"

"And you didn't think to tell me? What if I'm searching every inch of WiHi—"

"You're not. You're at Tony's. With Marci."

The surrounding din has sold me out. "How was your second day?"

"How do you think?"

The line goes dead. I give the freshmen the evil eye, as though one of them were my pain-in-the-butt sister. They look terrified, finish eating quickly and stumble away. Less than ten seconds later, Marci maneuvers over, juggling two slices and a couple of lemonades.

"A little help?" she asks.

"Sorry." I grab the cups before she drops one.

Marci slides into the booth. "Okay, Valerie, spill. What's the matter?"

I don't even ask how she knows something's wrong. "Bethany. She hung up in my ear."

Marci reaches for the jar of hot pepper flakes. "At least your sister hates someone besides me."

"Bethany doesn't hate you."

"Does, too," she insists.

"Does not." My best friend cocks an eyebrow. "Well, not more than she hates anyone else," I concede.

Folding my pizza in half, I shove it in my mouth. Tony's slow-simmered sauce, gooey melted cheese and crisp crust instantly improve my mood. "You know, he'll make a great anchor."

Marci chokes. "Jagger? Val—"

"It's my job as producer to use the resources of the team wisely," I say primly.

She rolls her eyes. "Right. Oh, and congratulations."

There's something so self-satisfied about the way it comes

out that it makes me suspicious. "Fess up, Marci. How were you so sure I'd win?"

She busies herself with the pizza, shaking oregano over the slice. "Because you deserve it. Because you're the best—"

The light dawns. "Because you talked Henry into voting for me. Marci Lee! That's cheating."

"Riigght. Like Raul didn't get there first."

I sit back into the wine-red banquette. "Are you sure? I mean, okay, I thought I saw him give the boys a look."

Marci nods. "Me, too. I think he spoke to them after class yesterday. *Before* I talked to Henry. So I don't feel the teensiest bit bad about it."

"What did you say—wait. Let me guess. You hit him with your killer smile and told him how much it would mean if your best friend got chosen producer."

She finishes chewing. "It's not as if you don't deserve it. Henry knows that."

"So you didn't have to promise him a date?"

"Valerie Gaines! You should kiss my cute little Asian feet right now, not yell at me."

She's right. I hoped I'd win because more people wanted me to be producer than Raul. Without Marci watching my back, I'd be wallowing in despair at this very moment.

"Thank you."

"You're welcome." She leans across the table. "The right person got the job, Val—as long as you stay focused. And you know exactly what I'm talking about."

I cross my heart. A double sign—of promise and of locking it up tight.

"Excellent." Marci grins. "And I promise that as long as I don't have to miss soccer practice or a game, I'll do anything you want."

"I'll cover for you in TV whenever you need it." I tip my lemonade toward hers.

"Always and forever," Marci replies, evoking our longtime sisterly vow with a return tap of her glass.

"Exactly the reason Bethany hates us."

A little after six o'clock, I barge into the bedroom.

"Mom sent me up here to tell you it's time to eat," I inform my sister.

The Gaines family, all six of us, live in a three-story brick row house. We occupy the first two floors. My parents rent the top apartment to a succession of young professionals, none of whom seem able to hold on to their jobs for very long.

Our kitchen, living and dining rooms are on the ground level. Three bedrooms take up the second floor. That means Bethany and I share, as do our six-year-old-twin brothers, Jesse and James. They think it's the best thing since the invention of the Oreo cookie; I'd live on the fire escape if Mom would let me.

Right now my sister's wearing earbuds. I know she sees me because I'm standing over her bed. Still, she pretends she doesn't.

I lift the buds. "Dinnertime."

"Not interested."

"Bethany, if you don't eat, Dad will start in on how you're so skinny and Mom will get crazy about anorexia—"

"I'm not anorexic," she whines.

"I know. You eat plenty after everyone goes to sleep."

"That's when I'm hungry."

"Tell it to the parents. Right now it's your turn to set the table. If I end up doing it, you wash the pans, whether you eat or not. It's pot roast. Emphasis on pots."

"I hate pot roast." Bethany swings her long, thin legs across the bed, kicking me in the shins before I can jump aside.

"Jerk," I mutter.

"Asshole," she says.

I start toward my sister like I'm gonna kick her butt. She takes off, which was my plan all along. Slamming the door, I throw myself onto my bed, next to the window and as far from my sister's as I can get it.

Bethany Ann Gaines. Her long brown hair is barely wavy, as if even her follicles can't be bothered to curl right. She inherited Dad's straight teeth, though, never needing braces the way I did. But now I have a perfect smile and Mom's auburn hair, just red enough to give me natural highlights. I keep it shoulder length like my fave TV reporter, Channel 5's Emily Purdue.

It's not only looks that separate us. Bethany is, well, boring. It would be totally cool to have a sister who scribbled angry poetry on the edges of her homework. Or a computer whiz who didn't have to ask me how to do every little thing. I'd even take a boy-crazy chick with awesome taste in clothes— but that's not her.

Then there are the twins. Jesse and James—my dad's not very funny joke—live up to their collective fugitive name by constantly getting into one mess after another. The amount of screaming, yelling and arguing that goes on in this house would send shy Henry to the loony bin for sure.

There is, however, one advantage to a large family that only-child Marci can never claim. As long as I make decent grades (I do) and don't get into trouble (I don't), nobody's in my business. It's not that my folks don't care. With the chaos of four kids and two jobs, the parents are overwhelmed.

Which is the reason no one knew how destroyed I was last year. Perversely, I stare at the ceiling and tick off Jagger's traits. Egotistical, manipulative and extremely charming. Pretty much a lethal combination. He has this way of talking to you like you're the only person in the world—

My cell rings.

"What do you think MP stands for?" Marci asks.

"Not Marci Lee. Why? Who's MP?"

"Phil called. After practice, he and the guys saw those two letters chalked all over the place."

Phil Colletti is Marci's boyfriend. He's a linebacker; she's the cocaptain of the soccer team. They make an interesting couple—the Italian giant and the Korean imp—but there you go. Brooklyn diversity in all its glory.

"I saw those initials, too," I say. "Chalked on the wall near the nurse's office."

"Got to be Marshall Prep. That's who the football team plays first."

"Okay. Why are you so upset?"

"Coming into our school, punking us before the game like that is so insulting."

"It's actually kind of lame, Marci."

"Not really. They got into the third floor without anyone seeing. It's bold."

My reporter instinct kicks in. "Let's do a story."

"Hell no. We are not giving Marshall the satisfaction of knowing it bothers us."

"Okay, then what—"

The door pounds. Jesse. Or James. "Mom said she told you to come right back down!"

"Gotta go. Call you later." Sneaking quietly across the room, I pull the door and stretch my arms. "Gotcha!"

James shrieks. "You scared me!"

"Dinnertime!" My zombie laugh echoes. "You, little man, look good enough to eat!"

James wriggles out of my grasp and runs down the steps, screaming. I chase him, laughing insanely. Dad, pulling off his tie, steps out of his bedroom. "What on earth is going on?"

From the kitchen, Jesse cries, "I want to play, too—"

Crash. The sound of breaking glass echoes throughout the house.

"Jesse Gaines!" Mom yells. "Why can't you be more careful?"

"You got milk all over me!" Bethany shouts. "Stupid idiot!"

Jesse wails. James laughs. Dad thunders. Drama at the Gaines Family Zoo. Drama at WiHi. Two days into the first semester and already it's obvious the year's going to be a wild ride.

3

The Media Center isn't set up like a regular classroom. The only "desks" are two round tables in the middle of the room. A row of computers, loaded with editing software and graphics programs, line the back wall. On the east side, there's a mini-TV newsroom. Somebody, some year, painted the front of the school on a backdrop—a very realistic, to-scale depiction. The station's call letters, WiHi, are printed at the bottom. The station's weekly anchorperson sits at an oval table directly in front of the painting.

Mr. Carleton keeps the equipment in several large, locked cabinets on the opposite wall. Cameras, microphones, headsets, lights. Sign-out sheets are clipped to a board. Next to the cabinets, two small glass-fronted rooms were carved out. One is the sound booth, the other the control room.

Attendance taken, B Team settles at our table. I open my *Campus News* notebook and wet my lips nervously. "Ideas?"

Marci speaks first. "I could interview the football team about their chances for the year."

I glance at my List of Possible Stories. Next to the line that says *Football/school spirit/hot dog stand,* I'd penciled in Marci's name.

"Excellent. Since it's the first game, can you add a bit about school spirit? And don't forget the senior hot dog stand. Money goes to prom."

She nods. "Can I work with Omar?"

Advanced TV Production works in teams of two. One person interviews, holding the mic, while the other runs the camera, wearing a headset to check sound quality. They switch roles for the second person's assignment.

"You're on, sista. But it's a lot of setups," Omar says. "Anyone got something easy for my segment?" His eyes flicker toward Raul as if *he's* the one in charge.

I jump in quick. "How about a Spotlight? There's that new assistant principal."

Raul laughs. "Mrs. Fairy?"

"Fahey," I correct.

"Like anyone's gonna call her that," Jagger snorts.

"Snap!" Omar gives me the wriggly eyebrows. "Spotlight works, Val. Always a good idea to kiss up to the new administration."

Two down. Time to take on the monster. "How about anchoring, Jagger? It's not hard—"

"Nah," he interrupts. "I don't want to be on camera."

Of course. I should have told him *not* to anchor. "Then what's your plan?"

"What do you mean?"

"If you don't anchor, you have to shoot and edit a piece. Do you have an idea?"

His eyes turn thunderstorm-gray. "Didn't know I had to think of one."

Omigod. Why is he even in this class?

Trying not to appear flustered, I glance at Henry. "What if you take the anchor position for the first broadcast? That way, you'll have time to help with the opening graphics."

He nods. "I could do that."

Thank goodness for Henry. "Cool. That leaves Raul with Jagger."

Jagger leans forward. "Why can't you and me be together?"

My heart jumps—until I realize he's playing me. Or is he? The sudden intensity in his eyes is confusing. It seems so... honest. The next instant, though, I catch myself.

Do not fall for the Voorham charm the very first day!

Omar, fanning his face with mock envy, raises his voice. "Hooking up during *Campus News!* That allowed, Mr. Carleton?"

The teacher, sitting with A Team, glances at us. "Whatever you say, Omar. As long as Work. Gets. Done."

Great. First day in charge. Jagger's making a fool of me, and Mr. C. thinks we're screwing around.

"Producer doesn't take a specific assignment the first week, Voorham." My voice has a frosty edge. "Except for directing anchor stuff and making sure everything else works out."

Raul must think I can't handle Jagger, because he jumps in. "Val's right. You're with me. How about doing something on the new skateboard park down by the river?"

Why didn't I think of that?

"Community story! Carleton'll love it," I tell him.

Raul smiles. At the same time, Jagger looks a bit...disappointed. Or maybe he's pissed that he didn't get his way.

I glance at Marci to see if she's paying attention, but she's filling out the Question Sheet for the football story.

Quickly, I get back to work. "That leaves only one segment to figure out." After checking my list again, I make a decision. "After-school clubs. It'll be good for the ninth graders."

Jagger snorts. "Clubs? I'd rather do something about MP."

Omar glances at him curiously. "Who's that?"

"Haven't you seen the initials chalked around school?" Jagger asks. "Got to be a tagger."

Marci pushes her paper aside. "MP. It's Marshall Prep. They're the first football team we play. They're messing with our heads. Something you know all about."

He grins. "Whatever. I'll do that. Talk to the usual suspects around school. If nothing pans out graffiti-wise, I know a guy at Marshall. I can try to find out if he's heard anything—"

"No way!" Marci declares. "Marshall Prep does not get one bit of publicity for punking us."

Jagger tilts his chair back so that it balances precariously on two legs. "Why are you so against me trying, Marcikins?"

Quickly, I shut my notebook. I need to take charge *right now* so the team doesn't blow up before a single frame is shot.

"It doesn't matter whose initials they are. Clubs are more useful for a first broadcast. Five hundred freshmen need to hear about them before sign-up day."

Jagger lets the chair down with a dissatisfied bang. "Whatever you say. But I'm willing to bet MP is a way better story than a group of lame-ass kids sitting around solving equestrian math puzzles!"

> What we need is hatred. From it
> our ideas are born.
>
> JEAN GENET

MP LOG

Six drops of blood. Oh yeah, they looked cool on the page. Real red. One drop for each of us. We sat in a circle and pricked our fingers. Even the chicks did it. Then we mixed them together for a blood oath. Watching each other's backs is the only way to survive.

This school is such bullshit, man. Ask anyone what they think and they'll say it blows. But the truth is, everyone's a phony. They say one thing, but then they join a team or sign up for some club they know is stupid. Not to mention sucking up to the teachers. MP's not gonna suck up to anyone.

Phantom and I are in charge because we thought it up. Everyone picked names. I'm Skeletor. There's Hell Girl, Frankenstein, Ghost Face and Zombie. We memorized the oath because that's how I want to start every meeting. Always a good idea to remind people of a sworn blood oath.

Then we talked about what's next. I explained my theory that you never do your best stuff first. Everyone agreed: start small and work up to some serious shit.

See, we're really not the same as the other kids at school. When *we* say WiHi sucks, we mean it.

I cannot wait to see their shocked faces when it all goes down.

4

Every member of TV Production focuses on the monitor. It's the Wednesday before the first broadcast. Presentation Day. The team has to show Mr. Carleton what we have so he can sign off on each segment.

Henry and I ate lunch in the Media Center for almost a week to work on the opening graphics. They're heavily Photoshopped, with a bit of anime that Henry, bless his over-achieving little soul, created.

When they finish running, we get the thumbs-up from Carleton. Next, Marci runs the football segment, which includes an interview with Phil. A few cheerleaders go on—and on—about school spirit. Then the senior-class president, Greg Martin, makes the pitch about the hot dog stand.

"An Irving dog is a deserving dog, dawgs," his on-screen image tells us.

"Lame!" Jagger grumbles.

"But it's in sync. And loud enough. Although the piece is a little slow, Marci," Mr. Carleton says. "Can you edit the girls? And that tight end?"

"Linebacker," Marci corrects. "As long it gets done in class. I can't stay after school."

I nod at my best friend, remembering our pact at Tony's. *Whatever you can't finish, I will.*

Next, it's Raul's turn. Eagerly, he clicks into the skateboarding piece. The thing starts crazy and keeps on going. Jagger's on a board, doing some amazing tricks. A sweet bank to the ledge before he blasts a kick flip looks pretty spectacular on the screen. Then the point of view shifts so it seems like the viewer's skating.

"Dude!" A Team's leader, Scott Jenkins, looks a little green with envy—or worry. "Where'd you get the music?"

"*GarageBand,* bro," Jagger says. "Put it together last night."

"Now, that's tight!" Scott murmurs.

I try not to gloat. *Score one for the newbie—and the team stuck with him.*

Mr. Carleton is not as impressed. "Camera work's good, boys. But it's a little light on specifics. For example, where's the park located? Hours. The boring *information* that actually constitutes news."

Raul laughs. "Don't sweat it, Mr. C. I'm planning a voice-over under the last trick."

"You could end with a visual," I suggest. "Didn't I see footage of the entrance sign in an earlier version?"

"I cut it because I thought we were long, but sure, I can go out on it. Along with the voice-over. Would that be okay, Mr. Carleton?"

The teacher nods. "What else do you have, Val?"

"Spotlight and club news. Omar, you're up."

He plays his interview with Mrs. Fahey. It's the least interesting thing we've got, but it's short. Still, it's the kind of piece Carleton loves because it puts the administration in a good light.

"Great job, Omar, although her audio's a little low. I'll show you how to boost it when we're done," the teacher tells him.

I tap Jagger. "Ready?"

He shakes his head. "I was helping Raul."

"You were supposed to work on the clubs—"

"No worries, Val." Raul tries not to yawn. "It'll get done."

Is he making the point that he'd be a more laid-back producer than me? Or am I paranoid and he's just trying to help?

Carleton stands. "Good start, folks. Valerie, you're shooting anchor tomorrow, right? Plus keeping track of time." He claps his hands. "B Team, you know what you have to do.

"A Team, I better see some equipment signed out. You're on the hot seat next week."

The class scatters. Scott's group huddles at their table. There's always some degree of rivalry between the two teams. If Scott wants to put in the effort, he and his team can definitely give me a run for the money. I won't find out how seriously they want to compete until their broadcast airs next week.

"Bring it, A Team," I whisper before moving to the computer Henry's staked out as his own. "Do you want to write anchor stuff or should I?"

"You do it," he says. "I'm not happy with the last two seconds of the opening."

"Looked fine to me."

Henry shakes his head. "Color's not tracking...."

I leave him to his screen. No sense wasting class time writing material, because I can do that at home. There are more important things to worry about.

Raul and Jagger are working on the skateboard voice-over.

"Can I see what you have on the clubs?" Jagger hesitates, so I get in his face. "Let me explain how Advanced works, Voorham. Points are taken from everyone if we don't run four segments. That's why there's a producer. It's about the team, not any one person. I'm supposed to work with anyone who needs help." I look to Raul. "You guys shot stuff, right? And imported?"

Importing footage to the computer takes forever. It'll help a lot if they've gotten that far.

"Yeah, we digitized." Raul stretches. "I got this, Jags. Can you find it for her?"

Jags? Don't tell me Raul's fallen under the Voorham spell. I'm pretty sure they never said a word to each other before last week.

Jagger strolls to a computer at the far end. Damn. Now it's just the two of us. He's wearing an emerald-colored tee today, tight enough to make even his skinny body look buff. I wonder if he realizes how that particular shade brightens the specks of green in his eyes—

Stop thinking about him. Concentrate on the job....

Pulling up a chair, I view the raw footage. The problem's fairly obvious. There's no focus. No angle into the story—and not a lot of time to get one. Part of that's my fault. It was too big an assignment for someone new to the game. It also didn't help that the boys got so into the skateboard story, neither of them cared about this one.

"Run it again," I mutter.

The second time through, I see a way to make it work. "Mind if I do a little editing?"

"Knock yourself out," Jagger says.

We switch chairs. "The interview with Mr. Sorren on his new European history club isn't bad, but he goes on too long." Jagger and Raul interrupted his class when they walked in. As the video camera pans the room, I see my sister sitting by herself. I'll never hear the end of it if Bethany gets into the piece looking like a friendless twerp. The first thing I do is cut her out.

See how I protect you? Bethany wouldn't appreciate the ges-

ture, so I won't mention it. But somewhere, on a huge whiteboard in the sky, someone's keeping track of my good deeds.
At least I hope so.

I fast-forward to a student interview. One of Jagger's skater
friends asks, "Why join anything?"

"Might be able to use this kid as a segue...." I want to try
an editing trick one of last year's seniors used. Repeat a tiny
section, in this case, "Why join anything?" between the interviews. It can give a piece momentum so it doesn't feel all
over the place.

"Jagger, get the Weekly Bulletin and scan the Club Schedule into the computer. You know how to do that, right? Then
blow it up, print it back out and we'll shoot it...."

The class ends before we're close to finishing, but at least
I have a plan. "I might be able to get a rough edit done during lunch." I glance guiltily at Mr. Carleton. I'm not supposed to do Jagger's work—but it's crunch time. It'll take too
long to teach him the ins and outs of editing before the Friday broadcast.

"You're allowed to eat in here?" Jagger asks.

"As long as we don't spill anything on the equipment. You're
supposed to sit at one of the tables, but no on actually does."

"Should I meet you in the cafeteria?"

No! No—

"I brought a sandwich."

"Then I'll come after I get through the line," he tells me.

Omigod, omigod, omigod...

"Sure," I mumble.

"Val?" His touch is light but every fingertip tingles against
my skin. "Thanks for helping."

He takes off. I walk to the B Team table for my backpack,
trying to figure out his game. Did Jagger take the class because

he thought it would be easy? That he'd be able to slack off while I do all his work? If so, he's in for a very rude awakening.

At the lockers before lunch, Marci has to relay every detail about last night's fight with her dad. Usually, I don't mind listening, but right now there's no time. Luckily, Phil shows up halfway through the replay. She turns to him for the kind of comfort I can't give. A sloppy lip-lock.

Released from best-friend duty, I burst into the Media Center. Mr. Carleton waves. Feet on desk, coffee in hand, he's watching something on his computer.

"Anyone from the team show up?"

He shakes his head. "Not even Henry."

I glance at the clock. Jagger's probably stuck in the lunch line. It's why I bring a sandwich every day. Pulling up the piece, I continue editing where I left off, working quickly. It's not until the bell rings that it occurs to me that Jagger stood me up.

Unbelievable! How can I possibly fall for his B.S. again? Instead of being hurt, I'm furious—at both him and myself.

At the end of the day, I head directly for the V row of lockers. Jagger always leaves school as soon as he can, and I want to catch him before he does. Laura Hernandez, she of the considerable rack and raven hair, hovers close to him, chatting a mile a minute. Instead of fighting for airspace, I shout from across the hall.

"Yo! Voorham!" He glances over, waves. "Talk to you? Alone?"

Jagger saunters over, probably so Laura and I are sure to notice how good he looks in his black jeans—front and back. I move to the gap in front of the band room. "What happened to lunch at the Media Center?"

His eyes widen in surprise. "What do you mean? You blew me off."

"Are you kidding?" His crap might work on someone else but not me. Not anymore. "I might have been a little late, but I asked Carleton. He said no one from the team showed."

"I never talked to him," Jagger tells me. "I peeked into the room, saw you weren't there, so I waited in the hall. After a while I figured you forgot."

"I wouldn't forget—"

He puts up a hand to still my protest. "Let's not fight! It's just one of those crossed-wire situations. Not like it hasn't happened before." He waits for me to nod reluctantly before asking, "Did you work on the piece?"

"Yes. But there's still plenty to do."

"What about music?"

"I was a little busy editing, Voorham. By myself."

He ignores the dig. "I don't have anything that'll work on the iPod, but there's a couple thousand songs on my laptop."

From across the hall, Laura yells, "Jagger! Coming back today or what?"

He looks annoyed and lifts a "one second" finger. "Don't worry, Val. I'll go home right now and find something good. How about I bring a bunch of choices tomorrow so you can pick what's best?"

Forget flowers or chocolate. Jagger knows the way into this girl's heart. No matter how well it's edited, a driving beat goes a long way toward disguising boring footage.

"Okay." I sigh. "It'll run at least two and a half minutes, so make sure the music's long enough."

He gives me the patented Jagger grin before going back across the hall. Laura immediately starts talking as if he never left. I know I should get to the Media Center, but I'm glued to the spot. Did Jagger tell the truth and lunch was just a missed connection? Is he really eager to create a sound track to brighten up the club segment? Or is listening to music a perfect excuse to make out with Laura Hernandez on that extremely comfortable bed he has?

That thought is what finally gets me to move away.

5

I stay late again on Thursday to tweak a few things. The broadcast runs 15:30—a perfect time. Omar shot the anchor ins and outs, so it's beautifully framed. Henry looks surprisingly comfortable behind the anchor desk. The edited flow, football to Spotlight, clubs to skateboarding, ends on a high note.

Battered briefcase in hand, Mr. Carleton barks, "Shut it down, Val. We were supposed to be out of here five minutes ago."

I press Save one final time, scoop up my backpack and head for the door. "I had one last thing to check...."

Mr. C. flips the light switch. "It's fine. A good first broadcast."

Fine? A good *first* broadcast. Like it would be way better if the team was more experienced? As soon as I get home, I text Marci. Her reply is no comfort: Great! An easy A.

All night long, I'm antsy. Bethany's got some test to study for, so she bans me from the bedroom. I give the twins a bath, watch a little CNN with Dad. Friday morning, I'm awake before the alarm rings. I dash into the bathroom before anyone else so I can wash and then straight-iron my hair. Back in the bedroom, I change clothes three times—nothing's right. I want to look good, but not as if I'm trying hard. In my dreams, not only does the show go off without a hitch, but people come up and talk to me about it. How *Campus News* is way better than last year. Or the year before.

Part of that's true. The show, airing in its usual first-period time slot, looks good. But not one single person at WiHi pays attention to the closed-circuit feed in any of the classrooms. I know this because everyone's talking about The Prank.

Even the TV Production teams.

It had to have been set up early in the morning. Or, I suppose, late last night. By the time I got to WiHi, all straight-ironed and looking good, a crowd had gathered at the front. Everyone's focus was up.

Is something happening on the roof? A jumper? Fire?

Nothing's there. Still, windows on all three floors are open as wide as safety latches will allow. Less than a foot, so even an idiot can't fall out. Faces pressed to panes watch… something.

Phil stands near the iron statue of the school's namesake. Washington Irving. Although he created the Headless Horse-man character, our statue has a head. I'm not sure it improves the guy's appearance, though.

I figure Marci must be standing next to the BF, so I make my way over. Amazing how predictable people are. "What's going on?"

She points to the flagpole. "Look at that!"

"Holy crap!"

I can't believe I didn't see it until now. The flag is gone, replaced by a row of undies flapping in the breeze. Mostly grandpa boxers and tighty whiteys, with a few bikinis and one bright red thong. The largest pairs have letters stenciled across them. The early-morning sun shines in my face. I shade my eyes with my hand to read the message.

WIHI SUCKS MP.

"Marshall Prep," Marci says smugly. "Told you that's who's doing it. The game's tonight."

The front door bangs open. Mr. Wilkins, the principal, strides out. Thin as a string bean and tall as a giraffe, he carries a portable microphone with an attached battery pack.

"Bell's about to ring," he announces. "Get to class, students."

No one moves, not even the ninth graders. That's because the head custodian, Mr. Orel, arrives at the same time. Hand over hand, he pulls the rope. With a squeak, the underwear sinks to the ground. There are jeers—and cheers. Depends on how you feel about undies. Or WiHi.

"Into the building," Wilkins shouts, "or you will all be considered tardy."

As if Mrs. Gribaldini, the attendance lady, can mark hundreds of kids late at the same time. But there isn't anything else to see, so the herd heads off.

Phil, linebacking a path for Marci and me, runs into Bethany. Literally. Her unmistakable voice screeching, "Watch it!" alerts me to her presence.

"Did you see that?" I ask.

My sister doesn't bother to answer the admittedly obvious question. Like the rest of the school, the prank caught me off guard.

Everyone wonders. During first period, and into second and third. Who had the bright idea? How did they do it without being caught? What happened to WiHi's Stars and Stripes?

That's the reason nobody cared about the year's first *Campus News* broadcast.

★ ★ ★

After school, a larger than usual crowd hangs around the flagpole. I stand close and eavesdrop. Several kids place bets on how soon Mr. Wilkins will get the flag replaced. Another group argues about which pair of undies they wish would permanently replace the flag. No one's discussing our broadcast. Not even the skateboard piece, easily the one with the most audience appeal.

Disappointed, I start for home. Henry's at the curb, talking to someone I don't know. She's kind of punked out—ripped jeans, combat boots, nose ring—not at all his style. Curious, I stop beside them.

"Hey, Henry."

"Hi, Val." After I glance at the girl, Henry takes the hint. "Do you know Toby? She's a junior."

"Not really. Nice to meet you."

She gives a sort of half nod. "Gotta go."

"Think about it, okay?" Henry says.

Toby bestows a "you're lower than a worm" look upon him before walking away. Ouch! I'd like to give her a good slap. How can anyone treat sweet Henry like that?

He doesn't appear to notice. "At least she didn't say no. If Toby joins Chess Club, we have a chance to win City."

"That girl plays chess?"

Henry looks insulted. "It's a popular game."

"Sorry. I hope she joins. We'll do a story."

"Cool!" He glances around hopefully. "Waiting for Marci?"

"Nah. She's got practice. I was by the flagpole. Everyone's talking underwear."

"It was different, that's for sure." He laughs. "By next week, I bet no one remembers. Something new'll pop up. It always does."

★ ★ ★

Never underestimate Henry's smarts. He's absolutely right. Very few people pay attention to the A Team broadcast the following Friday.

This time it's inside. Third-floor corridor at the west end. Past the double doors that separate the staircase from the hallway, there's an extra-wide water fountain. Made of chipped white porcelain, it has a pair of spouts on either end so two people can drink at the same time. Maybe in the last century, before they had water bottles and continual germ alerts, people might actually have done that. I don't know a single person who'd stick their face into any gross WiHi water fountain no matter how thirsty they are.

It's not the fountain people stare at. Right beside it, someone dragged over an honest-to-goodness toilet. Inside the bowl is the flag from the flagpole and a small plastic bucket, the kind little kids bring to the beach. Except it's not mud dripping over the side of the pail—it's streaks of blood. The words stenciled across the front jump out at me.

MP LIVES—Will U?

After a few seconds, I realize the "blood" is paint. I'm not the only one fooled. The kids who jostle for space beside me make the same initial intake of breath—followed by laughter a few seconds later.

The spot was wisely chosen. It's near the little-used stairway that leads down to the school's storeroom. Still, word gets out. Lots of kids take detours on the way to first period, though I don't see a single teacher. The school's adults are holed up in their classrooms, too busy gearing up for the day's torturous activities to notice what's going on.

As soon as A Team's broadcast ends, I call a team meeting.

The six of us head into the control booth for privacy. Henry and Marci are the only ones who saw the toilet, so I quickly describe it for the rest.

"This new stunt means MP isn't Marshall Prep," I finish breathlessly.

"You think?" Jagger says. "The game was last week. If they were behind the flagpole crap, they'd move to whichever school their football team plays next, and start punking them."

Marci can't do anything but agree. "Our guys killed, so why would they ever step foot on campus again?"

"Henry." Raul, sitting in the director's chair, swivels around. "Could the toilet be an art project? The flagpole stunt, too. Wasn't there some kind of art thing, fada or lada—"

"Dada." As the youngest of several geniuses in the senior class, Henry has the good sense not to show off unless specifically asked. "It made fun of the modern world. The meaninglessness of everything. They mostly targeted rich people and, like, posers. But I haven't heard of a single teacher giving out a Dada assignment. No one at WiHi's ever been that cool."

Raul gives me a look. Frustration? Anger? Is he telling me *he* would have made a different decision when assigning stories? Chosen MP instead of clubs.

Time to suck it up, Val.

"Okay, everyone. Jagger was right. MP is obviously somebody's initials, not a high school football team. And yes, it's a good story."

Voorham takes an exaggerated bow. "Hold the applause 'til the end of the magic act."

Asswipe, Marci mouths.

I ignore both of them. "We'll add the MP story to the next show. But what's the angle? We have to find a good way in."

Raul's on it. "How about the flag? Ties both stunts together."

The bell in my head, the one that tolls *good idea,* rings loud and clear. "That'll work."

Omar wriggles his fingers. "Hold on, sista. We're talking five segments."

"You're right." I make an instant editorial decision. "We can cut the piece I'm working on. Since the MP story was originally Jagger's idea, he takes it if he wants. I'll edit what he's working on."

"Do I get to pick my partner?" he asks.

"Unless they want to finish their segment."

Raul's already nodding, assuming he's the choice. Jagger stares at Marci. She opens her mouth to protest. Without taking his eyes off her, he says, "ValGal."

A shiver runs through me. For once, it has nothing to do with my ex-boyfriend. It's the thrill of the hunt. Not only do I *want* that story—I want to report its butt off.

"Henry, change the whiteboard, please?" The teams have to list all stories on the board so there's no duplication. "Just in case Scott gets the same idea. Jagger can pull equipment while I make sure no one messes with the toilet."

I gallop to the third floor. Excellent! The toilet display is untouched. Not five minutes later, several sets of feet pound up the stairs. All of B Team arrives. Either nobody trusted Jagger to sign out the right equipment or everyone wants in on the action.

They've brought it all. Lights, stands, camera, microphone.

"Not so loud!" I warn. "We don't want anyone to stop us."

Quickly, the team sets up. Immediately, however, a problem surfaces. Although we've got an extension cord, there's no place to plug in the lights. The hallway is too dark to get a decent image without additional illumination.

Raul turns toward the steps. "I'll get an extra cord from the cabinet. You guys figure out where to score some power."

Two classrooms are located around the corner. After a quick discussion, we decide to avoid teachers if we can. There is, however, a boys' bathroom halfway down the hall.

"Do the 'boys' have outlets in them?" Marci asks.

"One way to find out." Henry jogs into the bathroom, returns less than a minute later. "It's at the far end. Raul will have to bring a bunch of cords."

"No probs." I pull my cell from my pocket. Like all city high schools, WiHi has a firm no-cell-phone policy, but Mr. C. lets us use ours for stuff like this.

"Don't abuse it, folks," he warned. "I will not go head-to-head with Mr. Kuperman if anyone cheats on a physics test!"

Raul's reply is quick: Found 4. The instant he arrives, he, Omar and Henry gang the cords into one. They snake it along the edge of the hall and into the bathroom.

Turning to Jagger, I ask, "You know what to say for the stand-up?"

He shakes his head. I start to tell him how it could go, but he stops me before I finish a sentence. "You do it."

"I'll coach you. It's not hard."

"Uh-uh," he says. "I don't want to be on-camera."

Marci puts a hand on her hip. "Why not? *Campus News* not cool enough for you?"

Jagger avoids looking at me. "Hit the nail on the head, Marcikins. I needed an arts class to graduate. Doesn't mean I have to be on-camera."

The lights go on. Henry sticks his head out of the bathroom.

"All good," I tell him.

The boys tumble out. Raul wants to direct. Omar calls camera. Jagger and Marci reach for the headset at the same time.

"I got it first!" she says, appealing to me.

"Raul's directing. His call."

"Fine!" Marci throws the headset at Jagger and stalks to the opposite wall. Omar messes with my hair while I sound-check.

"Ready, everyone?" Raul asks. "In five, four, three—" He holds up two fingers. Folds down the first, then the last. My cue to start talking.

"Good morning, Horsemen and Women. I'm standing on the third floor of Washington Irving High School, in front of what might be considered a work of art. Or a prank."

I move to the side so Omar can get a clear shot of the toilet. As I narrate, he zooms into the flag. "For the last seven days, the WiHi flagpole lost its reason to exist. Today, that purpose has been rediscovered. The flag removed last Friday can once again fly high. But the mystery deepens. Who put this thing, um, object, in the hall—"

"Cut!" Raul says. "Start again, Val."

We shoot the stand-up two more times.

"I think we got it," Raul says.

"Audio's clear," Jagger announces.

"Cool." It's the first all-team effort. Except for the little tiff between Marci and Jagger, I'm happy with the way it went. "Let's get the empty flagpole. When the office finds this stuff and puts the flag back, we can reshoot the pole."

The toilet's gone by the end of the day. That's all right with me because the footage Omar shot is perfect.

Over the weekend, I make a list of people to interview. Jagger doesn't object when I suggest we start with the art teachers on Monday. Working the segment at the end of last week seems to have broken the iceberg between us. He's quiet, focusing his attention on the camera, letting me do the interviews.

All three teachers swear it's not a project they assigned. When I ask Ms. Cordingley, the department chairperson, if she has a student with the initials MP, she taps a charcoal pencil on the desk.

"I wondered about that myself, so I checked the rosters. No one with those initials is taking art. Not this semester."

"Okay. If you remember someone from last year, would you leave a note in the *Campus News* box? I check it every day."

In the hallway, Jagger asks, "Do you think she will?"

"Nah. But I had to suggest it. Like Carleton always says, leave no stone unturned when investigating a story."

On our way back to the Media Center, we run into Josh Tomlin, cast in every WiHi play since freshman year. He agrees to be interviewed. No surprise there, because the kid never met an audience he didn't like.

Jagger's behind the lens again; I've got the mic.

"It's not performance art," Josh tells me, "because you need a performer for that. But the toilet would make an awesome prop for a play."

"Do you have any idea who's behind it?"

Josh pauses dramatically. "Like everyone else, I wish I knew. I can't wait to see what's next. At least, I hope there's something else."

"Thanks." I turn to the camera. "That's what everyone wonders. Will there be anything more?"

The following day, Jagger and I interview a history teacher, Mr. Correra. An Army Reservist, he sponsors the school's Junior ROTC program. The teacher makes it clear that he's extremely upset at the "desecration of our national symbol, the American flag."

For balance, I insist we find a free-speech teacher.

"That'll be Mrs. O'Leary," Jagger says. "Had her for ninth grade English. Old-school hippy fer sure."

He's right. When I ask the teacher, dressed in a long flowered skirt, dangly earrings and Earth shoes, if she thinks the flag has been desecrated, she bristles. "I found the entire toilet seat display an especially incisive metaphor for our country in these troubled times."

"Some people are upset that the flag was stolen from the front of the school," I tell her.

Mrs. O'Leary pauses to get her thoughts in order. "While I cannot, of course, condone taking down Irving's American flag, sometimes dramatic measures must be taken to fight the powers that be. It should also be noted that the flag wasn't actually stolen. Borrowed, then returned." She smiles, proud of the way she tightroped the answer.

Jagger and I do one more interview. Tanya's one of those peppy girls joined at the hip to her best friend. We manage to catch her alone, scurrying back from the bathroom. Before agreeing to be interviewed, she flips open her cell to use as a mirror.

"You look great," I tell her. "Once we get rolling, introduce yourself and then tell us what you think about the flagpole and the toilet bowl." I stick the mic in her face. Tanya giggles through her name.

"Cut! Let's start again."

It takes five tries before she keeps a straight face. "I'm Tanya and I'm a sophomore. I just want to say how cool this school is. The first year I was here, which was last year, WiHi had *dancergirl*. This year, it's something completely different. I don't know who's doing all the MP stuff and I don't care. It's fun seeing what shows up." She sticks up her index finger. "Irving is definitely number one!"

"Cut!" I say. "Great, Tanya, thanks."

"Can I see it?"

"It'll air Friday on *Campus News*."

I wind the mic's cord as Tanya trots off. "We've got enough, Jags. Let's go back—"

"Uh-uh."

"What does that mean?"

"The student interviews are one-sided. Everyone's looking at the surface. It's something different to break up the daily grind." He gestures down the hall. "'Irving's so awesome,' but did Tanya actually read the message on the underwear? You'd think she'd be insulted."

"Not that I disagree, but we have to import what we shot, edit—"

"It's my piece." He holds up his index finger and then sticks out his thumb, turning the Irving *I* into an *L* for *Lame*. "I'm not going to put out only the rah-rah view. We need to find an outcast or two. See what they think."

I'm kind of impressed with the way Slacker Jagger's fighting to get what he wants—although there's no way I'll tell him that.

"Fine. I'll text Raul and get him to bring us another camera. He can start importing this while we find—" I make an O with my fingers "—outcasts."

Jagger groans. "Tell me you are not that dorky."

"I'm not," I repeat dutifully. "Usually."

He laughs. "Come on, I know where to find the peeps we need."

We gallop to the basement level. At the back of the school, an exit opens into the yard. Raul catches up to us at the door and we switch cameras. Jagger leads the way outside. Except for the gym class on the field, no one's around.

"Not much time before the bell rings," I tell him.

"So move it." Around the corner, on the far side of the building, a group of kids smoke forbidden cigs. The outlaws. The haters. The kids who ignore the rest of us. One of them glances over, sees we're not teachers and returns to his smoke.

Jagger moves to a pimply dude sitting by himself. "Liam.

I'm helping out a friend. Can she ask a couple of questions about the flag stuff going on? She's with *Campus News*."

He gets the finger for his trouble—and gives it right back.

"Such cooperation," I mumble. "Like any of these guys will go on camera. You won't even do it."

"He was a bad choice," Jagger admits. "The only screen Liam cares about is a computer screen. Someone else will talk."

I'm not so sure. Two kids stamp out their butts and shuffle into school without acknowledging our presence. Another pretends not to hear. I might as well be in my bedroom, talking to Bethany for as much good as this does.

I'm about to tell Jagger to give it up for the day when someone finally agrees to be interviewed.

The kid definitely fits Jagger's idea of an outlaw. He's got the tats, the earrings, the unwashed hair. He tells me he'll go on camera but won't say his name. I shrug. His choice.

Anonymous starts to talk as soon as I give the cue. "I didn't see the toilet bowl. But I don't know what all this crap's about. Who gives a shit?"

The bell rings. Anonymous takes off.

I laugh. "Happy, Jags? We can use it if I cut the last line."

"Do we have to? It was very poetic. Toilet, crap, shit. Mrs. O'Leary would love the use of extended metaphor." Jagger hands me the camera, the headphones, the mic. "You don't mind bringing the equipment back, do you? I have class on the first floor and I gotta finish the homework."

And he's gone. Leaving me alone, holding everything myself.

After school, the Media Center is quiet. I set up at one of the computers to start editing.

Carleton walks over. "Faculty meeting today, Val."

I groan. "Can I stay? Please. We want to add the new segment for Friday's show. I haven't begun to cut it."

He sighs. "Okay. But don't go broadcasting that I've left you alone. I'll be back to lock up at four-thirty *if* Wilkins can keep to the schedule. Do. Not. Leave. Someone's got to stay with the equipment."

No problem. Jagger and I shot a ton, so paring it down to four minutes will be a challenge.

I play the first several minutes of raw footage. Hit Stop. Rewind. Click through frame by frame. Something bothers me. It's not just the obsessiveness of the image. The precise fold of the flag. The way it's looped exactly equidistant from either end of the porcelain tank. It isn't the positioning of the toilet, either, placed in such a way that it can't be seen from the main hall. Or the pail—wait! That's it. Inside.

I stare at the overhead shot Omar took at the last minute. The entire pail can be seen resting in the bowl. Inside, across the bottom rim, tiny letters look like decoration. Then again, it might be a message. A secret note. Maybe a signature...

I blow up the frame as large as I can. Can't make out anything except *s o r*. There's not a first name I can think of with those letters. Last names, sure. Mr. Sorren, the history teacher. One of the outlaws I recognized at the side of the school. Craig Sorestsky.

But *s o r* doesn't have to be a name. It could be part of a word. Sore...sorrow...sorry. Hmmm. They're sorry. You'll be sorry.

Something in my gut—reporter's instinct?—tells me that's correct. Someone's going to be sorry.

"What are you doing here?"

I jump at the sound. A Team's Hailey Manussian stands behind me. Her perfectly round face, completely surrounded by dark wavy hair, looks irritated.

"You scared the crap out of me," I tell her.

"Door's not locked. Where's Carleton?" She glances around the room suspiciously, as if Mr. C. and I are having a secret rendezvous behind the anchor desk.

"Faculty meeting."

"He let you stay?"

I shrug the obvious answer. "He'll be here by four-thirty. Come back then if you want to talk to him."

She glances past my shoulder. "What's on your screen?"

I click it closed. "Something I'm working on."

Hailey gives me a stony stare. "You think you're so clever, ValGal. Best friend's on your team, so producer vote goes your way. Got the hot guy, too, because Carleton thinks you're the only girl in class who knows how to do stuff. I know everything you know—and more."

She stomps off. Hailey hasn't liked me ever since I screwed up a science lab in seventh grade—getting us both a shitty grade—but you'd think she'd be over it by now. That rant was on the vicious side. Even Bethany doesn't hate me *that* much. At least, I don't think she does.

I return to editing, but my mind's all over the place. As soon as Carleton enters, I head for the office. Mrs. Kresky gets Mr. Orel on the walkie-talkie. The custodian's mopping the language hallway.

"Mr. Orel. Remember the toilet and pail on the third floor? Were you the person who took it away?"

Not a rhythmic beat of mop swishing is missed. "One of the younger janitors carried it down."

"Where'd he put it?"

"Trash bin. Pickup was this morning."

"The pail, too?"

My disappointment must show because Mr. Orel stops cleaning. "Yes. But don't fret. The flag's fine. Ever since the incident, I take it down as soon as school ends. Come tomorrow morning, it'll be flying high."

"That's great," I tell him. What I'm thinking is: *Some reporter. Why didn't I notice the letters on the pail before today?*

> Power and Liberty are like Heat
> and Moisture; where they are well
> mixed, everything prospers.
>
> FIRST MARQUESS OF HALIFAX

MP LOG

So it was cool. We did the first two pranks. Just as I thought, everybody talked about them for days. People wondered who has the balls to do what we did.

In the third-floor hallway, I overheard someone say they wished they'd thought of this. But even if they had, they wouldn't follow through. The truth is, no one's ever done anything like what we're doing for two reasons. One: deep down, people are afraid. They think they'll get their asses kicked or their mothers will yell at them when they find out what they've done or they'll get sent to the office. And two: you have to be smart to pull off stuff like this without getting caught. It's brains, not muscle, that are important. You can always find the muscle you need, but you can't make yourself more intelligent. That's a fact.

Most times even the people who think they know you don't, because they only see what's on the outside. The outside's a flimsy cover that no one takes the time to lift so they can see what's really underneath.

Now people are saying they want to be MP—whatever MP is. It's hard not to laugh out loud because no one has ever wanted to be me before. It isn't only that I've become hard-core. It's that I know something no one else does—exactly what

MP stands for. No one else can understand because not one single person saw the message I left. If they had, they'd realize:

MP is power. The kind of power that sneaks up on people, smacks them in the face and makes them regret their sorry existence.

6

At last, people pay attention to *Campus News.* I know this because it's *Bethany* who says something at the dinner table.

The twins shoot peas at each other, using the engineering principle of spoon-as-lever. Dad is busy pointing out how advanced this is to an extremely annoyed mom when my sister clears her throat.

"Val was on TV."

The conversation-slash-argument stops. Bethany rarely initiates a dinner topic. She can barely manage a mumbled yeah or nah when asked a question.

"Excuse me," Mom says. "I'm so sorry. I didn't hear—"

"Val was on TV at school," my sister repeats.

There's a moment of silence as the parents try to figure out what Bethany's complaining about. She rarely speaks my name without whining about something I've done—or not done.

"*Campus News,*" I remind them. "I'm a producer. I told you guys...."

"Right," Dad says, except I'm pretty certain he has no idea what I'm talking about.

James sets his milk at the edge of the table. "Was it fun to see her, Bethie?"

"Don't call me that," she snaps. "It's knee. Beth-a-*knee*. I've told you a million times—"

"He's only six," Mom soothes, at the same time moving his glass inland to avoid catastrophe. "James, her name is Bethany."

"Nobody calls you Jimmy," my sister points out.

"They could. I wouldn't care."

"Jimmy, Jimmy, Jimmy," Jesse chants, accompanying himself with his favorite percussive instrument: fork-pounding-on-plate.

Dad holds up his hand. "We get the point, Jesse. What was Val talking about, Bethany?"

In any other household, the question would be directed to me because, well, I was the one on the screen. But here? Bethany speaks and the world stops spinning. It's like trying to get druggies to talk about where they score. You don't dare stop 'em once they start.

"Last week someone took the flag from the front of the school and replaced it with a bunch of underwear—"

Jesse shrieks. Bethany shoots him a superior glare. He clams up.

"This week someone put a toilet in the third-floor hall-way," she continues.

"A potty?" James shouts. "Did anyone pee in it?"

Despite Bethany's frown, he and Jesse laugh. My sister gets all huffy and refuses to say another word.

I jump in. "Sorry to disappoint, little dudes, but not a single person used it for, um, personal activities. There was a beach pail in the bowl." For whatever reason, that seems even funnier. The boys' whooping becomes contagious. Laughter circles the table.

"Okay, girls, don't keep us in suspense," Dad says, "Who's the culprit?"

Bethany shrugs. "No one knows."

For the first, and maybe last time in the history of the universe, I agree with her. "So far, nobody's taking responsibility. But it makes watching *Campus News* interesting, right, Bethany?"

My sister stabs a French fry, deaf once more. Too bad. The truce was kind of nice while it lasted.

Neither interesting, nor nice, is how Marci sees any of it. Especially when body parts show up. Not flesh and blood body parts, though from a distance, that's what it seems. Up close, it's obvious they're plastic. A department store mannequin pulled apart. An arm dangling high above the third-floor staircase railing; in a second-floor bathroom, a bald head and neck hang from a noose. An upside-down leg with a red high-heeled shoe, sticks out from a trash can at the side of the school.

Every part has the same message:

THIS COULD BE YOU.
MP.

"What's that supposed to mean?" Marci gulps.

"Just that someone watches too many horror shows. Jeez, look at the crowd." The crush of people surrounding the leg is three deep.

"Who cares about a crowd?" She tugs my arm. "Let's go."

"Not yet."

I push forward to check out the leg. No tiny letters that I can see. Being this close to a cut-up body, though, even if it's plastic, makes me feel weird. Like some kind of perv. Or maybe it's the flash of intuition that tells me Marci's right: MP's not all fun and games. Underwear and kiddie pails and secret writing meant to seem cool. He might be something else. Something darker. Someone evil. Goose bumps erupt all over my arms.

When I hit the Media Center, Raul, Henry and Omar are already there, looking three shades of gloomy.

"What's up?"

Omar tugs an earring. "Read the board. A Team's doing an MP story."

"What? That's ours!"

"It's not on our list," Raul points out.

"How was I supposed to know he'd get all serial killer today?" A glance at the A Team table tells me this was Hailey's doing. She can barely contain a superior smile. "I'll take care of it!"

I make a beeline for Carleton, quietly taking attendance. "A Team cannot have the MP story. It's ours."

Scott Jenkins scoots over. That doesn't surprise me. Passive-aggressive Hailey sent *him* to do her dirty work.

"We listed it like we're supposed to. Mr. Carleton approved it," he tells me.

Even though I'm furious, I keep my voice reasonable. Thanks to Bethany and Jagger, I've had lots of practice. "Guess you didn't realize we were doing follow-ups, Mr. C."

"No one knew," Scott says. "It's not on the board."

"We haven't finished planning the next broadcast. That's what today's for."

The teacher holds up a pudgy hand. "Don't fight—"

I refuse to let Hailey get away with this. If I lose, my team will never forgive me. "Mr. Carleton. On TV, the same reporter follows a story no matter how long it takes. They don't hand it over to whoever feels like working it that week."

"Puh-lease." Scott laughs. "This is high school...."

He continues to argue. I catch Mr. C.'s eye. With what I hope is a subtle tilt, I glance at the Emmy Award shelf. Mr.

Carleton's name is nowhere to be found. It's the last media teacher, R. Rosenfeld, who's listed as adviser.

When Scott pauses to take a breath, I jump back in. "Mr. Carleton's trying to run a professional operation. So we can move on to good media programs in college, get jobs, win awards…"

"Val!" Mr. Carleton admonishes.

Oops. Might have hit the award thing a little too hard.

"But Ms. Gaines is correct." Behind us, the room is silent. "A story should be followed by the originating reporter. Val, I didn't realize you were continuing to investigate. If it messes up your broadcast, A Team, I'll allow three pieces this week. No grade penalty."

Scott slumps over to Hailey. If looks could kill, he'd be heading straight for death row. I feel for him, but I'm glad it's not me who lost the argument.

Mr. Carleton lowers his voice. "Don't let me down, Val."

"I won't!"

The team piles into the director's booth.

"Way to get back what's ours, sista!" Omar hoots.

Henry and I fist-bump. Raul gives a short nod. Over in the corner, Jagger yawns. If I expected props from Voorham, I'm a fool. His short attention span hasn't increased by much in a year. Screw him.

"Let's get organized. Jagger and I stay on the story since I just made a big deal about it. But we need help."

"I'll anchor," Raul suggests. "Frees me up to do whatever's needed."

"Right on. I have all the footage shot and half-edited on the College Application story we didn't air last time. If someone wants to finish that, it's an easy second segment."

Marci speaks up. "I'll do it. MP creeps me out."

Omar grins. "All mannequins are creepy. But naked ones are waaay better."

I roll my eyes. "The rest of us split into groups. Omar and Raul. Henry, me and Jagger."

"You don't need three people," Henry says. "I'll help Marci."

"That's sweet," she tells him, "but we've got a week."

For a moment, he looks disappointed. Immediately, though, Henry cheers up. "We need more stories. I'll stay here and think of a couple easy ones. Marci can help me shoot next week."

"Fine. Whatever. Got to get going," Raul urges.

The team piles into the main room, ignoring the resentful looks Scott and the rest of his team send our way. I head for the equipment cabinet. "Marci, sign it out for us?"

"Aye-aye, ValGal." She salutes.

Expertly, I flip a case onto a table and pull the camera. "Jags and I shoot the yard. Raul, you and Omar get the inside stuff."

Outside, at least, the plastic leg is untouched. Jagger and I set up in front of the trash can.

"You're awfully quiet," I tell him.

Jagger shrugs. "What's there to say? Either you were going to get the story back—or not."

"Don't you think we should follow up? You're the one who wanted it in the first place."

He plugs the headphone into the camera. "All I said was that it would be a good story. Especially since *Campus News* is usually so lame—"

"Thanks a lot." I whip the mic cord out of the way. "Why are you even in the class if that's what you think? You could have taken Mechanical Drawing or the Fine Art of Cooking Crap or whatever that class is called."

Jagger gestures to the trash can. "Ready?"

"No. Me and *Campus News* might be lame, but you're… awful. A terrible person. You hang out with me all summer. Then the night of Sonya's party, I'm stuck babysitting the twins, so I say, 'Doesn't mean you can't go.' Every other boyfriend in the universe would tell me, 'I'll keep you company.' Not you. When I finally show up, you and Dawn Chevananda are tonguing like crazy." All the hurt bottled up inside gushes out. "You never said a word. Ever. Don't you think I'm owed an apology? An explanation."

A curtain lifts and his Tortured Soul look appears. Last year, whenever that happened, it made me want to hold him tight, tell him it would be okay, whatever *it* is.

"What's wrong?" I would whisper.

"Nothing," he'd always say.

So I'd let it go, thinking I was crazy. Or believing that my hugs—and kisses—would banish whatever problem he was having. Until I found out I wasn't enough at all.

"This is not the time to get into it, Val." Footsteps sound behind us. Immediately, Jagger's expression changes. Frustrated, he points to the leg. "Start talking or the bell will ring before we get a single shot off. Then you'll really be pissed."

Like I'm not now—but he's right. Mr. Orel heads straight for us, trash bag in hand. Stalking to the garbage can, I glare at the camera. To add to my rage, Jagger counts down as if he's been in TV Production forever.

"In five, four, three…"

Later that evening, after the twins are asleep, Mom calls me into her bedroom.

"What did Bethany tell you I did now?"

She laughs. "I don't know. What did you do?"

"Nothing."

"Good." Mom looks pleased. As if by using Advanced Interrogation Techniques she's managed to get something out of me. "I'm the one who wants to ask a question. About your sister."

"Go ahead." I sit on the queen-size bed, the blanket a lumpy mess from the twins' postbath read-aloud.

"Does Bethany have a boyfriend?"

"What? No!" That would be horrible. I haven't had a boyfriend since Jagger. How could she?

"You sure?" Mom asks.

"Not really. How would I know? It's not like Bethie talks to me. Ever."

"That'll change when you get older. Blood's thicker than water." Mom gets her canny Interrogation look again. "Maybe you've seen her with someone at school."

"Mother! Are you asking me to spy on my sister?"

She appears dutifully shocked. "Of course not. I was just wondering."

I prop up the pillows. "Now I'm curious. Why are you asking?"

Mom laughs. "No big deal. Bethie wants to go clothes shopping. Asked if I knew where to get cute shirts."

"She said, 'cute shirts'? Not tan shirts? Or baggy cargo pants? Boring brown sneaks...?"

"You don't need to go on, Valerie. But yes, that's why I'm asking."

The idea that Bethany has a boyfriend boggles my mind. "If I find out anything, Mom, you'll be the first to know."

Or not. Hoodie on, I wade through the dirty clothes and the rest of the junk Bethany's tossed all over the floor. Grabbing my cell, I open the window beside my bed and climb onto the fire escape, pulling the pane back down so she can't hear me. I have a private nest out here—three-inch camping mat and sleeping bag rolled up in a waterproof bag. It works great until the weather turns November nasty. I've got a few weeks of privacy until then.

Marci is horrified when I repeat Mom's conversation. "You cannot sell out your own sister if she doesn't want anyone to know about it. Even if the sister in question is Queen of the Sloths. What's that thing your mom says?"

"Blood's thicker than water?"

"Yeah." Marci pauses. "I don't actually think she's right, but—"

"Don't worry. You're more my sister than Bethany will ever be."

Marci giggles. "Okay. So maybe she is right. Which means you can't rat Bethie out."

"I'm not saying I'll tell on her. I only said that to appease Mom."

"SAT word!" Marci moans. "You're not studying, are you?"

"You kidding? I've got enough on my plate." Last-chance SAT is in a week—and then we start to apply to colleges. Neither of us wants to think about *that,* so I return to the discussion at hand. "It would be the ultimate revenge if Bethie has a boyfriend."

"Because you don't?"

"Yeaaah."

"I hope she does."

"Hey! Who's BFF are you?"

"Yours," Marci says. "Maybe this will get you to pay attention. I'm pretty sure Raul has the hots for you."

"Very funny. He thinks I'm doing a terrible job. That the team would be better off if he was producer."

"He told you that?"

"Not exactly. I can tell by the way he looks at me." I remember his half-assed nod in the director's booth.

"What about you? Do you like him?"

"I guess. Sure. He's cute, but it's not like I ever thought of him as boyfriend material."

She pounces. "Then who *do* you think of as boyfriend material? If you even breathe the *J* name—"

"Don't worry. I went off on him today."

"Hallelujah!" Marci breathes. "What did he say?"

The elm in front of our brownstone has begun its yearly transformation. Yellow leaves, like shots of gold, shimmer between the green.

"He didn't say squat, actually. You know Jagger. Doesn't care about anyone—or anything—except his own butt."

"That's what I told you. The guy never changes. Pretty on the surface, devil below. Maybe it's good he's in TV. Lets you see him as he really is."

Instead of answering, I contemplate the tree. For years, I assumed that leaves were naturally green. Then I discovered that chlorophyll, running through veins in the leaf, masks their true colors. Underneath, leaves are more beautiful than the surface allows us to see.

The nagging thought that Marci's wrong—that what's going on with Jagger isn't that he's shallow but that there's something hidden deep inside—keeps me up half the night.

1

"Hey, you! News Girl!"

Standing in a doorway, Ms. Cordingley beckons. I make my way through the crowd of kids hurtling toward second period.

She wears a paint-smeared smock. "Thought that was you. What's your name again?"

"Val. Valerie Gaines."

She nods, although the name means nothing to her. I haven't seen the inside of an art room since seventh grade. "I've been thinking about our conversation. MP."

My heart immediately speeds up. "You found someone taking art with those initials?"

"Not exactly."

"Then why—"

"Art History. That's why I didn't think of it right away. She took AP Art History last year."

"She?"

"Mirabelle Portman. A junior. Do you know her?"

Everyone knows Mira. She might be the prettiest girl at WiHi—if you like your chicks with porcelain skin, pixie haircuts and the most amazing eyes on the planet. Elizabeth Taylor eyes, violet, which I didn't think was an actual thing until Mira showed up.

"I forgot about her because she barely came to class," Ms. Cordingley says. "Took the tests, of course, aced every one."

"How can that be?"

The teacher shrugs. "Her mom runs the art department at City College. Mira knows more about the contemporary scene than me—or the critic at the *Times*. That's what made me think of her. The more we see of MP, the more it reminds me of found art. Some Dada, of course, and a little Banksy in the way—"

This is not the time for an art lecture. "Sorry to interrupt, Ms. Cordingley, but I have to get to class. Thanks for the tip!"

Mira Portman? She most definitely does not have that underwear/toilet/body parts kind of vibe. But maybe that's the point. Perhaps doll-like Mirabelle is a secret cutter. Or purger. Could this be a weird cry for help?

I find Marci right before she walks into her next class. She listens without interruption. When I'm done, she nods.

"You and I should talk to her at lunch without the others tagging along. Don't want to scare Mira off."

In math, I try to imagine dainty Mirabelle dragging a toilet up three flights of steps. No way. If it *is* her, she had help.

At noon, it's my soccer-playing best friend who spots her in the crowded hallway leading to the cafeteria.

"Mira!" Marci waves. "Can we talk to you for a minute? In private."

Her smooth face wrinkles in confusion. "It looks important."

"It is," I say.

A pair of doors stands behind us. Beyond that, a short staircase leads to an entranceway. A second set of doors opens to the street. No one's supposed to leave during the day, so the tiny foyer is quiet.

"What's up?" Mira asks.

"You must have seen those MP things—" Marci blinks as Mirabelle laughs. "What's so funny?"

"I wondered if someone would think of me."

"You're MP?" My voice squeaks. Did we do it? Find the right person?

"No," Mira says. "My initials *are* MP, but I'm not the person who did those stupid pranks."

"One of the art teachers thinks they're, like, cool pieces."

Mira laughs. "Ms. Cordingley? Hasn't a clue about contemporary art."

"She said that, too. Told me you know more than she does."

Mira's violet eyes brighten at the compliment, but then her face falls. "I'm pretty sure this isn't an art project."

"How can you tell?"

With a graceful wave, Mira suggests we sit on the steps. "Promise you won't say anything to anybody." She waits for us to nod. "We don't hang, so you guys don't know me. I'm afraid you'll think this is totally conceited. Everyone thinks I am, but really, I'm not."

Marci shakes her head. "We don't. What does knowing you have to do with MP?"

Mira hesitates. "Has anyone ever been in love with you? Totally, madly, completely—and you can't stand the guy?"

"Sure," Marci says.

I remain silent.

Mira searches for the right words. "It's possible—and I really do mean *possible*—that someone's doing this to get back at me."

Marci's eyes widen. "Because you dumped him?"

Mira shakes her head. "Never got that far. I ignored him. Ignore. Present tense included."

"I get that!" Marci tightens her ponytail. "The reason you think it could be this dude is because the MP stuff is on the arty side, right? And there's the initials. It's like people who hire airplanes to skywrite, 'Will you marry me, Louise?' If the name isn't there, it's a waste."

Mira nods. "It sounds completely crazy but he might be trying to impress me. Or hope I'll get in trouble. Of course, it could be a 'who needs you?' bitch slap."

"Sounds like a whole lot of effort to go through," I say.

"That's why I'm not sure. But see, Ms. Cordingley came up with my name. If he wants to get me in trouble, why not do it like this?"

Marci and I exchange a glance.

"Who's the guy?" I ask.

"Uh-uh. I give you a name, it could make things worse. I'm ignoring it. Crossing my fingers that you *Campus News* guys find out who it is. Maybe it's not who I think it is or the reason I said. Then I'd feel stupid, which is why I swore you to secrecy in the first place."

"Mira," Marci says firmly, "you have to trust that we won't go all whistle-blower on you. Val and I will find a way to talk to whoever it is without them knowing we spoke. If you want it to stop, you have to give us a name."

With a resigned sigh, Mira whispers, "Trey Lyman."

Marci grimaces. "You poor thing."

"Why?" I ask. "What's wrong with Trey?"

"Are you kidding? Trey Lyman in love with you?" Marci shivers. "The guy's had a creepy little mustache ever since fifth grade. Real hair, too, not some little pencil line."

"Oh, come on. How would you even know that?"

"I went to P.S. 27 with him. Before I knew you, Trey and I rode the magnet bus together. Boogers came out of his nose and milk bubbled from his mouth every morning. Nobody would sit next to him."

"Thank you!" Mira exclaims. "At least I'm not the only one grossed out."

"That was elementary school," I point out.

"It's hard to get the picture out of your head," Marci says.

Mira nods vigorously. "I met him at Hebrew school. Same boogers. Same milk. He never said a word to me until last year, but I always knew he liked me."

"Okay, Mira, thanks for the tip," I say. "Trey will never know we've talked."

After soccer practice, Marci and I walk to her house. She lives at Cadman Towers on the nineteenth floor. A corner deck overlooks downtown Brooklyn. Daylight saving time hasn't ended yet, so the late afternoon's infused with a last gasp of warmth. We settle on lounge chairs, a bag of chips and Marci's laptop on our knees.

"I need new boots," she tells me. "Brown. Mom said if I find a good deal, she'll buy them."

Marci's idea of a good deal is on the loose side. Ten dollars off counts as a major sale. It doesn't take long before we bookmark at least ten pairs, not one less than two hundred bucks.

"You didn't find any you like?" she asks.

"Are you kidding? The only way I get new boots is if I find them at the discount place on Fourth Avenue. In the sale bin. We have twins, Marci. They need new shoes, like, every other month!"

She brightens. "Why don't you tell your mom to buy them two, or maybe three, sizes too big? They can grow into them. Money saved goes to you."

I throw the bag of chips at her. "You'd make a terrible older sister."

"I guess." She shuts the laptop. "I was thinking about something all through practice. How are we supposed to interview Trey and *not* tell him we talked to Mira?"

"How should I know? It sounded good at the time."

"Do you have any classes with him?" she asks.

"Uh-uh. You?"

She shakes her head. "Maybe one of the guys. Gym or something. They could propose a 'girls who won't give you the time of day' story."

I reach over and grab the chips. "Cuts Jagger out."

Defiantly, she grabs them back. Her perfectly tweezed eyebrows arch. "Send Raul. I'm pretty sure he can relate!"

> Anarchism is the great liberator of
> man from the phantoms that have
> held him captive.
>
> EMMA GOLDMAN

MP LOG

I've been thinking about how modern man is completely tied down by rules and regulations. It's not like back in the day when you could do what you want when you want. Now all decisions are made by people you can't influence or talk sense to. It's exactly the same at WiHi. We've got to eat when they say and stand when they say and sit where they say and even get permission to take a shit.

MP has got to start changing things. That's what I told the rest of the group. We're the only ones willing to show the world it can be done. We should start with *Campus News*. Block them from broadcasting stories about us. Once that stops, once we break the power ladder in this school, it can't be put back together. It can't be controlled.

Phantom said, "It's cool to be on school news because nobody knows who we are. Everyone wonders about us."

I said, "Uh-uh, we need to control the informational flow. When we're ready, *then* we'll tell them what we want them to say. That shows our strength. Our priorities. Our total command of the situation."

Phantom's face had a skeptical look, but Ghost Face said, "Skeletor's right. That

Campus News girl is the type who won't stop unless we make her. If she finds out who we are, the school might break us up."

Ghost Face glanced at me while saying it. I'm pretty sure she likes me, not like most of the stuck-up bitches at this school.

"How are we supposed to stop her?" Phantom asked, all pissed off because people were on my side.

Hell Girl came up with an idea. I have a better one, but sometimes you've got to let chicks think they're smart if you want to keep them in check. If Hell Girl's plan doesn't work, we'll go for mine. Like I always say, save the best for last.

Once we got that out of the way, we started planning the next prank. That's what we call the stuff we do. Phantom read some old book about people doing pranks. It's part of the reason we're MP. In the summer, when we thought up the idea, Phantom wanted us to be the Merry Pranksters. I said, "No. We can't copy from that book exactly. We could maybe use the initials, MP, but it's got to mean something else—" That's when the idea came to me. "Masked Pranksters! All the people we ask to be in it can pick their own names from comic books or *manga* or even horror movies and then we'll get masks."

"What for?" Phantom asked me.

"We're going to need them. People feel freer behind a mask." Free to do whatever's needed.

8

"Whoa!" Marci whispers as we exit the third-floor staircase.

The hall looks like the East Village with concert announcements plastered across construction site walls. The only difference is that the papers taped to lockers aren't blasting info about the latest indie band. The flyers, if that's what they are, repeat the same words, over and over.

JOIN US.

Underneath the stenciled letters, a small group of birds gather. The drawing doesn't have many details. Hatch marks create messy feathers; darker lines make up legs and heads. Something about them looks cool, though, despite the fact that the picture is crude.

In the bottom corner, one bird stands alone. He's got a crooked wing and stares up at the flock as if he's just been attacked. On the other hand, it might be that the poor bird's desperate to join the rest. It could go either way.

"MP?" Marci whispers.

"Who else? The writing's the same. Call Phil. See if they papered his hall. I'll try Bethany."

My sister answers on the second ring. "If I get caught talking—"

Honestly, would it kill the kid to answer the phone nicely just one time? "You won't get in trouble. It's before first bell. Are you at your locker? Is the hall papered with MP flyers?"

"No. Is yours?"

"Yes. Go around the corner. See if anything's there. I'll wait."

It doesn't take long before she whispers, "I see them—"

"Which hallway? English or French?"

"I'm not sure. I don't know where all the classes are yet."

"What room are you in front of?" I ask.

"One eighty."

"That's French. Thanks, Bethie-any." I hang up before she can yell at me for screwing up her name. "First floor was hit. The language corridor."

"Phil's locker is clean," Marci reports. "What do you think? MP only had time to do a couple of halls."

"That'll be my guess. We should ask Mira—darn it!" I point down the hall. "People are starting to tear these down. I've got to get equipment!"

Just before sprinting to the Media Center, I make sure to reattach the flyer to my locker.

By the time first period ends, Omar and Raul have returned from their reconnaissance trip.

"MP did one hallway on each floor," Omar says. "My guess is there wasn't time to blanket the whole school."

"Any rumors going around about who did it?"

"Eryn Forrester, who's on Student Council, thinks it might be an advertisement," Raul tells us. "For a new gym or something."

"They can't do that, can they?" Henry asks. "Advertise in school?"

I perk up. "Wait! The Board of Ed is considering a motion to allow companies to hang banners in public schools. Paint lockers with their logos. They'd give the district a ton of money if it passes."

"How do you know?" Raul asks.

"Channel 5 did a piece about it last week. But I don't think the Board voted yet."

"How can Wilkins let some business put up weird ads on *our* lockers?" Marci's pissed. "Honestly, what does he *do* all day except go around with that stupid bullhorn and yell at people in the cafeteria?"

"Good point. We should get the administration view," Omar says. "I'll check it out with my new friend Mrs. Fairy."

"Cool. Go with...Jagger?" The boys nod. "Raul, Marci's got a long shot idea to tell you about."

"Wait up!" Henry gets tongue-tied the instant everyone turns.

"Do you have a suggestion?" I ask gently.

He shakes his head and points to the flyer. "A question. It says 'Join Us.'"

"Yes. It does." Marci wrinkles her eyebrows. "What are you—oh, I get it! *Us.* If MP is someone's initials, why didn't he write 'Join Me'?"

Henry gives her the puppy dog eyes. "Exactly. Who's us? 'Til now, we've assumed it's one person. And there's a second question. How does someone join? There aren't directions."

Marci chews the string on her WiHi Girls' Soccer sweatshirt. "Maybe this is the first flyer. There could be more with instructions."

"Hold on!" Raul points. "Henry, are you saying MP isn't the bird in the corner? It's the group of birds?"

"Flock," Jagger notes.

"Group, flock, whatever."

Henry's scruffy hair flies as he nods. "The flock's definitely MP."

"Why are you so sure?" Omar asks.

With a Sharpie, Henry traces a pattern on the flyer. "Check out the feet. See the two letters on each claw? MP. The corner bird doesn't have that."

Raul whistles. "I'd never have noticed that in a million years."

"Doesn't prove anything." Jagger taps the paper. "Maybe 'Us' means if you join *Me,* MP, then it's an us."

"Whatchu smokin', bro, and can I have some?" Omar laughs. "That makes no sense."

"It does. If it's rhetorical," Jagger insists.

"Rhetorical or not, you guys sign out a camera and talk to Mrs. Fahey during lunch so we can rule out a company looking for publicity," I tell them. "If it's a dead end, at least we have another way to go."

Skipping the cafeteria, I pop into the Media Center to digitize the locker footage during lunchtime. Just before the bell rings, the rest of the team appears. Nobody looks happy.

"What happened?" I ask.

"Mrs. Fairy told Omar that she won't be interviewed on camera again," Jagger says.

Omar lightens his voice for a very credible imitation of the assistant principal. "'What I can tell you right now is that Mr. Wilkins wouldn't think of allowing advertisements without the Board's approval. And I hope, no, insist, that *Campus News* refrain from spreading rumors. I refuse to speculate regarding the nature of the flyers.'"

Before we stop laughing, the intercom squawks. Mr. Wilkins.

"Teachers, please excuse the interruption. At this time, I need to remind all students that postering on lockers is not permitted. Approved flyers *must* be placed on bulletin boards designated for that purpose. Thank you for your cooperation."

Marci shakes her head. "Let's see if I get this straight. Cut-up plastic body parts are fine with Wilkins as long as they're not hanging from lockers."

I laugh. "The mysteries of WiHi are..."

"Mysterious. I know. But—" The bell cuts off whatever else she's about to say. Marci waits as I hit Save and then Close.

"Raul and I struck out, too, Val. Trey's got that horrible flu that's going around. The runs, the stomach—"

I hold up my hand. "No further details needed, thank you very much!"

"Yeah. Okay. He hasn't been in school all week, so he didn't put up the flyers. He's not MP."

"Are you going to tell Mira so she won't keep worrying?" She holds her phone. "Already texted."

Later that evening, I catch the news while the twins take a bath. Channel 5's Emily Purdue does a piece about roadkill jewelry, actually modeling a rat bracelet. Shows how far that lady will go for a story, even if it's fluff. I love the way she keeps her cool, though, never letting viewers know what she really thinks. Watching her on the screen, I fall into one of my favorite fantasies. A summer internship as Emily's assistant. How cool is that? My dream college in Syracuse has an extensive internship list, so it's not like it's out of the question.

That line of thought leads me upstairs. No sense sitting around when I have so much stuff to do. Narrowing down the list of schools that I should apply to. I could start the Common Application admissions essay. Or figure out a way to catch MP.

The door to my bedroom is closed. It's no surprise to find Bethany on her bed just…sitting there.

"What?" she snaps.

"I just watched the grossest thing—"

My sister blinks. "And you're telling me because…"

"I'm considering buying you a skunk necklace for Christmas. Just want to know what you think."

She yawns. "I hate skunks. Everybody hates skunks. Are you done with the TV?"

Honestly. Why bother trying to have a conversation? "All yours. Until the twins get out of the bath, that is."

Bethany shoots out of the room like a cannonball. Her feet pound the steps. Dad yells, "Who's running like that? I've told you kids a million times…"

Instead of starting the essay, I pull out my *Campus News* notebook and try to come up with a plan to unravel the MP mystery. A coup like that would go a long way with college admissions committees. Is it a group, like Henry thinks? If so, what does that mean? No lightbulb ideas hit, so I move to the computer. Bethie and I share, which means I can only get on when she's not. As producer, I'm on WiHi's announcement distribution list, so I try to check email at least once a day.

Two messages are in my in-box. Reading the second one sends a jolt of electricity through my brain.

Information is power. MP has the power. Stop trying to find out who this is or *Campus News* will be cut out.

Holy smokes. Actual contact! Never mind what it says. Sending an email means my stories have hit home. Maybe I'm closing in without realizing it.

The email address, mp@hotmail, doesn't help. Anyone can set up a Hotmail account. Leaning forward, it takes a couple of tries to craft the right response.

Can we meet to talk about this? Any time and place you say.

Imagine the scoop! Meeting MP, trying to convince him—or a group—to go public. The triumph when I tell the team. Raul will have to admit I was the right choice for producer. It won't matter whether Jagger smirks or not. I'll break the story. Student Emmy Award—and college of my dreams—here I come!

I cannot wait for the reply.

Which never comes. After two days, I give the team the go-ahead for a segment using the flyers-on-lockers footage. Everyone except Marci works on it. At the end, I ask the question: Is MP one person or a group? The camera cuts to a close-up of the flyer. Henry highlighted the faint MP on each of the birds' claws. Just as the piece comes to a close, the letters start to glow. We hear actual applause from the neighboring classroom when the broadcast signs off.

Raul gives each of us the WiHi fist bump. "Great show, guys."

"Agreed!" I say. "Best team ever!"

Marci's caught up in the excitement, too. "Let's eat lunch together. Never, in the entire history of *Campus News,* has anyone applauded."

Jagger laughs. "That's because everyone's asleep by the end."

She leans back in the chair. "Do you *have* to be such a jerk? Every time?"

"Can you two call a truce? Please!" The constant bickering between Marci and Jagger is getting to Omar. "At least during lunch. I want to talk Halloween. I'm having a party."

"Cool," I tell him. "Corner table by the far window?"

Everyone nods except for Jagger. Luckily, Marci's not looking his way.

Before heading to the cafeteria, I twirl my locker combo, fling open the door—and immediately slam it shut.

Tracy Gardner's got the locker next to mine. "What's the matter, Val? Forget your sandwich—"

"It's nothing." With a "no problem" wave, I barrel down the hall. "Marci!"

The screech is louder than I intend. Marci and Phil turn at the same moment.

"What's wrong—" she starts.

I grab her arm. "Come, too, Phil. You're not going to believe what I just saw."

The looks we get as I drag them through the crowd make me realize I need to slow down, stay cool. Just in case someone's watching. I pull the two of them into the gap by the nurse's office. "Wait until the hall clears."

"For what?" Phil asks, at the same time Marci says, "Tell me!"

"Hold on." I wait a bit before peering around the corner. Halls empty quickly at lunch. "We're good!" I move to my locker, turn the combo and swing the door open. "Voila!"

Marci pushes Phil aside and then shrieks, "What on earth—"

"Crazy, right?"

A dead bird hangs inside the locker. One end of a string is tied around his neck; the other end loops to the coat hook. The left wing droops crookedly.

"It's fake, right?" Marci whispers hopefully.

"Hell no," Phil tells her. "This is, or was, a real animal. Sparrow maybe. Or wren. Look at the eyes. That is not plastic."

"This is way creepy!" Marci says. "And disgusting."

Phil reaches into the locker. "I'll get rid of it—"

"No!" I breathe. "I mean, not yet."

"You don't want to keep this—"

Marci shudders. "She does. At least until she can shoot it."

The light dawns on Phil's face. "MP! He's the one—"

"Or they," Marci scolds. "Didn't you watch the broadcast this morning?"

My phone buzzes. Text message. "It's Raul. They're waiting for us in the caf."

"Give me that." Marci takes my cell.

Phil gestures to the locker. "Do you really want to show this to the whole school? It might give people ideas."

"Don't tell me you're advocating censorship!"

He shifts, confused. "Um, not if that's a bad thing."

I toss my head. "Yes, it's a bad thing. Marci, give me my phone back. I need to tell them to bring equipment—"

"They're on it." She shudders. "Can you at least shut the door while we wait? That thing's weirding me out."

"You're not going to faint, are you?" Phil sounds worried.

"I just need to sit." She settles on the floor, her back against Tracy's locker. "That poor bird…."

"I'll wet some paper towels," Phil says.

Marci watches her boyfriend jog down the hall. "So sweet."

"Uh-huh." He's a little too troglodyte for my taste, but I'll never say that out loud. "How do you think someone got into my locker?"

"What?" She looks startled. "I don't know."

Both Phil, carrying a boatload of dripping paper towels, and the team arrive at the same time.

"Ran into Jagger," Omar tells me. "He'll be right here."

Marci rolls her eyes. "After the work is done."

I pull open the locker door and Raul whistles. "Now, *that's* a visual."

Phil might have some caveman in him, but Raul understands news. After the lights are set, Omar starts to shoot. He gets straight on, side, and low angles.

Just as Marci predicted, Jagger strolls down the hall the instant we finish. "Miss much?"

"Take a look," Henry says.

Jagger takes it in without blinking before turning to me. He sounds concerned. "What are you going to do now?"

"Are you kidding?" Marci looks like she wants to gag. "Throw it away. Right this second. I can't imagine the diseases the poor thing has. Had."

"I don't think we should toss it. We need to keep it for proof," Raul says.

"Of what?" Jagger asks.

Henry says, "Foul play."

Jagger can't help laughing. "*F-O-W-L* play? Now, that's good, Henry."

Henry actually smiles. "*F-O-U-L*. As in, this is a seriously bad sign that MP wants Val to stop reporting."

"You're right." I dig into my backpack and pull out a copy of the email. "Got this a few days ago."

The group gathers to read. Marci blinks. "And you didn't tell us?"

"I didn't think they'd actually *do* something to me. Tell the truth. Does anyone here think we should back off the story because MP says so?"

"Give us a little credit," Raul mutters.

"Wait a sec. We *should* stop reporting it." Marci points to the locker, at the same time Phil throws me a satisfied look.

"Whoever did this is crazy. You're just feeding his, their…
whatever by giving MP all this publicity. Not only that, but
this is clearly a 'Locker Violation.' Wilkins will be pissed. You
should tell him."

"You can't be serious," I protest. "He might squash the
story. It's my locker, Marci. I get to decide whether or not to
keep quiet."

"Like that will ever happen," she mutters.

Phil holds up a hand. "It doesn't matter to me what you
guys do about *Campus News*. Right now you have to decide
about the bird. You can't leave it here or maggots will—"

"Phil!" Marci shrieks. "That's disgusting."

"But true," Raul says. "How about we find a plastic bag,
wrap it tight."

"And keep it where? Not in the Media Center or this is the
last you see of me." Marci pouts.

"Freezer," Henry suggests.

"Gross," Marci mumbles.

"I have twin brothers. If they see it next to the ice cream
or whatever, they'd dissect it in two minutes flat."

That pulls Marci out of her funk. "You should see Val's
fridge. There's no room to freeze a candy bar, let alone a bird."

"What the hell?" Raul says. "If we find a bag, I'll keep it.
Tell my mom it's a science project. She's seen worse."

Everyone except for Jagger goes off in search of a plastic bag.

"Looking a little pale there, ValGal." Although he sounds
lighthearted, his concern feels genuine. "You sure you're all
right?"

Before I can say "I'm fine," his arms circle me. Omigod!
I've forgotten what it's like to be this close to him. The body
wash, or aftershave or whatever he uses that smells so good.
The way my head reaches the soft part just below his shoulder. The shift as he leans into me, creating tiny bolts of light-

ning at every spot his body touches. Even though I know I should, I can't push away.

"I'm really sorry," he whispers.

Before I can ask if he means the dead bird or the way he treated me last year, we hear the excited chatter of the team just before they round the corner. Instinctively, I jump aside. Jagger winks before turning toward the team.

Our little secret.

9

In bed that night, I feel the events of the day swirling around my brain. The dead bird, Jagger's hug. Marci pushing us to back off the story, Jagger's hug. Was it a friendly "you found a creepy thing in your locker" hug—or something more? I consider calling him to ask, but that thought lasts about ten seconds. I'd feel really stupid if he doesn't know what I'm talking about. As in, I hug girls all the time, so don't think that was something special.

Then there's the lock mystery. It wasn't broken, so someone got the combination from somewhere. It would be easy for Tracy Gardner—locker to my left—or Lawrence Gold on the right—to sneak a look. But Tracy's headed for Harvard, so why would she have any part in hanging a dead bird? And Lawrence must have OCD. He has not one, but two boxes of antibacterial wipes in his locker, as well as a stock of mini hand sanitizers. If Lawrence heard Phil mention maggots, he'd have dropped out of school by now. Still, I plan to have someone from the team interview them.

Leave no stone unturned.

On my sister's side of the room, the steady rise and fall of the blanket tells me she's asleep. I sneak over to the computer. A second message from MP awaits.

Like the present? Stop putting us on the news. You don't want to be responsible for more dead birds. Or worse.

I take my time typing a reply.

I asked for a meeting and you ignored me. I'm asking again. If you're too scared to meet in person, perhaps it's chickens, not sparrows that should be on your flyers.

"Val?"

"Why are you sneaking up behind me, Bethany?"

"I'm not," my sister says. "I called your name three times, but you didn't hear."

That's probably true. Years ago, I learned to tune out the chaos in the house, especially when I'm concentrating. In an effort to shield the computer from Bethany's prying eyes, I stand in front of the screen.

"What are you doing?" she asks suspiciously.

"Nothing. Sending an email. Go back to bed."

"You know I can't sleep until every light in the room is out. Including the computer."

Honestly! What did I do in a previous life to deserve the Queen of Lame in this one?

"One second!" I mutter.

No chance to reconsider. With a pounding heart, and the click of a finger, my message to MP flies through the Net.

10

The scoop is humongous, outrageous, crushing. While we're busy spinning our MP wheels, A Team's next broadcast rocks the house. Literally.

They did an entire show about the Battle of the Bands going down Saturday night. On the whiteboard, Scott listed each segment differently so Mr. C. wouldn't catch on until too late. News story about the show itself, Spotlight on one of the bands, Community story about a benefit concert (that just happens to feature the third band—with their youth-obsessed thirty-year-old lead singer), and a fourth story he listed as Informational. Like anyone at WiHi doesn't know about death metal bands. Even if you live in a cardboard box under the Brooklyn Bridge, you'd have some sense of what they're about. The leader of Impaled on a Stick mumbled something about mutilation and necrophilia before Scott cut it off.

Even worse, after really short interviews, each band *played*. Hailey told Mr. C. that it wouldn't be fair if one band performed and not the others because it was a battle and they couldn't tip the vote. So what we basically got was a sixteen-minute music video. Forget applause. The hoots echoing down the hall are proof positive that A Team jumped way ahead of us in terms of popularity.

Jagger slaps Scott on the back. "Freakin' tight, man. How'd you mic Impaled so they sounded so good?"

Hailey gives me a *gotcha, bitch* grin. I walk over, smile sweetly. "Nice job. A little narrow in scope, but hey…if you don't have a lot of ideas, you gotta do what you gotta do."

"Look who's talking." She stares so hard that her eyes cross. "I bet you made it all up."

"Made what up?"

"MP. You needed an interesting story, so you got your friends to put up stuff around school."

The accusation is so shocking I can't even speak. That only seems to confirm Hailey's belief.

She lets out a breath. "Of course! How clever. MP! Marci and Phil!" She turns.

"Scott—"

I grab her. "Shut up! I would *never* fake a story. Not in a million, trillion years. So don't go spreading rumors that aren't true."

Before she can respond, Raul comes over. "Sorry, Hailey, we need Val." He pulls me toward the director's booth. "What was that all about?"

"Nothing. Hailey's an idiot. What's up?"

"Henry's got something."

The rest of the group is there when Raul and I enter. Jagger's jumpy, more excited than I've seen him all year.

"That was a cool show!" he says. "Wish we'd done something like it."

Marci gives him the death stare. "You can always play for the other team, Voorham. No one's stopping you."

Omar pats the chair next to him, grins wickedly. "Other team's just waiting."

Jagger winks. "Thanks. I'll keep that in mind."

Henry clears his throat. "Guys? I've been thinking about that bird all night. Who's got your locker combo, Val?"

"No one. I mean, besides me."

"Not even Marci?" Jagger asks.

She shakes her head. "Got enough trouble remembering mine. I keep doing last year's. Anyone else have that problem?"

No one answers.

I lean forward. "I thought about that, too, Henry. Somebody could have watched me work it."

He pushes hair out of his eyes. "You think you're being followed around school?"

"Not exactly. It wouldn't be hard for Lawrence Gold or Tracy Gardner to get the combo. They have the lockers next to mine."

Henry nods. "Do you want me and Omar to check it out? Lawrence is in AP Gov with us and Tracy and I have Spanish together."

Raul drums his knuckles on the table. "You should definitely talk to them. But there *is* another way to get the combo. Who's your homeroom teacher, Val?"

"Dr. Linet. Except homeroom teachers don't know combinations. All they do is give out the slips on the first day."

"Let's make sure. Because if teachers keep a copy in their desks, anyone who has class in that room could find it."

"Even if they don't, the office must have a list," Marci offers.

"You don't actually need that," Omar says. "Janitors can get into any locker anytime they want."

The hair on my arm rises. "How do you know?"

"My uncle. He's head custodian at LaGuardia. They have master keys. That's the reason he told me never to put anything dangerous in my locker."

"Like a gun?" Marci's eyes are huge.

"More like weed. The administration can open any locker without asking because it's the city's property, not ours."

"Good to know," Jagger says.

Omar grins. "Better clean out your locker quick, bro."

Jagger nods vigorously and the group laughs.

"A janitor makes sense," I say. "Access to school at night—and early in the morning. One of them could easily carry the toilet up to the third floor himself. Paper the hallways with flyers before anyone got here."

"Except Mr. Orel looked really pissed about the flag-pole stunt. Unless it's one of the other janitors and he doesn't know," Marci concedes.

Omar shrugs. "He could be acting. Any of them could. Like firebugs. Lots of times, they observe people watching the fires they set. Sometimes they call it in themselves so they can be the heroes. Or an abandoned building is lit up by a fireman who needs the overtime."

"How do you know?" Henry asks.

"My uncle."

"Wait. I thought he worked at LaGuardia High," Marci says.

"That's my uncle the janitor. This is my uncle the fireman. I have more than one, don't you?"

I wave the question away. "This is solid information. Let's split up. Interview Tracy, Lawrence and the janitors. Who wants what?"

Still upset about the bird, Marci forgets her vow not to work on any MP story.

"I'll go with you, Val. We can talk to the lady janitor, Shirley." She glances at the clock on the wall. "I bet she's in the cafeteria. She cleans up after the free breakfast kids fin-ish eating."

The team grabs cameras and splits up. WiHi's cafeteria is in the bottom level. A row of small windows lines up directly underneath the ceiling. Most of the light, however, comes from ugly fluorescents that turn everyone's skin a little green. During lunch, the old floor tiles and Formica tables make the room sound like Grand Central Station. Aeons of horrible school cooking have seeped into the walls. The barfy cheese smell is something I'm sure I'll remember the rest of my life.

The doors are locked. Marci stands on tiptoes and glances through a rectangular glass window. She waves. After a few moments, a door is pulled open.

Shirley's Jamaican-style braids, blond at the tips, are tied back in a loose ponytail. A set of keys jangles against her tan uniform. She gives us a quizzical look. "Lunch doesn't start for another couple of periods."

"We know." Marci turns on the hundred-watt smile. "My friend Val and I wanted to ask you a few questions for *Campus News*."

"You want to put me on the TV?"

"We're trying to find out about MP," I say. "You know, the toilet bowl, the missing flag, the flyers. All those plastic body parts—"

Shirley shakes her head. "I don't know nothing about that!"

"Wait! Can we turn the camera on while you talk? It's for a class."

She considers. "What do you want me to say?"

"We don't want you to say anything specific," Marci explains. "Val asks questions and you answer them however you want. Honestly. It's like a conversation. You can sit at a lunch table. Val will be right next to you."

"I guess." Shirley pulls the rubber band off her hair. The braids frame her face nicely. "Do I look okay?"

"Absolutely." I settle beside her and Marci starts recording. "Good morning, Ms. Johnston."

She smiles. "Oh, now, I'm not a teacher. Call me Shirley. Everyone else does."

"Okay, Shirley. You must have noticed strange things popping up around school. Do you or any of the other custodians know anything about it?"

She shakes her head. "We show up to Irving like you kids, and there they are. Pretty weird, huh?"

"Yes. Do you think one of the other custodians is doing it? For a joke? The stuff must be set up either after school or before it starts. Custodians are the only ones here at those times."

Shirley's braids shake. "Not true. Lots of teachers stay late. Or come in early. The teachers at this school work really hard. I don't think you kids appreciate that."

"But don't they have to be let in by you guys? The custodians, I mean."

Again, her head shakes. "Teachers have two keys. One for the front door and one for their classroom."

"Are you saying that MP's a teacher?"

"Oh no! I'm just saying the custodial staff aren't the only ones here before you kids show up. Or after you leave." She glances at the round wall clock. A steel grill protects its face. "That okay? I've got work to do—"

"One more question. Please. Custodians have master keys that open student lockers, right?"

She looks concerned. "Did something get stolen?"

"Oh no! No. We're not accusing anyone. In fact, it's the opposite. What if someone wanted to put something *in* someone's locker?"

Shirley blinks. "We couldn't."

"Why not?"

"We don't know which locker belongs to which student."

"What if Mr. Wilkins gets worried that there's something dangerous inside one of them? You could open it, right?"

"Yes. But he'd have to tell us *which* locker. 'Open 247 for me, please, Shirley.' I could do it, but I wouldn't know whose locker it is." She stands. "Now, ladies, I really have to get moving."

"Thanks for talking to us."

Out in the hallway, Marci sounds disappointed. "She wasn't very helpful."

"She was!" Unlike my friend, I'm excited. This is real investigative reporting. "What we just discovered is that janitors don't keep a list of students and lockers. The next step is to find out who does!"

"Mr. Wilkins," Marci says. "At least, that's what Shirley implied. Unless someone spied on you from, like, across the hall."

"Think about it. Every person stands directly in front of his locker to open it. Blocking it. If it's not Tracy or Lawrence next to me, a person would have to have binoculars to read the combo from down the hall." I shake my head. "I don't buy it. Let's go to the office and find out who has access to the master list."

This time, I lead the way. The main office has a large counter across the front, with a row of desks behind it for the secretarial staff. Mr. Wilkins's private office is to the left. Teacher mailboxes line the right wall. Marci and I wait for Mrs. Kresky, the office manager, to get off the phone. Automatically, I check the *Campus News* box.

"Morning, Val. You waiting for me? I didn't forget to put the daily announcement in your box again, did I?"

"Oh no, we got it. Marci and I are here for something different. *Campus News* is doing a piece on the way things work at WiHi."

Mrs. Kresky breaks into a laugh. "Kind of hard up for stories, aren't you? No one cares what we do in the office."

"Not true," Marci says. "Behind-the-scenes stuff is hot. Like the way they do the Oscars. And Kitchen Wars."

Mrs. Kresky shrugs. "If you say so."

"Not to say it'll definitely be a story," I add hastily. "We're doing preliminary work. Getting a feel for the possibilities."

She leans back in her chair. "What do you want to know?"

I pull my notebook from my backpack and pretend to read notes. "First, um, how are locker assignments given out? Who keeps the list? What if someone loses their combo and needs to—"

The office manager holds up a hand. "I can't answer any of that. Mrs. Gribaldini is in charge of locker assignments. She's the only person at school with the list. You need to talk to her if you want to find out about lockers."

Marci and I exchange a look. "Would you mind writing a note that says it's all right for Mrs. Gribaldini to talk to us? Otherwise…"

"Say no more." Mrs. Kresky scribbles on a message pad, tears the sheet off. "If Mrs. G. gives you a hard time, have her call me." The phone rings. "Washington Irving High School."

I wave and mouth, "Thanks so much."

She nods as she picks up the pen. "Can you repeat the name, please…?"

Out in the hall, Marci makes a sour face. "You know what I think of Mrs. Gribaldini. No way will I voluntarily step foot in her office." She gives me an evil smile. "How about I volunteer Jagger? If we're lucky, she'll swallow him whole and we'll be done with him forever."

"Tell him to hurry. I want to get it in before the period ends."

Marci must have been pretty insistent because Jagger shows up a few minutes later. It's the first time we've been alone since the hug, but I'm focused on getting the interview with Gribaldini. I hand him the camera, pull the door and walk in.

Folding chairs line two walls of the small office. Right now they're empty of truant students. I haven't been late or absent this year, so I haven't had the pleasure of running into the attendance lady, seated behind the counter doing paperwork.

"Get caught cutting?" she growls.

If students ditch, they get sent to her for the old "this goes on your permanent record" threat. Only at WiHi, it's not a threat. You'd think she could pull up your record on a computer, but the public school system hasn't changed since paper was invented. Gribaldini makes you watch while she waddles to one of the file cabinets lined up against the back wall, stiff marines eager to serve. Slowly, she pulls out the right folder. Writes on it with black marker so that for the rest of eternity, everyone will know what a terrible person you are.

"We're with *Campus News*." I nudge Jagger and he waves the camera. "We'd like to ask some questions."

She sniffs. "I don't let anyone take my picture."

Good move on her part, as it probably saves lots of lenses from cracking.

"We don't have to shoot it if you don't want. I have a note from Mrs. Kresky. It says you should answer our questions."

Mrs. G. is all about notes. She holds out a pudgy hand, reads the message carefully. Gives a put-upon sigh. "What do you want to know?"

"You're the person at school who keeps the locker list. So if someone loses their combo, they come to you, right?"

Disdain drips from her lips. "I see what this is about. You should have told me up front, instead of wasting time with all those camera shenanigans. Forgot your combination, did you? You're supposed to keep the numbers in a safe place."

"I do. But we were wondering. Did anyone come to you

this week and ask for a combination? We're doing a story about…" My voice falters. I can't think fast enough.

"Student responsibility," Jagger says quickly. "How many kids at school forget stuff like locker combos. Or the opposite. Someone's sick and asks their best friend to get their science book from the locker. But they forget to give them the combo—"

"I do not give out locker combinations without a note from the main office," Mrs. G. sniffs.

"We're not accusing you," I say quickly. "We just want to know if anyone asked this week."

She looks at us suspiciously, trying to figure out what we're up to. To her way of thinking, students are *always* up to no good. Subtly, I glance at the note in her hand.

"You're Gaines, right? The older one. Valerie Jane."

Man, she's good. "Yes."

"Well, Valerie Jane, nobody asked about any locker. Yours, his, anyone else's. Now get back to class or I'll write you up. And I'll be more than happy to get into it with Mrs. Kresky."

Before she can reach for the phone, Jagger and I beat a hasty retreat. Out in the hallway, he pokes me. "I didn't know your middle name is Jane. Jane Gaines? How very Dr. Seussical."

"Could be worse. Together, the twins are Jesse James Gaines."

"You should call yourself Janey Gainey instead of ValGal." Jagger goes high-pitched. "This is Janey Gainey, Channel 5 News, reporting from—wherever I'm reporting from."

I smack his arm as we enter the Media Center. The bell rings, but no one on the team moves.

"Anything with Gribaldini?" Raul asks hopefully.

"She insisted no one asked about my locker. What about you?"

"Marci told us what Shirley said. Mr. Orel gave us the same info."

"Tracy and Lawrence swear they don't know your combo," Henry says. "They wanted to know why, so I just said someone put something in there. Didn't tell them what."

Everyone looks disappointed. Score so far: MP 4, *Campus News* 0.

11

Music pulses all the way out to the street, making the small brick row house that Omar lives in easy to find. Underneath the stoop, three steps lead to the basement. A tidal wave of sound, heat and dancing bodies hits me the instant I push the unlocked door. The party's epic. A Halloween night that falls on a Saturday cannot be beat.

Costumes are the usual mix of comic book characters, assorted sluts and various types of hideous ghouls. Even without their masks, I'm pretty sure I'd have no idea who half these people are. Word got out. *Masquerade Party on Remsen. Wear a mask, BYOB and you're in.*

Omar stole the idea from some TV show. Maybe a movie. Either way, the place is decorated in 99 Cent Store chic. Streamers and strands of plastic beads fall from the ceiling. A row of squat candles line the folding table, holding bowls of chips and pretzels. Carved pumpkins, waxy light flickering through cutout teeth and weirdly shaped eyes turn the basement into a New Orleans vamp fantasy.

Omar and Jagger spent an entire class period creating a playlist. The crowd is anonymous—and amped. I told Marci and Phil not to wait for me as I had to shepherd Jesse and James, dressed as Tweedledum and Tweedledee, around the neighborhood for their annual greedy haul.

Bethany was supposed to come, too, but she bailed at the last moment.

"I'm going trick-or-treating with a friend," she announced.

Mom's eyebrows rose. Before she could ask *who* the friend is, my sister started to whine. "I don't see why I can't stay out past ten. Val doesn't ever have to be in until midnight."

"I'm a senior. When *you're* seventeen—"

"Everyone else in the world gets to stay out later," she said, pouting.

"Ten-thirty," Mom said. "Not a minute after."

Bethany grinned in triumph and scurried out before Mom changed her mind.

"She's got you wrapped around her finger, you know," I informed my mother.

She bit the thread from the needle. "Call the boys, Val. Hats are done."

The kids came running, so cute in their fat little costumes. The truth is I don't mind taking them around. The twins always give me their Special Darks, so it's win-win.

After I dropped them home, it was on to Omar's, six-pack in a paper bag. Everyone knows which bodegas in the neighborhood "forget" to card, so it's easy to score. Now I make my way to the tables at the back of the basement. Twist the cap off a bottle, hide a second one behind a pumpkin for later and put the rest in the ice-filled trash can.

"Lookin' good, Val." Omar is dressed as the Tin Man, with a silver mask and a matching triangular hat atop his head.

"How'd you know it's me?" I shout.

He points to my head. Right. The cat half mask I found at the drugstore covers the top part of my face but not my auburn hair. Once I found the mask, the rest of the costume was easy. Black shirt, black leggings, shiny belt, homemade tail safety-pinned to the back.

Omar points. "Dance?"

I gesture with the beer. "Just got here."

Dancing is not something I'm good at. I'd much rather hold up a wall and watch the crowd. Omar boogies back into the thick of things and I amuse myself trying to figure out who's who.

Marci would be easy to spot even if I didn't know she came dressed as Wonder Woman. She and Phil have staked out a spot on the make-out couch. No surprise there. Ever since last year, going to a party with Marci is pretty much going it alone.

Jagger's near the chips, talking to some girl in a dark kimono and a pale mask. It's not the half-white/half-black *Phantom of the Opera* mask he wears—more appropriate than he can imagine—but the tight black jeans that gives him away. But if Laura Hernandez is wearing the Sexy Pirate Wench costume and tiny bandit mask I noticed when I came in, who's the manga Hell Girl?

I could walk over and check it out, but why torture myself? Resolutely, I turn toward the center of the room. Some chick that's probably Zombie Hailey is totally trashed, grinding hips with…Trey Lyman? I search for Mira to see if I'm right. Either her costume's really good or this is not her kind of scene. I don't see anyone who could possibly be her.

I do catch sight of Raul. He told the team he was coming as a Thief. He's wearing a black T-shirt and dark jeans, but it's the handkerchief tied across half his face, which doubles as both costume and mask, that makes me laugh.

Watching him dance with a Fairy Godmother is the real surprise. Seriously, the dude can move. Raul comes across as a guy's guy, a cross between a shortstop and a cop. But on the dance floor, he's different. He moves effortlessly, completely in sync with the music. When the handkerchief slips down to his neck, the look of joy on his face is contagious. A gaggle of girls crowd next to him, showing off their stuff. No wonder Marci's been trying to push me into his arms. Muscles rippling, he's easy on the eyes.

The song ends. The music segues from house to metal, sending the crowd into jumping spasms of joy. Raul vanishes into the wild frenzy at the center of the room.

"Meow, Cat Girl." The guy standing next to me wears a skeleton mask underneath a hooded blue sweatshirt. "Want...?" The rest of the sentence is drowned out by a barrage of "Woot-woots."

"What?" I yell.

"Dance!"

Even if I wanted to, the guy's sweaty BO is not particularly attractive. I point to my ear, shake my head.

"Can't hear," I mouth.

Peeling away, I push across the room. If I can find Henry, I'll hang with him. Or I might check to see if Jagger's still talking to Hell Girl. A sixth sense, however, tells me to turn around. Skeleton Face is giving me the finger. Honestly. WiHi guys are such jerks.

Raul taps my shoulder. "...party!"

"Loud!" I yell.

He nods. "Your costume's..."

The rest of the sentence is lost, although I smile in the hope that it's a compliment. We stand for a moment, checking out the crowd. Drunk Fairy Godmother appears, waving her magic wand and dousing us with sparkles.

Raul laughs good-naturedly. As he brushes off his shirt, Fairy Godmother tugs at him for a dance. He shrugs at me and I wave him away.

My beer's gone. Nothing's left in the ice-filled trash can,

although my stashed bottle is still behind the pumpkin. Armed
with the fresh drink, I wander about. The room's hot, the air
thick. Smoky. Cigs. Weed…

Somebody pulls my tail, safety-pinned to the back of my
belt.

"When'd…here!" Jagger shouts into my ear.

"Half an hour?"

He pushes his mask up over his hair, grabs my beer. I know
his tricks. Given half a chance, Jagger will drain it in two seconds. I pull it back.

He coughs, eyes watery. "…some air?"

Before I can nod, there's some kind of commotion behind
us. Holy shit! It's not cigarettes making Jagger's eyes burn.
It's smoke!

A set of streamers dangling from the low ceiling is on fire.
The group closest to the flames push away. But with music
pumping and kids dancing, no one gets very far.

Screams penetrate the chaos. "Every…out! Fire! Fire!"

A moment of delay before true panic sets in. The crowd
surges forward. I struggle not to get trampled. In the crush
for the door, Jagger and I are separated. Wildly, I look to my
left. It's not Jags I see but Omar. Silver hat flashing, he's rac-
ing *toward* the fire. Something's in his hands.…

The claustrophobic squeeze of people behind, in front and
to the side overwhelm me. It's as scary as fire. The wave inches
forward. At last, I stumble outside. Arm scratched, chest heaving, I tumble to the sidewalk and take deep, appreciative gulps
of fresh air.

Outside it's chaos, too. People mill about, talking on cells,
yelling for friends.

"Valerie? Val…" Jagger lurches toward me. "You okay?"

"Omigod. Yes. You?"

Sirens cut off his answer. Marci and Phil, together with Henry, rush up.

"Val—"

"Marci! Thank God. Are Omar and Raul out, too?"

Heads shake. No one's seen them. The arrival of four red trucks accompanied by earsplitting sirens and tire squeals seems quick. Someone must have called while the rest of us were fighting for the door. Firemen pile out. In a rapid but organized sequence, one group attaches a hose to the hydrant as a second team heads for the building.

"Basement!" people yell.

My heart pounds. Several men scurry up the steps and pound on the front door. At the same time, three guys aim for the basement. One of them pulls the hose. I find myself clinging to Jagger as the firemen make their way into the building.

After what seems like minutes but is probably only seconds, Omar and Raul are escorted from the basement. The last ones out.

"Over here!" Marci yells.

The pandemonium is still monumental, so she runs to them. Omar, in earnest conversation with a fireman, stays. She does manage to drag Raul back with her. He reeks of smoke, but I don't care.

I move to give him a hug. "We were so worried when we didn't see you out here, Raul."

He squeezes back, muscles tight against my shirt.

The rest of the group clamors to find out why he and Omar got out of the basement so late. As I step aside, Marci gives me a quick, approving nod. For the first time, I seriously consider that she might have a point. Paying more attention to Raul could be a good thing. Nothing can ever happen if you don't give it a chance.

Just as that thought crosses my mind, I catch sight of Jagger. He glances away quickly, as if he doesn't want me to notice he's been watching.

My heart lurches. If I didn't know better, I'd think he was jealous.

My cell rings. Surfacing from what feels like an underground cave, I squint at the sunlight, then my cell. Not quite noon.

"Omar! Are you in trouble?"

"Whatchu think, sista?"

"But you saved everyone!"

The thing I'd seen in his hands as he rushed *toward* the flames was a fire extinguisher. By the time Engine Company 224 arrived, he and Raul had put the fire out.

Omar laughs drily. "Got a couple of points from Dad for not being the wuss he usually thinks I am—but not enough."

"Grounded?"

"Oh yeah. But I didn't call to bitch. I have to show you something. Can you come over?"

"When?"

"Soon as you can."

Even with the basement door propped open, the burned smell is nasty. Omar does not look like himself. He isn't wearing a single scarf or ounce of jewelry. Instead, he's got on dirty jeans, an old shirt, work gloves and a dorky pair of boots. Lumpy trash bags, buckets and sooty sponges fill the room.

Raul holds a mop.

"Didn't know you were here, too," I tell him.

"Stopped by half an hour ago. Just wanted to make sure everything was cool."

"That's nice of you." Remembering my thoughts after last night's hug, I shoot him an extra-warm smile.

He shrugs modestly. "I'm a nice guy. I was helping Omar fold tables when we found it."

"Found what?"

Omar points to the corner. The words are spray-painted across the bottom of the wall.

MP was here, suckers.

"Holy shit!" I cry. "They came to the party!"

Omar cocks an eyebrow. "At least one of them."

"Let's not jump to conclusions. Anyone from school could have written that," Raul points out. "It's not their regular writing."

"Oh, come on! Stencils take time," I say. "People would notice. Damn. Why didn't we think about this before? Of course MP would come to a masked party. It was the perfect place to hide in plain sight—" The next thought takes my breath away. "Omigod! Do you think one of them started the fire? On *purpose?*"

Omar blinks. "That would explain how it happened. I'm not dumb. I didn't hang decorations near any of the candles. So, really, how *did* it start?"

"People were smoking. Somebody with a match or lighter wasn't paying attention and whoosh—fire's lit." Raul shakes his head. "It's a big leap, guys. How do you go from hanging underwear to pyromania?"

"Don't forget the dead bird," I say. "Okay, maybe it started as a joke. A sick prank that got out of control. Someone in MP was fooling around, lit a streamer and didn't realize the whole mess would go up."

Raul picks up the water bucket he's using to mop. "I still think it was an accident. No one at WiHi is that stupid—or that evil—to burn down a house with everyone inside."

PART TWO

NOVEMBER

12

A Team puts together a broadcast on the fire.

"Your crew can't do it because it's a conflict of interest," Scott tells me after listing it on the whiteboard. He looks surprised when I don't argue.

"Go for it!"

Hailey interviews Omar, who "neglects" to mention what he found on the wall. Even though she and Scott shot footage of the basement, they don't see the writing. That's because Omar painted over the words so that his parents wouldn't see them. He took a few decent pictures before he did it though, in case we need them for a future broadcast.

Next, A Team talks to kids who "saw it all." Of course, by Tuesday, half the two thousand kids at WiHi claim to have been there. No one wants to admit that they didn't go to the most exciting party of the year.

For a Community Story, the captain of Engine Company 224 makes a plea for fire safety. The entire broadcast is well done.

"You got it together so fast," I tell Scott after the Wednesday presentation. "Impressive."

"Thanks. Of course, there isn't anything you guys kept from us, is there?"

"What's that supposed to mean?"

He gives me a shrewd look. "There was fresh paint on one of the basement walls. Not on the fire side. I wondered why."

I keep cool. "Did you ask Omar?"

"He said someone puked in the corner. He tried to wash it, then decided he should paint that section of the wall. Something about getting rid of the smell."

"So that's what happened," I say.

"Yeah, I guess that's it."

I wait until Scott goes back to his team before casually wandering over to our table. Omar's filling out a Question Sheet for his next story.

"You should have told me what you said to Scott," I whisper. "I could have blown it."

Omar puts down his pen. "What are you talking about?"

I repeat the conversation. Omar shakes his head. "He didn't ask about the paint."

"He didn't?"

"I would have made up something better than barf!" Omar snorts, then nudges me. Across the room, Scott's grinning at us. It's kind of creepy, actually, but I simply return the smile as if nothing's wrong.

Faking a yawn, Omar turns so no one on A Team can read his lips. "I do believe Scotty boy knows we're keeping something from him."

"You think?" I turn, too. "Do you feel bad about it?"

"Not really. I'm not the one who just lied."

"Okay, good. Then I don't feel bad, either." I tap the Question Sheet. "All's fair in love, war and journalism, right?"

"Pretty sure that's what Carleton would say," Omar tells me.

"I'm not going to ask."

"Neither am I, sista. Neither am I."

★ ★ ★

Exactly twenty-four hours later, Henry drags the entire team out of class.

"Wait up!" Raul says. "Do we need equipment?"

Henry smacks his forehead. "Sorry. Wasn't thinking."

We sign out what's needed and gallop down to the main hall. Henry points to the glass-enclosed case that everyone, including Mr. Wilkins, passes by every day.

"Don't know how long it's been there. I just noticed it," Henry tells us.

At first, all I see are the usual trophies: WiHi's 1994 Sectional Wrestling trophy, 1953 Citywide Baseball win, 2011 Girls' Varsity Basketball champs, Debate Team champions of 1966. There are awards and proclamations: Washington Irving High School Community Service Award, Irving High Certificate of Excellence for Most AP Classes Offered in a NYC School, Best High School Attendance. Several times.

At last, though, the fakes become apparent. Once I notice them, it's impossible not to stare at the two "added" to the case. They're the type of trophies a little kid gets after soccer season, but the first one is more menacing than anything from a recreational center league. A thin rope loops around the girl's neck. The other end is attached to the shelf above so that the trophy hangs. The original nameplate has been replaced with "Roving Reporter."

The second fake's scarier. The player's head is chopped off.

Raul whistles. "Right next to the office. That's bold."

"No stenciled letters but...broken-off body piece, hanging neck." Omar's eyes narrow. "Anyone see a pattern?"

"First they target Val, now me," Marci moans.

"Why would you think—oh, soccer!" Henry smacks his forehead for the second time. "How could I forget you're captain of the girls' team?"

"Cocaptain," I automatically correct. "But it doesn't mean MP's after you, Marci. A rec center trophy is the easiest thing in the world to find. Sidewalk sales, flea markets. They're in half the bedrooms in the city."

She doesn't look the least bit soothed. "We should tell Mrs. Fahey. Or Wilkins."

"No!" comes the choir of voices.

"Anyone remember *Punk'd*?" Jagger gestures down the hall. "Let's set up a camera in secret and tape people's reactions."

"No one will notice. Henry did but that's because he's Henry." Marci manages a tiny smile. "Detail-oriented."

"If one of us stands here and stares at the case, everyone that passes will, too," Jagger declares.

"Count me out! It's sick. Like voodoo dolls but without the pins." Marci's eyes widen. "What if MP is a coven? That could explain the bird in Val's locker! They needed, like, eye of newt for some kind of witchy spell. But who knows what a newt is, or where to get one? So they killed a sparrow instead. Then they decided, waste not, want not and hung it in Valerie's locker to scare her off."

"Not sure about the voodoo hoodoo," I say, "although I agree MP's trying to frighten us. But as long as I'm in charge, *Campus News* will keep reporting until we find out exactly who's doing this."

"Cool!" Jagger says. "Are we going to shoot this by getting surprise reactions? Because I'm tired of the old 'stand here and talk about it' interview."

An argument ensues. I make the point that punking people is not close to professional reporting. The boys, however, think it's a great way to cover the story.

"Henry found it," Jagger says. "He should do the piece any way he wants."

Henry's hair flops up and down as he agrees. It makes him look like a Muppet—and how do you tell a Muppet no?

"Okay, the guys win. Marci and I will go back to the Media Center and work on something else."

She links arms with me. "Help me edit the story on the new locator app in *Yearbook*. Carleton's gonna tell me it's long because I never know what to cut—and now I'm too upset to concentrate."

As we climb the steps, I wonder if the message in the trophy case is being sent to her...or me. *If dead birds don't scare you off, threatening your best friend might.*

As always with MP, you have to read between the lines. Or rope. Of course, I could be wrong. As if everything MP does is for my benefit. I burst out laughing, startling Marci.

I've been hanging around self-centered Jagger way too long.

The next day, Mr. Carleton calls me to his desk.

"This was in my box." He hands over a summons to the principal's office. "Take your crew. I'm pretty sure Mr. Wilkins has something to say."

"He wants to do an interview? The note doesn't say that."

"A little birdie told me." Mr. Carleton grimaces. "Sorry. Bad choice of clichés. I ran into Mrs. Fahey in the parking lot. She and Wilkins had a meeting after they saw the trophy case yesterday."

Carleton's right. The principal has us set up in his office. He looks straight into the camera and announces, "I've been very tolerant of these pranks up to now, but really, this has to stop. Any student with information or knowledge regarding MP must come to me. All tips will be kept secret."

We air the piece. Not a single person at Washington Irving High School tells him a thing. On the contrary, Wilkins does MP a favor by making them seem even cooler.

★ ★ ★

A few days after the interview airs, a metal box about the size of a physics textbook appears. It's chained with a bike lock to one of the basketball poles at the back of the school. Just like with the trophies, there's no fanfare. No flyers or hanging underwear to announce its appearance. That way the administration won't discover, and then confiscate, the box. Because of the Wilkins interview, the news is kept extrasecret, whispered from kid to kid.

Check out the basketball court in the backyard.

It makes every person who finds the box seem special. Gives the message stenciled across the top all the more appeal.

TELL US WHY YOU WANT TO JOIN.
PLACE APPLICATION IN SLOT.

The slot they're talking about is obvious. It's a slit cut into the metal lid—but there aren't any applications that anyone can see.

As soon as we hear about it, Omar and I go out, equipment in hand. The instant we get close, though, the few people staring at the box move directly in front of it. Protecting MP. Or rather, protecting the evidence that MP exists.

"What are you looking at?" someone yells.

Omar keeps walking. "Don't say anything, Val. Do not stare. You don't want to make a scene or give them anything to get crazy about. They probably think we'll get Wilkins to confiscate the box."

"We wouldn't—"

"*I* know that," Omar says.

The hostile glares following our retreat means he's right.

During lunch, I return to the yard but stand off to the side. No camera, no crew. I don't want to call attention to myself.

It's not the box I'm interested in, or the people checking it out. I want to see if I can figure out who's *in* MP. I'm hoping that someone is watching from afar the way I am.

No one is. As much as I'd like to, I can't stand here all day. First quarter is just about over and teachers are going crazy giving tests. Keeping up first-semester senior grades helps with college admission, the guidance counselor told us last year. Reluctantly, I head back inside. The instant the last bell of the day rings, I rush back out, but the box is gone.

The next morning, I'm in the main office, picking up the daily announcement sheet from the *Campus News* box, when a couple of boys walk in. Definitely freshmen, they check the stacks of paper lined up across the counter.

"Can I help you?" Mrs. Kresky asks.

One of the boys mumbles, "Do you have the application form?"

"Working papers are in guidance. Fill out *both* sides, make sure you get a parent's signature, bring in proof of birth and a doctor's note," she rattles off in a single breath. "You have to be fourteen as of the day you fill it out."

The boys flee. I'm fairly certain it's not work permits they're looking for. As if MP would leave applications with Mrs. Kresky. Or guidance. Or any other school office.

Several days later, the box appears once more. It's chained to the side fence instead of the basketball pole. This time, though, it vanishes by lunch, leaving *Campus News* as much in the dark as ever.

> You have kindled a fire which all
> the waters of the ocean cannot put
> out, which seas of blood can only
> extinguish.
>
> THOMAS W. COBB

MP LOG

It's like I said. Once we start to fuck with the power ladder and give people choices, you can't predict what they'll do.

When I turned the box upside down, all kinds of stuff fell out. We didn't actually expect anything because there weren't applications. It was just one more way to mess with people's heads. But the truth is, you can't stop a good idea.

It wasn't only letters stuffed into the box. One of those folded-up origami birds was there. An unused napkin. Even a five-dollar bill.

At first, everyone in MP laughed and said, "Stupid fools. We aren't gonna take anyone new into the group." But then I said, "Hold on. Here's an opportunity to prove that we are not like the people at the top of the ladder. That we're better than they are. We evolve."

Zombie looked confused.

"It's about change," I said. "That's the cornerstone of tactical thinking in combat, business and anything else interesting. The other side can't predict what'll happen next or how far we'll go. Transformation keeps them off balance so we can ascend."

We split the applications into two groups. No and maybe. The first one chosen for the maybe pile wrote:

```
No one knows. I started cutting again. But this
time, I'm better at it. I know how to keep it secret.
Not like last time. So if you choose me, I can keep
any secret you want.
```

The blue origami bird had one word stenciled on each wing. It was the same kind of writing we use for MP, but way smaller.

Pick Me.

The chicks went crazy for this one because of the last lines.

```
Dear MP,
I am a junior, age 16, and like to try new
things. If MP is fun, I want to join. If it is
work, I don't need any more of that. My mom puts
a lot of pressure on me to get straight A's. It's
hard right now because I don't get Chem. I have
to go to tutoring every Wednesday, so if you meet
on Wednesdays, I can't do it. It would have to be
another day. Oh, on Thursdays I have Leadership
and Mondays I am in Student PETA. We try to save
strays, but sometimes we can't. If you want a
stray, just let me know. Cat or dog, whichever you
want, I'll find you a cute one. I promise.
```

This was the opposite. Real short.

i wake up in the morning, never look in the mirror. i bet u don't either.

Scribbled across the crumpled napkin someone wrote:

> *Hey, fool! Who wants to be in your stupid groop? Ha ha. Just kidding. Me.*

And this one.

```
freEks! My tribe. I gotta know you cuz I
know all the freEks in skewl. Let me in. I
know I act like I don't want to join anything
but I'm down with this. Its kewl. Friend me
up, dudes.
```

This one was my personal fave:

You need to step it up. Read the anarchist's cookbook. Yeah, it's old school, but the shit in there works. Word. That's something MP should think about. If I join, we could have some serious fun.

As if I haven't stepped it up. But, man, there were good choices. Right before we voted, Zombie asked, "How do we know if we want them in forever? A piece of paper doesn't tell us everything. Maybe they aren't right for MP."

Ghost Face said, "How about we do an interview like for a job. Let them prove they'll fit in."

Frankenstein nodded. "We can wear our masks again so the person doesn't recognize us. After they leave, we vote. In or out."

That's when I got this amazing idea. I said, all casual, so no one would know how excited I was, "Once we choose, we'll have an initiation."

"What kind of initiation?" Hell Girl asked.

"Whatever it is," I said, "it won't be lame."

13

There's something sad about a rainy November night. That's when the last autumn leaves, plucky survivors desperately clinging to their branches, give up and flutter to the ground. I vow that will not happen to me. I'm determined to get to the bottom of a story wrapped in mystery, confusion and obvious attempts to make me stop.

"Val?" Bethany asks. "You up?"

"I am now."

Over in her bed, my sister leans an arm under her cheek so that she's half facing me. "You know those stories you're doing? The ones about MP? Did you find out anything yet? Like who they are?"

I sit straight up "Why? Did you hear we did?"

Outside, a crack of thunder. Inside, Bethany shakes her head. "I just remembered that box that showed up last week. The one that said put an application in if you want to join."

"You didn't drop your name in there, did you?" I ask.

"No!" She looks surprised—and then disappointed that she hadn't considered it. "I figured you have to be a senior or at least a junior."

"There's something weird about them, Bethany. Something dangerous."

Her mouth falls open. "There wasn't anything explosive in the box, was there? Why didn't you tell me? I stood really close—"

"Don't get carried away. Nothing blew up."

"Then what are you talking about?" she snaps. "What's so dangerous about them?"

"You know the story about the bird we did?" I ask.

Although *Campus News* aired the footage, Mr. Carleton insisted we leave out exactly whose locker it was. *"For your protection, Val. You don't want anyone else to get ideas."*

"Yeah, I saw it," Bethany tells me.

"That's what I'm talking about. It's not a smart idea to hang out with anyone who kills animals."

"I like animals, Val. Don't you know that?"

"Most people do." I sigh. "Bethany, if you never listen to a word I say after tonight, that's okay. But until *Campus News* learns that MP isn't some weird cult like we think it is, don't get fooled into thinking they're cool."

"When will you find out?"

I can't hide my frustration. "How should I know?"

She shakes her head, obviously disgusted with me. "What's the point of having a sister on *Campus News* if you can't ever figure anything out?"

"Sorry to be such a disappointment!"

She doesn't respond. I decide it's time to change the topic. "Bethany?"

"What?"

I'm about to pop "the boyfriend question," but the words stick to my tongue. For the past several weeks, my sister's gotten up early every day to wash her hair. She spends at least an hour the night before deciding what to wear. It's the most…

interested in anything I've seen her be since she discovered the Video Arcade a couple of summers ago. If that doesn't spell *B-O-Y-F-R-I-E-N-D,* I don't know what does. But she has a different lunch period than me, so I don't know who she eats with.

"Never mind," I say.

With an annoyed huff, she turns to face the far side of the room. After a few minutes, my sister's asleep. I, however, am wide-awake. Honestly. Even when Bethany isn't trying, she makes me feel like a piece of crap. Gossip buzzes around WiHi like mosquitoes at a picnic. It shouldn't be this hard to find a clue as to who's pulling pranks all over the school. Any clue at all.

As if my life isn't lame enough, Marci's been bugging me on almost a daily basis about Raul. "Boys are shy. If you keep treating him like just another guy on the team, he won't step up."

It's hard. I get that Raul's cute. But whenever I close my eyes, the arms I imagine wrapped around me aren't his. Not that Jagger's said or done anything personal since the hug at my locker. Still, I can't help what sticks in my mind. What I dream about.

I'm absolutely pathetic.

Outside the wind gusts, rattling the window. I brush my finger across the pane. The relentless storm has turned the glass ice-cold.

14

On Friday, everyone on the team, except for Jagger, is in a terrible mood. The rain hasn't stopped for two days. Our most boring broadcast airs. Without an MP story, we're just another dull news team.

"Cheer up," Jagger tells us. "MP will make a move soon."

"Did anyone consider the fact that if they hadn't started doing all this stuff, we'd have been forced to find something good to report about a long time ago?" Marci shakes her head. "We're coasting, guys. Waiting for MP to do something."

Jagger looks confident. "They will."

"How do you know?" Raul demands. "No one's heard from them since the box disappeared."

"Think about it." Jagger drops his tilted chair forward with a bang. "You don't do all that stuff, get away with it and stop. You keep going. Come up with bigger ideas, take more chances."

Marci unwraps a cough drop. Like half the kids in school, she has a wicked cold. "You think they're planning something creepier?"

"Makes sense."

Intent, I lean foward. "Jagger, if you know something you're not telling us, fess up right now!"

"Okay, okay. I'm MP," he says.

Everyone stares. Not a single breath is taken. The silence around the table is so thick I feel like I'm at the bottom of a well.

Jagger laughs. "Gotcha!"

Henry blinks. Raul looks pissed.

Omar shakes his head. "You really are an asshole! Cute— but an asshole just the same!"

Before Marci seconds the opinion, I say, "Moving on. Does anyone have any ideas about how to get the story going? My sister, who barely talks to me, accused me of being stupid. We need to get back in the hunt!"

"It's what I'm trying to tell you. MP has the power right now, but once they start pulling new stunts, they'll slip up. That's how we track them down." Jagger laughs. "Or not. Sitting around moping and making dumb accusations won't do us any good. Instead, we should be setting stories for the next broadcast."

I push my notebook forward. "Go for it."

Jagger thinks a moment before accepting the challenge. "How about a Spotlight on Alicia Ruffino? I heard her talking in Trig. She's choreographing the musical. Or starring in it. Something like that."

"Ali won't be interviewed," I tell him smugly. "I tried last year. She turned me down flat."

"Maybe you should have used a little more charm."

Marci scoffs. "Like you? Puh-leeze."

Henry, however, lights up. "I'll go with you. Ali's pretty." He shoots a sidewise glance at Marci. I bite my lip to keep from laughing. Is the kid trying to make her jealous?

"Sure." Jagger pats Henry on the shoulder. "I'll show you how it's done."

Marci rolls her eyes and turns to me. "I haven't directed yet and Omar's only anchored once, so we'll team. That leaves you with Raul."

I give her *the look*. "You have it all worked out."

"Don't you want to be with me?" Raul asks with a mock-hurt expression. At least, I hope he's faking it.

"Of course I do," I say hastily. "I love working with you. Seriously."

"Oooh...." Jagger mimics my voice fairly accurately. "Love working with you."

"Child! Can you be more annoying?" Honestly, the minute I think Jagger's serious about *Campus News,* he proves me wrong. Unless that's his reaction to Raul and me working together. Jagger won't have me—but Raul can't, either?

Not fair, Jags. Not fair at all.

Across the room, Mr. Carleton calls out, "Everything okay?"

Jagger waves him off. "We're oh so excited to get to work."

Mr. Carleton peers over his glasses. "Glad to hear it! Too many of you just sitting around..."

Raul starts to toss out ideas. Henry and Jagger begin to fill out a fresh Question Sheet. They'll probably get that interview with Ali and make it kick-ass just to prove me wrong.

Raul nudges my arm. "Which story do you like better?"

Startled, I turn. I haven't heard a single thing he said.

It takes another couple of days before the storm pushes past Brooklyn. Rain-slicked streets, bare branches and a bitter wind are all that remain. The official start of winter is more than a month away, but the weather is an unruly toddler who can't read a calendar.

I stay late to work on a piece about Academic Decathlon. Passing Tony's Pizzeria on the way home, I notice Jagger and Henry sitting at a window table. Henry sees me at the same time and waves me in. Curious, I stop at the counter to get the special before making my way over to them. Jagger's got his legs sprawled across his side of the booth. I couldn't sit beside him even if I wanted to.

I slide next to Henry. "How's it going?"

"We're celebrating. We got an interview with Ali. Plus, she let us shoot rehearsal."

"Really?"

"Really!"

Jagger watches us quietly.

"Good for you," I say. "Did you remember to return the camera?"

Henry pats his backpack. "Tomorrow."

Jagger glances out the window. "Maybe you should get home before it's too late. You don't want to be walking in the dark with expensive equipment in your backpack."

For someone so smart, Henry's eating out of Jagger's hand. "Good thinking, Jags. See you guys tomorrow."

I wait until he's out the door. "I'm asking nicely, Voorham. Don't corrupt the kid."

Jagger grabs Henry's leftover crust. "I'm not. But he's a senior like the rest of us. You all treat him like a Chia Pet."

I keep a straight face. "If he were a Chia Pet, he'd get a haircut once in a while."

Jagger laughs. "You stay late to edit?"

"No ESP points. I'm predictable. It's you that's the shock. You actually hung around after the bell to work on a class project?"

He shrugs. "Ali invited me to rehearsal. And—"

"She's soooo pretty," I say.

His eyes crinkle. "Do I detect a bit of jealousy?"

I take a bite of my pizza. "None whatsoever."

He gets a satisfied *I don't believe you* look. All I can think is *Please don't do this. I can't go through it again. The way my insides melted whenever you looked at me. Waiting on pins and needles for your call. Insane happiness when it happened. Horrible numb feeling if it didn't....*

Jagger slurps my lemonade.

"Hey!"

"I left you some." Jagger gives me the cup and his hand brushes mine. "I— Damn." He glances at the tacky Leaning Tower of Pisa clock on the wall. "Gotta go. Talk to you tomorrow."

He's out the door in less than twenty seconds. Without glancing over his shoulder, Jagger waves, arrogantly certain I'm watching. Disgusted with myself, I sink into the booth, staring out the window. The gray day has morphed into a surprisingly soft evening. Colors splash across the still-wet asphalt: stoplight-red, neon purple, fruity-orange. People exit the subway wearing slickers with a rubbery sheen. Brooklyn Heights, now a watercolor painting, pulls me deep into thought.

Why can't I figure him out? Every time it seems like Jagger's about to apologize, or explain or maybe beg forgiveness, he cuts it off. He was the one who pushed me away—but lately it's like he's not sure that's what he wants.

Except I can't go back. I never, ever want to feel so hurt again....

The insistent wail of an ambulance jolts me into the present. The emergency vehicle flies down Montague, heading urgently toward the Promenade. The light atop the roof flashes garishly. I take it as a sign from whoever runs the universe, telling me that staying away, keeping my distance from Jagger, is the right thing to do.

> *Power is pleasure; and pleasure sweetens pain.*
>
> WILLIAM HAZLITT

MP LOG

Yeah, man, this is what I'm talking about. The world is a swirling mass of energy, all boxed up. Once you let it out, you can't control it. You never know what's going to happen, but it'll definitely be better than what came before.

The initiation was an easy ten out of ten. When you hit that high mark the first time out, man, there's nothing like it in the world.

We found a spot on the Promenade where a rock wall curves down from the street above. It's a couple stories high. We told the new girl to get there first and stare at Manhattan across the river. Then we snuck out from our hiding places and warned her not to turn around. I brought my camera and started snapping pics while one of the chicks blindfolded her. The new girl took the oath of silence, stood on the wall and then, just like we planned, Frankenstein told her to start walking down.

The rain ended about an hour before, so no one got wet. I kept snapping pics, following her. I leaned in close. Then boom, pow, her foot slipped—and she flew over the wall. A cracking sound echoed as she hit the ground.

In that moment, it became crystal clear to me. The alignment of our power is almost complete. It cannot be stopped.

At the bottom level, a metal fence separates the Promenade walkway from the rock wall. In between the two, there's a group of bushes. That's where she landed.

Phantom climbed the fence and took off the blindfold. The new girl was crying, saying, "It hurts so bad." Without asking anyone, Phantom called 911. That's when the new chick stopped for a minute and said, "I won't tell what happened. I took the oath. I still want to be in the group, so can I?"

I said, "Hell yes, if you say you were by yourself when you fell." She nodded. I said to the rest, "Get going. Phantom, you have to stay because you called the cops. When the ambulance shows up, just keep saying like you did on the phone that you were taking a walk and found her."

Just before I left, I snapped a couple of pictures of her leg. The bone stuck out and there was all sorts of blood. When I got home I blew up the photos on my computer.

Best pics I ever took.

15

Mom's on the phone when I get home. She waves me into the kitchen and tells the caller, "Val just got in. Call when you're on your way." She disconnects. "There you are!"

"Here I am. Stayed late to work on something for *Campus News*." It occurs to me that the house is unusually silent. "Where is everyone?"

Mom runs a hand through her hair. "I got stuck on the train for more than an hour. Some kind of stall ahead of us. Dad'll be late, too."

I'm confused. "Where are the twins?"

"That's the problem. I texted Connie as soon as I had reception. Asked her to pick up the boys when she got Robby from after-school. If you get them from her place, I'll start dinner."

"Why do I have to? I'm not the only teenager in this house, you know."

Mom throws an apron over her navy blue power suit and starts to chop an onion with short, quick motions. "Bethany's sick. Oh, that reminds me, I need to find the thermometer—"

"If she gives me that disgusting cold going around, I'll never speak to her again. Marci coughed so much at lunch, green crap came out of her *mouth*."

"Valerie!" Mom stops midchop. "The boys?"

With my fist, I pound the counter. "Just once, I wish Bethany would do something around here besides complain! Or get sick at the most inconvenient times. I've got homework!"

I stomp into the hall, shrug back into my coat. Honestly, the kid gets out of doing everything. In my next life, I plan to be the youngest. Or an only child.

It's not quite six o'clock, but already the night has that damp chill that settles deep into your bones. Connie and her son live four blocks south. I scurry down the sidewalk, dodging peeing dogs and their impatient owners, as well as pedestrians carrying grocery bags and briefcases. I'm checking building numbers when something makes me glance across the street. I stop so fast that the woman behind me literally bangs into my rear.

"Sorry," she says.

"My fault." Ducking my head, I slip into the shadows of a doorway. After a few seconds, I peek out.

Jagger's across the street, talking to a girl. When she laughs, her face shifts slightly. Ali Ruffino! The chick choreographing the musical.

Great. He leaves me flat at the pizzeria to meet her! My cheeks burn with anger. I don't have to text Marci to know what she'll say.

Once a flirty jerk, always a flirty jerk.

> Fear is maintained by a never failing
> dread of punishment.
>
> MACHIAVELLI

MP LOG

I called an emergency meeting. We had to get together because of what happened with the new girl.

We sat in a circle like always. The chicks started in right away, not even waiting for the oath. They're scared they'll get in trouble. They think the new girl will tell someone what really happened. I said, "Smarten up. It's been three days. You would have been called to the office by now if that's what she was going to do." I looked around. "Any of you been summoned?"

Heads shake. "See? You really don't understand how powerful we are. She wants to be part of us. She knows she can't if she tells. End of story."

After a bunch of grudging nods of agreement, I shifted the conversation. "Since we're here, we might as well get started on the next prank."

Out of the blue, Phantom said, "I quit. I don't like how this is going. When that girl fell, one of us was awfully close to her."

Everyone turned to me, but I know my circle. I understood the look in their eyes. They're scared but not about the new girl anymore. They're worried I'm going to flip out or say, "Okay, no more group" because they know Phantom and I started MP together.

None of them wants MP to end.

I laughed, which is not what anyone expected. In situations like this, it's always better to do the unexpected, to keep everyone off balance. I said, "I don't care if you quit. Go ahead, but you can't tell anyone about us."

"Yeah, yeah," Phantom said. "I took the blood oath, so you don't have to worry about me snitching or anything."

I have these two sharp teeth and if I open my lips a certain way, I look like a wolf. I gave the group my *Canis lupus* smile. "I got another reason you won't tell, Phantom. Why no one will tell." Like a magician with a hat full of rabbit, I pulled out the pictures from the initiation and fanned them across the floor. "Every one of you is in at least two of these pictures with the new girl. But not me. So if anyone says anything, I'm going to send these to Wilkins. Anonymously."

Phantom looked at me with eyes full of fear—and respect—and then said, "I told you, I'm not gonna tell and I won't, but I'm outta here. If the rest of you have any brains at all, you'll follow."

After Phantom left, no one said anything. Nobody got up to leave, either. Then one of the chicks asked, "We still got a group, right?"

"Yeah," I said. "We still got a group."

16

"Why won't you shut off the light?" Bethany whines.

It's after eleven. She's been out of school for a couple of days. It wasn't a cold, but a virusy thing that was making her extra cranky.

"Just a minute." I type the last sentence of my history essay and don't even proof it before hitting Print. While I wait, I click over to email. Holy crap! A new message. It's from a Gmail account, though, not Hotmail.

If you want to know more about MP, meet me at the Promenade playground, 4:00 tomorrow. Don't tell anyone. I will know if you disobey. Come alone.

My immediate response: I'll be there. By myself.

Even though the time elapsed from reading the email to sending the reply is probably no more than sixty seconds, I feel my sister's eyes on my back. Sure enough, when I turn, she gives me a pouty stare.

"If I'm still sick tomorrow, it's your fault."

I don't get into the science of germs with her. Like the fact that they have a specific life span and keeping the light on five more minutes won't make a lick of difference to her health. Instead, I gather pages from the printer.

"Done! Go to sleep."

"Shut the light!" she commands.

I flip the switch on my way to the bathroom. That means I have to feel my way across the Sloth Queen's Cave of Darkness upon my return. It's not like I'm falling asleep anytime soon, however. A million questions run through my mind: Who sent the email? What will the person tell me? Why the playground?

Every night, before going to sleep, I pull the curtains together in order to get the room dark enough for my sister. Long ago, I discovered that if I shift the fabric in a certain way and lean against the window, the light from the streetlamp shines only on me. Without waking Bethany, I slide my *Campus News* notebook out of my backpack and come up with questions to ask. My assumption is that MP will freak if I whip out a notebook so I memorize the list.

Once that's done, it's hard not to pick up my cell, charging on the desk, and text Marci. Or someone else on the team. But if I do that, I've broken my promise. Gone public with something private. When you're investigating a story, "off the record" is the hardest thing to deal with. It means the reporter's not allowed to name the source who gave up the information. The problem is that no one can double-check the accuracy of what I'm saying. I could be accused of lying like Hailey had done.

There are other reasons to keep quiet. I could be getting *Punk'd*. No one shows up and I look like a gullible twerp. Or they do show up and I can't convince whoever's meeting me to agree to an interview—or get them to go public—so I can report it. Better to not embarrass myself in front of Jagger and the rest of the team until I find out what's up.

Still, I'm so excited. I stare at the moon.

"I'm meeting MP!" I mouth, knowing the moon, at least, will never tell.

At school, I'm antsy all day. Jagger uses the computer station next to mine to edit his Spotlight interview, but I barely notice. It's only when I hear Henry say, "The stuff on Ali's rehearsal tape is really great," that I glance over.

"What rehearsal tape?" I ask.

"Ali gave Jagger video of a rehearsal that Mrs. Malmgren shot," Henry tells me. "She brought it home to check how the dances look. Ali's in the show *and* she's choreographing."

"Guess she's doubly talented. When did you get the tape, Jags?"

He looks up. "What? Oh, after I left Tony's. That's the reason I ran out of there so fast. Ali said she'd meet me in front of her building at five forty-five and I didn't want to be late. Why?"

Wow. I'd completely misinterpreted the situation but at least I hadn't said anything to him. "No reason."

Jagger shrugs and shifts his attention to the screen. "Henry, do you think this part is a little slow…?"

Happy to dodge *that* bullet, I return to my list, reviewing the questions I plan to ask my MP contact and adding a couple of new ones. I want to be ready for anything the contact says.

What I'm not prepared for is the envelope propped on the shelf in my locker at the end of the day. It's not as creepy as finding a dead animal, but being reminded that MP has my combination—and is not afraid to use it—makes me furious.

It's a plain white envelope, the kind all parents have on their desk, and that any kid can take without it being missed. Nothing's written on the front or the back. Inside, the typed note is brief:

```
Change of plans. Tonight at 9. Same place.
Remember—not a word to anyone. Do not come
one minute earlier.
```

"Damn!" I breathe.

How scary is a playground in the afternoon, with parents and nannies alert for any whiff of danger? Not very. Nighttime, however, is a whole different story.

My immediate thought is to email MP, tell him I can't go at night and ask for another afternoon. But if the past is any example, there won't be a reply. I could skip the meeting, but that ruins any chance for an interview.

Someone's cleverly thought this through. If I want the story, I have no choice but to do what I'm told.

When I get home after school, I discover the Cub Scouts are having a spaghetti dinner fundraiser at the elementary school. Mom's on the committee and she made Dad come home early to help.

For once, I'm the daughter who whines. "Nobody told me about this! I've got stuff to do."

"We bought you a ticket," Mom says.

"Is Bethany going?"

"No!" my sister shouts from the living room couch. "I hate spaghetti dinners. Gross pasta and hard garlic bread."

"See?" I look to Dad for support. "Come on, Dad, tell Mom I shouldn't have to do it."

He shrugs. "I don't see why you have to go. But it's your mother's decision."

Mom throws up her hands. "Fine! Eat leftovers, girls."

Bethany scoots into the kitchen. "No way. I am not eating meat loaf again. It was disgusting the first time."

"Then come to the dinner. Those are your choices." Mom

stomps out of the room, yells up the steps, "Jessie! James! Time to go."

Dad puts a finger to his lips and pulls out a couple of tens. "Get a pizza or something."

My sister grabs the money and grins at Dad. "Thanks!"

"Frank!" Mom is on the front stoop. "We're late!"

"Have fun, guys!" I shout. After the door closes, I hold out a hand for my share of the dough. "Nice going, Bethany!"

She shrugs. "I hate meat loaf."

"So does Dad."

"Then why do we have it?"

"That is an excellent question."

She looks to see if I'm messing with her. I'm not, but Bethany isn't sure.

"I'm going to order Chinese when I get hungry," she says. "Do you want something?"

Bethany knows I hate Chinese, so it's not a surprise when I say no. She gallops happily upstairs. I finish my homework in front of the living-room TV, watch a rerun and then the news. Emily Purdue interviews a Wall Street dude about the stock market dip. She's focused and polite. When the guy doesn't answer a question and shifts the conversation to what *he* wants to say, she rephrases. A useful tip—and one I'm eager to try.

The delivery guy shows up about seven o'clock. It's against house rules to eat anywhere except the kitchen or dining room, but Bethany doesn't care. She takes the bag and starts back upstairs.

"If cockroaches show up in our bedroom tonight," I shout, "I'll kill you!"

Her reply is a door slam. It's not only roaches I'm worried about. Now the room's going to smell like Kung Pao chicken. Suppressing the urge to run up and choke my sister, I head for the kitchen. I don't hate meat loaf as long as there's ketchup.

If I eat that now, my share of the money is saved for after-school pizza emergencies.

Half a meat loaf sandwich later, my stomach, tied up in knots from nerves, rebels. I toss the rest into the trash and check the time. Restless, I go through my backpack. Phone charged, new pen, small notebook in case the contact person lets me take notes. Check, check and check.

After reviewing my questions for the hundredth time, I run halfway up the steps—no way am I stepping foot into the bedroom until my sister's done eating—and yell, "Bethany, I'm going out for a little while!"

Five minutes later, I'm on the way to my first-ever interview with an unknown source.

The little park that's the rendezvous point is next to the Promenade on Pierrepont Street. The Statue of Liberty, the East River and Manhattan are visible from the top of the slide. The twins still look for Easter eggs there during the annual hunt.

What surprises me, though, is just how dark the playground is at this hour. Twisting branches of maple trees block the streetlamp, creating shadows within shadows. The benches are vacant. It's not like I thought I'd see kids swinging on swings or making sand castles. Still, it's a surprise to find the place completely empty.

The play area itself is small, surrounded by a spiky metal fence that reaches my shoulders. There's only one gate into—and out of—the playground. The sign says Open 7 a.m. to 10 p.m. I check my cell. It's 8:59.

The final minute is taken up with trying to open the gate. Did MP screw up? Does the city lock it early? Finally, it occurs to me that I have to reach *through* the metal bars, twist my hand and slide the latch from the inside edge.

Dead, crinkly leaves drift across the walkway. The gate clangs. I glance over my shoulder, but it's only the weight of the metal set to close each time someone enters. No one's behind me. My gaze sweeps the area. The usual assortment of swings, teeter-totter and slides are off to the side. In a central pit, a large structure made of wood, rope and plastic has climbing steps, bridges—and several hiding places.

"That's close enough!" Coming from either inside or behind the play structure, the voice is distorted. There's an app for that. Given the Gaines girls' lame phones, we aren't able to download it, but I've seen it before on Jagger's phone.

"I told you to stop!"

It's too dark to see any movement ahead of me. I'm not sure the person is even *in* the playground. He could be on the other side of the fence, hiding behind the bushes.

"Come out, come out, wherever you are," I shout.

"Go to the Starbucks on Montague. Second table on the left. Look inside the napkin holder."

"I thought we were going to talk—"

"If you don't get there by nine-fifteen, the note will be gone."

I check my cell. Eleven minutes to go. Even if I charge forward like Phil blitzing an opposing quarterback, I can't get out of the playground. The fence is impossible to climb. By the time I move back through the gate and run to the other side, the person will be gone.

There go all my carefully crafted questions. With no choice but to hike down Pierrepont, I scan the side streets for anyone scrambling away. No luck. I swerve onto Montague. Starbucks is two-thirds of the way down, not far from Trinity Church's school auditorium.

With barely a minute to spare, I burst into the coffee shop completely out of breath. A few weird looks from people drinking chai lattes and mocha cappuccinos get thrown my way, but nobody says anything. It's Brooklyn. I'd have to have a bloody face or bullet in my arm for anyone to actually speak to me.

I check out the tables. Is it two from the back—or front? It seems logical to count from the door. I walk up to the balding man sitting at the second table.

"Excuse me. I have to switch this." The man, focused on his laptop, barely looks up as I replace his metal napkin holder with one from another table.

In the corner, an empty leather chair beckons. Hunched over, I pop out the napkins. Fan them carefully. Nothing. Either my contact lied, or he's counting from the back.

The couple at the second-from-last table when I first arrived is gone. I do the same pull-the-napkins routine. Stuffed behind the last one is a note.

```
Your broadcasts are right. MP is not a
person but a group. We chose someone from the
people who put stuff in the box and told her
she could join as long as she went through
an initiation. She said yes, but it went
wrong. Now she's in the hospital. It changed
everything. I could get in big trouble for
telling you this. Don't let anyone know I
contacted you. Spies are everywhere.
```

The house is dark when I slip back in, twins and parents tucked away in bed. That's a happy surprise because it means I don't have to explain where I've been.

Despite the fact that Bethany cracked the window about an inch, my bedroom smells like a Chinese restaurant. Apparently, being the Queen of Sloth is an unusually tiring occupation because she fell asleep before getting rid of the leftovers.

The takeout carton sits on the night table between our beds. With visions of roaches skittering across my pillow, I grab the box with two fingers and toss it into the downstairs trash.

Now that I'm sure everyone's asleep, I decide to reread the note in the full light of the kitchen. The news hasn't changed. Someone's in the hospital. Joining MP isn't a game.

What to do? I lay out three options: say nothing, tell the team or show the note to an adult. Mr. Carleton, Mrs. Fahey or Wilkins. But something nags at me. It's still possible to be the victim of an elaborate *Punk'd* scheme. What if the note's a setup? A lie? I go ahead, broadcast the story—and then somehow they prove it false. That would make me look unreliable. To the school, Mr. Carleton and the team.

What I need is a second source. In Intro, Mr. C. screened *All the President's Men*. The whole point of the movie is that the reporters had to confirm every piece of information discovered two ways—or their editor wouldn't publish the articles.

"I'm holding you to the same standards," Mr. Carleton told us. "*Campus News* is not gonzo journalism. Not the Grunge Report."

The good part is I'll be perfectly safe broadcasting a story as long as I find one other person to verify the information in the note. That way, I haven't burned my source and I can't get in trouble for not checking things out correctly.

Then the adults at school can take over and actually *do* something about shutting MP down—instead of making stupid announcements in the middle of class. B Team will get that story, too, so it's win-win.

How I find the second source, though, is what makes being a reporter interesting—and really, really hard.

17

"I want to do a story about accidents," I announce the next day.

Raul perks up. "Car? Snowboards? Walking under a ladder and then falling into a hole—"

"That's a superstition," Marci tells him. "Like breaking a mirror."

"Not superstitions!" It comes out harsher than I intend. "Sorry, Marci, didn't mean to yell. I want to find kids who are in the hospital because of an accident. Any kind."

Jagger looks at me curiously. "Isn't that kind of...random?"

"Not really," Omar says. "It's like a Spotlight but with more than one person."

"I'm in," Marci says. "Nice idea, Val."

"Since when is *nice* one of a producer's qualities?" Jagger asks a bit too innocently. "I thought they're supposed to be hard-hitting, a little bossy—"

Not for the first time, Raul rides to my rescue. "If the girl wants to do a puff piece, she can. Change it up, right, Val?"

Marci kicks me under the table just as Henry asks, "You sure there's anyone to interview?"

"Definitely," Marci says. "There's the girl who got into a bad accident last week. Our goalie knows her—"

"Got a name?" Raul asks.

"I can find out."

"Don't bother. I'll check with the attendance office," I say. "Who's up for a trip to the first floor?"

Raul pops up. "I'm not afraid of Mrs. G."

Marci smiles brightly. "Great!"

I slip my backpack over my shoulder. "Don't bother to sign out a camera, Raul. Gribaldini refuses to let us shoot in her office, but it won't matter because all we need are names. The rest of you know what you're working on?"

At this point in the year, we've got stories in all stages of development; some ready to roll, a few half-finished, a couple just getting started. Chairs scrape as the team scatters. Raul and I walk out of the Media Center side by side.

"How'd you come up with the idea?" he asks.

"Oh, you know." I wave a hand vaguely. "A 'late at night can't sleep' thought."

"Mine always suck. I'm positive that whatever I think of at midnight is fantastic, but in the morning, the idea doesn't hold water."

"Hopefully, this will!"

In the main hall, I hesitate. "Maybe we should get another note from Mrs. Kresky so Gribaldini will talk to us."

"Nah. I got this." Raul strides confidently into the attendance office. "Hey, Mrs. G. You have a minute?"

She looks up. "Raul! Nice to see you."

Nice to see you?

I look at Raul, astonished, but he's leaning against the counter, explaining what we want.

He finishes up with, "It's a 'well-wishing for the injured' kind of thing."

Mrs. Gribaldini doesn't break a sweat. Four names are inside the Rolodex in her head. "Two freshman—Alexis Abbot and Pablo Ruiz. One junior, Taneisha Woods, and the senior football player who got hurt in the game against Kennedy High—"

"Tristan Hannity," Raul says. "We're in Lit together. Thanks. If you think of anyone else, would you leave a note in the *Campus News* box for me?"

She actually smiles. "Will do. It's a nice idea. Bad accidents are tough. Now, don't forget to say hello to your mom, Raul."

"Back atcha for Tommy. He graduate from City yet?"

"Next year." Gribaldini quivers proudly. "Tommy's doing real good."

"I bet." Raul gives her a warm salute. "We've got to get back. Thanks for the info."

In the hallway, I breathe a sigh of relief. "Not so hard."

"She and my mom went to Irving together. Her oldest kid, Tommy, used to babysit me before my grandmother moved in."

"Bet Mrs. G. doesn't give *you* a hard time when you're late."

He laughs. "I don't get the Voice, if that's what you mean. How do you want to work the piece? We could talk to Tristan first—"

"I think we should start with the freshmen. Move up from there."

"Sure. We still have to find out who's in what hospital—or if they've been released to their homes."

"Let's split that part up. How about I take the two girls and you work on the guys? Did you keep the copy of the directory they gave out in September?"

"I can get an extra from the office," Raul says.

"Cool. Let's see what info we can find out tonight and sign out a camera after school tomorrow. If we're lucky, a couple of the kids might be in the same hospital."

"Lucky for us," Raul says. "Not sure that's what they'd say."

Embarrassed, I duck my head. Sometimes my reporter instincts make me sound awfully cold.

The instant I get home, I check the Starbucks note. It does say, "*She* ended up in the hospital." I glance at the girls' names in my notebook. My first real lead! One of them has to be MP's choice to join the group.

Kids in the WiHi directory are listed by class year. You can choose not to have your information added, though, so there's no guarantee I'll find what I need. I do a quick check; to my relief, both names are there.

Downstairs, Bethany gobbles cookies before Mom gets home. That may be the reason she's never hungry at dinnertime—though it's none of my business.

"Do you know a girl named Alexis Abbot?"

She washes the cookie down with milk. "Why?"

"Can't you just answer a simple question for once? She's in your grade."

"What does she look like?"

"I don't know. That's why I'm asking. We're doing a *Campus News* segment about kids who've been in accidents." Bethany doesn't say anything, so I add, "It's a human interest story."

"What does that even mean? Mrs. O'Leary says all humans are interesting."

"Do you know Alexis or not, Bethany? She's been absent a couple of days."

My sister brushes crumbs from her mouth. "I'm not Mrs. Gribaldini. I don't keep attendance records."

"Why do I bother?" I snap.

Upstairs, I dial the listed phone number. After a few rings, a sweet voice answers. "Hello."

"Alexis? This is Valerie Gaines. I work for *Campus News*.

We're doing a human—um, a story about WiHi students who've been in accidents."

"Why?"

"Sort of like a fancy video get-well card."

"Oh." There's a pause. "That's nice, I guess."

"Yeah. Can you tell me exactly what kind of accident you were in?"

"Okay. It was right after all that rain. The streets were still wet." Alexis hesitates, as if afraid to relive the event. "I was riding with my dad and some guy skidded through a red light. He smashed into my side of the car. It's lucky I was wearing my seat belt or I'd have hit the windshield."

"That's terrible!" Sympathy for her mixes with disappointment that she's obviously not the person I'm looking for. "You okay now?"

"I have a broken clavicle and punctured lung, but it could have been worse."

"What about your dad?"

"He's fine. But the guy who T-boned us had a heart attack."

"What a nightmare. Is it all right if we come by after school tomorrow to interview you?"

"I'm pretty banged up."

"That's okay. You'll be doing people a favor. You know, reminding everyone to wear seat belts."

"I guess. Sure."

"Great. Is this your cell? Are you in the hospital?"

"No. They finally let me out. I'll give you my address."

"If it's the same as the one in the directory, I've got it. See you tomorrow."

I put a line through Alexis's name. Unless I'm completely off base, there's only one person it could be. Eagerly, I flip the directory pages to the *W*s and find Taneisha's number. It goes to voice mail.

"Hi, Taneisha. This is Val Gaines. Could you please return the call? It's sort of important."

When she doesn't call back by dinner, I try again. She doesn't pick up this time, either. I decide not to leave a second message and risk scaring her off.

Luckily, it's Bethany's turn to scrub pots. Taking the steps two at a time, I consider an investigative plan of action. First assumption: the initiation happened close to WiHi. That means the ambulance would drive to a nearby hospital. There are only two possibilities: Brooklyn Hospital and Long Island College Hospital.

Long Island's the obvious first choice. It's on Hicks Street, a few blocks south of the Heights. I call the main number and ask for Taneisha's room.

"Hold on, please." After a moment, the operator declares, "We have no Woods."

"Has she been released? I'm a school friend and I'd like to know if she's all right."

"Hold on." A moment later, she comes back on the line. "Sorry, dear. No Taneisha Woods admitted in the last week. Try Brooklyn Hospital."

"Thank you."

I find the number. The operator gives me the same "Hold on, please" comment. Then she says, "Room 503. Do you want me to transfer you?"

My breath quickens. "That's all right. I'd rather visit."

"Visiting hours end at eight, so you'd better hurry if you want to see her tonight."

It's 7:15. From the Heights, it will take two trains to get there. There's no way I'll make it. "What time do they begin tomorrow?"

"Eleven to eight every day."

"Thank you."

I hang up, quite pleased with my investigative skills.

"I hate hospitals," Raul says.

"Me, too!" For no reason whatsoever, we're whispering. It seems appropriate as we cross a reception area filled with puke-colored chairs. None of the people hanging around the lobby look even the tiniest bit happy. Raul and I take our place at the counter in front of a sign that states Visitor Sign-In Here.

"Can I help you?" a pleasant lady asks.

"Yes, we're visiting Taneisha Woods. Room—"

"Five oh three." She looks up from the computer. "Over fourteen?" Raul and I nod, too nervous to be insulted that she can't tell we're almost eighteen. "Sign in and I'll give you a badge. Red line to the elevator."

I stick the visitor tag on my jacket. The red line starts parallel to the yellow and green lines but then veers into its own corridor. It leads to a wide elevator. When the doors whoosh open, we hesitate. A male nurse stands beside a rolling bed. An old person lies on it, covered by a white blanket. He's hooked to a tube attached to a standing pole and liquid-filled bag.

"Plenty of room," the nurse says cheerfully.

Without a word, Raul and I step inside. At the third floor, the nurse says, "Getting out," and competently pushes the bed/person/tube affair into the hall. Raul lets out a relieved breath. On five, the doors open once again. A sign on the wall has arrows.

"503 is to the left," I announce.

Raul looks more and more uncomfortable. "She knows we're coming, right?"

"Not exactly. Taneisha didn't return my call, so I got the room number from the hospital operator last night."

"Oh. I didn't catch that. Maybe you should go in first. Make sure that, um…"

I understand. Nobody wants him barging into the room if Taneisha is not ready for visitors. "I'll get you when we're ready."

He puts the camera case down gratefully, leans against the wall to the left of room 503. "I'll be right here."

Softly, I knock on the open door. "Taneisha? Can I come in?"

A woman's voice answers, "Of course. Neish, you didn't tell me a friend was coming to visit."

Each of the two beds that take up most of the room has a curtain that can be pulled to create privacy. An older lady in the first one is asleep. On the far end, by the window, a woman, probably Mrs. Woods, sits on yet another puke-colored chair. Taneisha's hospital blanket is rumpled. Her short, straightened hair is uncombed, and she's got on one of those blue-and-white cotton hospital gowns.

The instant Taneisha sees me, she puts down the *Masters of the Universe* comic she's reading. A series of thin scars on her left arm, like tiny railroad tracks, peek out from under the loose, short sleeve of the nightgown. She's a cutter, I realize, although I'm not sure if that relates.

Taneisha notices my glance, and immediately pulls the blanket up to her neck.

I give her my camera-ready grin. "Hi, Taneisha. I'm Valerie Gaines from *Campus News*."

"I know who you are," she mumbles. "What do you want?"

"Neisha!" her mom scolds. "That's not polite—"

"It's okay, Mrs. Woods." Taneisha's mom is as rumpled as the blanket. Clothes wrinkled, face creased with exhaustion, she looks as if she's been sleeping in the chair for days. "I didn't get a chance to tell her I was coming. But I'm here now, so if you want to take a break or go to the cafeteria or something, I'll be glad to keep her company."

Before her daughter can protest, Mrs. Woods nods gratefully. "That would be wonderful. Just a few minutes. Be right back." She mouths *Thanks* before hurrying out of the room.

Taneisha glares. "Really. What do you want?"

"To ask a few questions. *Campus News* is doing a piece on accidents and we'd like to include you."

Taneisha shakes her head. "I don't want to be in it."

"It's like a video get-well card. Isn't that cool?"

"No. Can you go now?"

I lean over. "Taneisha, I know you got hurt because of MP—"

She rears into the hospital pillow as if I slapped her. "Why would you say that?"

"I can't tell you how I know, but—"

"You don't know anything. I was doing something stupid right after it rained and I slipped and fell. That's all. That's it—"

"I won't say anything if you don't want me to. I just need to know the truth."

"Get out!" she screams. "Now!"

The lady in the other bed stirs. "Something wrong, honey? Push the button."

Taneisha's blanket falls to the side. Her left leg is in a cast from foot to thigh. A steel rod goes from one side of her leg to the other, right under her knee. It looks extremely painful.

"Everything's fine," I reassure the old woman. "I'll leave now, Taneisha. But if you change your mind and want to talk—" I scribble my cell number on a page from my notebook. "Think about it. Please."

Before she yells again, I hurry out. Raul's exactly where he said he'd be. "What happened? I heard shouting."

"She doesn't want to be interviewed. But I told her mom I'd stay—oh, good. Here she is."

Mrs. Woods hurries down the hallway, Styrofoam cup in hand. "Everything okay?"

"Taneisha got kind of upset. I'm sorry—"

Mrs. Woods shakes her head. "Don't worry about it. She's been cranky ever since the accident. It's what they call a tib-fib. Two broken bones."

"Ouch. I'd be cranky, too," Raul says.

Mrs. Woods looks at us curiously. "Thanks for visiting...."

Before she asks how we know her daughter, I grab Raul's arm. "Hope she gets better soon."

Taneisha's the only one of the four accident victims still in the hospital. Raul and I stop at Tristan's brick row house to shoot his interview. I don't hear a word he says, even though I'm the one working the camera and have the headphones on. I'm still thinking about Taneisha. I couldn't tell if she's terrified by MP—or protecting them.

"Thanks, Tristan. We got enough." Raul asks, "Val?"

"What? Oh, sorry. Yeah, it's good."

Outside, the sun has set. Raul nudges me. "Up for a burger? I need food before interviewing Alexis."

"We don't have to do them all today."

He gestures to the camera. "We've got the equipment. Didn't you tell me Alexis lives on Joralemon? We have to pass the Burger 'n Bun to get there."

"Now that you mention it, I am hungry."

Raul breaks into a grin. "Thought so. You seemed a little spacey at Tristan's."

Burger 'n Bun is one of the few restaurants in the Heights that hasn't been renovated, refreshed or turned into an overpriced hipster joint. A narrow place, there's barely room for a well-used grill and fryer combo behind the yellowing marble counter. A set of round, patched-leather stools face the grill. Three wobbly tables line the back wall, but no one sits there if there's a choice. The counter's the place to be. We take the end stools, leaving a couple of empty seats between us and an elderly man drinking coffee.

"Hey, Dave," Raul says.

Dave's run the place forever. The large-bellied cook flips burgers, scrambles eggs and fries potatoes to near-perfect crispness.

"Afternoon, folks. What'll it be?"

There aren't menus at Burger 'n Bun. Just a faded list on the wall that no one bothers with. There are never specials of the day, no new items. Nothing ever changes, which might be the most comforting thing about the place.

Politely, Raul lets me go first. I wave him on while I decide.

"Cheeseburger and fries," he orders. "With a root beer."

"I'll have a grilled cheese with fries. Rye bread and tomato, please. Lemonade if you have it."

Dave grunts and gets to work. He's not a talky guy, but he's a magician with a spatula. For a few minutes, we watch the show. Fries, burger, bun. Bread for my order is slathered with butter and plopped onto the grill.

Raul swivels his stool to face me. "You going to Winter Formal?"

"Uh-uh. A Team's got that story. They're doing ticket sales next week, and then they'll cover the dance in January. It's on the board."

Raul clears his throat. "I don't mean for *Campus News*. I meant, you know, to go. To dance and shit."

Before I can answer, Dave slaps chipped white plates onto

the counter and brings drinks with paper-covered straws stuck to the outside of the glasses. "Need anything else?"

Raul shakes his head. "Thanks. That's it."

I get busy unfolding a napkin and then reach for the ketchup. Next thing I know, a wrapper hits my cheek. Raul's resorted to the ten-year-old "blow the straw paper at your neighbor" trick to get my attention.

Turning toward him, I notice the expectant look on his face. I pass him the plastic bottle. "You could have asked."

"I sort of did. Will you go to Winter Formal with me?"

My fork clatters to the floor. "I'll get it."

I jump off the stool before Raul can move. Never mind the embarrassment of groping about on the floor. It gives me a moment to think.

Wow! Marci's right, after all. He does like me that way. It's not hard to figure out what she'd tell me to do: *just say yes*.

She's right. I can't spend the rest of my life dreaming about Jagger. It's not like Raul and I don't have a lot in common. We do. We could talk camera angles all night. Plus, he's cute. Yes, I haven't felt that special spark the way I do even now when I'm with Jagger—but maybe that takes time.

I resurface with the fork. Raul hands me a clean one.

"Thanks." I swivel the stool so that I'm facing him. "Sure, I'll go with you. It'll be fun."

His anxious look melts into a grin. "Excellent. 'Cause you know, Latinos can dance."

I hold up a hand as if I'm being sworn in at a trial. "Full disclosure. I'm really lame at the whole dance bit."

"I'll show you."

I laugh. "Right. Mr. Carleton will be glad to give up class time for salsa lessons."

Raul squirts ketchup onto his burger. "I'm not thinking about doing it in class!"

"Raul!" I pick up a sandwich half. "Okay, if I don't start eating, this grilled cheese will turn to rubber."

He laughs into his burger.

Honestly, Val. Can you possibly be more of a dweeb?

> Power is not a means, it is an end.
>
> GEORGE ORWELL

MP LOG

This is what happens when things don't get done right. The new girl called me from the hospital and said she had to talk to me. Alone. She sounded really scared, so I said, "I'll be there at seven. Make sure your mom, or whoever is visiting you, is gone. I don't want to run into anyone."

At 6:45, I slipped into the lobby wearing a gray windbreaker, the boring kind that nobody notices. My hair was combed neatly. I ignored the desk with the notice that said Visitor Sign-In Here. Instead, I stood by a trash can. Didn't take more than a few minutes before someone tossed their visitor sticker. Easy to stick it on my jacket.

When I got to the room, the new girl told me she'd had a visit from that news chick who *knew* she got hurt doing something with us.

I kept my voice low and calm because you never want to show you're surprised.

"Did you tell her anything?" I asked. "Anything at all?"

She looked terrified, like maybe I wouldn't believe her. She said, "I swear, all I said to that Val girl is I don't know what you're talking about and you better get out right now. She wrote down her phone number in case I changed my mind and wanted to talk to her, but I threw the paper in the trash. Is that okay?"

"Yeah that's good," I said, "but how did she find out? Did she give you an explanation?"

"I have no idea," the new chick said. "That's why I called you. Because I wasn't the one who told her."

Then the new girl started crying and asking, "Do you believe me and can I still be in the group when I get better because it's not fair to punish me when I did what you said to do."

I said, "Nothing changes as long as you keep quiet." She swore she would, so I said, "Okay, you're still MP."

But now we've got this problem. At the next meeting, I said, "One of you broke the blood oath. I'm going to find out who."

Everyone looked shocked when I told them about the hospital visit and they all swore on a second blood oath that it wasn't them.

"What about Phantom?" Hell Girl asked. "Maybe Phantom talked to *Campus News.*"

Frankenstein shook his head. "Why? Skeletor has pictures of Phantom like he has of the rest of us."

Ghost Face looked thoughtful. "Maybe Phantom wants to make sure we never meet again. If the new girl caved and told *Campus News* what actually happened, we couldn't blame it on Phantom."

That made sense.

"We're okay," I told them. "If it was Phantom, it's not like that *Campus News* chick was told all that much. She didn't know anything for sure."

I hit them up with the wolf grin and said, "But if I ever find out it was one of you, that person will be really, really sorry."

Everyone nodded. Word. It's spine-tinglingly cool how much control I have. Especially since Phantom quit. I said to the group, "Now we're going to pick someone else to join."

Talk about shock and awe! One of the chicks said, "What about the new girl? You promised her she can be in the group."

"She can but not for a long while. It's not like she can hang around with us in a cast and crutches because everyone will notice. So first we'll plan another prank just so the assholes at school don't forget about us. Then we'll choose someone else to join. I saved all those applications from the box, so it'll be easy."

What I didn't say to anyone is that after we choose this second person, we'll have another initiation. I'll make sure it's even better than the first one.

Just because I can.

18

Exactly as Jagger predicted, MP resurfaces. This time, the target is Mr. Washington Irving himself. WiHi has two statues: one at the front of the school next to the flagpole and another near the ball field. A small plaque on the second one says *Donated by the Class of '28*, and it's really, really ugly. The guy looks like he can't decide whether he's constipated or about to let out a big one.

MP draped the nastier of the two heads in a hood, and then hung a rope around the statue's neck. **DIE, SUCKERS!** was painted across the chest in bloodred letters.

The hood and rope are gone within two minutes of its discovery. The painted words stay until Mr. Orel can figure out how to get it off without ruining the finish on the statue.

Lucky for us, Raul got a shot of it on his cell before the hood was removed. What we also get are gossip, rumors and just plain anger. Omar and I set up a camera during lunch, and a crowd gathers.

"This isn't funny anymore. I heard there was a hood and rope around the neck. That's definitely a racist statement against African-Americans," Cleve Watson, the captain of the AV squad, tells us. "Mr. Wilkins should find the culprits and kick them out of school."

One of Omar's lesbian friends in the LGBTQ Alliance agrees. Her nose ring flares angrily. "LGBTQ stands against any person who trashes someone else's rights. A noose around a neck has bad connotations like Cleve said. But what we in LGBTQ want to know is why nobody got upset by those body parts that were left around campus last month. Even if they were plastic, they were female parts. We find that to be just as offensive, especially to the women in this school."

A senior, holding tight to his sophomore girlfriend, wondered, "If Washington Irving is white, and there's a noose around his neck, does that really dis African-Americans? Or boring writers?"

Over on the side, watching intently, is a thin, pimply dude. Omar motions him over. "Want to be on *Campus News?* We're asking people what they think of the latest MP prank."

The kid ducks his head, mumbles, "Uh-uh," and shuffles off.

"Sure looked like he was waiting for his minute of WiHi fame," I say.

Omar shrugs. "People get camera-shy."

Shy, however, is a word Mr. Wilkins has finally discarded from his vocabulary. The principal makes an emergency announcement over the PA. "Please excuse the interruption. Anyone involved with defacing and vandalizing the old Irving statue will be punished. I ask all members of the Washington Irving community to cooperate with campus police as they investigate the matter."

In an on-camera interview, Mr. Wilkins explains further. "I was tolerant of those first pranks because I didn't want to trample any student's free speech rights."

"Are you saying you didn't want a Manhattan High problem?" I use my best Emily Purdue voice. "You know, when their principal broke up a legal student protest last year and the parents got him transferred?"

Mr. Wilkins gives a tight-lipped smile. "I was not thinking about that situation at all, Ms. Gaines. My policy is to allow students the full amount of First Amendment rights to which they are entitled. The original MP incidents could not be considered vandalism in the *legal* sense because no school property was destroyed. The actual defacing of the Irving statue, however, changes things."

"That's a fine line," Omar huffs indignantly. Back in the Media Center, the rest of the team watches the interview on the monitor. "I don't think Wilkins cares about free speech at all. He's just covering his ass."

"Totally," Marci says. "Besides all that, how much does the noose on the statue remind you of the bird in Val's locker? And the trophy in the display case? Those were warnings. Is this one, too?"

Henry brushes hair out of his eyes. "Who are they warning by messing with the statue?"

Jagger gives me a curious look. "Val? You're awfully quiet."

I didn't realize my silence was so obvious. In my head, I'm having a fierce argument.

Tell them about the secret agent, the meeting in the playground....

Uh-uh! Remember the note. "I could get in trouble for telling you this. Don't tell anyone. MP has spies everywhere."

Not that I think anyone on the team is a spy, but so far, MP's been awfully good at finding out stuff. Locker combo, my email address. I do not want to be responsible for outing the secret agent. Not yet.

"I'm as much in the dark as the rest of you," I tell them.

Technically, that cannot be considered a lie.

★ ★ ★

The doorbell rings. Footsteps pound as the twins race to get there first. I'm in the dining room, college catalogues spread across the polished wood table. The task is to choose my top nine—three reach, three safe, three "I really want to go here, but can my folks afford it if I don't get a scholarship?" schools. Narrowing it down is tough. Plus, the journalism programs require extras. A kick-ass *Campus News* segment that nails the MP story would really help.

Jesse—or is it James?—shouts, "Val! It's for you."

I'm happy for the interruption—until I see who it is.

"Can I come in?" Jagger's wearing an aviator jacket with a fake sheepskin collar and a multicolored scarf. Not an outfit everyone can pull off. He, of course, looks great.

Jesse and James swarm around us. "I'm Jesse," James says.

"No, you're not." Jesse tackles his brother. "He's James...."

Clearly, staying on the first floor is not an option. "Let's go upstairs. Find a little privacy."

But where? Bethany, as usual, is in the bedroom. It'll be a month of pot washing to get her out of here.

"Hey, Bethie. Remember me?" Jagger asks.

For a moment, I'm not sure how she could. It's not like I brought Jags around when we were together. The house is too loud and too crowded; it was easier to hang out at his place. But then I remember the July afternoon I had to get Bethany from the Arcade because she had a doctor's appointment. Jagger came with me. At the time, he barely looked at her. Now he gives my sister the full Voorham treatment.

"Got yourself all grown up, didn't you?"

"Ninth grade," she mumbles.

"Cut your hair, too. I like it." She shrugs as if she doesn't care, but I can tell she's pleased. He shoots her a dimpled smile.

"You think you could give me and Val a few minutes alone? I need to tell her something and it's kind of private."

"Okay." Bethany scoops up her iPod and closes the door quietly behind her.

"How do you do that so fast?" I laugh. "I figured I'd have to bribe her to get her out of here."

"Natural charm." Immediately he turns serious. "I really do have something to tell you." He pats the bed beside him. "I won't bite. Or do anything else."

I pull out my desk chair. "I'm fine here."

He shrugs. "Whatever."

There's an awkward pause. "So? What do you have to talk to me about?"

"Remember the MP box?" Jagger asks. "The one that said 'Join us'?"

I perk up. "You found it?"

He shakes his head. "I put in an 'application.'"

"Wait. What? There weren't any."

Now that Jagger has my attention, he takes his time, puts a pillow behind himself and leans comfortably against the headboard. "Right. Not formal applications. I scribbled something quick and slipped it in."

"Don't tell me they asked you to join."

Jagger grins. "Got the word today."

"You want to be a member of MP?" My voice gets more than a little screechy. "Are you crazy?"

"That's how we get the story, Val. What exactly is MP? Who are they?"

I lean forward. "It doesn't make sense. Why would they let someone from *Campus News* into their club? I mean, they hate me especially, but I'm sure they're not in love with the rest of us."

"Exactly!" The dimples on his cheeks widen. "But no one

knows I'm in the class. I've never been in front of the camera, never anchored. Invisible the entire year—just like MP. You have to appreciate the irony."

I roll my shoulders to get rid of the tension tightening my muscles. At the same time, I'm frantically sorting through what I know—and what to say.

"What's wrong?" he asks.

"Don't do it."

Jagger's brow wrinkles. "Why not? I thought you'd be happy. I mean, okay, I didn't tell you I put in an application, but that's because I wasn't sure anything would happen. Plus, the fewer people who knew I did it, the better."

Omigod! I lean forward. "Do you think someone on B Team is a spy?"

Jagger laughs. "Are you downloading secret agent books in your free time? Of course I don't think anyone's a spy. But word gets out. Henry and Omar talk about it in Calc, Marci tells Phil in the cafeteria. Someone sitting next to them hears. You know how that goes."

I do. The WiHi rumor mill is fierce. That's why the MP story is so frustrating. Equally worrisome, though, is what the double agent told me: a girl ended up in the hospital after joining. But I'm sworn to keep that information secret. A crazy dilemma.

"You can't do it, Jags."

"Give me one good reason."

Urgently, I move to the bed. "Because they're crazy. And dangerous. You can't trust them."

His eyes flash. "Boy, are you transparent! Jealous because I'll break the story and you won't. I can't believe I've been fed a line of crap all semester. 'It's all about *Campus News*. Not any one person. We're supposed to work together.'"

"It is. We do—"

He gets to his feet. "Unless the we is me. Okay, I know I fucked up the night of Sonya's party. I was drunk and Dawn came on to me big-time. I'm sorry. But it's stupid to hold it against me the rest of my life."

"I'm not!"

"You are! What's worse is you're letting the best story of the year slip through your fingers for personal reasons. I refuse to let it happen."

He storms from the room. Bethany must have been in Mom's bedroom, because she walks in less than ten seconds later.

"You and Jagger have a fight?"

"None of your business!" Despite the cold, I lift the window and climb onto the fire escape. Jagger stalks down the steps of the building. This time he doesn't bother to wave.

19

I pull the books for morning classes from my locker. Feeling someone behind my back, I turn. Jagger waits for Tracy to get out of the way before he moves in.

"Change your mind?" I ask hopefully.

He lowers his voice. "I want to make sure you're not going to tell anyone."

"Jagger—"

"Valerie. Did you tell us about that email the instant you got it? The one that warned you to stop investigating?"

"That's different."

He laughs. "Only because you're the one who kept quiet. Don't you see? If I get caught telling anyone, I'm out before I get in—"

"What's going on?" Marci's usual cheery face is stony. "I hope you're talking about *Campus News,* not anything of a personal nature."

"Since when did you become captain of the Conversation Police?" Jagger counters. "Wait. Cocaptain. Seriously, Val, you need to find yourself another BFF."

"Like you?" Marci retorts. "Whose only interest is himself—"

"Enough! I got the message, Jagger, but I wish you'd change your mind."

He walks away. Marci looks upset. "Val, you promised!"

"We're not getting back together, if that's what you're worried about. Especially now."

Marci scurries to keep up as I stomp down the hall. "What happened?"

"You were right. I made a huge mistake. I should have asked Carleton to switch Jagger to A Team in September. Go ahead. Tell me you told me so."

"I told you so."

We enter the *down* staircase. "Happy?"

She shakes her head. "Not really."

"Why not?"

"Because whatever's going on, it's making you miserable."

Miserable is an understatement. I don't know what to do. Jagger's right—and wrong. His way may be the only way to get the story. But he's wrong when he says I want it for myself. Everyone on B Team's worked it at some point. All of us stand to benefit by cracking MP's circle of silence. Not only B Team but the entire school, as well.

Is it wrong to keep my mouth shut about the double agent—even though I promised? Or is it worse to let a golden opportunity slip through our hands? I could insist Jagger be careful. He knows they're unpredictable, so it's not like it would be a surprise.

There's something else. Jagger's changed. Marci would argue the point, but it's true. He wants this as much as I do. Taking it from him might be almost as harsh as what he did to me.

After dinner, another cryptic email awaits.

Tomorrow. Same place. Same time. Don't be late or think about blowing me off. I have something really, really important to tell you.

20

Lying, spying—I've turned into someone I wouldn't have recognized three months ago. I have to keep reminding myself that what I'm doing is standard operating procedure for an investigative reporter. You can't go around telling people about a source until the story's locked down.

I'm out of the house by six o'clock, several hours before I'm supposed to meet the double agent. Mom thinks I'm working on an English project with Marci. She has no reason to doubt me. After all, I'm the daughter who never makes waves.

Slipping into Starbucks, I check the napkin dispensers in case it's a repeat of the other night. I'm hoping the note's already hidden.

No such luck—but it's early. Like all good reporters, I have a backup plan. Directly across the street is a Middle Eastern fast food restaurant. A narrow eating counter runs the length of the front window. I settle into one of the tall stools. It's not a bad place to try to catch the double agent leaving the note. It would be easier if I could actually sit in the café, but I have to assume everyone in MP recognizes me because of the broadcasts.

Munching a falafel, I settle in for surveillance. By seven, my enthusiasm for investigative reporting starts to ebb. It's *really* boring just staring out a window. I order a Coke to keep me awake, and then a sticky pistachio-covered dessert.

Finally, a little after seven-thirty, there's some action. A kid from Irving enters the coffee shop. I recognize him because he and Bethany went to elementary school together.

I slip my dad's small bird-watching binoculars from my backpack. I've been here so long, nobody notices me. I fiddle with knobs until the freshman comes into focus. He's at a table—and he's not alone. The dude's talking to a girl a little older than me. When I lower the binoculars to see what they're looking at, an open textbook comes into view.

Realization hits. This is not some secret spy meeting; it's a tutoring session. The chick's a college student, earning extra dough teaching high school kids just enough geometry to pass chapter tests. Disappointed, I lower the binoculars.

Only one other possibility appears. This kid is tall and his face makes a distinct impression. Jake Crenshaw. Raul interviewed him last year when the basketball team lost the city semifinals. Jake rushes into Starbucks. Before I get my binoculars focused, though, he's out again. Too quick to order a drink—or hide a note in a napkin holder. I assume he was supposed to meet someone and was late. Or his date never showed.

At 8:40, I use the restroom—two Cokes have done their work. I check my cell. Fifteen minutes to go. It doesn't take more than ten minutes to get to the playground, but I don't want to be late.

I play the game exactly the way I'm supposed to. At 8:55, I walk past the playground to the Promenade itself. Concentrate on the view. Across the river, Manhattan twinkles like New York's version of a country sky. Skyscraper and bridge lights, strung like jewels across a woman's neck, substitute for real stars.

Sightseeing, however, is not the plan. Every few seconds, I check my cell. The instant it turns nine, my breath quickens. Just as before, no one waits for me. I pull open the gate, step into the playground.

"Stop right there," comes the command. Again, the sound is distorted by the altered voice app. No way to recognize it.

"We're not doing this for a second time, are we? You told me you had something important to say. Come out so we can talk!" I can almost feel the hidden head shaking. "I promise I won't tell anyone who you are. You have my word you'll stay anonymous."

The request is ignored.

"Go to *Heights Videography*," the Voice tells me. "Find *Animal House*. There's a note inside the box."

I stamp my foot. "This is ridiculous—"

"Do it! You've got fifteen minutes or it will be gone. Trust me, you don't want that to happen."

Outmaneuvered again.

No wonder I didn't see him go into Starbucks. By choosing a different place, the double agent made sure to stay ahead of the curve. Here I am, thinking I'm soooo smart. If boy-genius Henry wasn't a member of my own team, I'd wonder if it wasn't *him* behind the play structure.

As I run down the street, a question occurs to me. Why does the secret agent send an email sometimes, but then make me go through all this crap to get an actual note? Unless he's afraid the account will be hacked by someone in the group. Or his laptop has a virus. Maybe he doesn't even have his own computer so he has to use the free one at the library. There's no way to know.

I barrel into *Heights Videography*, with its huge collection of hard-to-find-videos, startling the guy stocking the shelf.

"Where's your comedy section?" I ask breathlessly.

He straightens. "Oh, hey, Val!"

"Charlie!" Charlie Liu's taken every film class Mr. Carleton teaches. You'd think film and *Campus News* kids would hang together, but it's art vs. journalism. They're pretty much lone wolves who want to do everything themselves. We're team players. At least, most of the time.

"Didn't know you work here," I say.

"That's because you're not a member. You can't take out a flick unless you join. Do you want—"

"No!" He looks surprised by my outburst. "Sorry. Didn't mean to yell. I'm doing research for a *Campus News* story and I need to see the *Animal House* box."

"You didn't have to come all the way here. Go online and check *IMDB*—"

"Charlie! The comedy section?"

He points. "Just trying to help."

"I know. Thanks."

I walk to the correct aisle. It's not hard to find the movie. A small envelope is inside the box. I check to make sure Charlie isn't watching before slitting it open. My hand shakes as I read three short sentences that change everything.

```
The second initiation is going to be way
more dangerous than the first. I am not
kidding. You HAVE to find a way to stop it.
```

21

"This is ridiculous," I mumble.

I've been up and down the block three times, trying to work up the guts to climb the steps that lead to a buzzer with Voorham printed underneath. It's not like I haven't done it before. It's just that I haven't been here for over a year.

I also needed to rehearse what to say. Find the right words to convince Jagger that he absolutely, positively can't have anything to do with the initiation.

It's the wind that finally drives me to the apartment building. Gusts of cold air shoot wickedly off the East River and set my teeth to chattering. Despite gloves, the tips of my fingers are freezing.

A light glows behind the shade of an upper window. Jagger's room. Instead of ringing the bell, though, I text him. Banished long ago from my cell, I still know the number by heart.

I'm downstairs. Need to talk.

His reply is brief: K.

He buzzes me in. Thunder, a gray tabby with Z-shaped stripes, tries to slip past, but I'm on it.

"Not so fast, missy! Thought I forgot about you?" I give the cat a cuddly squeeze. "She's getting fat, Jags."

"I guess. You look cold, Val."

I wonder if he watched me walking back and forth. "I've been outside for a while. I've got something to tell you."

He lifts his cell. "So you said."

Despite the weather, he's wearing a white tee and torn jeans. I can pretty much bet that he combed his hair before buzzing me in, though. He looks good—which will only make the conversation that much harder.

"In private?"

"Oh yeah, sorry. Come on." Jagger leads the way through the living room and into his bedroom. He's got a laundry basket full of dirty clothes, band posters taped to the walls and a bunch of Little League trophies. The kind you get just for being on the team.

I busy myself with my jacket. Fold it neatly across the back of the desk chair I know he never uses. I turn the chair so that it faces into the room. Jagger seems amused as he lounges across his bed.

"Want a baseball bat to hit me with if I get out of line?" he asks.

"This is serious."

"If you've come to tell me not to join MP again, you're wasting your breath."

"Jags—"

"Val! You're the one who's always going on and on about 'the story.'"

"But what if 'the story' puts you in danger?"

That gets his attention. "What are you talking about?"

"What if I have information that the initiation MP is planning isn't so innocent? That it could put you in…what's the expression?"

"Harm's way?" he suggests.

"Exactly."

"Do you know that for sure?" When I nod, he asks the obvious follow-up question. "How did you find out?"

"What if I told you that it's a protected source?" On the street, I'd rehearsed the answer several times.

"I'm on your side," he snorts. "You're supposed to *share* info with me—not hide it."

I wind the fringes of my scarf around my hand. "Can't you just trust me?"

"Oldest line in the book."

"You should know!"

He punches the blanket. "Honestly, if this is still about us breaking up—"

"We didn't break up. You ditched me."

He gives me a wounded look. "How many times do I have to say I'm sorry?"

I refuse to get sucked into Tortured Soul world. "This isn't the time to talk about it."

"Then when is?" His voice rises.

"How about right after it happened? You didn't even look at me for weeks after, asshole."

"I know." He balls a pillow into his stomach. "I hate myself, Val. It *was* an asshole thing to do."

That's the moment Thunder darts into the room. Jagger gets up to shoo her out but then decides to let the cat stay. He closes the door. "Did you ever meet my dad?"

The change in direction takes me by surprise.

"No. Your folks were already divorced by the time we… got together. He'd already moved out."

"People say I look exactly like him when he was my age. Sound like him, too. My grandma still can't tell the difference on the phone." Jagger sits on the edge of the bed. "It's not only physical things that remind people of him. It's the attitude. The jokes. For years, I watched him turn on the charm

whenever it suited him. Somehow, I picked that up. It's like
I channel him even when I don't want to."

Sensing Jagger's distress, Thunder jumps into his lap. It takes
about a minute or so before Jagger speaks again.

"After he left, my mom found out about *all* the women he'd
been cheating with. Not just the last one. I swore I'd never
be like that." He blinks. "It got pretty bad, Val. I came home
after school one day and found her unconscious. She'd taken
too many pills. I had to call an ambulance...."

"God, Jagger, I'm sorry. She's okay now, right?"

"Yeah. She still refuses to date, but at least she figured out a
way to move past him." He pushes the cat away. "That night
at the party, I swear it was Dawn who came on to me, not the
other way around. Yes, I was drunk, but the truth is I could
have stopped it. Stopped her. I wasn't that far gone."

He takes a breath, lets it out.

"And then I felt so...*sick* when you showed up. Here I go
promising myself I'll never be like Dad—and the first opportunity I have, I fucking blow it. That's why I couldn't face
you. When I finally got the guts to apologize, it was too late.
You refused to talk to me. I even begged your sister to ask
you to call me."

"You came to the house?"

"Video Arcade. She was by herself. I walked over to the
machine she was playing, but she wouldn't look at me. She
barely even responded. I figured she heard from you how
much of a jerk I am."

"No one at home knew what happened, Jags."

He nods, understanding that the deeper the pain, the more
we suffer in silence. "It was a mistake, Val. I knew it then. I
know it now. Can you forgive me? Please?"

"Yes—if you promise not to join MP."

"Are you kidding me?" He stares as if trying to figure out

what the hell I'm hiding. "I've just been completely honest with you. Don't I deserve the same? If you want me to stay away from them so badly, give me the real reason. I know there's something you're not telling."

Agitated, I walk to the window. Pull up the shade, stare at the street. Screw the double agent! Jagger has a right to know.

I turn to him warily. "This has to be between us."

"Sure."

"Say it."

He lifts a hand. "I promise to keep my mouth shut. Feel better?"

"Not really. And you won't after I tell you what I found out."

He stays quiet as the story spills out. It's actually a relief to unload it all: the playground, the hurried run to Starbucks, the visit to Taneisha.

"That's why you wanted to do the accident piece," Jagger interrupts. "I *knew* it had to be something other than being nice."

"I couldn't figure out any other way to find the injured kid."

He shakes his head. "But she didn't cop to it. You don't know for sure Taneisha's the one who went through the initiation."

"You didn't see her face when I mentioned MP. Honestly? It's her."

Jagger drums his fingers against his knee. "Let's say you're right. It doesn't mean I'll get hurt. Taneisha slipped off a ledge. I won't."

"What if they make you do something else? Something more dangerous."

"Valerie!" Jagger knows me all too well. "What are you leaving out?"

"I'm getting to it." I reach into my pocket, unfold the second note. "Someone in MP doesn't agree with what's going on. But he's afraid to tell anyone. You'd be an idiot not to pay attention."

He scans the page. "You have no idea who's leaving these?"

I shake my head, so frustrated I want to scream. "I get messages telling me what time to meet, but it's a B.S. email address. I've replied. No one answers."

Jagger moves the pillow. "Sit. Please. You're making me nervous walking around like that."

"Promise you won't go through with it," I say softly.

He shakes his head. "I can't, Val. Especially now."

"Why now?"

He leans close, as if afraid the walls will hear. "What's to stop MP from choosing another person? Someone without a friend to warn him not to join. Don't you see? It would be irresponsible to drop out now."

I give a rueful snort. "Since when are you this concerned with responsibility?"

"Since when do you not want to get the story?"

He's right. I want the story so much it's like a splinter under my fingernail, bugging me practically every waking hour. Still... "I couldn't stand to see you get hurt, Jagger. And that's for real."

He pulls me close. "Me, neither. We'll be smart. We'll make a plan."

I catch the "we." Despite everything, my heart soars. "What are we going to do?"

"Right now?" he whispers into my ear. "I could think of a few things—"

I push him away. "Jags!"

"Just kidding!" He holds up a hand. "The deal is I meet

the group first. They can reject me if they don't like me for whatever reason."

"Fancy that."

He laughs. "As long as Marci ain't in the group, I'm golden."

"How do you know they won't do the initiation that day?"

He shrugs. "No way to tell for sure. But if they wait, they keep me in suspense. MP is all about controlling the situation."

"Hold on." I grab his hand excitedly. "This could work out. After you meet them, you'll know who they are. So it's not like you have to go through with the rest of it. You can stop right there and report the story."

Jagger shakes his head. "Don't count on it. MP is not dumb enough to blow it like that. They must have some way to interview me so I won't find out who they are."

"Wish we could ask Taneisha."

"She didn't talk the first time. If either of us goes to her now and she runs straight to MP, I'll never hear from them again."

I nod. "So, you think that after they vote, someone tells you where to show up for the initiation?"

Idly, he traces a circle on the back of my hand. I should pull away, but I can't. My hand is frozen—and on fire at the same time.

"That's exactly how I think it goes down," Jagger says. "All we have to do is document it."

"*All* we have to do? How about keeping you from ending up in a hospital?"

"I can take care of myself."

I wish I could burn the cockiness right out of his eyes. "You've got to take this seriously, Jags. MP reminds me of the twins. Jesse and James do much stupider stuff together than when they're alone!"

"I didn't know you care so much."

"Don't be a jerk. You know I do."

"I wasn't sure...." With a slow, gentle touch, Jagger runs a finger down my cheek and across my lips. Then back again. My pulse quickens. I know what comes next.

Get up, Val. Walk out of this room. Go right now—

Some things never change. As soon as our lips come together, I melt into him. How does he do it? His kisses are so sweet, yet so very, very hot....

22

The next morning, Marci catches up to me at my locker. "I can't believe you didn't tell me."

"Tell you what?"

Jagger? The secret meetings? The kissing? How would she know—

"Winter Formal. Don't tell me you forgot!"

"Oh! Well, yeah. I mean, with everything going on…" I hang my jacket on the metal hook. Forget? The fact that I'm supposed to go to the dance with Raul has been wiped from my memory bank. "How'd you find out?"

"How do you think?" Marci pouts. "Raul told me the other day. I was waiting for you to say something, but there's been sort of a deafening silence coming from your side of the friendship."

"Sorry, Marci. I didn't want anyone on the team to know. So no one accuses me of, you know, favoritism."

"I'm not anyone!" Immediately, though, she brightens. "We'll shop for dresses together. In the Village—hey, Raul!" She waves him over. He turns out of the slipstream of kids heading off to homeroom. "We were just talking about you."

He looks pleased. "Yeah?"

Marci grins. "Val and I are going to shop for Winter For-mal together."

"Cool!" He grins shyly. "Don't forget to tell me the color, Val."

I manage a smile. What on earth should I do? Tell Raul that last night I fell into the Voorham Vortex, so forget you? That's flat-out mean. But how am I supposed to pull off danc-ing with him? What if Raul tries to kiss me? After last night, Jagger's touch is all I can think about.

Best friends were invented to figure out stuff like this, but if I even *hint* that Jags and I might get back together, Marci will clobber me with her history book. And I wouldn't blame her one bit.

Second bell announces the end of homeroom. Dashing into the Media Center, I settle at a computer and start editing quickly so I don't have to talk to anyone. When I'm done, I play the get-well video card through. It's terrible.

"What's terrible?"

Startled, I glance at Raul, two stations down from mine. I hadn't realized I'd spoken aloud. "The piece. It's lame."

"Let me see."

Within ten seconds, Marci and Jagger gather around, too. At the final frame, Marci nudges me. "I think it's sweet. All you need to do is write a good intro and find some music."

"Uh-uh." Jagger gives us a gravelly look. "Camera angles are boring and repetitive."

"Thank you, Mr. Carleton," Raul says drily. "It just needs a bit of cutting. Like Marci said, the instant you lay in music, it'll brighten right up."

Jagger shrugs. "You ask for truth, I give it to you. You don't like it, it's no skin off my nose."

"That's your opinion," Marci snaps. "Not every segment has to be heavy. I bet lots of people will love this."

Raul taps my shoulder. "I can help tighten it if you want."

Instead of snapping, "I'll figure it out myself," I take him up on the offer. Stupid to let my newly complicated personal life get in the way of the help I need.

He smiles broadly. "Let me save the stuff on my computer. BRB."

Jagger checks to make sure no one's looking before he winks.

Just playing the game.

I give him the briefest of nods. "You think you can find music that isn't sickly sweet?"

"Sure. Come over after school. We'll figure it out."

I never make it to his house. Jagger finds me after sixth period, walking glumly out of a bio test I'm sure I tanked. He pulls me into the stairwell.

"Got the summons," he whispers excitedly. "I'm supposed to meet MP after school."

"Today? Are you sure you—"

"It's just the 'meet in person and decide if they want to let me in' meeting, Val. I'm gonna be so charming they can't say no. Then we'll blow the lid right off their stupid club." He grins. "Honest to God, I get why you love *Campus News*. This is way more exciting than figuring out the back beat of a song."

"It is." I pull him close. "But I swear to God, if you let them talk you into doing anything dumb…"

"Relax." Jagger runs a hand along my spine. "It's going to be okay."

I want to believe him, but it seems too good to be true. Break the MP story and be with a more honest Jagger? Does anyone ever have it all?

23

I'm at Starbucks, sitting in the back of the store where no one on the street can see me. I've been sipping a cup of hot chocolate for about an hour, anxiously waiting for word from Jagger. When my cell rings, I snatch it quick. "You okay?"

A laugh. "Of course I'm okay."

"Raul? Sorry, I was expecting another call."

"Should I be jealous?"

Yes.

"Ha. What's up?" I ask.

"You're not going to believe the double bill at the Quad this weekend. *All the President's Men* and *Broadcast News.*"

"My two favorite movies. How'd you know?"

"I figured. You want to go Friday night?"

My cell clicks, signaling a second call. The fastest way to end the conversation is to take Raul up on the offer. "Friday's good. See you at school tomorrow."

I switch over to Jagger. "Everything okay?"

"I'm aliiiive."

"Don't fool around. What happened?"

"I got out about five minutes ago. You home? I'll come over."

I didn't want Bethany to figure out that Jagger and I are up to something, so I never went to the house. "I'm not home. Going there's not a good idea."

"Meet you at my place?" he asks.

"No." As much as I'd like to, I can't do that. Not after just agreeing to go to the movies with Raul. "Not good, either."

"Too distracting?" Jagger laughs. "Okay. Tony's is too popular. What about Burger 'n Bun? It's on—"

"I know where it is!" I take a breath. "Too close to WiHi. Someone from MP might be sitting on the next stool and we'd never know."

"Then it's got to be the bridge. Half an hour."

It's not until I hang up that I realize what I've agreed to. The Brooklyn Bridge is where Jagger took me on our very first date.

The pedestrian walkway that spans the bridge might be the most romantic spot in the world. It's easy to imagine couples promising undying love while down below, boats sail, silent witnesses to the pact.

Jagger puts his arm around me. "Warm enough?"

God knows I want to snuggle into him, but I need to focus. Carefully, I slide a few inches to the right. "I'm good. Dying to know what happened. Who they are."

He shakes his head ruefully. "They wore masks."

"The whole time?"

Jagger laughs. "Yep. They think they're oh so scary. Frankenstein, Zombie, Skeletor—"

"Who's Skeletor?"

"*Masters of the Universe?* Skeleton face, cape thing with a hood—"

"Holy crap!"

Jagger blinks. "What?"

"I know him." Jagger's mouth falls open in astonishment. "I mean, not *who* he is. Some kid in a skeleton mask and hoodie tried to get me to dance at Omar's party. Of course, it might not be the same person—"

"What color was the hood?" Jagger asks.

"Blue. Darker than sky-blue but not exactly navy."

"Letters or pictures?" he asks.

I shake my head. "Plain."

"So was the one he wore today. What's his voice like?"

"The music was so loud I could barely hear. Do you really think someone from MP tried to pick me up? That's insane!"

He gives me a look I can't read. "Not so insane, Valerie."

"If that kid's in MP, it was a goof. Getting off on me *not* knowing who he was." I stare at the long strip of land that's Brooklyn. "What happened next?"

"I gave them exactly what they want."

"Which is?"

He lightens his voice. "You're so awesome. I really want to be in the group. I have lots of ideas for things we can do."

Before the meeting, he and I came up with a list of pranks in case that was part of the interview. "Did you give it up?"

"Nah. I told them they have to let me into the club first. Like we planned. Dangle the carrot, let them grab for it."

"Did they?"

"Oh yeah. Had them eating out of my hand by the time I left."

I snort. "So you say."

"You'll see. I'll get in."

Down below, a tugboat pushes an oiler. "How many are there?"

"Five."

It's killing me that I wasn't with him. "Could you tell if there's a leader? Someone they're afraid of."

"Not sure. If I had to pick, I'd choose Skeletor. He was pretty quiet, but the others kept looking at him. As if trying to figure out what he was thinking." Jagger shakes his head. "The hardest part was not laughing. They kept calling each other by their mask names. I'm supposed to choose one for myself if they vote me in. How dorky is that?"

"Actually, it's smart. The masks hide who they are." Something tickles my brain. "Taneisha had a *Masters of the Universe* comic at the hospital. Wonder which character she chose."

"They never mentioned her or anyone else."

I poke him. "Did you pick a name? For when you're initiated?"

Jagger laughs. "You choose. What about Gollum from *Lord of the Rings?* Or the one all the girls think is hot. What's his name?"

"Legolas."

"Great! That's who I'll be."

"Egomaniac!" Laughing, he starts to protest, but I wave him off. "Seriously, we have to plan. They might give you fifteen minutes to get somewhere. That's all I had to find the notes."

Jagger's eyes are bright with anticipation. "You've got an idea, don't you?"

"Yes. But you have to promise to follow it."

Unexpectedly, he turns me so I have no choice but to look directly at him. "Valerie, please tell me last night wasn't some freak accident. That you really do forgive me."

"I told you. I do. But what's important right now is stopping MP. Let's do that first, and then figure us out."

He grabs my scarf and pulls me close. "That's exactly the reason I want to be with you. You're the most driven person I know. Interesting, exciting…"

I back away. "Now you're making fun."

"I'm not! I mean it. And I'll prove it to you, if you'll let me." He holds up his hand. *"After* we get the story."

With the wind ruffling his hair and bridge lights reflected in his eyes, Jagger's a city sprite swearing undying allegiance. It's heady, beyond anything I ever imagined—but we have to get back to business.

I take a step away. "Here's what I think we should do. Did you see that little camera some company donated to Mr. Carleton? He wants people to try it out...."

The plans get made. When we're done, I let Jags take my hand for the walk back. Just like he promised, he doesn't push for more.

I'm not sure if I'm relieved—or disappointed.

24

It's weird. I find out when and where the initiation will take place before Jagger does. I wish it had to do with some awesome reporting on my part, but it doesn't. The message is in my in-box late Thursday night. No time for the secret agent to play his annoying hide-and-seek game because it's planned for the very next day.

Flag Pole, little park by the river in Red Hook, 5 p.m. Friday.

I know the place. From the Heights, the bus travels south through Cobble Hill and Carroll Gardens before it crosses under the Brooklyn-Queens Expressway. On the other side of the BQE, it's a different world. Mostly warehouses and factories, mixed with blocks of identical brick buildings turned into low-income projects.

It can be dangerous, especially at night. Some of the warehouses were converted into artist studios and lofts, although many are abandoned. A tiny park stands at the river's edge. The East River empties into the ocean less than a mile away, so the wind goes arctic awfully quick. Once November hits, the park is empty.

The perfect place for an MP initiation.

★ ★ ★

Jagger and I meet in the Media Center during lunch. The team's latest broadcast aired earlier that day, so we don't have a specific reason to be there. Mr. Carleton's reading the paper, however, and isn't paying attention.

We slip into the control room and keep the lights off.

"You're sure the camera's charged?" I ask nervously.

The white camera is about the size of an iPod. A little thicker, maybe, but not by much. Jagger and I tested it yesterday. The images are clear—and the audio rocks. The small mic built into the cam picks up voices from across a room.

"Positive," he tells me. "Checked again last night."

"Good. I'll get to the park by four and hang out in the garden. Watch it happen from behind a bunch of plants or something."

"Be careful," Jagger says. "If anyone sees you, they'll shut the whole thing down."

"Don't worry. You be careful, too."

He smiles with the self-confidence that's pure Jagger. "It'll be fine. You've got your cell. If I do this—" he tugs his ear "—call 911. But only if I give the signal."

We've gone over and over this. I can tell he's as excited as I am. If we really do pull this off, we'll have the story of a lifetime.

"Meet back at my house after it's over and we'll check the footage…together," he whispers.

That, too, has been arranged. We don't want any MP dawdler to see us together.

Jagger and I plan to rough-edit over the weekend and show it to the team on Monday. From my hiding place in the garden, I'll set my still camera on zoom and photograph each MP member who shows up. Then we'll intercut the pictures with whatever footage Jagger gets.

"What do you think they'll have you do?" I wonder.

That, too, is a question I've asked incessantly. Jagger nibbles my ear. "We decided not to worry about it, remember?"

I pull away. "Promise me one more time that you won't do anything stupid." Silence. "Jags?"

He grins. "Only if you do something for me now."

It's hard to suppress a smile. "And that is…"

"One kiss. For good luck."

How can I say no? No one sees us. Nobody knows what we're doing.

By the end of the day, I'm so focused on my part of the plan that I jump half out of my skin when someone taps my shoulder. "Sorry, Raul. Didn't hear you behind me."

"Next time I'll wear a bell." He grabs my backpack as I stick my arms through my jacket. "Should I come by at seven?"

"What?"

His face falls. "Double bill at the Quad—"

"Omigod, I totally forgot."

My face feels flushed. It's not only that I failed to remember that Raul asked me to the movies. This is precisely the moment I should tell him what Jagger and I are doing.

I don't say a word. Two people sneaking around the garden doubles the danger. If we get caught, Jagger will never forgive me.

"I'm so sorry, Raul. I can't go tonight."

He tries not to look crushed. "*Mañana?*"

How can I do this to him? I *have* to explain. But right now Red Hook awaits.

"Tomorrow's fine. I'll call you after lunch and we'll work it out."

He lights up like a Fourth of July sparkler, which makes me feel even worse. I suck so much.

★ ★ ★

At the bus stop, it's an easy switch from guilt to worry about not getting into position in time. When the bus finally comes, it's crowded. I pull my beanie over my hair and slide into the last empty window seat. With my face turned to the street, the hope is that no one recognizes me. Any of the people riding the bus could be MP, getting to the initiation before it's scheduled to start. Exactly the way I am.

By the time the bus crosses under the highway, all the high school kids have gotten off. At Coffey Street, I press the yellow strip lining the window. The driver pulls to the curb, brakes hissing in protest. The afternoon is blustery but not too cold. Pillowy clouds skip across the sky. They don't linger, and neither do I.

The street is rough, built of hard cobblestone. It's one of the strangest things about Brooklyn. For some reason, the city never got around to laying asphalt in this part of town. Walking around Red Hook is like stepping into another century. Rocky streets, old-school brick buildings. The air smells of the sea, salty and fresh. A bell clangs, seagulls screech.

The flagpole is easy to spot. Tall, like a ship's mast, it's surrounded by grass. An American flag flies at the top; a second one, with a nautical theme, flaps on a crossbeam.

Head down, I move into the garden. Three large juniper bushes provide sufficient cover while giving me the view I need. Past the flagpole, the narrow path widens into a semicircle overlooking the river. Maritime Park. Benches are set every few feet along the fence. The Statue of Liberty is so close I can see her copper-turned-green teeth.

Not a single person is there—which means I made it in time. Now comes the hard part. Jagger had me promise not to call or text. With nothing else to do, I put in my earbuds and set the music low so I can still hear the world in a vain attempt to calm my nerves. I read tags on plants. Sit on the side of a planter, and then stand to stamp my feet. The afternoon is not getting warmer.

Time drags—and drags. I amuse myself by trying to figure out the initiation ahead of time. Maybe they'll make Jagger climb the flagpole. Or ask him to tightrope-walk the ledge over the East River....

Low laughter gets my attention. Finally! Somebody's shown up. My heart beats fast. Carefully, I peek around the plant. False alarm. A couple of fishermen, dressed in bulky coats and earflapped hats, carry buckets and poles. I've never understood why anyone would eat fish caught in the dirty East River, but it doesn't seem to bother the men. Casting poles into the water, the two settle onto a bench, content to watch the sun sink into the horizon.

This is definitely a problem. MP missed the opportunity for an audience-free initiation. It's a huge mistake, something that's never happened before. If anything, the group overplans. That's why they haven't gotten caught.

The second problem is mine. Unless MP shows up soon, my camera will flash when I take pictures. If I disable the flash, it won't pick up faces. That means the visuals won't be clear enough for *Campus News.*

Ten minutes after five.

Where are they?

My stomach burns with tension. Nothing adds up. At least one MP member, if not all of them, should be here. No one except the double agent, perhaps, would want to miss a moment of the initiation. Why isn't Jagger by the flagpole? If the ceremony's been called off, he'd let me know. I didn't miss a call, didn't get a text.

5:15, 5:17, 5:20... Something's definitely wrong.

Leaving the safety of the garden, I circle the small park as fast as possible without calling attention to myself. Jagger is not here.

Did I lose him?

I check my cell one last time to make sure I didn't miss a message. That's when something clicks. The locator app in *Yearbook!* When Marci did the story, the entire team accepted the app to try it out. Did Jagger turn his off?

I don't have internet access with my lame-ass cell, although Jagger does. What I do have is my iPod. All it needs to connect to the internet is wireless. But of course, whenever you really want it, there's no signal. As I'm moving toward Coffey Street, my mind makes one of those leapfrog jumps: Coffey—coffee. Artists have to have their coffeehouses. Every one of them has wireless. There *must* be some kind of café in the neighborhood.

I dash down the rapidly darkening street, oblivious of any danger hidden in doorways or shadows. Up ahead, there's a lighted window. An old-man bar. Probably been there since the dawn of time. Not a chance in hell they've got internet.

Keep looking.

My instincts pay off at the next corner. A neon light flashes Open. Exposed brick on the walls, curved steel tables. A hipster restaurant that almost certainly has Wi-Fi.

A couple with matching nose rings drink beer and give each other kissy-kissy eyes. Neither bothers to look over as I barrel through the door. The only other customer is a guy at a small table in the back. He stares at his open laptop, so it's a good bet I'm right.

Connection never looked so sweet. In less than ten seconds, the iPod gets me to *Yearbook*.

"Can I help you?" The waitress has jet-black hair, many earrings and amazing tats running down her arms.

"I need your wireless for a sec. My, um, boyfriend and I got separated—"

"Bastard!" she says. "Cheating on you, huh?"

"I'm just lost."

She grins, not buying it for a second. "Go ahead. But don't stand in the middle of the aisle." She points to an empty table. "Over there."

The chair scrapes as I pull it out. I press the iPod and it relights. Scrolling down, I look for Jagger's name—yes! His app is enabled.

"Find him?" the waitress asks.

I look up. "Four eighty-two Van Brunt."

She crinkles her nose, glances at the clock behind the bar. "It's all warehouse down there. The workers are gone for the day. By five it's dead...."

I'm already out of the chair. "Thanks."

"Be careful. Red Hook's not a place to wander around by your lonesome. Especially at night."

I raise a hand—*I'll be okay*—and scoot outside. It's almost six o'clock. A whole hour since Jagger was set to meet MP. Sixty minutes in which I was supposed to stop whatever's happening. My stomach churns so much I want to puke. Ignoring the feeling, I dash down the uneven street, past drunks and the occasional homeless person camped out in the doorway of an empty building.

Jagger. Jags! I told you not to do it. Begged you...

A bunch of thuggish-looking guys hang around the edge of an alley. They notice me at the same time. It's precisely the kind of group that's best avoided by crossing the street before you get very close.

I'm in too much of a panic. Ignoring their catcalls, hoping they're too high to chase me, I careen past them.

A block later, I reach Van Brunt. Frantic, I glance at buildings, but the numbers are hard to read. Several precious seconds are wasted figuring out that they're higher to the right. Toward the river.

Peeling paint in doorways, overflowing garbage cans. This part of the Red Hook is especially sketchy. A graffiti mural proclaims **SOME WALLS ARE INVISIBLE.**

Decrepit apartment buildings glare at me from behind cracked sidewalks. Empty factories bounce my footsteps so that it continually sounds like I'm being followed. I touch my face, wipe away the salty droplets that run down my cheek.

The occasional apartment building dotting the street ends. Now there are only warehouses. One or two stories. Flat roofs. Some are in use during the day. Those buildings are cleaned up, brightly painted signs announcing the products sold. The rest are abandoned, windows mortared tight with cinder blocks.

474, 478, 480. There! A red dot, with a black 482 stenciled inside the circle, tells me I've arrived.

My breath comes in shallow gasps. A sharp pain stabs my side. The dilapidated building takes up the entire block. Windows run the length of the warehouse, every single one covered by metal sheeting. A steel door is surrounded by cinder blocks. Graffiti squiggles decorate it, **ARSON** spelled out in red paint.

If Jagger's in the building, he didn't get in from this side. I follow the sidewalk to the end of the block. The yard, littered with hulking pieces of machinery and Dumpsters, is surrounded by fence. Spiky metal circles loop across the top. Anyone attempting to climb over it would get their clothes—and skin—torn to shreds.

How did he get inside?

Rounding the corner, I come across a chain threaded between the fence and a gate. It's locked with a thick padlock.

Frustrated beyond all reason, I kick the gate. The chain rattles and I realize it's not as tight as it could be. There's some give. I push hard, widening the gap between the gate and the fence. It's just big enough to squeeze through.

The yard is silent. No one talks, laughs—or screams. Still, this feels like the right spot. The emptiness, along with a sense of decay, is the type of place MP would love.

A streetlamp gives off a semibright, orangey light. It helps as I pick my way around broken glass and empty cans. Something brushes my leg. Cat? Rat? Caught by surprise, I stumble and crash into a piece of machinery. The *clang* echoes loudly.

Rising quickly, I limp into the shadows, staying frozen. To my relief, no one comes to look for me. When I'm sure it's safe, I sneak to the building's edge. Somewhere, somehow, there has to be a way in. I check each window, looking for a loose metal covering. Crumbled bricks. An actual hole into the building.

There! At the far end a small, unobtrusive door is set into the wall. The padlock's broken. Not only that, but the door itself is ajar—as if someone entered hurriedly and didn't bother to pull it shut.

Carefully, I inch the door inward. I don't shout for Jags in case I'm paranoid and everything's going fine. Instead, I slip inside. The place is pitch-dark with that musty, rat-poop smell peculiar to closed-up buildings.

There isn't a sound. Did I miss the entire initiation?

Stepping forward, I turn my head. There! At the far end, a beam of light spills across the floor.

"Jagger?" I whisper.

No reply.

"Anyone here?" My panicked voice, now uncontrollably loud, echoes off brick walls.

The need to find him overwhelms me. Moving forward,

I stumble over something soft. Using my cell as a light, I see that it's a backpack. Jagger's backpack.

"Jags!"

My feet pound as I head for the cone of floor light. Scooping up the flashlight, I swing it around. The next sound I hear is an unearthly scream that practically shatters my throat. Then—absolute silence. Mouth open, I stand frozen in horror.

Jagger dangles in front of me, swinging gently, a rope around his neck.

25

I have no sense of the time. The waiting room is quiet at last.
Everyone's left to go...somewhere. EMTs, Jagger's mother,
the doctors. Even a pair of cops. One of them didn't look very
old. You'd think maybe he'd get it—but it was like talking
to a brick wall.

"It *wasn't* attempted suicide," I said fiercely. "It was MP.
They're a secret group at school. They made him do it."

The young cop, Officer Chen, showed me a piece of paper
that an EMT guy found on the warehouse floor. Instructions
for Pass Out, downloaded from the internet, complete with a
diagram of someone "hanging."

"Did Mr. Voorham tell you he was into this?" Chen asked.

I shake my head. "He wasn't. Like I told the EMT guys,
it was an initiation into the group. They're like a club, but
no one knows who's involved. They call themselves MP. We
were working on a story for *Campus News*. Jagger was un-
dercover—" The cops exchange skeptical glances. "It's true!
That's how I found him. You have to figure out who's in MP.
Stop them before someone else gets hurt...." My voice cracks
at the thought of Jagger lying in the ICU. Barely alive.

Mom shows up minutes after the police leave, Bethany at her side.

"I can't believe it," my sister keeps repeating. "How could this happen to someone from school? Someone you know?"

"Take her home, Mom," I beg. "Please! She's not helping. Marci's coming. She'll be with me." When Mom hesitates, I wave my cell. "I'll call if I need you. I promise. I can't leave right now. I have to stay a little longer...."

After they're gone, I sink into a hospital chair, completely numb. Finally, a voice pulls me out of the fog. "Omigod, Val, he tried to kill himself!"

Marci puts her arms around me, but I shake her off. "He didn't! I've been trying to tell people that all night. It was Pass Out—"

"What?"

I wet my lips. My mouth can barely form words anymore. "It's that choking game. You know, to get high—"

"Are you kidding?" Marci's voice squeaks in disbelief. "Jagger can get weed whenever he wants!"

The clomping of feet is jarring as Raul, Henry and Omar rush into the room.

"We checked with the nurse," Raul says. "He's still not awake...."

"Omigod." Tears, which have been coming and going all night, break through again. "Omigod, omigod..."

Omar settles on one side of me, Marci on the other. Henry looks ready to sob along with me.

Raul stands, uncomfortable, as if he'd rather be any place but in a room full of hysterical people. He offers to find water. My best friend digs into her backpack and pulls out a pack of tissues. She hands them out to everyone. Raul returns with paper cups filled with water. As I drink, Marci relays what little I told her to the guys.

Omar twists his ring nervously. "That doesn't sound like Jagger."

Henry nods in agreement.

"What I don't understand is how you found him, Val," Raul says. "How did you know where to go?"

Yet again, tears overflow. How to begin? Where? The story's so awful…

"Let's leave," Raul suggests. "Jagger's mom is here. The nurses won't let anyone else into the room tonight, so it's not as if we can see him. We'll come back tomorrow. Early. Hopefully, Jagger will be awake by then."

Marci nods. "We can go to my house. My folks will be asleep by the time we get there. It'll be quiet.…"

The team surrounds me in the subway, then circles protectively as the elevator rises nineteen floors to Marci's apartment. It isn't until we settle in the living room that I notice the stares. They can't help it. I found Jagger in an abandoned warehouse in Red Hook. I called the cops. They know there's a story—if only I can pull myself together to tell them.

They wait as patiently as they can until I start. From the beginning. The emails, the secret meetings. The way Jagger put an application into the MP box without telling anyone, got accepted and made me promise to keep quiet.

The walk to the flagpole, the long wait, the frantic search. In halting sentences, I explain what happened after I saw Jagger swinging on the rope. The way I rushed forward, pushing him *up* toward the ceiling. Hoping the rope would loosen and he'd wake up. After a couple of seconds when nothing changed, I realized I'd have to get him down myself. The rope was tossed over a ceiling pipe and then attached to a radiator. It took a superhuman effort to release Jagger and let him hang again. I ran to the wall, untied the end hooked to the radiator. Jagger crumbled to the floor the instant it loosened.

The team sits silently, horrified.

"I'm not exactly sure what happened next," I mumble. "I called 911, got the rope off his neck…but it's kind of a blur."

Marci's mascara etches black lines down her cheeks. I look at her oddly, not sure how that happened, until I realize she's crying.

"Lucky you were there," Henry mutters.

Omar is furious. "I can't believe you didn't tell us. It was stupid—"

"Don't yell," Marci says sharply. "She's been through enough—"

"I begged him, Omar. I swear. Begged, yelled, pleaded. Tried everything to stop him."

"Then it was even stupider to keep quiet. We all would have been there—"

"And done what?" It's Henry who comes to my defense. "Hide next to Val in the garden? Wave a bunch of branches in front of our faces like that army in *Macbeth*? If MP *had* shown up at the flagpole, it would be obvious what was going on the instant they saw five of us trying to cram behind a bunch of plants."

"Jagger said that, too," I mumble. "He thought it had to be just him and me—"

Raul slaps the coffee table, as pissed off as Omar. "We would have spread out, Val. From the bus stop to the park. So if, or when, they changed the plan, one of us would have followed."

That catches Marci's attention. "What do you mean, change the plan?"

"Val said they never got to the flagpole. That means they headed him off at the bus stop. I bet MP never planned to go to the park." Raul shoots me a dark look. Is he upset that he wasn't there to save Jagger? Disappointed that we blew the story? Or jealous because I spent so much time with Jags? "The only reason MP told Jagger to go to the flagpole was in case he spoke to someone else."

As soon as he says it, it's obvious. Once again, I've been outmaneuvered. I can't look at Raul. He's absolutely right. I made all the wrong choices.

It's two in the morning. Marci insists that I stay overnight. After everyone leaves she offers to take the air mattress, but I make her sleep in her bed. I figure I'll be awake all night, so why not let one of us be comfortable?

Quietly, I take her laptop, prop it on my knees and sign in to my email. Nothing from MP. Furious and devastated beyond belief, I decide that this time I'll be the one to make contact. It's not like I expect an answer. But I have to let the double agent know the consequences of his betrayal.

I waited at the flagpole. No one came. Why did you lie? How could you leave Jagger in the warehouse, in the dark, with a rope around his neck? I found him, but it might be too late. If he never wakes up, I want you to know it's as much your fault as mine.

It takes two days before they let me into the ICU. Jagger's completely still, almost unrecognizable.

His face is puffy and swollen. An angry red mark circles his neck. One end of an accordion-like plastic hose attaches to a tube that disappears down his throat. The other end is hooked to a machine. He can't breathe without it.

Seeing him frozen in the twilight world of a coma is more than I can bear. The nurse walks me out. She smells like coconut, her dark skin soft as she puts an arm around me. She speaks with a New Orleans lilt.

"You the girl who found him?"

I can barely nod. "Will he be all right?"

"Nobody knows, *cher*. He could wake up tomorrow with little or no damage. Depends on how long his brain was deprived of oxygen. Or…" She hesitates.

Part of me does not want to know what's on the other side of that sentence. But another needs to find out every bit of information. Not as reporter, but as punishment.

We stop in the middle of the hallway. Doctors and nurses pad softly around us, giving us space. They're used to tragedy.

"Tell me," I whisper. "I have to know."

Quietly, the nurse utters words I will never forget. Once said, they can't be taken away.

"He could stay like this. Not livin', not dyin'. A persistent vegetative state is what they call it." She gives me a look with eyes that have seen it all. "You don't want that for him, *cher*. Trust me. You don't."

PART THREE

DECEMBER

26

It's funny how you can get to be a high school senior and never really understand the word *crisis*. Not that I haven't lived through plenty of bad days. Zits and flunked tests and, oh yeah, getting cheated on by my boyfriend. But nothing, until now, has come close to the literal meaning of the word. Zero hour, point of no return, doomsday, death's door. The last an all-too-real reminder of what's actually going on in hospital room 225.

The team lives in a fog. None of us can do much except go through the motions. WiHi, hospital, home. Any moment we expect, hope…pray that Jagger will get better. Homework, tests, deadlines. None of it means a thing. Thanksgiving arrives, and then it's history. The weather is a merry-go-round of slushy rain, bright sun, snow flurries—but Jagger's condition does not vary. He's living, if you can call it that, in a time warp of nothingness. Can't move, can't speak, can't seem to wake up.

After two weeks, the time comes when even I have to stop the daily pilgrimage to the hospital. Marci drags me to her house at the end of the day to force me to write the paper Mrs. Orapessa assigned.

I stare at the book. "My brain is mush."

"Come on, Val. The extension runs out tomorrow."

"So I'll flunk. Why does it even matter?"

Marci throws a pillow at me. "Jagger would not want you to blow senior year. Colleges look at first-semester senior grades. You know that—"

"And I don't care. No college should accept someone as stupid as me. Someone who let Jagger go through with that..."

The obsessive guilt loops constantly. In the waiting room, during all-too-brief visits with Jagger, in bed at night.

"Valerie!" Marci's voice is sharp. "Jagger chose to put his head into that rope. They didn't hold a gun to his head."

"How do you know?"

She looks directly at me, slumped beside her on her bed. "I *know*. The members of MP might think they're cooler than Italian ice, but they're not the Jersey Mafia. Jagger thought if he played along, finished the initiation, you and he would break the story."

"Since when are you a Jagger expert? You don't even like him."

Marci's pissed. "I'm not gonna vote him Most Popular, but the dude almost died to get the story. It's impressive, okay? I understand why you're in love with him—"

"I am? You do?"

"Yes." She sighs. "But I'm not sure how to tell Raul."

"Omigod, Marci, I've been sick about that, too. I don't want to hurt him. He doesn't deserve it. The only reason I said yes to the dance is because I decided to try...to see if maybe it would work out—"

"The whole thing's my fault, Val. I pushed you into it." She pulls the hair band from her ponytail and shakes her head as if some brilliant thought will wriggle loose. "We'll figure something out—"

Mrs. Lee knocks on the door. "Turn on the TV, girls. Channel 5. They're doing a story about your friend."

In a flash, Marci's got the remote. Emily Purdue, makeup perfect, suit immaculate, stands in front of Brooklyn Hospital.

"...teen, playing Pass Out, discovered hanging by a rope in an abandoned warehouse weeks ago, has been in a coma ever since. The game, considered autoerotic, led to at least two teenage deaths last month. Is this the new high? Will it turn into an epidemic?" She looks directly into the camera. "For more information on this dangerous fad, click the 'See It on TV' link on our website. Emily Purdue, Channel 5 News."

Hot lava erupts in my veins. For the first time in weeks, a burst of energy gets me moving. Within seconds, I'm on Marci's computer.

"What are you doing?" she asks.

"Looking up the phone number for Channel 5 News. We need to talk to Emily Purdue. *I* need to talk to her. Tell her she got it wrong."

The members of TV Production huddle in the cafeteria. Raul nibbles a greasy cafeteria calzone. I haven't touched my sandwich; Marci's taken maybe two bites of salad. Henry's making milk doodles across his tray, using his straw as a pencil. Omar's uncharacteristically subdued. For the last two weeks, he's been as devastated as I am, as if somehow he should have *sensed* what Jagger and I were up to.

Despite my attempt to reach Emily Purdue, which consisted of refusing to get off the phone until I was transferred to her voice mail—"Please leave a name, message and valid contact number"—Channel 5 rebroadcast the segment during the ten o'clock news. By morning, text messages, like smoke signals, have crisscrossed the Heights. Every kid at WiHi, it seems, has seen the piece, setting off the gossip mill like never before.

"She made Jagger seem like such a loser," Henry moans. "When really, he's a hero."

Raul drums his fingers against the tray. "We need to get back on the story. Get it right. Unlike Channel 5."

"Val and Jagger tried," Henry says loyally.

"That was then. This is now."

"Why are you being so harsh?" Marci asks.

"Because this is the answer to MP's prayers," Raul tells her. "*Campus News* doing nothing, too upset about Jagger to work the story. Or have us doubting ourselves after watching the way Channel 5 reported it. Either way, we've backed off."

"You think that's how Emily Purdue got the story in the first place?" I push my sandwich away. "Someone from MP tipped her?"

Raul shrugs. "Or the cops. If it's the third bad Pass Out incident in a month, they'd want the public to be aware. Parents, kids."

"You must have *some* idea what to do next, Val." Omar leans forward. "Where's their weak point? What's the angle?"

"I wish to God I had something. The only thing I can think of is someone should talk to Taneisha again. Maybe she'll feel bad and spill. I *know* she's lying about how she got hurt."

"Jagger found out she's in MP?" Henry asks. "That's something, at least."

Exhausted, I rub my eyes. "Not specifically. The only thing we're positive about is that he was the second person asked to join. There was an accident during the first initiation. Taneisha's the only one who fits. Type of accident, right time frame."

"Were they playing hangman with her, too?" Raul asks.

The bluntness of his words makes me flinch. I glance at Marci. Does Raul know about Jagger and me? She shakes her head slightly. Still…

"Taneisha refused to talk to me, Raul. Her mom said it happened on the Promenade near the globe statue. You know how that end of the walkway is below street level? Taneisha *said* she was by herself, tightrope walking the sloping wall after the rainstorm. It's a steep curve and everything was still wet. She slipped and fell. So no. It wasn't Pass Out. They saved that wonderful activity for Jagger."

Omar crumples his napkin in disgust. "It's not just an activity, Val. It's some kind of criminal."

He glances at Henry.

"I looked it up," Henry says. "Reckless endangerment is the least of it. Someone could make a case for attempted manslaughter. Maybe murder. They left Jagger hanging. That's a lot more than a 'fun' initiation stunt."

"Not if Jagger agreed to do it," Raul argues. "If you voluntarily do something stupid, it's your own damn fault if you get hurt. Look at it from the cops' point of view. It's the third time in a *month* some kid gets hurt trying Pass Out. They jump to the obvious conclusion. Jagger heard about it and found a vacant building with a group of other kids. They were experimenting. Daring each other. Being dumb teenagers."

"But we have proof it's more," Marci says. "Maybe Val didn't have it with her then, but you kept the note, right? The one the kid wrote telling you about the first initiation and how it went bad."

"Yes. Of course I saved it."

Raul clears his throat. "But the note's anonymous. Just like the writing in Omar's basement. Police work's got to be the same as reporting. Unless the cops verify the source, what can they do? Especially since there's no actual threat involved. Even we don't know for sure if the note's telling the truth. Someone could have made it up."

Henry looks thoughtful. "Did Jagger read it?"

"Yes! Trust me. I *begged* him not to go through with it."

"Then Raul's right. If he did it willingly, understanding he might get hurt, it's on him," Henry says reluctantly. "The police can't do anything to them."

Marci shakes her head. "Not true. MP left him like that."

Omar hits the table impatiently. "Hold on. Why is everyone assuming the cops are ignoring what Val told them? I bet they at least checked it out. Asked Mr. Wilkins. 'Yes, some group appeared out of nowhere. I tried to find out who's involved, but you know how kids are.'"

"Which means it was the *police* who went to Channel 5." Raul looks around the table. "So far, there haven't been any arrests at school. That's not the kind of thing that stays secret for long. Obviously, the cops are stumped, too. Let's do something useful to help them. Get at least one name. Nobody cares about this as much as we do."

"What if I visit Taneisha?" Marci says. "If she leads us to a second source or proof that MP is behind the initiations, we could go to the police *and* run the story. That would make everyone happy, right?"

Around the table, heads nod.

"If you go to the hospital or her house, Marci, someone else should go back to Red Hook," Henry says. "Talk to the warehouse guys next to the abandoned building. One of them might have seen a bunch of kids hanging around. Maybe we can get a description."

"That's what I'm talking about," Raul says. "Action. I'll go with you. Omar, how about you team with Marci?"

I can tell Raul's concerned about sending Omar to the macho part of Red Hook. The artists who live there might be cool—but they're outnumbered by warehouse and factory workers. The kind of guys who might decide Omar's a bit too flashy for their taste.

No one, including Omar, wants to deal with that.

"What about you, Val?" Marci asks.

My anger at Taneisha is so intense I'd probably break her other leg if I talked to her. How could she be loyal to people who hurt her? What kind of spell, or charm or just plain charisma, does MP have? If she'd told the truth in the first place, Jagger would not be in a coma right now.

"I won't be much help," I say.

"That's fine," Raul tells me. "Henry and I could really use you. Except for buying stuff at Ikea with my dad, I've never been to Red Hook."

"There's another thing we could try." Henry's learned not to get flustered when everyone looks at him. "You know those emails Val got? The ones telling her where to meet? I can show them to someone I know."

"Computer geek?" Raul asks.

"Yeah. My friend Toby. She's a chess-playing computer genius. She might be able to get the IP address." He glances at the look of confusion on Marci's face and adds, "Every computer has a specific one, like a fingerprint. Hopefully, Toby can track down who sent the emails."

"That would be awesome!" I say.

As if to punctuate the feeling, the bell rings. Kids spring up, laughing, pushing. No one at our table moves, however. Everyone's focused, hell-bent on stopping MP. It's not only the story the team wants. Or making sure no one else gets hurts. It's personal. Without anyone quite knowing how it happened, Slacker Jagger burrowed his way into each of our hearts.

The blood-dimmed tide is loosed,
and everywhere
The ceremony of innocence is
drowned.

W.B. YEATS

MP LOG

No one noticed me watching the parade. Doctors, nurses, red-eyed mother, sobbing WiHi assholes.

It's extremely amusing. *Campus News* spinning their wheels for so long trying to find me. And there I was. Fifteen, maybe twenty feet away. Watching. Listening. Laughing my ass off.

I sat in plain sight across the hall. "Grandpa's so out of it," I told the nurse, "he doesn't recognize me." She agreed it was very sad.

After everyone left, I slipped across the hall. Took pictures of him all tubed up. Close-ups of the bruises around his neck because that shit's awesome.

The genie's out of the bottle—that's for sure. And there's no way he goes back in. Been out ever since the new girl slipped on the ledge. Phantom thinks I pushed her, but I didn't. I got in close, and maybe she felt something and moved too much to the right, but I can't take credit. Just a lucky accident that proved how easy it can be to terrify them. To show the world how meaningless their petty lives are.

A rope. A box. A plan.

It's all I needed to make a nightmare come true.

27

The bus pulls up in front of the glass-topped bus shelter. The door hisses open and the three of us exit into a partly cloudy afternoon. Not much wind, the temp hovers somewhere in the mid-forties. I go straight into reporter mode, lock my feelings up tight and lead the boys through Red Hook's narrow streets.

"That's it."

Henry takes in the unused building, the fence. "How'd you get inside?"

"I'll show you."

At the side yard, I point out the loose, rusted chain. Push the gate to widen the gap. Henry slides in first. He helps Raul, who's got at least twenty pounds on him. I slip through last, and they fall in behind me as I move toward the back door.

Something's changed.

"That's a different lock." The new padlock is made of thick, shiny steel. "The other one was broken and sort of hanging."

"The cops must have contacted the owner," Henry surmises. "Told him to make sure no one gets in again."

Even though I'm desperately trying to focus, my mind swirls. *What if* I'd been ten minutes later? *What if* Jagger hadn't kept his locator app enabled? *What if* I hadn't noticed the back door in the dark...?

Henry senses I might lose my shit. He must also know that Raul asked me to Winter Formal because he says, "How about you and Raul stay together? I'll cross the street and try to find someone who saw the kids. Maybe we'll get lucky."

Swiftly, he retraces his steps.

"Val, if this is too hard—" Raul starts.

"Take out the camera." Silently, I wait for him to get ready. After he nods, I start speaking. "It was dark by the time I found the place. Probably should have used my cell for light, but I was in a rush and not thinking clearly. An animal brushed past me and I fell into that pile of rusted machinery."

Raul swivels to capture the scene. "Which made a lot of noise, so you hid."

"Right. Behind that trash can. No one came to look for me. By the time it felt safe to continue, I saw that the back door was half-open. I didn't notice anyone leaving. Don't know if they heard me and got out when I was hiding or if they had a lookout. Maybe the plan was always to leave Jagger alone."

Raul stops shooting. "That doesn't seem right. The point of an initiation is that as soon as it's over, you're a member of the group."

"Unless they were suspicious of Jagger the whole time. Who's to say one of them didn't follow him to the Media Center and realize he's in TV? They might have figured out he was doing it for *Campus News*."

"This is some truly evil shit." Raul restarts the camera. "What happened next?"

"I pushed the door slowly so it wouldn't squeak. I hoped the initiation was still going on, that everything was okay. Except for a small streak of light across the floor, it was pitch-black. Completely silent. I called out. No one answered. That's

when I panicked. I ran into the room and tripped over Jagger's backpack." I'm moving backward, showing Raul where
I'd gone on the other side of the wall. "About here. I picked
up the flashlight and that's when I saw…"

I can't go on. Raul moves forward and puts his arms around
me so that I don't fall. It feels familiar—although the hug I
remember isn't his. It's Jagger's. At my locker, after I found
the bird…

"Hold on a sec!" Pushing Raul aside, I dump my backpack
onto the ground. Paw through the contents.

He squats beside me. "What are you looking for?"

I sit back on my heels. "Remember how we couldn't figure
out who got my locker combo? I just realized it wasn't Mrs.
G., Lawrence or Tracy Gardner. It was me."

Raul cocks his head. "Who'd you tell?"

"No one. I mean, not specifically. But Marci and I always
keep the combo sheet we get at the beginning of the year in
our backpacks, in case we forget the numbers." I point. "It's
not here."

He gives me a skeptical look. "You could have tossed it by
accident."

"No! Somebody got a hold of it. Maybe MP planned to put
the bird in my backpack, not the locker. But then they saw
the combo. Decided it would be scarier to tie a string around
the poor thing's neck and hang it."

"Okay," Raul says, "but I still don't see how this helps.
Anyone at school could have found the numbers."

"Not really. I keep the backpack with me every second of
the day—except for one class. We all leave our bags—"

"In the Media Center." Raul blinks. "You don't think
someone on the team—"

"Not us. A Team."

His brow furrows. "Really?"

I remember a line from one of the emails: *There are spies everywhere.*

"Think about it. Suppose one of the people on A Team is in MP. They check the list of stories on the whiteboard. They're at the Wednesday presentations. They go back and report it to the group. That's how MP knows we haven't figured out who they are. That's the reason they keep going, getting bolder each time."

Slowly, thoughtfully, he puts the camera back into the case. "It's possible. Anything's possible. But it's hard to believe anyone on A Team hates us so much that they'd leave Jagger in the building, alone."

"Hailey can't stand me. Never could. Still doesn't explain why she'd do that to Jagger—"

"Unless she has a thing for him—and it wasn't returned."

"Hell, *that* explains something." I tell him about the conversation in the Media Center. "Hailey was mad at me for no real reason. If she knew Jagger and I went out last year…" My voice peters out. Raul doesn't notice the slip—or if he does, he decides to ignore it. Hurriedly, I add, "She accused *me* of making it up just so I could get the story. She could be doing that thing magicians do. Focus my attention someplace else so I don't notice what's in front of me."

"Let's think this scenario through slowly," Raul suggests. "Hailey's in MP. She's also in love with Jagger, who couldn't care less. He shows up in class at the beginning of the year, gets put on our team. *Your* team. MP starts doing all that stuff. We work the story hard, which pisses Hailey off even more. She tries to blame you—"

"But that doesn't work. So she steals the locker combo from my backpack, hangs the dead bird in my locker. Tries to scare us off the story—along with a personal screw-you."

Raul nods. "Jagger puts the application in the box—"

"And Hailey gets MP to choose him. So she has a better chance of hooking up."

Raul leans against the building. "First flaw in the logic. Jags thought they chose him because they don't know he's in TV, right?"

"Unless they knew and were playing him. Or Hailey didn't care or didn't think it mattered. She might have thought he was trying to mess with our team. That he was turning on us. On me. What does it matter?" I sling the backpack over my shoulder. "If Hailey's in MP, any explanation is possible."

28

The team gathers at Marci's. She throws a bag of chocolate chip cookies on the coffee table and slumps onto the couch. "We got nothing. No matter what Omar or I said, Taneisha refused to talk about MP or the accident."

"She acted completely clueless. But I get why Val thinks she knows something. There's something fishy about that girl." Omar tears the bag open with his teeth. "What about Red Hook? Anything?"

Henry shakes his head. "The guys I talked to said it's a ghost town after five. MP could've used the building a hundred times. As long as they met after work hours, or on a weekend, they'd be invisible."

Raul and I exchange a look. "All we got is a theory. Val?"

I repeat what I told Raul. The team is so desperate for a lead, any lead, that no one questions the possibility. The only concern is how to approach Hailey. We finally decide that a surprise attack, when she least expects it, is best.

Just before everyone takes off, Henry's phone pings.

"Hold on, guys," he calls out.

Marci leans over to read the text message. "What does 'K Pawn to e4' mean?"

"It's an opening gambit. Toby wants me to call. She obviously found something." Excited, Henry hits the reply button. "Come on, come on—hey, what you got?"

We wait impatiently as Toby goes through an obviously obsessive explanation of how she tracked down the email address. After a few minutes, Marci does a hand-circling "Get on with it" gesture.

Henry ignores her, listens some more, then asks, "You sure?" Pause, then, "Owe you a game."

Marci bounces impatiently on the couch. "Finally! What did she say?"

"Whoever sent the emails routed them through Val's computer."

"What?" Marci asks.

"It appears as if they were sent from her own computer," Henry explains. "To herself."

"That's ridiculous!" I protest. "I wouldn't do that."

"Of course not." Henry's voice has more than a touch of admiration. "It's not the hardest thing in the world to do if you know anything about hacking. At least that's what Toby said. The original IP address was switched out for your computer ID, Val. Insanely clever. That way, no one can track down who sent them."

Raul looks thoughtful. "After we talk to Hailey tomorrow, a couple of us should speak to Toby. Find out if she has any idea who at WiHi has mad hacking skills and can fake an IP address!"

Orange Street is quiet, a few blocks north of the heart of Brooklyn Heights. Before school the next day, the team meets opposite Hailey's building. The air is chilly. Marci looks particularly miserable that she had to get out of bed earlier than usual. No one speaks until Omar raises his voice.

"Hailey! Over here!"

She looks surprised, and then amused, as we surround her. "If you're trying to kidnap me for ransom money, you're out of luck. My folks don't have a dime."

"Funny." Marci pulls her into the alley.

"Can someone tell me—" Hailey turns pale. "Did something happen to Jagger?"

"He's the same," Henry mumbles.

"That's a relief." Nobody responds, because it's not a relief at all. "What's this about?"

"We need the truth," I say.

"Please," Marci adds. "It's not like we're accusing you of doing it by yourself—"

"Doing what by myself?" Hailey seems genuinely confused. "You think I'm the one who got Jagger to stick his neck in a rope? I don't do that kind of stuff."

"He wasn't playing Pass Out," Henry says. "He was getting initiated into MP."

Hailey blinks. "Oh-kay. Someone's going to have to explain."

"Maybe you should. What were you doing that night?" Raul demands. "The night Jagger got hurt."

Hailey's eyes flick around the group, then land on me. "You fucking bitch! You think I had something to do with it? That I'm MP?"

"Are you?" Henry asks. "Maybe someone else on your team—"

"Are you nuts? Besides the fact that nobody on A Team would *ever* do that to anyone, none of us has time to freaking breathe, let alone join some secret society and plan weird-ass pranks. Benny's aunt is sick, so he has to pitch in until his mom comes back from Florida. Both Leni and Scott took two days off to finish their early-deadline college applications.

We're one segment short this week—" She looks around the group, hate making her body rigid. "If anything, it's Val who set this up. You guys ever consider that? She'll do anything to get ahead!"

"Let's not do this," Raul says. "I believe you when you say it's not you, but it's not Val, either. You understand why we had to ask, right? We figured the only way everything makes sense is if there's an insider in TV Production."

The fight leaves Hailey as the impact hits. "Jagger did it for the story?" She leans limply against the wall. "Put his neck in a noose and…damn!"

"Yeah," I say. "It's crazy."

"When was this exactly?"

"The Friday before Thanksgiving. Why?"

"No reason," she says. "Just, you know, I didn't remember the exact day." She gives me a funny look. "Don't you have tape?"

"Excuse me?"

"When Jagger met MP. Didn't you shoot it? That's what I would have done."

"I couldn't. I wasn't there—"

Immediately, I shut up. I should have realized something long before this moment.

We pass the bagel shop on the way to WiHi. Raul nudges me. "Got a couple of dollars? I didn't eat breakfast—and don't have any money."

"Sure." Waving the others ahead, I dig into my backpack. "What kind do you like?"

"Sesame." He grins.

The store is warm, windows steamy with morning goodness. It's too bad I don't drink coffee because the scent of fresh-made smells delicious. Not burned, which for some reason is the way Mom seems to brew it.

Raul and I settle at the table farthest from the door. In front of us, two toasted bagels are smeared with cream cheese. He takes a huge bite of his, chews it down before saying, "Okay, Valerie, spill."

"First, when did you start sounding like Marci? And second, I don't know what you mean."

"I saw your face when we talked to Hailey. Something upset you. Besides the fact that she called you a bitch."

I lean back. "She's right. Jagger planned to shoot as much of the initiation as he could with Mr. Carleton's little demo camera."

"And…?"

"In the confusion, I forgot about that."

"How was he going to capture anything without them knowing? Did he hide the camera in his jacket?"

I shake my head. "Backpack. He was afraid he'd have to take off his coat."

Raul swallows another bite of bagel. "He couldn't have gotten the camera going. The cops would have watched the footage. They'd realize something's up because MP would have to tell Jagger what to do with the rope. He didn't know ahead of time."

"Except the police might *not* have found the camera." Raul's eyebrows rise like double question marks. "Jagger hid it pretty well."

"Cops aren't stupid. I'm sure they checked."

I laugh grimly. "Jagger worked it out himself. He was very proud of the idea. Said he read some James Bond novel where the spy hides a gun inside a paperback."

"No way," Raul breathes.

"Way. He took his copy of *A Separate Peace* and hollowed

a space big enough for the camera. Then he cut a hole on the cover exactly where the lens is. He showed it to me. You'd have to know what to look for to notice it."

"So, what was he going to do? Take out the book and say, 'Go ahead and initiate. I'll just sit here and read my English assignment'?"

"He put it in the side pocket." I lift my backpack. "It's mesh like this one. All he had to do was press Record. He practiced in the mirror so he could do it without anyone noticing."

"Genius," Raul admits. "You think the police missed it?"

"What else could it be? The camera is so light, even if a cop picked up the book, they might not notice. Actually, they probably didn't even take it out of the pocket. Jagger's in high school. They'd expect him to have a book."

"Mrs. Orapessa's going to be pissed it's ruined," Raul mutters. It's the kind of random thought that's been beaten into us throughout thirteen years of public school.

"There are extras in the book room. What we need to worry about is finding Jagger's backpack."

Raul glances at the painted bagel-clock that hangs behind the counter. "It's early. If we're lucky, Mrs. Voorham's still home. It's closer than going to the hospital."

First period's almost over, so why not ditch the rest of the day? "I know where he lives."

"I bet."

Uh-oh.

There's a definite undercurrent in his voice. Does Raul suspect something went on between Jagger and me? Getting up to throw the paper plates away, I pretend I didn't hear.

My first impression of the woman who opens the door is that we're looking at Jagger's grandmother. But then the voice, dull with exhaustion and worry, greets me by name.

"Come in, Val."

"Hi, Mrs. Voorham. This is Raul. He's a friend of Jagger's, too."

"How is he?" Raul asks gently.

Jagger's mom sinks into a living-room chair. Without being invited, Raul and I take the couch. "They took out the breathing tube yesterday."

"That's good, isn't it?" I ask.

Helpless, her shoulders rise and fall. "He's breathing on his own but still unresponsive. No one knows what'll happen next."

Jagger's story about his mom makes me worried. "He'll be okay, Mrs. Voorham. You have to hang in there. For Jagger's sake. That's what we're all doing."

She nods and I pray that means she'll be all right. The silence in the room hangs like a cloud, dark and heavy. After a few moments, Raul clears his throat.

"Mrs. Voorham, Val and I were wondering if you have Jagger's backpack."

"What?" She makes an effort to focus. "His backpack? I don't know."

"Maybe the police gave it to you," I say. "After, you know, at the hospital."

"Did Jagger have it with him when…?" She can't continue. Her face is so pale.

"Why don't I get you some water?" I ask. "I know where the kitchen is."

"Ummm…" Even that is hard for her to decide.

"I'll be right back."

The kitchen is separated from the living room by a half wall. I run the tap, fill a glass and glance back to see Jagger's mom and Raul talking quietly. Taking advantage of her distraction,

I step into Jagger's room. Perhaps Mrs. Voorham forgot she put the backpack in there.

Standing in the bedroom is impossibly hard. Jags actually made his bed because we were supposed to meet here to transfer the footage to his laptop. Swallowing hard, I glance around the room. No backpack. That means the cops have it. A huge obstacle. It'll be harder for Raul and me to convince them to give it to us than it would be Jagger's mom.

She takes the glass with a soft "Thank you."

Raul stands. "We'll visit him later today. You should try to get some sleep, Mrs. Voorham."

She hesitates, not quite able to let us go. "The kids have been great. So many of Jagger's friends stopped by the hospital. I don't recognize half of them."

"He's kind of popular. Really, if you ever want company, or you need something, please call me. I live close." I scribble my phone number on a piece of paper and place it on the coffee table. As I move to give her a goodbye hug, I notice Raul staring at the half-open coat closet. I follow his eyes. There, on the floor, is exactly what we've been looking for.

"You did get Jagger's backpack!" I say. "It's in the closet. Would you mind if I look through it? Jagger, um, borrowed something I need."

"Oh." She rubs her eyes. "I can't remember. Everything's so confusing...."

The backpack lies on its side. I check the pocket. The book is exactly where I hoped it would be.

29

We're on the way to my house when my cell buzzes. I look at the readout. "Omigod!"

"What?" Raul asks.

"It's Emily!"

"Emily who?"

I hold up my hand to silence him, take a breath and accept the call. "Hello."

"Emily Purdue speaking. You left a message."

"Hi, um, Ms. Purdue." Raul's eyes widen. He leans in to listen. "This is Valerie. Valerie Gaines. Thanks so much for calling me back."

On the phone, her voice has a higher pitch than when she's on camera. More impatient. "You said it was 'extremely important.'"

"Yes. It's about a story you reported. You got it wrong." As succinctly as I can, I start to explain what happened at the warehouse. She cuts me off before I get very far.

"Listen, sweetie, that's old news. If the kid in the hospital dies, okay, let me know. Maybe I'll follow up. Not promising."

Without another word, she hangs up.

Raul whistles. "That's cold, Val. Sorry. I know you like her."

The last bit of the world that I trusted, the part desperately clinging to the belief that reporters want to get a story right, crumbles before my eyes.

"Do you think she realized what she said? How...awful that was?"

Raul sighs bleakly. The disaster that's become our lives is wearing him down, too.

"I don't know." He shifts Jagger's backpack, hooked over his own, higher on his shoulder. "Let's see if there's anything on the camera. The only way anyone will take us seriously is if we have proof of what went down."

We walk the rest of the way to my house in silence. After unlocking the door, I push Raul ahead of me.

"You sure this is okay?" he asks.

"No one's home, but the neighbors are nosy."

Once we're inside, I open Jagger's book and pull out the camera that's been securely taped into a well of cut pages. Nothing happens when I press *Play*.

"Dead battery," Raul observes. "That's good. It means Jagger had it running at some point."

"Computer's upstairs." I gallop up the steps, then pull to a dead stop. "Wait here. I share with my sister."

I pop in to check for stuff like random underwear thrown onto the floor, which would be totally embarrassing. I'm lucky. Bethany has finally taken to dropping her dirty clothes into the hamper. Although both beds are unmade, there's nothing especially cringe-worthy lying around.

"Okay. Come in."

"This isn't so bad," Raul tells me. "You should see my room."

I plug the camera directly into the computer. It takes a moment to power up. A couple of mouse clicks later, the transfer starts.

"Not sure how long it'll take. There's ninety minutes of memory." I peer at Raul. "You can take off your coat, you know."

"Yeah. Thanks."

"Do you want something to drink? We have everything. Soda, milk, juice…"

"Juice is good," Raul says.

Breakfast dishes, milky glasses and crumpled napkins are all over the kitchen table. The garbage can overflows.

Raul quietly checks it out. "How many brothers and sisters do you have?"

"Three, but the boys are twins." I open the fridge. "Apple or orange?"

"Whatever you want."

I pull two glasses from the cabinet and rinse them in case there's crud inside. Raul says, "I can clear the table if you want."

"Are you kidding? That'll totally make my mom suspicious." I hand him a glass of cider. "Or give her a heart attack."

"Wouldn't want either to happen." Raul gulps half the cider, and then stares at the glass.

"Is there dirt inside? I'm so sorry, the dishwasher's really old." I reach out. "I'll get you another glass."

"It's fine."

I lean forward. "Then it's Hailey that's bothering you, right? Wasn't it a little strange the way she wanted to know the exact day Jagger got hurt? And the question about the footage. What if we're right, after all, and it *is* someone on A Team but not her? Scott lied about Omar's wall when he shot the fire piece." Raul gives me a look. "He told me he asked Omar about the new paint, but he didn't."

"That's not it."

"Oh. Then what..."

Raul gestures toward the glass. "I was thinking about Jagger's mom. When you got the water. You seem to know the apartment pretty well."

"Yeah. Well, I mean, it's not a secret that Jags and I went out at the end of tenth grade."

"But you broke up." He waits for me to nod before continuing. "That's why I thought it would be okay to ask you to Winter Formal. And the reason you said yes."

"Raul—"

"Because after Jagger wakes up, and after all he did to get the story, maybe you'd rather go to the dance with him."

At last! The time to confess. But the thought of seeing one more person hurt right now is too much for me. In the room directly above us, a camera transfers the footage that will show how Jagger slipped into a coma. A coma he may never come out of.

Across from me is a guy who's working as hard as he can to uncover the truth. For Jagger. If you asked which he'd rather have—Jagger waking up perfectly fine and losing me or the other way around—Raul would certainly choose Jagger. He's liked Jags from the moment they did the skateboarding piece. Yes, I complicate things, but the fact doesn't change. Raul is as upset by what happened as the rest of us.

How can I knowingly wound a guy like that?

"Will any of us feel like going to the dance if Jagger's still in the hospital?" I ask quietly. "I know I won't...."

Raul's hot cocoa eyes widen. "God, Val, you're right. I just assumed he'd be better by then.... Jesus, I'm a jerk."

I lean across the table. "You're not. I've hardly ever seen you be less than the most considerate person imaginable. Everyone knows you care. About a lot of stuff. Your family. *Cam-*

pus News. Jagger. What we need to do right now is find out who did that awful thing to him—and then pray he wakes up. Nothing else matters."

He nods—because the truth is, Raul may be the nicest person ever.

Climbing back up the stairs feels different. As if we've reached another level in our relationship. Real friendship? The comfort of people who want the same thing? Whatever it is, neither of us feels the need to talk about it.

By the time we get to my room, the footage has transferred. Instantly, we're all business. I pull Bethie's desk chair next to mine. Raul reaches for the keyboard.

"Ready?"

"Do it."

At last we find out who's in MP! The idiots who left Jagger with the rope around his neck. My heart ticks fast as the image on the screen moves. It's shaky. We can see the street in late-afternoon light. I catch a glimpse of a jean jacket on the person walking next to Jagger. Just like the one I wear—along with half the kids at WiHi.

Jagger's voice is loud. "Why aren't we going to the flag-pole?"

"Change of plans," a girl replies.

Her voice is clear, although I don't recognize it. Raul shakes his head. He doesn't know who she is, either.

"Where *are* we going?" Jagger manages to sound annoyed, not worried because he knows I'm waiting.

"You'll see when we get there."

After some jostling, the footage abruptly cuts off.

"Damn," Raul says. "You think she found the camera?"

"My guess is Jagger shut it down because he didn't know how long it would take to get to the next place. Didn't want to run out of memory." I point to a second thumbnail image on the computer screen. "The camera saves each start-up as a different file."

"Got it." Raul clicks the mouse, and the second section begins. Same girl's voice. "In here."

"That's the warehouse," Raul mutters. "I recognize the walls. That tiny camera's pretty good, Val."

"Except we aren't getting her face."

"Don't worry. It's early. I'm sure—"

"Shit!"

"What?" Raul looks startled.

My stomach drops. "We're not going to get picture. It was pitch-black inside."

"Oh, man," he moans.

Even a tiny camera needs light.

On-screen, the back door swings open. Jagger and the girl step inside. Just as I predicted, the computer screen goes dark. In an eerie echo, both Jagger on the computer, and Raul next to me, swear.

All we get is sound.

"Lights?" Jagger lightens his voice. "I'm afraid of the dark."

"No electricity. But we have a flashlight." She raises her voice. "It's Ghost Face. Shine the light this way."

It doesn't help. The camera needs way more illumination than a single flashlight to capture images. Footsteps shuffle. It sounds like several people are moving into position.

On-screen, someone says, "Let's begin." The chant bounces off empty walls, echoing eerily.

"Blood of the untamed
Runs through our veins,
Power that forms
Cannot be contained.
Cold winds will rise

Increasing the pain
Yet our circle of silence shall always remain...."

I blink. "What the—"

"It's some kind of oath," Raul mutters. "Or warning. Keep quiet or else!"

To me, it sounds like a curse. The hair on my arms goes electric. The creepiness pouring from the screen is almost too much to bear.

The chant ends. Eagerly, a boy asks, "Ready, dude? Skeletor found a good box. Look how we set it up."

I imagine the flashlight shining first on the box—and then the ceiling.

"What the hell?" Jagger's first glimpse of rope, looped over the pipe, finally makes him sound nervous. "What's going on?"

Run, Jags! Get out. Now!

"It's for the initiation," Ghost Face says.

No one snickers *duh*. Instead, a titter of excitement makes its way around the group.

"This is sick," Raul mutters.

"Not so fast." A new person. A guy. "He needs to sign."

"Skeletor?" Now Jagger's pissed. "No one told me I had to sign anything."

"Yeah, well, new rule." A paper rustles. "It says you're doing this of your own free will. No one's making you."

"What exactly am I doing? All I see is a rope thrown over a pipe in the ceiling. And a box underneath it. And, like, five of you standing in a circle."

"He's narrating," Raul breathes. "Jagger knows the camera isn't picking up picture."

The first guy speaks again. Totally amped. "It's Pass Out. It'll be fun, you'll see."

Ghost Face pipes up. "I've got a pen."

Don't take it! Get out of there—

"Let me read it first. Hand me the flash."

My hand grips the desk. Beside me, Raul barely breathes.

Jagger laughs. "Whose father's a lawyer?"

The group shifts, but no one answers.

"If you don't sign, you can't be in MP," Skeletor states.

"Why doesn't he leave?" Raul grabs my arm. "He must know who they are by now."

I shake my head. "Jagger told me they wore masks the first time. Probably have them on again. Maybe there's some stupid ceremony where they take them off after the initiation's over."

"Give me the pen," Jagger mutters.

"Sign at the bottom." Skeletor's cocky, not at all surprised by Jagger's surrender. He knew Jags would give in, just like he knew he'd show up for the initiation. In some primeval recess of my brain, the one that got created when cavemen discovered poisonous snakes, a message throbs: *watch out for this guy. He's vicious.* But Jagger's not getting the same message. Or if he is, he thinks he can handle it.

"How's it work?" he asks, in full reporter mode. "Tell me everything."

A third boy takes over. He's the one who either did the research or played before. "First, you step on the box. Then you go up on your toes with the rope around your neck and let yourself hang. The rush comes in just a few minutes."

"Why's it called Pass Out?" Jagger asks.

"Because you might pass out. Not everyone does. That's why the box is there. So you can get down."

Raul notices my head shaking. "Val? What is it?"

"The box was on its side when I showed up. There's no way he could reach it."

Raul clenches his teeth. "Which means Jagger either kicked it when he tried to get down or someone knocked it over."

For the next few minutes, we listen to a plan designed by a devil. The members of MP get Jagger up on the box, bring one end of the rope over to the wall, tie it to the radiator and make sure it'll hold. Beside me, Raul looks like he wants to punch the screen. I grip the arms of the chair, steeling myself for the final descent into hell.

At last, they're ready. It's hard to tell by sound alone if Jagger puts the rope around his neck himself or if someone helps. Then…nothing. The entire group seems to have stopped breathing. The eerie silence goes on—and on. Finally, there's a shout: "He did it. He passed out."

A new voice speaks up, someone we haven't heard before. This person must be in the back, because it's hard to hear. I think the words are "It's done. Can we…down—"

Crash!

Raul glances at me. My mouth is so dry, I can only nod. That's me falling into a piece of equipment.

"Uh-oh." It's Ghost Face. "Somebody's here."

Skeletor yells, "Evacuate. Now!"

Instantly, we hear the sound of retreating feet and a *bang* when the box falls. The next voice we hear, just a few minutes later, is mine. Calling Jagger's name. Full of fear—yet not even close to understanding the horror that's to come.

I would do anything to hit Pause and then Delete, Delete, Delete. If only I could make what happened vanish with a click of the mouse.

The camera's memory runs out sometime during the ambulance ride. When it's over, Raul paces. I stare at the screen. "I can't believe I let him go through with it—"

"He was going to do it no matter what you said, Val. All you did was try to help."

"A lot of good that did," I mutter.

He waves my self-pity aside. "Focus, Valerie. Did you recognize any of the voices?"

I shake my head. "It was hard to hear everyone clearly."

"What do you mean?"

"Jagger said there were five people. Four did most of the talking. But there was someone who hardly said anything until the end." I find the spot on the computer, play it back. It's the low, whispered voice. "Sounds like 'It's done. Can we get him down?'"

Raul stops pacing about and sits on my bed. "That could be their weak link."

I move to him. "Meaning…?"

"Since he didn't say a word until that point, it could be someone who wasn't into this particular initiation."

"Why didn't he do something to stop it?" I ask.

"Same reason Taneisha isn't talking. They're afraid."

"Okay. So, what if that's who's sending me emails?"

"Exactly." Raul's jumpy, all keyed up. "Remember Jagger's mom saying she didn't realize he had so many friends? What if one of those people visiting is MP."

"Why? The hospital's the last place I'd go if I were in the group."

"Think about it. You're the person who isn't happy with Pass Out as the initiation, but you get outvoted. Or no one asked your opinion in the first place. However it happened, once Jagger ends up in the hospital, wouldn't you feel guilty? Wouldn't you need to see for yourself if he's getting better?"

I feel myself nodding slowly. "We could camp out at the hospital, see if we recognize any voices from the tape."

"Or get a look at the visitor log. Maybe a name will pop out."

"There's something else," I tell him. "Right after it happened, I thought the double agent played me. Told me the initiation was at the flagpole so I'd go there while they brought Jagger to the warehouse. But maybe he didn't know, either. Maybe he thought it was supposed to be at the flagpole and it got changed at the last minute."

"Because Skeletor doesn't trust anyone. Or he doesn't trust the double agent. Listening to the footage, it sure sounds like he's the leader."

"The last email I got said there are spies everywhere and it's too dangerous to email again. So yeah, Skeletor might suspect someone."

Raul grabs his jacket. "I'll go to the hospital while you send an email. Tell the double agent we can help, that we'll keep his identity a secret if he talks to us." He holds up a hand to still my protest. "I know you think he won't answer, but it's worth a try. Stay here in case there's a response."

I take my time composing an email. I want to get it right.

I know you want to stop the MP madness. The dangerous initiations. It's not hard to figure out that's why Jagger participated in Pass Out. So please. We have to meet. Wherever you say—but we need to do it soon. I'll protect you. I promise. No one needs to know your name. Ever. Contact me any way you can.

The hours go by. Raul texts to tell me he's going to wait for Jagger's mom to come by. I'm about to crawl out of my skin when Bethany barges into the room. She stops when she sees me. "What are you doing here?"

"I live here."

"Funny. I mean, what are you doing home before me? You never get back from school first."

"I didn't go today. Got halfway to WiHi, felt sick and turned around."

She looks at me suspiciously. "You've been here all day? Alone?"

"Of course. Why?"

"I don't know." She crinkles her eyes, looks around the room as if there's something she should figure out.

Damn! Two pillows sit side by side against the wall. Casually, I move to the bed, grab both pillows and fluff them together before randomly tossing them back onto the mattress. "I hope I'm not getting what you had a few weeks ago. Or that terrible flu."

Bethany gives me a piercing stare. "You don't seem sick."

"That's what sleeping half the day gets you." That's when I remember that the only thing I ate was a bagel. "I'm going to get something from the kitchen."

She plops on her bed. "And I care because…"

"I am your one and only sister and you love and worship me."

"Ha!" she snorts. "Wait, Val! Any news about Jagger?"

"They took him off the breathing machine."

She sits up. "They did? When?"

"Last night. He still hasn't woken up, so no one knows if it means he's getting better for good."

She plucks the sheet. "I was afraid, when I saw you home…"

"Yeah. But no, he's the same."

Something flickers in Bethany's eyes. *Omigod!* The clothes, the haircut, the not telling me Jagger talked to her at the Video Arcade. Showing up at the hospital with Mom…

"You're crushing on him, aren't you?"

My sister gets defensive. "Just because he's the only one of your friends who ever talked to me doesn't mean I'm in love with him."

"Marci talks to you."

"Like I'm a baby. Jagger treats me like I'm his age."

I can't decide if I should pity, be pissed at or be amused by my sister. I go for letting her down gently. "Don't be fooled, Bethany. Jagger's a flirt whenever a girl's around. He can't help it. It doesn't mean anything."

She looks so angry I dodge out of slugging range. "See what I mean? You act like I don't know anything. I know lots. I know it's your fault Jagger broke up with you last year—"

"Why would you even—"

"How long did you think it would last when you act so superior all the time? Jagger left you for that Dawn girl." She gives me a gotcha look. "Don't tell me he didn't."

It takes every bit of self-control to keep from beating the crap out of her. How dare she act all high and mighty, as if she's in a secret relationship in which Jags confides his innermost feelings to her?

"Bethany Ann Gaines, you know nothing about anything. When you get a boyfriend, if you ever do, we'll see how long you stay together."

I clatter down the steps, stomp into the kitchen—but I've lost my appetite. Grabbing my coat, I slam the door good and hard.

Standing on the street, I'm not sure where to go. My insides are so steamed the cold barely affects me.

I'm the one with attitude? Does the Queen of Sloth have any idea how she comes off?

Doesn't matter which way I choose. Heading east, I clomp past brownstones and apartment buildings decorated for the holidays. Christmas lights, plastic Santas, Hanukkah menorahs. I haven't spent one second thinking about the holidays.

Usually I leave plenty of hints about what I hope to get, but not this year. The only present I want is something my parents can't give me: Jagger listening to music, doing some crazy tricks on his board, laughing at us in *Campus News*...

Even as that thought crosses my mind, dark whispers crowd it out. *What if Bethany's right? Jagger said it was his fault, but what if I drove him to it? Did I really act so superior that, deep down, he wanted to see what being with Dawn was like? Could it happen again? Will Raul and I still be able to be friends if Jags and I do get together?*

It's only too easy to remember what it was like to get dumped. At the time, I came up with plenty of reasons: Jagger wished I was prettier, I'm too interested in *Campus News,* I'm not enough of a party girl. But arrogance? The thought never occurred to me. I couldn't possibly feel superior around him. It's the opposite. Deep down, I always knew he'd leave me. Even so, when it actually happened, I was surprised. That's not arrogance. It's stupidity.

Streetlamps blink on. My toes are numb. Reluctantly, I head home. I've got to check email—even if Bethany's in the room. To my relief, my sister slouches on the sofa, playing a video game. She gives me a hostile stare. I return it before heading up the steps.

Crossing my fingers, I sign on to my email. Click the message that awaits.

Told you before. Can't meet you. Ever. Do not email ever again. It's not safe.

30

The B Team meeting the following day crackles.

"I talked to Toby," Henry announces. "She said the only person at school who knows enough to hack an IP address is Liam Dolan."

"Who's that?" Marci asks.

Henry shrugs. "I don't know, but—"

"Hold on! The name sounds familiar. Liam, Liam…" With open palm, I pound my head, trying to shake the memory loose. "Got it! He's one of the guys I tried to interview after the toilet bowl prank. Before I could even start, Liam gave me the finger and stalked inside. We ended up shooting that other dude."

Marci nods. "Potty Mouth. I remember."

"Right. Someone should talk to Liam. Maybe there'll be others after we play this." I take the flash drive from my pocket. "I copied the footage Jagger took at the initiation so we could all watch it."

While I set up the computer, Raul says, "Listen carefully, guys. It's our only shot. The hospital told me it's against regulations to show the visitor log to anyone. We won't be able to find MP that way. Hopefully, someone recognizes a voice."

Marci closes her eyes. Omar moves in front of the speakers. Henry puts down the pencil he's doodling with.

Raul hits Stop after the part where I find Jagger.

Marci looks sick. "Wish I hadn't heard that."

"I know," I tell her. "Did you recognize anyone? Anybody?" All around the room, heads shake. The tiny ember of hope that flared when Raul and I found the camera in Jagger's backpack dies a quick death. "Damn! After all he went through, the footage is a waste."

"There's *got* to be some way to use it," Omar tells us.

Raul sighs. "I'm out of ideas."

"It's maddening!" I pace in front of the monitor. "To be this close. That kid who whispered, 'Can we get him down?' might be exactly who we're looking for. The double agent. The weak link. *Why* does it have to be the quietest voice in the room?"

Omar extends a hand. "Give me the drive. Mr. C. showed me how to boost sound back in September. I'll see what I can do. We can talk to Liam after that and see if his voice matches."

"Cool."

Henry stares at the darkened monitor. "That's a good idea, Omar. But why *can't* we also broadcast some of the footage? Do an *America's Most Wanted* thing."

"You mean—" Raul shifts into a deep announcer voice "—if you recognize any one of these voices, notify *Campus News*. All leads kept confidential." He goes back to his regular voice. "I don't know. Could it work with no picture?"

"It's a waste of time," Marci says. "The footage is useless. You can't figure out who's who. My mother could be on that tape and I wouldn't know for sure."

I lean forward. "Maybe all we need to do is shake them up. Get the group upset so that they make a move. A panicked, not-well-planned move that'll bring them down."

"I agree," Henry says. "MP can't be positive no one will recognize a voice. *They* know who's talking, so they might assume everyone else does."

"Might be worth a try." Raul glances at me for confirmation. "We can show, say, a minute and a half. Announce that more footage will air next time. In the meantime, if anyone knows anything—"

"Put a note in the *Campus News* box or contact any reporter!" I jump up. "I'll tell Mr. Carleton we're changing the show. You guys choose a section that runs straight through. No edits. The last thing we want is to be accused of messing with the footage."

"Hold on!" Omar stops me just as I reach the control room door. "Think about it, Val. If you go rushing off to Carleton, he might freak."

"Why? Mr. C. *wants* us to get the story—"

"Who's to say the school isn't responsible for what happened? Jagger was doing something for a class. As the teacher in charge, Mr. Carleton might be the person they hold accountable if his mom sues the pants off everyone. If I were Mr. C. and you came to me right now, with Jagger in a coma, I'd tell you to shut it down."

"He's not like that," I protest.

Marci nods at Omar. "Why find out? Or get Mr. Carleton in trouble? Let's bring it to the cops instead of playing Channel 5 News. Let them deal with it."

"That's not what Omar said," I protest.

"Not this second. But everyone in this room promised that if we got something solid, or anything close, that's what we'd do."

"It's not like the cops don't know about MP but have you seen even one of them asking questions?" Raul shakes his head. "You still think the police are going to sweep through, Marci, find out what we can't and save the day. This isn't Small Town, Montana, population eight hundred. Eight *million* people live here. Someone gets robbed or raped every hour of every day, and cops don't do shit—"

"That's not true," Marci protests.

"It is! It's happened to people I know—" Raul freezes, shocking even himself. The control room gets deathly quiet. Nobody moves; no one knows what to say.

He squares his shoulders, lets out a breath. "You live in a nice, safe doorman building, Marci. Your folks probably pay half a month's rent just to keep their car in a lighted garage with security cams all over the place. So you don't realize that unless it's murder, whenever anything happens and the person can't be identified, it's pretty much 'really sorry you had to go through that, we've got your statement and where's the front door again?'"

"I'm sure it's not how they want it," Henry protests. "There's only so much cops can do…."

"Which is why going to them with footage that doesn't have a single face on it is a waste of time," I say. "Like you said, Henry, we'd do better showing it on *Campus News.*"

"But then we run into the Carleton problem," Omar argues. "If we *tell* him ahead of time, we take the chance he says no."

"What else is there?" Marci gasps. "You don't think we should air it without saying anything, do you? Sneak it into the broadcast and hope Carleton won't get mad?"

Nervously, Omar twists a stray paper clip. "I'm not saying that's what we should do. But yeah, it's an option."

"With serious consequences," Henry mumbles.

"Like what?" I tick them off on my fingers. "Getting kicked off *Campus News?* Suspension? Expulsion?"

"Who knows?" Omar says.

I look at the team. "Then Marci's right. If we're afraid to

air it, we *are* just playing at being reporters. Because the guys on TV make hard choices all the time. How far into the war zone should I go? What if the hurricane sweeps me away? Will I get radiation poisoning if I do one more story near the broken reactor?"

Nobody says anything.

"Who votes to air a section of the video without permission?" I ask.

"Count me out!" Marci says. "I am not willing to screw up senior year for something I don't think will work. Sorry, Val. Not even for you."

"That's okay. I get it."

Marci blinks nervously. "What do I do if you show it? Quit?"

"No." I sigh. "If you leave right now, before anything gets decided, you can swear you're not part of it. And it would be true."

To my surprise, she stays in her seat. "Listen to me, Val, please! You're making a big mistake. Airing that footage might be the *worst* thing you can do. Who knows what MP is capable of? We don't even know if the publicity we've given them is what caused the warehouse mess. This might put them over the edge. Someone else could get hurt. One of us."

"We'll be careful," I tell her.

"Isn't that what Jagger said?" She looks at the others. "I want to find out who left him in that building as much as anyone else, but I think going back to the police is smarter. Even if, in the end, it doesn't do any good, at least we tried."

"Give us a couple of days," I plead. "After we run the footage, you can take it to whoever you want. The cops, Channel 5, whatever."

Her expression is so grim I'm sure she'll turn me down. But years of being best friends count for something. "You've got two days. Clock starts the instant the piece airs *if* that's what you all decide to do."

The oxygen in the room is sucked out as Marci exits. Henry's head falls to his chest; Omar slumps in a chair. Raul leans tiredly against the wall.

"You guys out, too?"

Omar can't look at me. "I'm up for a full ride at Cooper Union. Photography. All four years. If there's a hint of trouble, or I make a 'bad choice' and things get screwed up—my dad will kill me. I'm counting the days until I'm out of the house, Val. You know that."

"Henry?"

He stares at Marci through the control booth window. She sits at the B Team table, rigid, her back to us. "I think she might be right."

Given the choice between Marci and anyone or anything else, it's a Henry no-brainer.

"Then leave with Omar." I take a deep breath. "Raul?"

"First, we need to talk."

Omar and Henry can't wait to get out of the room. After they're gone, it's my turn to slump into a chair. "What just happened?"

Raul shakes his head. "Reality? Fear? Jagger's freaking us all out. Not just you."

"I know." I take a breath. "Tell me the truth. Is Marci right? Did *Campus News* make it worse from the start?"

"We didn't do anything wrong. It's not like we put MP up to any of it. All we did was follow the story. Like we're supposed to."

"Jagger didn't just follow the story," I moan. "He applied—"

"And had no idea they'd choose him. He's like that chick in the American history book. Nellie Something. The reporter who got herself committed to the insane asylum just so she could write about it."

"I can't believe you're comparing Jagger to Nellie Bly."

"Getting into MP was as much of a long shot as pretending to be crazy. As much of a long shot as airing the footage will be." Raul's face creases with worry. "One that could lead to a whole lot of trouble with nothing to show."

"But it's my choice, isn't it? You'd go to the cops with Marci if I back down."

"Back away, Val, not down. There's a difference."

Moment of truth. Whatever I choose changes lives. Good or bad, I'll never be able to say I didn't know what I was doing. Because if there's one thing I learned over the last few weeks, watching tubes and machines keep Jagger alive, is that there are consequences to every choice we make.

Even though I know I should wait for Omar to boost the sound, I can't help going to the outlaw corner during lunch. It's a carbon copy of the last time, although the weather is colder. Kids hunch against the wall, each in their own world. The haters not only hate the rest of the school; they hate each other, too.

I'm in luck. Liam's there, hand cupped around the smoke he's trying to light. Without looking at anyone, I make my way to the wall. Take a spot close—but not too close—to him. I get a couple of sideways glances, but nobody says anything. I desperately want Liam to talk—I want *to* talk to him—but can't figure out what to say. I can't confront him without proof.

I never heard him speak. Last time, all he did was give Jagger the finger. I'm not sure how they know each other. Maybe he's a skater. Along with outlaw, hacker, hater, skater, should double agent be added to the list?

Liam says something so softly I almost don't realize he's speaking to me. "You're Voorham's girlfriend, right?"

"No—well, yeah. I mean I was."

"He okay?"

"Not really." I lower my voice. "Do you know anything about it? What happened in Red Hook? *Please tell me.* I'll keep it quiet...."

For several moments, Liam does nothing except finish his smoke. I don't say another word. Don't want to blow it....

He drops the butt at the same time the bell rings. All around us, kids reluctantly start to move. I grab Liam's arm. "Wait—"

"Check your tape," he whispers. "You got more than you think you do."

"What does that mean?"

He shakes his head, pulls away. How does Liam know Jagger shot the initiation? Unless he's the double agent. The hacker. If he's good enough to change a computer's IP address, who knows what else he can do?

> Yet understand the exact
> and tribal, intimate revenge.
>
> SEAMUS HEANEY

MP LOG

I zoned out listening to the usual boring crap on *Campus News* until I heard someone say, "Right, Skeletor?" I glanced up. The TV screen was all black with two words stenciled across it: *Listen carefully.*

For the first few seconds, I was confused. I heard the others talking but still didn't see anything. That's when it hit. The initiation! I looked down quick so no one could see my face. My mind was whirling. I was trying to figure out what was going on and then I realized someone used their cell to record what happened in Red Hook.

Somebody in MP sold us out. Again. Phantom didn't know anything about the second initiation so another person is to blame. Someone told that news bitch a few details about the initiation—but not everything. Because if they told her everything, MP would've been shut down by now.

Just as I was thinking that, she came on the screen and in her fake reporter tone said, "If you recognize any of these voices, leave a note in the *Campus News* box in the office or talk to me, Valerie Gaines."

That meant I was right. She couldn't name names. At least not now. That was good, but I wasn't sure how long it would last. I snuck a look around, but no one was staring at me. Yet.

My blood boiled as I remembered the oath and how we promised to keep quiet. I'm pretty sure I know who the traitor is.

If I'm right, I can kill two birds with one stone.

31

At the end of the day, Raul waits by my locker. "Carleton's looking for you." I'd ducked out of class as soon as the broadcast began. "You have to talk to him sometime, Val."

"I just want a couple days. The same time Marci's giving me. Then I'll confess."

I twirl the combo and pull the door. A piece of paper, folded in half, sits on the top shelf.

```
Stay tuned.
```

"What's that supposed to mean?" I snap.

Raul crumples the note in disgust. "Just the usual controlling MP crap. But I'll walk you home in case it's something more."

Outside, the sky is what everyone calls 9/11 blue. Cloudless, sunny, crisp; the afternoon is more September than December. The year's first major snowstorm is scheduled to blow in by sunset, though, so it'll get cold soon enough.

"I hate this, Raul. Waiting for their next move."

As if in answer, my cell vibrates. Raul's does, too. He gets to his first.

"Omar got that section with the whispering kid boosted." Eagerly, he holds up his phone, presses Play. "Let's hope it's Liam!"

The instant it plays, it's obvious that it's not. Raul's face colors with frustration.

"It's clearer," he says, "but I don't know who it is."

It's funny. He doesn't ask if I can identify the voice. He must figure I'd say something if I do. The shock of recognition is so strong I'm literally stunned into silence.

At my side, Raul babbles on. "...hospital and ask Mrs. Voorham to listen. What do you think, Val? Maybe she'll know who it is."

"Um, sure. Okay. But you'll have to go by yourself. I want to stay home in case 'stay tuned' means MP is planning to contact me there."

"Let me know if they do." Raul waves his phone. "This didn't work out the way we thought, but we're close. Something's going to break. I can feel it!"

He waits until I unlock the front door before hustling down the street.

The house is quiet. Taking the steps two at a time, I burst into the bedroom. Bethany's not home yet. Quickly, I check email. Nothing from MP, although Omar sent the audio in a file so I could listen at home.

With pounding heart, I press Play in the dim hope that from the computer's speaker, it will sound different. Be different.

It's done. Can we get him down—

The voice hasn't changed because the person's the same. Bethany Ann Gaines.

My world spins crazily, a kaleidoscope of confusion. My own *sister's* a member of MP? It doesn't make sense. She wouldn't leave Jagger in the warehouse. She couldn't. She's in love with him. Sinking onto her bed, I take a couple of deep breaths. Try to think it through step by step.

As much as I fight it, the logic is undeniable. The secret emails that came from this very computer. It wasn't some sort of genius hacker trick; it was Bethie, sending them to me when I wasn't home.

Making me go to Promenade Park first and then leaving notes all over the Heights. She had to do that so she'd get home before I did.

I also figure out how she changed her voice to make me think the double agent was a guy. It wasn't a phone app. Grandma bought the twins a microphone toy last year. It shifts tones higher or lower. The boys played with it for weeks until they got bored. Left it lying in the toy chest....

A fury unlike anything I've ever felt runs through me. I wham Bethany's pillow against the mattress. Over and over and over again. It isn't until a piece of paper falls out of the cotton pillowcase that I stop. My combo! She freaking stole it from my backpack! That's how MP got into the locker to hang the bird.

I've been such a fool. Blind to everything. *She's* the double agent, not Liam. But what I can't figure out is why she didn't tell me straight up when she wanted to get out of MP. It's not like we're the closest of sisters. Still—we *are* sisters. Why go through all the double agent B.S.?

The answer hits seconds later. Bethany's terrified. Afraid of what'll happen to her if Taneisha talks. If MP gets caught. If *Campus News* breaks the story. She got in over her head and then couldn't find a way out without owning up to what she did.

The plan for Jagger's initiation freaked her out. She kept giving me clues, hints—hoping, praying I'd talk him out of joining. She didn't actually want me to find out she's in the group because she's as guilty as the rest of them. What she hoped was that the initiation would end before it began.

An all-too-familiar feeling of guilt hits. Big Sister couldn't do the one thing Little Sis asked.

Something else occurs to me. I move to the computer. To my dismay, this last piece of evidence proves it once and for all. The footage Raul and I downloaded from Jagger's camera is gone. There's only one explanation. As soon as Bethany saw it on *Campus News* today, she snuck home and deleted it. Perhaps she hoped it was the only copy. If it's gone, we can't do what we said—play another section during the next broadcast. But Bethany has no idea I did it without telling Carleton. That I might never be able to show anything again—because as of Monday, there's a good chance I'm off the team.

Somewhere in the house, something creaks.

"Bethany?" I scoot across the floor and step into the hall. Complete silence. "Bethany! Are you home?"

No answer. I clatter down the steps. Her coat's not hanging in the entranceway. I check the kitchen, although I'm pretty sure she's not there. I'd hear the fridge opening, milk being poured, the crinkling of the cookie package. My sister isn't in the living room, either.

I could have imagined the sound. Or the top-floor renter moved a piece of furniture. As soon as I'm back in the bedroom, I look around. What am I missing? Nothing's out of place. Nothing's gone. Still, I can't shake the feeling that something's wrong. Bethany really should be home by now.

My gaze focuses on the corner. The closet! Perhaps that's where the noise came from. Is someone inside? Waiting to spring out…?

With pounding heart, I tiptoe across the room, jerk the doorknob. No one's there.

My cell rings.

"Bethany! Where are you—"

"Maritime Park," she whispers. "Come right now. Alone. No cameras. No tape recorder. *Don't* tell anyone or I'm screwed."

"Wait. What's—" The only sound that comes from the phone is the hum that signals a broken connection. I call her back. Text twice. No response.

Oh, man. I never want to set foot in that park again. The garden, the flagpole, the benches next to the river. Just thinking about it makes my hand shake. Why does she want to meet *there?* Unless Bethany has proof that outs the rest of MP—and gets her off the hook.

My stomach tightens as I check the time. Not yet four o'clock. If I hurry, I might be able to get there before both the early December nightfall, and the promised snowstorm, arrive.

That hope is soon dashed. Standing impatiently inside the glass bus shelter, staring mindlessly at perfume and clothing advertisements, I text Bethie: Waiting for the bus. Be there as soon as I can.

No response. Why doesn't she get back to me?

Ten minutes later, I get a text, but it's from Raul: Important. Have to talk.

I shove the cell into my backpack as the bus finally pulls up. I can't tell Raul what I'm doing because I'm not about to sell out my sister. Not without talking to her first.

By the time I get to Coffey Street, thick clouds cover the dying rays of the sun. Yet again, I find myself making a nightmare run. Only this time, it's *toward* the park. Just as I reach the flagpole, my cell buzzes. Bethany must be someplace she can spot me, although I don't see any sign of her.

Wrong. It's not my sister but Raul. Ignoring the call, I shout, "Bethany? Are you here?"

Like a scene in one of those end-of-the-world movies, the

park is eerily empty. The first snowflakes, drifting from gray clouds, look as forlorn as I feel.

A clanging sound atop the flagpole gets my attention. *Please, no!* With a mounting sense of dread, I glance up. Let out a breath. No one's painted a message on underwear; nobody hangs from a rope.

A flash of movement. A trio spills out of the garden. My heart lurches. All three wear Halloween masks. Frankenstein. A zombie. The Ghost Face from *Scream*. None of them is Bethany. I'd recognize her coat, her shoes…her whole being.

"Where's my sister?"

The answer is a laugh.

"Where the hell is Bethany?" A rough push is the response. "What did you do to her?"

"Start walking," commands the voice behind the Frankenstein mask.

He attempts to shove me past the flagpole, but I grab the back of a bench. "I'm not going anywhere until you tell me where Bethany is."

"Shut up, bitch! We're taking you to her."

With no real choice, I release the bench and allow them to guide me past the grassy area. The lights of the Verrazano Bridge are directly ahead of us. *We're heading west.* Not that I know if that's important, but the knowledge is something I can cling to.

"Who are you? Where are we going?" The questions are automatic. Nervous instinct. I don't expect an answer—nor do I get one.

The hill begins to slope downward—straight for the waters of New York Harbor. Red Hook is the spot where the ocean mixes with the East River. Dangerous currents. Deep eddies.

To my left, a hulking building looms. Another abandoned warehouse. No way do I want to be forced into that building—but how do I know Bethany isn't there? That they haven't done something terrible to her?

My knees buckle at the thought of my sister hanging from a rope.

"Watch it, clumsy," Ghost Face says.

A few steps farther and it becomes clear that the building isn't where we're headed. Instead, I'm pushed toward the fence separating the warehouse from the edge of the water. It's supposed to stop people from getting to the river. Problem is, the chain link is no more than shoulder high.

"Climb," the kid wearing the zombie mask tells me.

Are they planning to throw me into the river? In December? No one would last more than a few minutes.

"And if I don't?"

My answer is a finger point. Through a thin curtain of snowflakes, and the dimming of light as dusk descends, I can make out an old dock. At the far end, broken-off posts, like sharpened daggers, rise from the water. Two people wait. One is my sister. Even at a distance, her slightly hunched silhouette is unmistakable. I have no idea who's with her; he's too far away for me to recognize.

Silently, the three MP members and I climb the fence. Scramble across a rocky barrier. The uneven stones, slick with a glazing of snow, make getting to the dock hard.

The wooden wharf creaks as soon as the group steps onto its weather-beaten boards. A terrifying vision flashes before me: the entire dock collapses and *everyone* ends up in the water. In the dark. During a storm.

About halfway down, we stop. The guy standing next to Bethany wears a skeleton death mask. A flash of blue hoodie peeks out from underneath his jacket. Skeletor. The kid at Omar's party who gave me the finger. Probably the dude who set the fire—

"Move it, News Girl!" he yells.

Frankenstein shoves me. "You heard him."

"You do everything he says?"

"Yeah. If you're smart, you will, too."

He pushes me once more. Carefully, I move forward, stepping across cracks and holes in the old wooden planks. At the end of the dock, Bethany shivers like crazy. That's not surprising since the wind picks up speed as it crosses the harbor. It's at least ten degrees colder here than on land.

I also can't discount the fact that she's terrified.

"Bethie, are you all right?" No response. "Bethany! Say something."

"Shut up!" Skeletor yells.

He's obviously talking to me because my sister hasn't said a word. I stop moving and give him what I pray is a steady, *I'm not afraid of you* stare. "How about we get to why I'm here so we can go home? It's freezing."

The guy takes his time. "How many copies of the tape did you make?"

"Excuse me?"

"The tape your sister shot. The one you played at school."

"She didn't shoot it." Confused, I stare at Bethie. "Why would you say…"

The group bristles. Everyone starts talking at once. Skeletor yells, "Zip it!"

Immediately, they all shut up—except for me. "Bethany did not shoot that footage. Jagger did."

"Yeah, yeah. That's what she said." He puts a hand on her shoulder. Bethany flinches. "Point is—it's her fault. She told you stuff."

"She did not!"

"Don't lie. She confessed."

Has Bethany lost her mind? Moved past terror to…I'm not

sure what to call it. It's hard to imagine what Skeletor did to force her to lie like that.

"Okay, fine," I say. "But the footage on my computer's been deleted. As of today. You were probably in the bedroom when she did it."

Skeletor shrugs, meaning: *big deal. You figured that out.* "She said you always make a backup copy. Who has it?"

"My friend Marci." Defiantly, I toss my head. "She's giving it to the cops—"

"Giving?" He sneers "Or gave?"

Shit!

"I don't know. She wanted to go to the cops from the beginning, but I wouldn't let her. We made a deal. She'd wait until after we aired the piece."

"How long?"

I glance at Bethany. "I'm not exactly sure—"

"My guess is she hasn't gone yet. All you *Campus News* freaks would make her wait. See if some asshole at school rats us out." Skeletor points a skinny finger at me. "Here's what you're going to do. Call your friend, tell her to leave the copy on the stoop of her building, or the lobby, or whatever she has, and bring it back here. Someone will trail behind you to make sure you follow directions. That's when I'll let your traitor sister go."

"Listen to me! It doesn't matter whether you get the copy or not. It's still on the school's server."

He laughs. It's a nasty sound. "Not anymore."

Surprised, I wipe snowflakes from my eyelashes. Someone deleted the footage? Who would do that? Who has access—

Skeletor takes a menacing step forward. "What are you waiting for? Get going."

Forget the server. Focus on the danger in front of you.

"I'll never get to Marci's." I spin the lie with as much certainty as I can. "I called the team before getting here. *Campus News* will show up in five minutes. Maybe less. With cameras and everything else. So you might as well let Bethany and me leave before you get into real trouble."

"You didn't call anyone," he tells me.

"Oh yeah?"

"Yeah." He jerks his head. "You wouldn't. Not until you talked to your sister. Something about blood being thicker than water. Just to prove I'm right, one of you check her cell."

Ghost Face yanks the backpack from my shoulder. Roots around, finds the phone. "She got a couple of calls and texts from someone named Raul. She didn't reply."

Behind the mask, I can feel Skeletor's *gotcha* smile. "Told you. Lying runs in your family."

"I'm sorry," I say quickly. "You're right. It's just so cold right now. Why don't we go together? It'll take more than an hour to get to Marci's and back. You'll end up with frost-bite if you stay here."

The snow's falling at a steady pace. It would be beauti-ful—if I wasn't so scared. I've finally figured out the reason Bethie isn't moving. Her arms, which have been behind her back the entire time, must be tied to the pole sticking up from the end of the dock.

"Don't worry about me." Skeletor sneers.

He's no dope. He'll find someplace to get warm while I run around Brooklyn like a maniac. And he's evil enough to leave Bethany on the dock until I get back.

Just as that thought hits, a blast startles the group. A tug-boat makes its way up the river. All heads turn—except for mine. Instead, I jerk my arms from Frankenstein's suddenly slackened grasp and race forward. There's no way I'm leaving my sister with a bunch of psychos.

Someone shouts. Skeletor moves to block my way. As I

swerve, my boots slip on the damp wood. I hit the deck hard, unexpectedly sliding past Skeletor on my stomach.

"Shit!"

The end of the dock is less than two feet away. Momentum, and a thin layer of melting snow, defies the law of friction. Skidding forward, I can't stop—

Just before I plunge into the cold, dark waters of NY Harbor, Bethany sticks out her leg. The front of her shoe hits my shoulder hard enough to keep me from going over the edge.

Scrambling to my feet, I turn to face the members of MP. "Back off, assholes! If either Bethany or me ends up in the water, you'll be arrested for murder. Is that what you want? Life in prison?"

The three at the back have the brains to hesitate. But Skeletor's out of control. He screams as he lunges for me.

"Don't call me an asshole!"

We struggle, locked in a tight, back-and-forth motion. The dock is not very wide and I don't want to slip again. Skeletor grabs a lock of my hair and pulls hard. I collapse onto my knees. A sickening *boom,* like a gunshot, scares the crap out of me.

A large crack fractures the dock. At the same time, Skeletor's foot crashes through the wood. He lets go of my hair as he falls. Lucky for him, the plank's splintered gap isn't wide enough to allow him to drop all the way through. He dangles awkwardly, one leg in the hole. His other leg and butt are splayed against the wooden deck.

The dock sways and groans. Any second now the thing will break apart, plunging us all into the chilly depths of the East River.

Skeletor screams at the masked kids, "Don't just stand there. Help—"

"Everybody freeze!"

The voice is familiar. I'm pretty sure I've lost my mind when I see Raul standing at the land edge of the dock, hands cupped to his mouth.

"Val? You all right?"

How on earth did he find me?

"Valerie!"

My voice trembles. "I'm okay. But I'm worried about Bethie. And this thing is really shaky!"

"What about me?" Skeletor yells. "My leg——"

"Nobody moves," Raul shouts. "Nobody panics. You'll have to get off one at a time." He points to the person closest to the edge. "You first. As smooth as you can."

I hold my breath as Ghost Face inches forward. When she gets to within inches of Raul, he extends a hand and pulls her off. Raul nods to Frankenstein. "Now you."

He moves quickly. Instantly, the dock quivers.

"Slow down!" Raul yells.

Frankenstein freezes. Legs shaking with fear, he starts again. After what seems like half a lifetime, he's off the dock, too. Now it's just one more person before only Bethany, Skeletor and I are left.

Gingerly, Zombie makes his way through ever-thickening snow. He finally hits land, which is the moment Skeletor loses it.

"I can't feel my leg anymore!" he screams. "Help me!"

"Hell no! Bethany's next," I hiss.

Ignoring Skeletor's pleas, I tap my sister. "Your turn."

Her teeth rattle so much she can't speak. Carefully, I lean over the edge. In the never-quite-dark of a New York City evening, my stomach drops.

"She's tied up, Raul!"

"Stay calm, Val. Go ahead and undo the knot."

"I can't. My fingers are cold. They're stiff——"

"You have to," he commands. "I can't get there. Concentrate. It's just like editing. One step at a time. Find the end of the rope...."

He keeps talking, nice and calm, as if standing on a crumbling dock trying to save my sister's life is a regular part of any day.

The faster I untie the knot, the faster Bethie gets off the dock. That's what I tell myself as I work the rope. *Then it's my turn. We'll both be safe.*

With a final twist, the rope comes undone. Quickly I unwind it from Bethany's wrists, and then drop the rope into the water. Within seconds, the current takes it away.

"Move your legs," I beg. "Please! We can't stay here much longer."

Painfully, my sister makes an effort. She bends one leg, then the other.

"That's great. Go on!" I urge.

She takes two tiny steps, but her knees wobble. Afraid she'll fall, I prop her back against the wooden pole.

"C-c-can't d-d-d-o it! V-V-Val...."

"Okay, we'll go together."

I wind my arm around her shoulders to sort of lift her. We don't take more than a few steps before the rotted pilings underneath begin to creak. The dock sways. I'm afraid to go any farther.

I give Raul a horrified, beseeching look.

In the face of looming disaster, he continues to remain calm. "Bethany? I'm Val's friend. Raul." He takes off his jacket, holds it out. "You can put this on when you get here. It'll warm you right up. Doesn't that sound good? Just get close enough to me and I'll help you the rest of the way. You can do it."

"He's right, Bethie. Go!"

Her thin legs move awkwardly. She takes a step. Then a second, a third... At the same time, Raul gingerly slides a few feet down the dock from his end. I hold my breath. About three feet from land, they meet. He says something I can't hear before leading her to safety. Puts his coat around her shoulders and shouts, "You're next, Val!"

Skeletor screams, "No! You can't leave me alone!"

I hesitate, but Raul waves me forward. As I move, a hand grabs my ankle and holds on tight. I pull Skeletor's head, violently, to get him to release me. His mask comes off in my hand and my body jerks backward. Off balance, I step down hard to keep from falling. The dock shakes, groans—and splits apart.

Omigod!

In a sort of slow-motion panic, I realize that I'm falling, falling, falling... The intense shock when I hit freezing water takes my breath away.

"Val!" Raul screams.

Frantic to stay afloat, I flail about. But I'm wearing boots, a jacket.... The swiftly moving current eddies around, pulling me down. It's impossible to breathe. In some part of my consciousness, I hear screams, see flashes of light...

As I slip underwater, the last thing I see is Skeletor's face floating beside me.

If I thought I'd recognize him, I'm wrong. Stripped of his fright mask and the power the others give him, he's nothing special. The kind of kid you pass in the hallway every day—and never, ever notice.

It's the last thought I have before the world turns black.

32

The chaos over the next few hours is colossal. To my immense good fortune, Raul called the cops the instant he saw us on the dock. By the time it falls apart, the police have arrived.

That accounted for the flashing lights and the yelling. After going completely underwater the first time, I managed to struggle back up. Gasping for breath, I see an orange tube float beside me.

"Grab it!" voices shout. "Hold on!"

Somehow I manage to grasp the tube and wrap my arms around it. Immediately, there's a sweet tug of rope as the police reel me in. As soon as I'm close enough, they drag me onto land. Coughing, sputtering, I feel my knees give out when I try to stand. Before I hit the ground, however, I'm scooped into strong arms. They carry me from the water's edge. The cop places me on a large, flat rock. Fingers press gently against my throat. I hear, "Pulse is good." Within seconds, thick, warm blankets wrap my body.

One of the uniformed men squats down. He has a black mustache and kind eyes. "Can you talk? Do you know your name?"

"Val Gaines. Where's my sister?"

He points. "We're keeping the other kids back there—"

The wail of an ambulance interrupts. I look over. Skeletor has been fished out of the water, too, but he's lying, not sitting, on the ground.

"Is he okay?" I ask.

A walkie-talkie squawks. In my dazed state, I can't make out the words.

The cop shrugs. "He's got a deep laceration on his leg, so we called the paramedics." He squints. "How about you? Can you stand? If not, we can send you to the hospital with him—"

I shake my head vehemently. "I'm fine. I need to see my sister. And Raul."

"Let's go to my car and then I'll find them," he says. "You'll warm up faster inside."

From the backseat, I watch Skeletor being carried on a stretcher to the ambulance. I still don't know who he is.

By the time Raul and Bethany get into the car, the heat's blasting. Raul takes the middle, Bethany the far side. Either because it's tight in the backseat, or because he feels the need to protect us, Raul wraps one arm around Bethany; the other hugs me. Despite the fact that she's still wearing his coat, he feels warm against my side.

"His name's Arnold Clemson," he tells me. "Mean anything?"

The shiver at the sound of the name has nothing to do with the fact that I'm soaking wet. "That's Skeletor? Uh-uh."

"Yep. I heard the cops talking."

I stare out the window. I don't recognize Ghost Face or Zombie, either. Two more people who manage to stay under the wire at school. Wraithlike, they float down hallways and settle into their seats, invisible to the rest of us. They don't raise their hands, don't cause trouble. Just like Bethany, I imagine, they go home after school, munch on cookies or chips, listen to music, do their homework—but they do it alone.

There is one person that I've met. Frankenstein. He's the dude Marci called Potty Mouth. The kid who gave what I now realize was a totally bogus interview, pretending he didn't give a crap about MP.

The Channel 5 News van shows up. High school kids plunging into the icy East River is news. Good old Emily Purdue, hair not quite perfect in the night wind, wants an interview. Raul, Bethany and I refuse. Determined, she heads for the others. MP can make up any lie they want. Emily can get the story wrong. I have no sympathy for her.

The cops string yellow caution tape barriers to alert people to the dangerous half-submerged dock before we get rolling. A second car, carrying the three MP members who originally surrounded me, follows. At the police station, parents descend. In the bathroom, I exchange the heavy blankets for the dry clothes Mom brings.

Names, addresses, stories. The cops talk to everyone separately, including Bethany and me. They write down everything, no matter how contradictory. A couple of lawyers show up. Since everyone's under eighteen, the final outcome of the evening is that we're released to our parents. Specific criminal charges to be decided next week.

With Raul by my side, the Gaines family exits. I think I'm holding it together pretty well until I discover that my folks took the car, even though the police station isn't far from home. Now we have to walk to where Dad parked, drive to Connie's apartment, wait for the twins to pack up their toys and *then* go home.

"I am not doing that!" I say.

"Val—" Mom starts.

"No! It's much faster to walk home. Raul will take me, right?"

He looks uncomfortable, clearly unhappy to be in the middle of a family fight. "I'll be glad to walk you home if it's okay with your parents."

Mom opens her mouth to protest, but Dad stops her. Saving at least one daughter, if not two, from certain death gives a guy major cred.

"She's got a point, Kate," he tells Mom. "No sense in all of us crowding into the car. You sure you're all right, Val?"

"Yes. I really want to walk. The police station was stuffy."

"Okay." Dad looks at Raul. "Be careful. Have her call the minute you get inside."

"Yes, sir. I will."

With a wave that's more cheerful than I actually feel, Raul and I head off. The snowstorm's moved on, leaving a half-inch blanket of crystals sparkling in the clear night air.

"Tell the truth," Raul says. "Are you really okay?"

"I guess. I just can't sit in the car with the twins and Bethany. Or my parents. I don't feel like answering a million more questions."

"I hear you," Raul says.

After a few minutes, though, I'm the one who breaks the silence. "The cops asked me something I couldn't answer. How did you know where to find me?"

"It wasn't hard. I got worried when you didn't respond to any of the texts or calls. I used the locator app like you did when you were looking for Jagger. Red Hook came up, but that didn't make sense. You were supposed to be waiting at home. Why would you leave—unless you'd been contacted by MP?"

"Bethany told me I had to come alone."

That's the moment it hits. How close I came to drowning. My body quivers with pent-up fear—and rage. I stop in the middle of the sidewalk. Raul gives me a concerned look before guiding me to a stoop swept clean of snow. It's dry. Gratefully, I sink down.

He takes my hand. "Oooh, cold." He rubs both sets of fingers with his large, much warmer, palms. "Better?"

"Mmmm." I let him fuss over me for a few moments, too tired to protest. The truth is, it feels good. "I'm sorry I didn't call you back. It's just—"

"You had to talk to your sister first. I understand." He blinks a few times. "I swear to God, Val, watching the dock collapse was the worst thing I've ever seen. I was ready to jump in after you. If the cops hadn't shown up…"

"Let's not go there." I try a smile. "I'm not sure I thanked you. If you hadn't called them when you did…"

"You're welcome," he whispers.

He leans over and kisses me. It's so unexpected that I just sort of…let it happen. But even though Raul saved my life—he isn't Jagger. As soon as that penetrates my still-confused state, I pull away.

"Raul—"

"Sorry, Val. I know. It's not the right time." He doesn't look at me as he stands. "We should go. Your dad's gonna worry."

"Wait!" Thinking about Jagger sparks a question. "Why did you text from the hospital? Did Mrs. Voorham recognize Bethany's voice when you played her the tape?"

He hesitates a bit too long.

"Raul?" My voice catches. "Omigod, is it Jags? Is that why you called? Did something happen…?"

His nod is practically imperceptible—but it's there. My stomach drops in anticipation of the worst news of the night. With a reluctant breath, Raul releases the last of our kiss. The expression in his eyes isn't sad as much as defeated. As if he knows he lost.

"Jagger opened his eyes, Val. He woke up!"

33

Pushed off the southern edge of WiHi's roof, I try to grab something. Ledge, window grate, flagpole. My fingers claw madly, but I'm moving too fast. The ground rises. Just before impact, I jerk awake.

Breathing hard, I stare at the ceiling. It's not only terror that overwhelms me. It's this horrible feeling that I've missed something important.

I glance at my cell. *Damn!* Almost ten. I'd set the alarm for nine just before collapsing into bed last night. I wanted to be at the hospital the instant visiting hours began. I don't remember hearing the cell ring, let alone shutting it off.

Lying in bed, Bethany stares at me. "The alarm woke me up."

"Sorry." I throw the quilt to the side. "I'll be out of here in a few minutes. You can go back to sleep when I'm gone."

"It woke me up!" she repeats, as if I didn't hear, or understand, the first time.

"I said I'm sorry!"

Unbelievable! It's like yesterday never happened. Just as I fell into the deepest sleep ever, it occurred to me that things would be different. That she'd change. That *we'd* change. Become better sisters, closer, despite MP—or because of it. But there she is, lying on her bed as if *I'm* the one who did something wrong.

I don't have the time, or the energy, to fight. Rising without a word, I cross to the door. The reflection in the dresser mirror stops me. Dark circles ring my eyes and an ugly bruise purples my cheek. I don't remember hitting anything when I fell into the water. One of the broken wooden planks must have caught me on my way down. Or my face dragged against a rock as I was being pulled to safety.

My hair's a mess. Frizzed by icy water, I'd hooked it behind my ears at some point. There's something about it that reminds me of Emily Purdue when she concentrates. It gives me a shiver. I vow to cut it as soon as I can.

Behind me, Bethany's started to sob in that really quiet way she has. She *should* cry—but it ought to be loud and clear. It's the damn silences that nearly got us killed.

That's when a flash of recognition hits. I glance back into the mirror. Maybe I'm more like Emily Purdue than I know. Than I want to be. The real MP story was in front of me the whole time—and I never saw it.

"Move over?" I climb into my sister's bed and fix the quilt so that it covers us both. I hand her a tissue from the box on the nightstand, wait for the crying to stop.

"It's over, Bethany. I'm not mad." She picks at the blanket. "Talk to me. Please."

"What do you want me to say?"

"Whatever you want. Tell me why you joined MP. Why you made me run all over the Heights instead of talking to me when it got bad."

A sly look crosses her face. "Got you, didn't I? You had no idea it was me."

"*No* idea. *Campus News* was desperate to figure it out. We even gave a copy of the emails to a computer whiz at school, but she told us a hacker wrote them."

"She?"

"Henry knows her. Toby—"

"You showed them to *her?*" Bethany screeches.

"Yeah. Why…"

My sister's voice turns hollow. "We called her Phantom."

"Hold on!" I stare at her. "Toby's in MP?"

"Was. She quit after the first initiation."

Holy shit! Wait until Henry finds out! My mind whirls for a moment, but then I think I understand how it all fits together. That's how Arnold knew the footage on the school server had been deleted. He probably threatened Toby to get her to hack into the system.

"*That's* why you wrote those notes!" I say. "You were afraid if you sent the initiation information by computer, she might find out."

Bethany refuses to look at me. "I didn't want to take extra chances. I'm smart, Val, smarter than you think."

"I never said you aren't."

"You don't have to say it," she tells me, pouting.

"I know you're smart. You get better grades than I do. Besides, it's not like you care what I think. What anyone thinks."

"That's not true!"

"Is that why you joined? Because you think I don't care?"

"I did it because… I don't know why, okay?" She swings her legs over the bed.

"Wait!" I reach out to stop her. "Don't get mad. Please! I'm just trying to understand."

Bethany hesitates, and then she slumps morosely into the bed.

Some walls are invisible.

The declaration painted across the Red Hook mural finally

makes sense. Why couldn't I see that Bethany's darkness was her very own wall? Built day by day, brick by brick to shield her loneliness?

Skeletor saw it. *That's* the power he had—and the prize he dangled.

He met them all at the Video Arcade. Loners who hate being alone. He offered each the chance to join MP. To be a part of something. To *be* someone.

"Listen, Bethany." Gently, I put an arm around my sister. "There is one good thing that happened yesterday. Jagger woke up."

Eyes red, nose runny, she turns. "He did? When?"

"Sometime in the afternoon. That's why Raul kept trying to get hold of me. And why I set the alarm this morning. I want to get to the hospital as soon as I can."

"Can I go—" She interrupts herself, not quite able to face him. "Will you tell Jagger I'm sorry? Please! I'm so, so sorry about everything...."

"Of course. And when I get back, we need to start trying to be better sisters. To help each other even if it's hard. It might take a while, but we have to find a way."

By the time I shower, get dressed and take the two trains to the hospital, it's lunchtime. Luckily Jagger's mom isn't there. As I slip into the room, my heart races. I'm not sure who I'll find. Sarcastic Voorham? Confident Jags? Or a Jagger damaged in ways that can never be fixed?

He's propped up on the pillows, eyes closed. Oh so gently, I place my hand over his. Behind pale lids, his eyes flutter. He struggles, blinks and manages to swim to the surface.

"Hey," I say quietly. "You're up."

He doesn't recognize me. The thudding in my chest threatens to knock me over. "It's me, Jags. Valerie."

Another long moment and then…a smile. My heart lifts, a hot air balloon released from its mooring. Jagger wets his lips, tries to speak. Not a single sound comes out.

"It's okay, Jags. I got you where I want you. No back talk."

He blinks. It's not a regular blink but a long, purposeful one. Immediately, I'm on my feet. "Water? The nurse?"

He shakes his head. Tries to say something, but words refuse to come. Frustrated, he lifts a hand to his cheek.

"Oh! The bruises." I sink back into the chair. "I'm okay. We caught them. *You* caught them. It was the camera…."

Quickly, I give him the highlights. His eyes widen when I tell him that Bethany left the notes.

"She feels terrible. She blames herself for what happened."

He shakes his head.

"You want me to tell her it's okay?" I ask. "That you're not mad?"

A brief nod.

"Omigod, Jagger, she'll be so happy. *I'm* so happy. You can't imagine how worried we all were."

My voice catches. Jagger wets his lips, glances at the nightstand.

"Water?"

He nods. Carefully, I place the straw in his mouth. When he's done sipping, I resettle the glass. Jagger looks at me. Even though he can't speak, there's no mistaking the message.

The kiss isn't long. But in those few moments, every bad thought I've ever had about him dissolves. Joy pulses between us. It's real and honest and we had to go through hell to get here.

From the look on Jagger's face, he feels it, too.

May

The award, in all its shiny glory, arrives in a plain white box. Mr. Carleton spends most of first period pulling everything from the shelf above his desk. Methodically, he dusts and puts it all back, making sure there's space in the center. Both *Campus News* teams admire the trophy before he sets it in the place of honor.

The plaque on the front reads Student Emmy Award, Public Service Reporting: *Dangers of Pass Out*. Producers: Scott Jenkins and Hailey Manussian. T. Carleton, Adviser.

The irony doesn't escape any of us. After all that happened, it's the almost-an-afterthought story A Team submitted that won. To be fair, it was well done and delivered an important message. I keep a bright smile on my face as we high-five all around. I mean it when I tell them, "Great job!"

The bell rings. Raul and Hailey continue their conversation as they walk out. I wouldn't be surprised if they end up going to prom together. From what I saw at Halloween, Hailey can certainly keep up with him on the dance floor.

Omar practically floats out of the room. He's been on an

incredible high since he got into Cooper Union, his life about to change in ways he once only dreamed about. Henry's wait-listed for Yale, with offers from half a dozen other schools. The rest of us have at least one decent acceptance—even if it's not first choice.

I hang back for a moment. Jagger stands behind me, arms circling my waist. "Tell the truth, Val."

His larynx, bruised by the rope, has all but healed. The rasp in his voice is just about gone. So is his arrogance. Jagger has plenty of saucy comebacks, but they're no longer mean. It makes everyone, including Marci, love him so much more.

"Tell the truth about what?"

He gestures toward the trophy. "You're not the least bit jealous?"

It takes a moment to sort through the rush of feelings.

"Maybe a little." He squeezes me. "Okay! A lot."

Jagger laughs. "I might be more sympathetic if I hadn't heard there's other news to cheer about."

I whirl around. "Who told you?"

"Who do you think?"

I pull the email from my pocket. I've read it so many times since printing it out this morning that the page is already crinkled. "Bethany's almost more excited than I am! I was planning to tell you at lunch, so we'd have a little more time to…celebrate."

He extends an arm, takes the paper and reads the words I prayed so often to hear. "Congratulations! The Syracuse University Admissions committee is pleased to offer you…"

Jagger lifts me up and swirls me around. "I am so proud of you, Val!"

In that moment, it's triumph, as well as understanding, that shines through. It doesn't matter whose names are on the trophy. It never did. Jagger and I, along with the rest of our team, did more than break a story. We broke through the barriers that trapped us all.

If some walls are invisible, so are some masks.

The actual masks MP wore weren't all that different from the ones we hid behind. *Reporter, Slacker, Queen of the Sloths*... We all had our roles and we played them well. They protected us from feeling adrift in hallways and classrooms—but they also kept us apart.

If Bethany had come to me—or I to her—she never would have had anything to do with the ugliness of MP. Marci and I should have invited my sister to Tony's for pizza; we could have hung out with her at the Video Arcade.

Instead, my sister found her own place to belong—until it all came crashing down. After the night on the dock, everyone in MP blamed everyone else. It wasn't until the police confiscated Arnold's journal that the court understood: Bethany and the rest were pawns in Arnold's increasingly sick game. Months of community service are a lot better than the time he's spending in juvenile hall awaiting sentencing.

And then there's Jagger. Hiding behind arrogance was his way of protecting himself—until even he grew sick of it. If he hadn't tried, and tried some more, to knock down walls and make amends, we would never have gotten here. The lessons learned, the love found.

Second period is about to begin. The students taking Mr. Carleton's Intro class swarm into the room. There will always be stories to report and deadlines to meet. For now, however, I don't want to think about anything except the warm hand holding tight to mine.

My sincere thanks to Sally Nemeth and C. Leigh Purtill, YA writers who have kept me out of the weeds too many times to count. Dr. Marilyn Mehlmauer made sure my characters were properly diagnosed. Zack Blatt, John McGorty and Robert Leventer were my skater/fireman/legal consultants. Genna Rosenberg, along with Adam Wilson, Janis Van Tine and Stephanie Carroll, helped in myriad ways. The Cashin-Maeby-Tanzman families provided spaces on the East Coast for quiet writing time. At Harlequin Teen, T. S. Ferguson did the heavy editorial lifting, for which I am extremely grateful; Natashya Wilson's keen eye made an impact throughout the writing process. Erin Craig and Tara Scarcello created the sophisticated art design and are among many on the Harlequin Teen team who helped guide the book throughout its journey. As always, fellow writers Jack and Liana Maeby managed to provide just the right advice, as well as laughter, when it was most needed.

* * * * *

The Spellbound Novels

In this contemporary series of spells and magic, curses and love, new-girl Emma Connor faces snobs and bullies at her elite Manhattan prep school. When the hottest boy in school inexplicably becomes her protector, Emma finds her ordinary world changing and a new life opening to her, filled with surprising friendships, deadly enemies and a witchy heritage she never suspected.

AVAILABLE WHEREVER BOOKS ARE SOLD!

The Clann

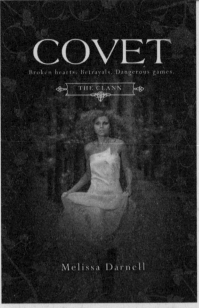

Available Now

Coming October 2012!

The powerful magic users of the Clann have always feared and mistrusted vampires. But when Clann golden boy Tristan Coleman falls for Savannah Colbert—the banished half Clann, half vampire girl who is just coming into her powers—a fuse is lit that may explode into war. Forbidden love, dangerous secrets and bloodlust combine in a deadly hurricane that some will not survive.